BONE CHILLS

FATED CHILLS SAGA
BOOK ONE

MAXWELL J SMITH

Paperback ISBN: 979-8-9947910-0-4

EPUB ISBN: 979-8-9947910-1-1

Cover by InvertSilhouette on VGen

Illustrations by InvertSilhouette on VGen

First edition 2026

CONTENTS

For my husband,
I couldn't have done this without you.
Forever thankful for you.
p.s you're gay <3

THE FATED CHILLS SAGA

The Fated Chills Saga is a dark tale of two deeply flawed, morally-grey men. It is doomed and toxic. It is not a romance.

It is a tragedy.

A Quick Note...

THE FORMATTING OF THIS NOVEL IS A <u>STYLISTIC CHOICE</u>.

IT IS A DIRECT REPRESENTATION OF THE NARRATOR'S MENTAL HEALTH.

PLEASE VISIT THE AUTHOR'S WEBSITE FOR A FULL LIST OF WARNINGS.

https://www.ledpaintsoup.com/fated-chills-series/warnings

PROLOGUE

THERE ARE TIMES WHEN I AM FILLED WITH AN ALL-CONSUMING shame for my part in it all. I can only hope that the Skalds sharing the tale know the truth; *I did what I thought necessary to save our people.* What I thought to be honorable was a lie, and I did not realize until it was too late. **Some men are unredeemable,** and *it is foolish to believe they can change.* Joining the rebellion was one of the *first* decisions I'd made to ensure I never became unredeemable, though I'm not sure how well that worked in my favor. The true start of my tale begins years before I'd first seen him. **He was the catalyst.** There were many years that I wasted and regret fills me as I look back on it all. It's been a long time since then. *Some details can be hazy these days.*

I began to see how corrupt my father was at a young age. Yet, I still tried to see a glint of pride in his eyes. I did dishonorable things in hopes he would love me as a father should. *I blamed myself for the way he treated me deeply into the later years of my life.* My father was more than the man who taught me lessons with his cruelty.

He was the first unredeemable man in my life, but he was not the last.

He smiled at starvation and laughed at the stench of death.
He held Sidirna underwater and watched our people drown so he could fill his pockets with coins.

He was a twisted and conniving man that I underestimated in the end. I would change many things if I could go back and do it all over again, but I'm stuck with the choices I made.

Those choices brought me to where I sit now, telling the story of my life as if the trauma does not still exist inside of me.

THE BEGINNING OF THE END BEGAN ON A WARM SUNNY DAY WHEN I WAS 16 YEARS OLD.

It was far from the first time I had seen the headsman, Amin, do his job. That day felt so different from the others. I'd learned the hard way, *through my father's fist*, to not show how disgusted I was when the axe separated a person's head from their body. Even then, I understood why the people flocked to the rebellion. **They wanted more than they were allowed to have.** I kept a lot of those feelings to myself then. There was a *twisted* feeling inside of me as I saw a member of the rebellion for the first time. I can still remember the way his bruised and bloody body held no fear as he kneeled with his back straight and eyes forward.

I'd longed to hold such honor in my beliefs, but my young self held on to my father's vision of how I should feel. *It was an idiotic thing to do, and one I regret deeply.*

I had kept the bored expression on my face as I sat on the left of my mother, with my father's Jarls standing in a line behind our seats. My father did not tolerate much, and I was used to keeping my face devoid from emotions. We sat above the platform that held the accused man. *Why was he so silent?* It was usually then that the accused begged for their lives, but this man must have known his fate was held by the Norns. **No words would save him.** I'd admired his resolve as much as I could, though I regretted the fact he was to die. I am ashamed that I was complicit in his death. He held himself as a warrior and one day I would pride myself the same way he had.

Though it was <u>many</u> years before I could be considered as such.

I am Alfrikr; the first son of Alfrikr the Wretched, who was the son of Alfrikr the Ferocious.

Each Alfrikr in my bloodline was known for their brand of a cruel, oppressive, and bloodthirsty rule. I'd known from a young age that I wanted to undo what each before me had done. It took me many years to get on the right track, but I'd eventually found my way. My name comes from two words of the Old Language; Alfr and Rikr, loosely translating to Elf King.

I was born to take the title of Rikr, ruler of Sidirna. I was destined to change Sidirna,

and this tale will prove that.

It is a horrible name. If I could choose a new one, I'd pick a simple one like Erik.

I could not help but stare into the accused man's eyes as the *smack* of Amin's axe severed the muscles with a sharp squish. My father was the Rikr to insist that beheadings be done facing him so he got the best view, and not the common folks. The blood was stark against his golden hair; *it was easy to imagine myself in his position through our similar appearances.* I could picture myself kneeling there with slumped shoulders. *How I would stare at the ground as I awaited my fate. I would never have the same resolve as him, and I hated that.* My gut churned from the onslaught of empathy that I felt for the man.

He'd only wanted a better life, and now he'd lost his head for it.

The man's head fell forehead first as his body slouched and tumbled backwards. It smacked the wooden platform with a *thump* that I felt rattle through the boards under my feet. His head tumbled before settling with his eyes to the sky. **He blinked thrice before his eyes settled wide open.**

The Gods had accepted him into a hall... I was sure of it.

When I led Sidirna, I'd save beheadings for only the worst men. The ones who were unredeemable. I would put the ones who cursed others to an ill-fated future up on that platform and laugh as their head rolled. **Beheadings would not be for a poor man who had dealt in knowledge to fight against oppression.** *There was redemption for all men with honor.*

My mother leaned over as the crowd cheered, "May Valhalla accept his soul."

I nodded my head, careful to avoid my father's attention. He did not approve of his heir having any relationship with his wife, my mother. My father was an insecure man who acted as a tyrant leader as well as a tyrant father.

I MET A SECOND MEMBER OF THE REBELLION ALMOST A YEAR LATER; Cor was a Thrall who belonged to Jarl Danr. I was born the winter before Jarl Danr's twin sons, Dallen and Doran. They were both to one day be my closest advisors. Cor had come from a small village near Ymir's Mountain, where he had been born into servitude, and sold by his previous Jarl at 23. He was the only male Thrall near our age, and the first to ever look me in the eyes. **I respected that about him.** Doran joined the rebellion weeks after Cor came to the stronghold, I joined another 2 months later, and I'm not sure Dallen did until we left. Dallen held himself to his standards, not to be confined by labels or loyalties. I still admire him.

At first, I was to share everything I knew. I would tell Doran, who would tell Cor, and Cor would spread it until it got back to Ivaldr, the leader. Slowly, more specific requests filtered back from Ivaldr. *I'd felt so important back then; like I was saving our people by listening in on my father's conversations.*

How stupid I was to think that the man would never know.

I was caught spying a fortnight before my 18th birthday, I left the same day.

I PRESSED my ear to the door, hoping to catch even one word through the thick oak slab. My father had called a meeting with the highest Jarls this morning. Though I tried to shadow my father during that day, I was asked to leave before the Jarls arrived. I'd run into Doran shortly after leaving, and he was the one who put the pressure on me to go spy. I flexed my palm against the door, *I could use my Sacredness to thin the door.* My father would notice, but if I did it quick enough, I could hope my Sacredness signature would be gone before the end of the meeting. I could always lean on his idea of me; **a cutthroat and ambitious heir.**

He'd once appreciated that about me.

I heard the rumble of voices. Too many were suddenly talking at once and I couldn't make anything out. I thought about how I could make the gap under the door bigger, but *knew it would not work.* I heaved out a sigh, trying to press my ear further into the door.

Cor would be expecting more information before night fell, and I had failed at getting anything worthwhile. Doran had harped on me to get something because anything would be useful to the cause. *I'd felt nervous at that moment, as if my father had known exactly what I was doing lately.* He typically never held his tongue, but I'd noticed how often his meetings were when I was doing my studies and training. Doran got more information than me, and *I hated feeling lesser.*

I yelped as I lost my balance, the door flinging away from my body. My face hit the soft chest of my pudgy father, his hands coming out to shove me away before he stomped down the hallway. *Hello father*, I'd wanted to snark in response.

"Follow me, boy." Jarl Danr said, almost gently, as he ticked his head in my father's direction. The way his face seemed to screw together for a brief moment before going back to blank was worrisome.

The tone of his voice ignited my worry until it consumed

the entirety of my body. My fatal flaw is how easily I get stuck cycling through my inner thoughts. My emotions and thoughts have always consumed me. They swirl inside of me as they take away my ability to think rationally and calmly. It was obviously not the time to have been caught snooping based on my father's behavior. *Did he know I have been spying? He knew. He had to know. I was done for. This would be my last day in this realm. He would not hesitate to place me up on the platform and have everyone watch as Amin beheaded me. No, I couldn't let it consume me. He did not know. He would not know. I had to hope he would only chastise me for being too curious.*

A single hit to the gut, a few specks of spittle on my face from his yelling, and a lesson on how to do it better next time would be my future. Father would often send me to spy on his Jarls, though I was always more careful. It was less worrisome to spy on them, for they were duller than my father was. I knew that he would figure me out, but I could only hope and pray to the Gods that he did not know the truth.

It wasn't the first time I had been caught trying to see what my father was doing. I could take the lashings for it with a smile, as long as I got something to tell Cor. Would Cor know if I had made something up? Something about the fall harvest would suffice. He was still at Jarl Danr's estate in the hills, how was he to know the truth? I would not have to worry about that much longer, though I did not know it then.

I was lost in my thoughts, spiraling about getting informa-tion. I had not realized we were at the headsman's platform until I stood upon the dais. There were no chairs to sit upon, though I knew I'd never sit based on who kneeled before me.

*My lungs emptied, my heart froze, and my soul
shattered as I looked down upon Cor and my mother.*

They kneeled side by side, a second more regal block had
been brought out for my mother. She looked pitiful as she
kneeled there with her shoulders trembling. Her usually pristine hair was a mess of wild tangles. I couldn't think straight,
nor at all, but my back straightened as my father came before
me. I knew better than to let him see any weakness. I gave him
a bored expression, the best I could muster as my heart pulsed
erratically in my ears. A hateful grin was plastered on his regal
face. His head bobbed twice as his mouth moved, but I was
unable to stop from looking over his shoulder at my mother.

At Amin sharpening his axe behind her.

Cor's shoulders shaking.

"Alfrikr!" He boomed, breaking through my frozen state.

"Yes, father? I don't want to miss the show." I droned out,
forcing a sly grin. He enjoyed it when I acted like a miniature
version of his hateful self. Though his face had scrunched at
me suspiciously.

"Your mother is an adulterous, rebellious, whore. What do
ye have to say?" *No, she was not. She couldn't be? Why wouldn't
she tell me? We could have worked together.*

"Why is there no trial?" *She was entitled to a trial, all had the
right. If I could get her a trial, then maybe I could break her out. I
could leave with her. Esmeren would come with us, so would Doran
and Dallen. I couldn't think of life without my mother.*

I was back in a daze as I met my father's eyes, and it was
then I noticed the complete lack of soul shining in his blue
eyes. Would I grow to be the same as him?

Soulless and wicked? Only time would tell, and by the end of my tale you will know.

"WE HAVE TO GO!" I shouted, my eyes flitting between Doran, Dallen, and Esmeren. "They know. They have to know!"

No one spoke as I looked between them all. They were weak foolish cowards. Dallen grimaced as he slid the knife down and cut the core from a sliver of apple. Esmeren's eyes were on the floor of the old grain building, her fingers toying with the hem of her dress. Doran frowned before stepping closer to me, a hand coming out to rest on my shoulder. I cringed away from him as I huffed out a breath.

"Tell us again what happened?" Doran asked gently, a mimicry of his father's voice that morning.

I wanted to slam my fist into his mouth until it was coated in his weak blood and his teeth wiggled in his mouth. I wanted to tie them all up and drag them behind me as we left. They were all meant to be loyal to me, yet they questioned me? They were meant to follow me! Their future Rikr! I'd already told them how I had watched as my father cut my mother's head off. How her lips seemed to grimace as her head rolled to the platform. How Cor had gone first, my mother watching her lover, and how it took many swings from my father to behead him. Each swing made him angrier than the last.

Esmeren had cried, but now refused to meet my eyes. Dallen had gagged before throwing up behind the apple crates he was leaning against.

I should have paid more attention to Doran then, seeing the way the wheels turned within his head.

I was due to meet with my father in an hour, and I just knew that Cor had ratted me out. Ratted us all out. While Esmeren was not happy with our involvement, she did keep our secret and provided little bits of information here and there.

"I'm leaving. With or without you." I finally said, digging the toe of my boot into the ground. I wanted to scream. I wanted to shake their shoulders until they did what I said. I wanted to chain Esmeren's wrist to my own and drag her away with me always. She was my betrothed, and I was meant to take care of her. How dare any of them disobey and question me?

"I-I'm coming." A voice said from the shadows, behind a stack of broken crates. Merelda, Esmeren's younger sister, stepped into the faint light. She was two years younger than us, and always wished to be included in our group. Doran moved towards her quickly, his hands finding each of her shoulders.

"How long have you been here, stupid girl?!" He whispered harshly.

The thought of Merelda being implicated in this lodged a boulder in my throat. She was a young girl with little station. She could not weasel her way out of anything if we were caught. Her older sister would be spared because of her standing as my betrothed. My hands shook as I forced myself to suppress my anger. Why did I care so much about the Karls and Thralls? Why couldn't I be as heartless as my father, throwing lives around like they meant nothing? I wished I could talk to my mother now. Sadness enveloped me as I settled on the fact I would never do so again. She was gone. I was alone. My friends wouldn't leave with me.

What is worth the cost of a person's joys, life, and existence? Sidirna needed to change. We were treating them like the sheep, letting them fuck and breed like animals so we have more stock. We reaped the benefits of their labor as we looked down upon them. The privileged sat high up on the cliff with bellies full as the people of Sidirna starved beneath us. My father was aging, in his early 40s now, I could have bid my time until he croaked. Made changes when I took power. I could not do that if he suspected me of treason. I didn't know the lengths he'd go to erase these thoughts from my brain. I would lose all of my friends, I knew that for sure.

I kept my gaze down as I weighed my options. I could watch everyone I care about get beheaded, or I could run away to play a bigger part in the rebellion.

The decision practically made itself.

THE END OF AUTUMN

I

DREADFUL AND COLD

There was not much that had happened during the nine years I'd lived with the rebellion. I spent years simply existing, which I would come to regret soon. I don't remember the exact day, only that it had been autumn when my fate had begun to change.

9 YEARS LATER...

My entire body shuddered as I thought of the cold gaze of those eyes, how the soul seemed to have left them entirely. The iciness of all-consuming dread consumed me after he left. Frozen pain hovered above the sickly feeling in my gut. The raid had gone well that night, until it had not. Esmeren's face lingered in my mind still. A singular thin stripe of flame curled towards my index finger, and I hissed at the slight sizzle of my finger pad. The fire was simply like recognizing like, despite my Sacredness being drained. *Maybe it was the Gods punishing me for living life so stagnantly.*

The flames swirled beneath my fingertips, reaching out towards my wrist as if they were shackles of my own creation. The haze against my skin made the filth stand out more. *I need to bathe.* Yet, the thought of leaving the warmth, stripping, and stepping into the river was one I could barely justify. I could have almost talked myself into it. I twisted my neck around, stretching the muscles as I dazedly rubbed at the center of my chest with my free hand. Something was wrong with me, but I couldn't explain what exactly it was. My intuition screamed that the Gods were displeased, and that I had made the wrong choice.

A sickness twisted its way into my body where the cold ache had set in hours before. I shuddered as another wave came over me. Cold, how was I this cold in front of the fire? Why did my chest ache so deeply? My gut twisted with an anxious swirl as I tried to move my mind from the memory of him.

"Alfrikr?" The deep rumble of a voice had startled me, my hands swatting the flames as I turned my head towards the archway. Sacredness was not meant to be used so sparingly, and I was lucky it was Doran who stood in my entryway.

"You know when you get a chill in your bones, and it won't go away?" I greeted as I turned my body to face him. Doran's lips tightened in a grimace, a look that rarely graced his uptight features. The anger that lived within me flared in jealousy as his face dropped back into his calm, neutral expression.

I should have killed him then for simply reminding me of his father.

"What happened out there?" Doran asked softly as he approached the fire, the flames casting his skin a few shades darker and transforming the copper swirling in his eyes to a haze. His back stayed straight as mine slumped. Doran's cautious approach enraged me. As though he thought I would attack at any moment.

"When you feel the ache to your core, and no matter how many layers you put on or fires you sit in front of, you're still chilled to the bones?" I whispered as he came to stand beside me. Another shiver wracked my body and I wanted to scream at the Gods to leave me be.

"That's what it's like looking into his eyes," I finished, wincing as Doran patted my shoulders. I shuddered at the thought of those cold eyes meeting my own. The cold ache in my chest flaring at the memory.

He did not respond, but instead stared at me with an unreadable expression. Doran's hair was braided back and his tunic was pristinely hanging to his knees. Jealousy surged at his regal look in comparison to myself. He was not affected in the same way as me, and I almost wished him to be in my place. There was a deep anger within me as I sat there shivering against the warmth I could not feel.

"You know it isn't your fault," he cautiously said.

I was not sure what to say as I turned and let my eyes fall to the logs that fueled the flames. Yes, it was not my fault that the Norns hated me that night. While the rebellion had its win, I had personally lost. The thought did not soothe the deep chill that had latched onto my bones. I worried the chill could kill me, but the severity of it had not settled in then. He spoke as if he were approaching a wounded animal, much like his father had the day my mother died. I was often brought back to that fateful day when I looked at the man. Doran was like his father in many ways. *He saw me as weak,* and I hated it. His demeanor was not what I needed.

I needed to be reprimanded, I wanted to be torn down, and I knew I would be the only one to do so to myself.

I knew he was coaxing me into believing he was here to help, but also that the boys had most likely drawn sticks to see who would come and talk to me. There wasn't a reality where he had come because he cared about how I was. Nobly bred men didn't have that urge to comfort others, but the rebellion had changed Doran the most. Doran had such a calm to him that always made me feel odd. I wished it would have been Dallen, Doran's twin brother, who drew the short stick. While Doran was filled with a quiet grace, Dallen was not. It was an odd trait for us in the rebellion; the rebellion believed love outweighed hate. It was as if I'd never truly belonged anywhere I've lived; *I was too gentle for my father and too vicious for the rebellion.*

The boys were difficult to tell apart, with both having burnt coppery speckled brown eyes, dark brown skin, and pristinely shaped runes. Runes littered each of their forearms, as did anyone with Sacredness. Theirs were an identical match. Their personalities could not have been any different. They were both the pristine image of carefully bred Jarls sons. Doran and Dallen had chosen me in the end, but I had thought they wouldn't. I spent days walking and running towards Ymir's Mountain in hopes of salvation, but filled with anger that my closest friends hadn't chosen me. They'd left after me and caught up with me many days later, with Merelda trailing behind them.

Much like myself, the twins were born into the upper class of Sidirna. Their father was the head Jarl to the Rikr, my father. There was not a time in my life where we were separated, aside from my birth the Winter before. We had not grown up with the suffering of others within the rebellion. All of us had seen how corrupt my father and the people within my father's circle were, regardless of our upbringing. Though, we were never truly accepted in the rebellion due to our upbringing.

While they were the spitting image of their father, I was unfortunately the same with my father, albeit my skin was marred with more marks than he had ever seen. My hair was the same shade of gold, my blue eyes swirling in the same shade of copper specks he once had, and my skin the same pale. Though, I thought my runes were more legible than his. It is said that the Gods blessed the most loyal, strong, and honest with the best runes.

My hand shook as I reached for the knife on my belt, feeling Doran's eyes scrutinizing my every move.

Did he think I was going to attack him?

Maybe he thought I would end it all right here.

Part of me wanted to end it all, and every so often I wish I would have.

It would have saved me from the horrors that came after that night. The pop of the fire echoed through the cavern as I brought the knife up slowly. The urge was strong within me, but I second-guessed my right to do this. I gripped my hair in my left hand tightly before I silently hacked off the braid at my nape. The silence between us was deafening. I'd wish I were alone. In one hand, I now held my hair, still braided and tied with a leather strap. I felt the rush of air as what was left of the hair fell, cascading over my ears. Three smaller, singular braids still hung around my left eye, the interwoven beads threatening to blind me.

I felt as if the Gods were watching me, and perhaps they were.

"Well, that was dramatic," Dallen called out from behind us.

I spun around, poised to fling my knife at him. He was always skulking around, and he knew all that went on. He dealt in knowledge and information, but I knew this moment would stay between us. The twins never liked to be separated for long. No doubt, he could not hold off on some remark to anger me.

A distraction, just what I needed.

"He's mourning, brother," Doran's voice quivered out, as his eyes darted between us.

Doran was always the voice of reason of the three of us. He was also the one filled with the most fear. I blamed his weakness on the fact he'd spent much time inside the stronghold as a sickly child. With Dallen being the instigator and I being the agitator. *Who would crack first?* I sighed, lowering my knife. My chest flared in pain again. Cold rushed out into my veins and seized my breath.

"Better burn it," Dallen had now reached the fire, standing between his brother and me. The dirt spattering his tunic was a mirror replica of my own. He splayed his fingers in front of the fire, wiggling them almost carelessly. A flame wove out and around his hand, close enough to feel hot, but not enough to burn him.

"Don't want Froggy getting a hold of that."

I knew he was right, but a part of me almost wished that the half deranged old man would have used my hair to curse me with warmth. Could Froggy tell what was lingering in my bones? Nothing could be worse than the hand I was just dealt by the Norns.

Perhaps I had already been fated to die.

"You're right," I sighed. "I caught him picking hairs out of my pillow once."

Froggy was a fate worker who relied on blood Sacredness to fuel his spirits. Hair, blood, bone, and whatever else he could get from a person. It was tricky work and part of the reason that the practice had been lost in the histories. Even so, the old man whose voice sounded like a croaking frog was one of the last known people who knew the craft. Nobody was sure whether it worked because Froggy prayed to Loki, if his greatest desire was to be a jester, or if he truly knew the craft. Blood Sacredness enabled him to do wicked things, but he was content on giving people eternal dripping noses or prematurely graying hair. I let the braid fall into the fire, crinkling my nose as the smell wafted throughout the cavern.

"What the Hel's happened?" Dallen urged, earning an elbow to the side from his brother. He grinned at me before urging the flames to snap at his brother's clothes, burning slight holes as they both fought for control of the flame.

"What the Hel's happened indeed," I muttered as I watched the flames overtake my hairs at the base of the fire. What had been a planned raid of the winter food stores meant for the Rikr's stronghold had quickly become the worst night of my life.

"At least we have enough food for winter," Dallen urged, wiggling his eyebrows. He did not take much to heart, always jesting. Doran now controlled the flames, weaving them down to catch the rest of my hairs.

"Yeah," Doran's face twisted slightly, "And there's a feast tomorrow to celebrate the victory."

"With Finnian's stew! Say no more, please." Dallen exhaustedly groaned. "I don't want to hear about a feast until it's in front of me."

Their attempt at normalcy almost settled me, though I appreciated their attempt more than they knew. Dallen was right, the hunger that pained one's stomach after that raid was like no other. I still found myself uncomfortable. Here we were, pretending that nothing had happened. Pretending that my body was not screaming in pain, that a cold had not latched onto my bones. *I just wanted to lose the sick chill within me. Or maybe I wanted to scream at the Norns to take back what had just transpired.* I ran a hand down my face with a sigh.

The Gods hated me.

"Right, Alfrikr!?" Doran exclaimed, throwing me from my cycling thoughts.

"Huh?" What was I getting involved in? Most likely it was something ridiculous.

"You should let Jezebel shear your hair to the scalp," Dallen said loudly, grimacing at the state of my hair.

"It's been almost nine years since I've had my hair sheared." It was a rite of passage for one to shear their hair after a life-changing moment. It was meant to signify to others to be gentle with you that your life was currently going through significant changes. Marriages, deaths, babies being born, and other significant moments were always followed by a shearing.

Yet, I had no intention for anyone to be gentle with me. *I deserved anything flung at me for what I had allowed to happen. I'd* already hacked most of my hair off, and I knew they were right.

"It would show that you don't accept the happenings of the night," Doran's shoulders shrugged as one eyebrow quivered towards his hairline. I did not accept it in the slightest. "You know how rumors flow…and you look scary right now with your hair all…" He gestured to my head with a look of disgust briefly on his face.

"We're nearing dawn," Dallen added. "Best to let all see it happen." He exchanged a look with his brother before adding, "We're going anyway."

He was right. They both were. I needed to show everyone that I was indeed mourning the pain to my soul, and fix that hasty urge that came over me.

Nine years ago, I sheared my head to show that I was mourning the loss of my mother and leaving my home. With my heart heavy, at nearly 18 years old, I had left the luxury of the stronghold. There were many who disagreed with my decision to leave because I had been easily able to pass along information about the Rikr to the rebellion. Yet, in the almost two years that I fed information, nothing was acted upon. 9 years later, headed the same results with new information from spies within the grounds.

We'd all overlooked it as we settled into a routine within the mountain.

With the loss of my mother, it meant my father, Alfrikr the Wretched, would find out about my role as he did hers. Much of the rebellion reluctantly trusted me with simple things now. Though the whispers that I had defected only to share the inner workings of their revolt still angered me all these years later. Not that their revolt had done much. The rumors flowed through these caves much like the streams that ran through them. The rebellion lived and thrived inside the inner workings of Ymir's Mountain. Babies were born, boys became men, and that was about it. There was no pillaging, fighting, nor other entertaining activities besides working. The rebellion had never done anything drastic towards those in power. We simply existed as if the outside realm did not.

The boys and I had lived in a small section of the cave near the back, far enough that if we were to sneak out, others would see. The hustle of everyday life thrived down here, from the markets towards the entrance to the homes near the middle to the training center towards the bottom and up to the political rooms near the top. Sacredness was a beautiful thing, and Sacredness thrived inside that mountain while I withered away.

A CROWD LINGERED around the outside of Jezebel's cave, a quarter of them with sheared heads. A quick scan of the crowd showed me that all of those with shaved heads had been on the raid with us. Though, a few were the families or partners of those who had been lost last night. Dallen and Doran stood silent on either side of me, and I was sure they were using their twin connection to speak within their minds. They were two halves of the same person, and twins were revered within Sidirna. While both were powerful, had they been born a single babe, they would have surpassed even my power. I was sure they had to have had at least one golden edged rune on their body. Though, I wasn't as power-hungry as I used to be.

"Alf?" I spun on my heels, knowing the voice of one of the few I trusted with my life. Though that did little to settle the anxieties I felt in a crowd, I knew she was on a mission to find out what happened.

I knew better than to have this conversation with prying ears nearby. Merelda stood before me with her fingers clasped in front of her. Her dark hair was twirled back with intricate braids, beads clanking together as she turned her head up at me. She looked so much older at that moment. My mind still clung to the image of her hiding behind those crates years ago. She was 26 now, and still followed us around constantly. Merelda wanted to be revered as the best healer within the stronghold as a child, but that had changed to the best healer within the rebellion as she aged.

Merelda had left her friends, family, and studies to join us all those years ago. She'd claimed it was because she believed in the cause deeply. While I knew she did in fact fight for the rights of the lower classes, I also knew that her heart longed for Doran much more. They'd been together for the last three years, which made things awkward at times. Doran was controlling, even if he was a quiet man.

I had been betrothed to her eldest sister, Esmeren, until she refused to join the rebellion with us. I saw glimpses of Esmeren in Merelda often enough that it no longer bothered me. The first few years were the hardest. The thought of Esmeren brought her face flashing into my head, the pain in her eyes as she kneeled at my feet and begged.

The sickness that now consumed my body.

I had heard rumors on the walk back from the raid that she was now betrothed to the captain of my father's Varangian guard, Loreth. Loreth was a man that I never wanted to see again. The memory of his icy-cold black eyes meeting mine made me suppress a shiver. I felt an odd pulsing in the depth of my chest, the same cold that met my bones when I had locked with his eyes the night before now lived within me. I would soon learn exactly how cruel the man was. I hoped to kill him one day if fate allowed me.

While the crown had mostly brushed off our cause during the years; beheading the spies they'd find, but never coming to the mountain to thin our numbers. He had sworn to hunt us down before retreating with the few guards he had arrived with. I believed that he would.

I would be prepared.

"Yes, I saw her." I said quietly as I stepped closer to Merelda. "She has joined the guard." I added, my voice barely above a whisper. Esmeren had worn the armor of the guard. The pristine eldest daughter of the second-richest Jarl's family in Sidirna, my childhood best friend, and my former betrothed charged into the grain's storage.

"Was she-was..." Merelda heaved a deep breath, straightening her shoulders. "Was she condemned?" I could see the terror milling throughout her attempted straight face. Her eyes dated between Dallen, Doran, and I. The boys conveniently averted their gazes, Dallen turning his back to the conversation entirely.

Condemning was something that the Rikr would force upon those he felt deserved it. There were no broken written laws that brought one to condemnation. They were trials to prove their gratefulness of the Rikr's mercy. While my father was a powerful Rikr, he was incredibly petty. So much that a perceived look on one's face could send them to the trials. Those acquitted were left with a singular brand on their neck, the sigil of the Rikr. I shook my head slowly, her neck had been clean.

"I spoke to her, Merelda." Her shoulders slumped as the words spilled out of my mouth. I wouldn't soon forget the shakiness of Esmeren's once strong voice, nor the bruises that mottled her skin. I heaved a shaky breath before taking a step closer to her. "I can't say anymore out here." It was an excuse, and we both knew it. Yet, there was a fear that consumed me, as I worried that my loyalties would be questioned if people found out.

Merelda hummed out a soft growl before spinning on her heel and pushing herself through the crowd without a single word.

"Alright," I muttered as I turned back towards Jezebel's cavern.

I felt no remorse for keeping a tight lid on my encounter with Esmeren, it was too delicate of a subject to discuss out in the open. Merelda would have to wait, though I knew that Doran would track her down if he hadn't already. Dallen turned around, back towards his brother and me with a slight nod before Doran sheepishly smiled at me.

"I think we should hold off on sharing your conversation." Doran whispered as he held up his hand to block his lips.

I knew what he meant, and I knew the repercussions of not sharing such a development with Ivaldr. The man was a force to be reckoned with, despite the way the crown did not take his rebellion seriously. Especially after I left to join the cause. The rumors circled throughout the Karls, Thralls, and Jarls, but my father never publicly commented on his defected son.

"I agree." Dallen added, quite loudly. "Besides, it's almost your turn."

I looked up behind his shoulder at the thinning group. It was too late to go back, but a part of me would mourn the loss of what little hair I had left. I was utterly exhausted as I nodded my head. The adrenaline of the battle had worn off, and I was left physically, mentally, and emotionally drained. I still needed to wash myself, my clothes, and oil my blades.

2

BLIND BATS AND MILDEW

I PULLED THE CURTAIN BACK AND PEERED MY HEAD INSIDE, NOT daring to enter without announcing myself. Jezebel stood hunched near the back of her cavern, with her mangled hands clutching a knife as she sharpened it on a stone. A rush of cold flowed down my body that made my knees feel weak. I didn't know what was wrong with me, but the cold still threatened to overtake my entire body. It took everything in me to not associate the dark of Jezebel's cavern with the deep dark eyes that peered straight into my soul. My stomach churned with a threat trickling up my throat as my mind brought the image to the front.

He would find me. He would kill me.

"Who's there?!"

I cringed at the shrill tone of her voice, clearing my throat before responding, "It's Alfrikr."

She didn't turn to face me, not that I thought she could see me very well anyway. The boys and I always found it humorous that an old blind bat was the one who cut and braided hair, but she was good at her craft. I took that as an invitation to enter. A shiver wracked through me as I carefully maneuvered my way through her hoard of items, cringing as I trudged over piles of people's hair. The chair was coated in a thick layer of hair of all colors. I hoped she would ensure no one got a hold of the hair, but I wasn't quite sure that she ever cleaned her cavern. I worried that my hair would be used in some sort of blood Sacredness.

Not that I knew much about ancient magic then.

I tried to relax in the chair, but couldn't help but shiver as another wave of cold overtook my body. I was filled with regret as I brought a hand up to touch the hack marks I left in my hair. Nine years of growth gone in the blink of an eye, and I longed for it back already. I knew that the others would look at me oddly if I had not. That knowledge did nothing to quell my feelings. We had not lost many, but the few lives we had were at the hand of the Varangian Guard. It was enough to have everyone on the raid mourning. I wasn't sure exactly what had happened to the three people who had disappeared entirely. They never met back up with us, and I could only assume where they were now.

I jolted as bony hands landed atop my head, petting me much like one would a cat. The warmth I would expect from her hands did not come, as I shivered again.

This sickness would pass. It needed to. I could not die yet.

"What the Hel happened to ye? Did ye get in a fight with a knife?"

I felt my face heat in response, glad that she could not see me. I shook my head no, knowing she would feel the movement as she clutched my head harshly. "I was filled with grief, the urge overtook me." I said quietly.

"What?!" Jezebel yelled in my ear.

I repeated myself, louder this time. I would not be judged for something that had been part of our culture; the urge to cut off our hair. Worry still filled me as I thought of how I would be judged for it. *Was I deserving of this moment? Had I suffered enough?* It was common for people to hack their hair off when overcome with great feelings. Another shiver wracked my body that lingered in my bones. It felt as if a ribbon of ice had been wrapped around each bone in my body, tightening until all I felt was the sharp cold pain.

"Sit still!" She hollered as she brought the knife to my scalp, efficiently shearing the hair. I sat as still as I could as I felt her guide the knife with one hand, and bits of hair fell off and into my eyelashes.

"Why do ye smell like that?"

"Like what?" I responded, hoping that the journey did not linger on my skin. I was sure that I smelt of sweat, but I had not realized I was that ripe.

"Death." Jezebel muttered.

I huffed a laugh before responding, "I haven't washed yet, the trek was long."

She paused for a moment and inhaled deeply, "No, it's something else."

Another shiver flowed through me; one that I could not tell if it was from the tone of her voice or the cold that had latched onto me. I sat patiently as Jezebel finished in silence. My knees were weak as I moved to stand, brushing off the hairs from my lap.

This sickness would kill me, or he would.

"What do I owe you?"

"Two pieces of hack silver and a bit of knowledge."

"I'll leave it in the bowl." I hesitantly responded. Knowledge? What did I have to offer? "The rumors are true. He was at the raid." I mumbled out.

Jezebel gasped in a way that made me shiver for a new reason. Her response was immediate as she began to whisper prayers to the Gods. I dug into the bag attached to my hip, pulling out what was owed. I dropped it into her overflowing bowl as I hurried to pull the curtain aside.

"There he is!" Dallen shouted, his newly sheared head

shining in the light from the torch on the stone wall. I gave him a reluctant smile as I walked over to him and his twin. Jezebel's reaction sat heavy in my mind.

"You only sheared the sides and back?" I questioned Doran as I came to stand beside him.

"Aye," Dallen responded for him, nudging the quiet twin roughly. "Tell him why."

Doran shifted from foot to foot, clearly nervous. He stuttered a bit before responding, "I don't want people to get us confused even more. At least if I keep some hair, I'll not be followed around by the flock of people trying to smack Dal around for leading them on."

Dallen and I laughed as Doran's cheeks heated. Dallen was known to sleep around with whomever he pleased, though he did have standards when it came to those who were already married. It wasn't unusual for someone to confront him for his wandering tendencies. It was obvious that Doran's priority had been to clean himself and return to the pristine image he cared so much about.

I tilted my head as I looked at Doran, "Are you going to the river soon?" My muscles ached as I stood there trying to shift my weight in a way that brought relief.

"Do I stink?" He lifted an arm, sniffing obnoxiously into the pit of his arm. Doran cringed at his brother's antics, taking a step away from him.

"I've got to go find Merelda." He said before slinking off through the crowd.

"Just us then." I shrugged at Dallen before turning and heading in the direction of my cavern.

"I'll meet you there?" Dallen said as he fell into step beside me.

I'D NEVER LOOKED at Dallen in such a way, but I could appreciate his toned body as he stood waist deep in the cold water. My body had been sluggish as I walked to my cavern and collected my soap and clothes. The walk to the river had almost taken what little energy I had completely. I reluctantly stood at the bank, slowly undressing through the urge to walk in fully clothed. Dallen's back was to me as he scrubbed his body, the sun shone off his flexed muscles as he reached an arm above his head to scrub the pit of his arm. His dark skin reflected the light and at that moment I wished I were an artist so I could capture his beauty in such a simple moment.

Dallen could be a God among men based on his beauty alone. Jealousy burrowed deep inside of me as I stared at the man—my best friend, and brother. These feelings were wrong, but I'd wished to be more like him. He was fun, outgoing, and good-looking. *While I was stuck inside my head, angry, and scarred.* My steps sloshed as I tread in his direction, my eyes still appreciating his beauty in envy. There was no other way to feel, as I appreci-ated his skin that was clear from scars. He was healthy, toned, and carefree. *Everything that I was not.* The envy was not a twisted one that caused me to mistreat him. Instead, I felt only the urge to be closer to him so I could almost feel as worthy as he was.

Dallen had an air about him that caused others to radiate to him; even if he was as low in the rebellion as I was. His anger of the rebellion had always been deep, but they'd welcomed him in a way they did not welcome me. I gave him a nod as he met my eyes.

This sickness will kill me. He could be watching from the

shadows now, waiting to take me down. Crouched in the bushes waiting for me—

"Did you get lost? Or just too old and slow?" He joked, knowing he was only a few months younger than me.

I rolled my eyes at him, "Wanted to give the water a chance to smell better, smelly."

I am going to die soon. This sickness will take me.

"That makes no sense," Dallen quipped back as he dropped his body low into the water. "The river is always moving; you're never touching the same water twice. Plus you're upstream."

I splashed him in response, laughing as he sputtered. "So, you get my smelly water?" I mocked him as I lunged to avoid the responding splash.

The sickness will consume me.

I had just begun to wash my body when a wave of chills shuddered down my spine. There was a small pulse of pain that seemed to beat in my chest alongside my heart. My knees felt weak as I bent down to wash my legs, and I could only hope that they did not give out while I stood in the steady flow of the river. A large cascade of water suddenly dropped over my head, drenching my cold body—Dallen! I whipped around with a glare, narrowing my eyes as I met him. He grinned foolishly as he gave me a small wave.

"Dishonorable!" I shouted to where he sat on the bank. Such a careless display of magic, one that was not necessary. He threw his head back in a laugh as if it were the funniest thing he had ever heard.

"Y-... You look... Like an egg!" He finally said between laughs. "Yer head is so shiny!" He added as he sent another splash in my direction.

I rolled my eyes, not that he could see it, and resumed

washing myself. *I didn't look like an egg!* I'd say that perhaps I looked like a freshly washed carrot; long, white, and a little ugly. I was exhausted by the time I had finished. The sun had steadily risen, and I'd guess it was between morning meal and midday meal. My legs shook as I carried myself to the bank; drying myself with a clean linen before dressing. I plopped onto the ground beside Dallen, who now lay on the ground as if he had not just washed himself.

"Are ye as tired as I am?" He asked, his voice full of the same exhaustion I felt.

There were moments where I had a burst of energy, but the aftermath of walking, hauling grains, and the cold that had latched onto me felt brutal. I nodded my head in response as I resisted the urge to do what I had just judged Dallen for.

"I would rather not move." I admitted. With a groan, Dallen moved himself to sit up.

"How are you holding up?" He asked solemnly, and I wished he hadn't. I took a moment to try to gather my thoughts, and I settled on giving him a half shrug in response. There were no words to describe the chill that swirled in my body. "That bad?" Dallen asked, reaching a hand out to pat my shoulder.

I jolted away from him, giving him a look. "That's weird," I huffed out. "Don't do that. Just say something foolish and we can move on."

"Thank the Gods!" Dallen yelled, raising his hands towards the sky. He turned to look at me, "She sure picked an ugly one, didn't she?"

I couldn't help the nervous laugh that bubbled out as I thought of seeing the man in person. Loreth was a God among men for a very different reason than Dallen.

He was a vicious, dishonorable, and unredeemable man.

However, I could agree that the broad man had a look about him.

"Did you see the size of his thighs, though?" He tacked on, licking his lips dramatically.

WE CHATTED on the walk back to our caverns. I had somehow found the energy to make it back, though it had left me as soon as I eyed my bed. With a groan, I turned away from my bed to grab my sword and dagger from where I had dropped them on the ground when I'd first returned. I was sloppy, and quick, as I dribbled the oil onto the blades and rubbed them with a cloth. I knew I'd come to regret it, but I could always do better in the morning. The cold had seeped further into my bones by the time I was done, and the fear settled in as I found myself alone for the first time.

Sick, I was sick.

I laid in my bed, covered in furs, but still chilled to the bone. The shivers that consumed me were enough to build the fear in my gut tenfold. My mind drifted back to the look in those onyx eyes; how they'd lacked the copper flecks we all had. Our souls shine through our eyes through the warm orange, making it easy to see who is cruel and dishonorable. Those eyes were black as night without a single fleck. My own were a rich blue; one that others said reminded them of the sky on a shiny day. My soul marks were not as fluid and rich as others, but at least I had a soul. Another shiver wracked my body and I curled further into the blankets.

It had been many years since I'd laid awake in fear. I couldn't lie to myself and say that I was unable to sleep because it was the middle of the day. The truth was a flaring flame that roared in my head. *Would I die from this chill?* I did not know. *Could I give this freezing cold to others?* I wish I knew. If there was a chance that I would spread this, then I would have to leave. I would rather die alone than know that I had caused pain and anguish to so many. My father would be one who would spread it willingly so he could laugh and celebrate the aching cold that flowed through peoples bodies. I knew I was nothing like my father, but the fear still existed that I might one day turn out to be just like him.

I wrenched my eyes open with a gasp as a sudden pain began to pulse in my chest. Had my heart frozen completely? Was this the pain of death? I tried to heave a breath into my lungs, but it stuttered out as everything went black.

A raven croaked loudly, but I could not see.

Or was it gone.

Death. This was death.

The sickness took me.

My vision was hazy as I opened my eyes; only making out the dark shapes of my surroundings. I must have fallen asleep, or passed out, during the pain. I was laid in my bed, I think? It felt more plush than when I had laid down, and I could only assume that was because of the aches in my muscles. A raven kraa'd somewhere in my cavern, its deep guttural tone reverberating through the chill in my bones.

I tried to roll my body over, but it would not move.

I tried again and again, but I could only lay there blinking with my eyes never adjusting to my surroundings. Dread seemed to consume me even further, though it felt like a foreign feeling brewing inside of me. The raven clicked its beak so loudly that it sounded as if it were above my head.

Something touched my hair — no, I touched my hair.

I ran my fingers through the tangles. I was worried about something that I could not remember. I only knew that it was important. Kraa, Kraa, Kraa. Where was the raven, and how had it got in? I ran a hand down my face, rubbing my tired eyes. I needed to sleep. Tomorrow was crucial, but I could not remember why. I didn't know what was going on. I knew that something had gone wrong, not the way I had expected.

Kraa, Kraa, Kraa.

"Shut up!" I shouted, but my voice did not sound right. Sleep, I needed to sleep.

I was not sure what I would do next, nor did I know why I was worried about that.

When I opened my eyes again, the mattress beneath me felt as lumpy and uncomfortable as I remembered. The ache in my muscles had seemed to lessen, though my chest still pulsed with a faint pain. I was cold as I laid there and adjusted to being awake. I had no idea what time it was, only that my stomach growled with fury. My head felt fuzzy as I blinked at the ceiling, faint memories of a raven swirling in my head. It must have been a weird dream, though I hoped that the Gods had sent me a message. If Odin had known what had happened, maybe he could fix the cold that had latched onto me. I shivered at the thought.

The Gods had left us long ago, though no one could truly pinpoint when, only that they had not been seen walking Sidirna since the borders had closed. Many wondered if they still visited the other lands in our realm; though we would never know. I knew of at least two other countries; one full of Ljosalfar and the other full of Dokkalfar. I was certain there were more than we knew of, but our knowledge of the outside realm was limited. My father controlled what the people knew, but his grandfather had been the one to truly ensure that the lower classes of people were kept without knowledge. What they did not know was how poorly that had worked, and if the knowledge of Sacredness had been passed by word of mouth since then.

I heaved myself out of bed with a groan, stretching my arms above my head for relief. While my muscles were sore and my body was chilled, I knew I needed a quick meal and a trip to the mountain's library. I'd learned a lot since coming to the rebellion, things that I had never found within the confines of my father's library. I could only hope to sort through the mess of books and find an answer about what had happened. As I pulled my trousers on, the cold pain began to pulse in my chest again. It was an odd feeling; one that I couldn't quite explain yet. It seemed to flow as if it were a living thing exploring the inner-workings of my body. Not only that, but it poked and prodded at my bones in some places, but twisted and curled inside of them in others. I brought a hand up to the core of the pain, hitting my chest hard as if it would dispel it from my body.

Knowledge. I needed to find knowledge of this, though I was doubtful that any existed if it were blood Sacredness.

This sickness could not have me.

3

TOMES AND BLOOD

THE WALK TO THE LIBRARY FELT LONGER THAN USUAL, AS IF MY energy was so depleted that it could not renew itself. My knees felt weak, and my hands shook as I pushed open the thick curtain and stepped into the damp, mildew-y air. It was worse than the last time I had been here, which regrettably had been months before. Books were thrown carelessly about, while some were stacked nearly to the ceiling. There was a steady drip sounding from somewhere; the last time I had been here, I had struggled to use my ground magic to repair the hole in the stone that the water leaked from. It was by far the worst place to keep these books; Ivaldr did not know how to read, so I was not surprised he allowed books to be treated this way.

I'd never thought much about the fact the man could not read. He couldn't lead a group of people, either. Ivaldr had a personality that drew people in. He was good with words, and it was a shock to hear he wasn't able to read. I'm not sure how much of it was true, though, as I had heard through a rumor Dallen had heard. I hummed to myself as I slowly walked through the chaos, a tune I had not thought about in years. My grandmother would always hum the same lullaby tune to me, and it was as if the sound were placed within my mind. I did not have to think as the sound enveloped my mind. It was safe, comforting, and natural.

A feeling I had not felt in many years.

I stopped to examine the oldest looking books before moving on. The sickness inside of me was one that I did not want to admit to the healers, so it was up to me to solve. I could only hope to find something that mentioned the cold ache that came and went. The humming stopped as I picked up a thick tome, and a feeling of fear slithered into my body. I dropped the book as fear began to consume me. There was something wrong with that book, and I would not deny my intuition. I could not risk picking up some cursed tome and being cursed on top of the sickness within me. Cursed items were rare, but how was I to explain this feeling without the knowledge? I hated to be faced with the truth, but deep down I knew it was some type of sickness that would kill me. It was after I saw him that this sickness began.

"Where, oh where, could you be?" I mumbled to myself as I turned in a circle.

The book would need to be older, though perhaps it was not bound in leather? It was not that black book, but perhaps it was near the book? *Was I being drawn towards the book because of blood Sacredness, or were the Gods guiding my hand?* I turned towards the stack of books where I had abandoned the tome.

A dark, deep, and guttural growl sounded from somewhere within me. My mind seemed to echo with the growl as my body shuddered.

"**No.**" A deep voice seemed to growl within my mind. I jolted as I turned to look over each of my shoulders. There was nothing there. No one was in here but me. I shivered again as fear slithered through my veins. *Something was happening, but I wasn't sure what.*

"What the Hel?" I muttered as my heart raced rapidly. Something was here, but I didn't see anything. *Was it a warning from the Gods?* The Gods had to be looking upon me and guiding me in the direction they wanted. I shivered before turning away from the books. They wouldn't hold what I needed, the Gods had declared it.

It felt as if I had searched for hours within the library, and I was sure I had. With exhaustion and disappointment consuming my soul, I came to a stop at the last pile of books. The stack was only knee-high, and searching it was quick. **Nothing!** I wanted to yell. An urge flowed through me to destroy. To knock every book over and tear out every page, and if I had the energy to do, so I was sure that I would have. With a heavy sigh, I turned on my heel and stalked towards the entrance.

"Stupid, piss-poor library." I grunted out as I kicked a stack of books as I passed.

Deep down, I knew that it would be a fruitless endeavor, but I had hoped to find at least one book about this sickness. My only other option would be to hunt down Froggy and trade him for information. I shoved another stack over with a grunt, almost feeling more angry that it brought me no relief. The books boomed as they hit the stone floor, bringing me an insignificant amount of joy.

"I should have never-" A single page fluttered from the rubble, landing at the toe of my boot.

Were the Gods looking at me with favor? I snatched the page off the ground, turning the blank side away from me so I could examine it. I didn't know it then, but it was important. The color was faint, but it still showed a crude drawing of a bind rune. The runes fell down in a straight line; *algiz, gebo, and dagaz.* I crumbled the paper and threw it across the room.

I was a fool. The Gods weren't looking at me with favor. They were certainly laughing at my stupidity—we existed for their entertainment, and I was sure they were laughing at what a fool I was. I turned to look at the mess of a library, hoping that I would see the black tome that I was warned away from, but was met with only disaster.

With a huff, I turned on my heels and stomped towards the exit. I raised my arm to quickly pull the curtain aside when everything went black.

Drip. Drip. Drip.

There was no way to tell if my eyes were opened or closed as thick darkness enveloped me completely.

Drip. Drip. Drip.

Something was somewhere nearby, but turning to look felt impossible. The library. I'd been in the library.

Drip. Drip. Drip.

I floated in the darkness with nothing. Somewhere deep inside myself, I knew I was safe. I was protected. This was not my end.

Drip. Drip. Drip.

"Please—" A man's voice rang out, cut off by a sharp smack.

Drip. Drip. Drip.

"You lie. You may speak when you..." I began to respond, trailing off as fear shot through me.

Drip. Drip. Drip.

The darkness began to lift slowly, as if it were a fog blowing away. I blinked once. Twice. Thrice.

Drip. Drip. Drip.

I could feel the damp air on my skin, smell the tang of blood, and hear the sounds of chains rattling. The library? This was not the library.

Drip. Drip. Drip.

Opening my eyes felt impossible as I continued to float in the darkness. The muscles of my face felt heavy, weighed down. It took all of my strength to finally wrench my eyes open fully. *Why was there a beaten man kneeling at my feet?* He looked familiar in a way, but it was difficult to tell through his swollen and bloodied face. *Where was I? What had I done?* Without a thought, I kicked my boot into the man's face before turning and stalking out of the room. This was not the library. *Fear.* My heart thundered as fear and anger coursed through my entire being. Feelings so deep that they threatened to consume me entirely.

Who was that man? Why had I beaten him? Where was I?

The heavy door was loud as it slammed behind me, the latch creaking as I struggled to place it with shaking hands. It was only moments before my feet were abruptly running down the dark hallway. The walls were familiar, but I couldn't place where I had seen them before. They almost looked like the walls of my father's dungeons, but the walls held no paintings as they once had. I did not think as I rushed with pounding footsteps, my body moved entirely on its own.

Was this a memory? Had I fallen asleep only to remember some- thing I had forgotten?

I'd beaten many men for information in the past, but I'd spent years trying to forget the sounds of their waling. A wave of pain clutched my chest. It pounded, pulsed, and twisted an icy path through me. My hand shot out to catch myself against the wall, my body tumbling soon after. I did not feel the pain of hitting the wall, but I groaned all the same. My eyes squeezed shut on their accord as the pain ripped through me.

As quickly as it came on, it disappeared as everything faded to black.

My eyelids were heavy as I shivered and groaned in pain on the cold, damp stone floor. The ceiling swirled and swayed above me as it brought a wave of nausea on. *Where was I? What the Hel happened?* The muscles in my neck screamed as I turned my head. *The library.* I was in the library. *What the Hel happened?* The weight of my arm was almost too much as I shakily brought my hand to press into the tender spot of my temple, pulling it away to see the blood streaking my trembling fingers. **It was a dream.** I'd blacked out, smelled my blood, and had a dream.

There were many times that I had dreamed of the horrors I had committed while I was within the stronghold. The Thralls I beat, the men I sentenced to death. Years had not done much to quell the ache of losing pieces of my soul to those atrocities. My body wavered as I heaved myself up to sit. I was a dishonorable man once, and I could only hope to redeem myself.

Embarrassment flared through me as I took in the way I had raged through the room I had once tried to keep safe. I was just as bad as Ivaldr, if not worse. *Shame.* That's what settled deep into my gut as I turned on my heel with wobbly knees. This sickness could not take me before I could right my wrongs. I needed to do something, but it all felt like too much.

The echo of my steps felt loud as I stumbled my way through the halls and common caverns. They weren't as beautiful as they'd once been. Tomorrow I vowed to appreciate the beauty as I once had. *Tomorrow. I will be better tomorrow. I would **not** give in to the anger within me. I would **not** allow those pieces of lost soul to corrupt me any further.* Years had gone by, my anger had faded, and I was a new man. I was no longer crafted in the image of my father, but the fear still slinked its way into my mind whenever it could. *Would I one day lack my soul in the way he lacked his? Would my eyes be the eery blue that shone down at me as his fists flew?* My heart picked up as my breath stuttered in and out.

Weak. I was weak. There was no time to be weak. I could not sit in this weakness. I must keep moving. *Living.* This cycle was not new, and I knew how it would end. I would vow to change everything. *Do more. Do better.* Then I would fall right back into the cycle of hating myself for not doing more while I actively did nothing. *This time would be different, it had to be different.* The sickness inside of me seemed to swirl in laughter as pain radiated deep into my bones. The Norns had dealt me this fate, and I would laugh in their faces as I figured out how to purge this sickness from my body. My body shuddered through another deep shiver as I folded my arms over my chest.

Sleep. I needed to sleep this off. Rest would do me well, right? My feet felt heavy as I trekked through the twists and turns with my head down. I knew that no one would try to speak with me, but the fear remained. *What was I to tell people? How was I to explain that I was sick in a way I had never felt before?* **Oh yes**, I imagined myself saying, **I looked into the cold eyes of a soulless man, and it had brought that coldness to my body**. I huffed out a laugh as I turned the corner, nearly running into a woman.

"Sorry." I muttered out as I stepped around her.

"Alfrikr," Her voice was a melodic tone that tugged deep inside myself. My steps faltered as I turned my head over my shoulder to look at her. I didn't recognize the small woman, but I gave her a tight smile anyway.

"Fight it." She whispered before hurrying around the corner.

Fight it? What was I to fight? It made little sense, but I didn't have it within me to cycle on something else. I was full of thoughts that encouraged the fear building within me, and consumed by the ever-pressing dread.

I was sick, scared, and weak.

"Alfrikr." Doran called out as he strode out of the passageway to my left.

"Doran." I nodded at him as I stopped to stand in front of him.

He wasn't who I wanted to see, but I hadn't wanted to see anyone right now. I wanted to go lay down, sleep the fear away, and have dreams that weren't littered with my past actions. Yet, there was comfortability in seeing the man, and it would be good for me to be with someone I trusted.

"Who was that?" He asked, nodding his head towards where the woman had gone.

"Dunno." I shrugged my shoulders as my eyes never moved from his face. He said more with his face than he realized, and I knew better than to ignore his reactions.

"Hmm," His eyebrows furrowed as he continued to gaze down the hall. "Where have you been?"

It wasn't an odd question for him to ask, but the tone of his voice set me on edge. Doran was a shadow to Ivaldr, one that went around gathering information and tracking Dallen, and I's movements. It was an odd thing to know that my best friend was detailing my every move, but that was just how our relationship was.

"Was going to the library, it was trashed, and so I left." I lied. I don't understand why I lied, but the urge to dampen my sickness was strong.

"Why is there blood on your face?"

"Wasn't watching where I was going." I shrugged as I brought my fingers up to scratch at the crust along my temple. "Opened the curtain and tripped over a book. Got up, and left."

"Hmm, is that so?"

"Why wouldn't it be?" I questioned back with a raised brow.

"Have you gone to see Ivaldr?" Doran changed the subject abruptly, as he often did. Interacting with the quiet man was odd. There was no in between with him. He was either a weak man who shuddered as he spoke, or he was the regal Jarl's son who spoke with confidence. There was much that went on in his mind, I was sure.

"Why?"

Doran didn't respond for a moment, and I knew he was racking his brain to say the perfect thing. It was frequently that he did that, and I knew that it wouldn't be long before something disgustingly regal came out of his mouth. His eyes stared directly into my own in such a way that it made me feel foolish.

I knew why, he knew I knew why, but I couldn't help but pretend I did not.

"There's nothing to tell him." I finally caved, sighing as I moved to lean against the wall. The pain had gotten stronger as I stood, and my knees threatened to buckle under my weight.

"I'm off to see him now, you're welcome to join."

"I've got plans…"

"With?"

"My bed?"

Doran scoffed as he turned on his heel, "May the Gods be with you, Alfrikr." His voice was an exact replica of his Jarl father's condescending drawl.

I cringed as the memory of my mother's beheading flashed to the forefront of my mind. *How her shoulders had shaken as my father beat at Cor's neck with angry grunts. The way it had grimaced at the sky. How I had never once felt her presence since then, and how it often made me doubt that those with the God's could look down upon us.* I missed her as much now as I did as soon as she had died. I shivered as another wave of nausea rolled through my gut. Life had gotten odd, and I wasn't sure how to navigate it right now. I'd seen Esmeren, gotten sick, trashed the library, and now I'd have to go speak with Ivaldr.

Doran wouldn't let it go, and I was sure he was on his way to tell Ivaldr all about how I'd seen Esmeren. *How aggressive I'd been with her. What sort of dishonor I'd brought on the rebellion because I didn't tuck tail and run.* It was a slippery slope that I'd fallen down, one that would consume my thoughts until all I could think about was what if's. My cavern felt cold, empty, and lonely as I pulled the curtain back. *How could I long to be alone just as much as I ached for company?* I wanted to come home to someone, but I knew there was no one like that for me. How nice it must be to never be alone with my thoughts. I almost longed for a twin at that moment.

Another half of myself who would be there for me always.

4

FOOLS AND MEETINGS

ONE TENDS TO FORGET, ESPECIALLY AFTER NINE YEARS, THAT sheared heads and fabric do **not** mix well. I stood in the middle of my cave with my arms locked above my head, and the crown of my head stuck like a burr in a wolf's tail. The struggle was futile, much like being in an open body of water. The more you struggle, the more you seem to suffer. The edges of my vision had seemed to fade as cold pain tore through my body.

Did all those who sheared their heads yesterday morning currently stand entrapped in their clothing as well?

Perhaps I was just a fool.

I could almost hear the Gods laughing at me; their deep rumble of a laugh echoing inside my head. I shivered as I stood there freezing cold with my arms stuck above my head. The sickness felt worse, as if it had burrowed deeper into my bones. Though a fool I may be, I grinned as I finally pushed my head through the hole of my tunic, the chill had not yet seemed to recede from my bones. Those dark obsidian eyes had locked onto mine through my pitiful attempt at more sleep after the library. Whether I was awake or asleep, all I could think of was those soulless eyes.

There had been a hatred surrounding them that could have only been formed by Hel herself. A bitter cold surrounded the lack of his soul, one that I could feel from paces away. One that had latched onto my body and seeped into my bones. As if the sickness within him had flowed from his body into mine. My intuition tugged as I thought of the sickness, *I knew he had done it.* The center of my chest felt tight as I stretched my arms backwards, it had to have been from carrying my shield two days ago. Though, the feeling was unfamiliar and felt too cold to be a knot of muscles. *Has the cold shifted to a different part of my body?* I feared it would overtake me completely.

While my body ached and my mind felt shattered, I relished the burning in my muscles. It had been far too long since I had done anything productive. If there was a way into Valhalla through being patient, I would have won nine times over. Though, I did enough sparring to be ready for battle, even if it was entirely with Dallen. I was weak.

I had finally given up on trying to regain enough energy to feel full. *Would my Sacredness always feel this depleted? Would my energy take ten times longer to replenish for the rest of my days? Would my runes continue to ache as though I had rubbed ice upon them? What would it take to drop this sick feeling that consumed me?* All of these feelings made me want to swing my fists until my knuckles bled, or maybe go for a walk in the woods. These were equally pleasing ideas.

Perhaps I could find some sorry soul to spar with and beat into a pulp.

Ivaldr had dropped by sometime in the hours of dawn, alluding to the fact he knew more than I wanted him to. He may have been a dull man who could not read, but there was an uneasy sneakiness about him that it seemed only Dallen and I could see. Not that I was hiding anything, but the knowledge I had learned was nothing substantial, and I hated knowing that he knew of the cold swirling inside of me. Something important was amiss within me, and I would figure out what it was. He was usually harsher when it was just him and me, but I am certain my bloodshot eyes and sheared head is what made him give me grace.

"After mid-meal," he'd said as he turned on his heel. His runes on full display, as always. Ivaldr was proud of his swirled, patchwork runes. I often fought through my father's voice in my mind, insisting that people like him were lesser. I admired his resolve and confidence, even if I despised the man. He was a balding, bastard child of a Jarl, though no one knew who. I had a few suspicions, there were a few who were known to make their way through brothels. Only his left arm had runes pristinely etched into his skin.

Those of Karl or Thrall blood tended to have translucent runes, the darkness varying depending on levels of power. Generations ago, there were not such drastic differences in their Sacredness' power. Slowly, but surely, the Sidirnians were losing Sacredness. Thralls were typically born into enslavement, but one who owed too many debts could be sold into Thrall-hood and condemn all in their bloodline under them. I had heard rumors that Ivaldr's mother had been the sister of my mother, but I would never know the truth. It sounded like a rumor to bring him closer to royal blood. If he were my kin, I would feel no different about him. Unlike most, Ivaldr always kept his hair neatly sheared, claiming he would only grow it out when the Rikr and Jarls had been torn from power. I knew it was because he was losing his hair.

If the light shone just right on his shiny head, you could see the lack of hair that grew upon the top of his head. *I almost felt bad for him.*

While he claimed to want to rip evil men from power, there was a direct opposition to his actions. He wished to sit and braid daisy chains instead of charging through the stronghold's keep. He thought that we never had enough numbers, even if we were constantly building more and more to house all of those within the rebellion.

If it were up to me, we would have bloodied the ground with the Jarls blood years ago. Instead, we sat on our arses.

I ran a hand down my sheared head with a heavy sigh, the itchiness would set in soon. Hair was a part of a person's life song; as if a bard had written a song through the strands on our heads. The longer one's hair was, the more peaceful their life was, and single braids were often decorated with beads woven into them. Those with shorter or sheared hair were given grace, those surrounding them would approach them with love and kindness.

Not all within the rebellion were willing to put aside their biases towards the nobly bred and treat us with kindness.

I gave my cavern a quick glance through, knowing that even if someone were to enter and fiddle with my belongings, I would not know. Their Sacredness might leave a signature that I could never track. The cavern system within the mountain made it easy enough to swirl Sacredness signatures into one tangled string. Yet, I would not put it past Ivaldr to have someone search my quarters while I was meeting with him. He played a fool to me, but I still felt the prickle of his doubts. His pettiness knew no bounds, and he loved to irritate me. Especially drawing on the fact I was not allowed to play an active role within the rebellion.

Doran, Dallen, Merelda, and I were still working through a so-called trial period. Though we'd been here nine years, and had clearly proven our loyalty, we were still left in the dark on many things. Doran was more privy to knowledge, yet he only shared plans for harvest, population numbers, and nothing that would truly assist us in real change. The rebellion did not take drastic measures, though I had suggested many. They felt the most peaceful route was the way to win, yet they seemed to just tread water. Never truly gaining more rights nor land. Even still, we mostly found ourselves working the crops or mining out new living spaces. Though, Merelda had found herself a small group of healers and was first to deliver a new babe.

I stepped out of the mouth of the cavern, and onto the main path. Meeting with Ivaldr couldn't wait, as much as I wished for it to. The largest part of my brain was cycling through the different ways he would kick me out of here. *What would I do when I lost my home? What if I had to leave because others would catch this chill? What if it were a curse?* The only other place I could go would be out in the wilds. I now had the knowledge of survival skills, but would that be a life worth living? I drew my fist to my chest, digging the knuckles of my left hand in, sighing through the flare of icy pain.

The sickness.

Ymir's Mountain could be easily compared with the structure and layouts of a fine stronghold. The hallways throughout the hideaway were at least three arm lengths wide, and the ceiling vaulted up decoratively. Many of the main pathways had intricate carvings into stone, but the hall leading from my cavern was by far my favorite. It was as though you were walking through the body of a snake, like Jörmungandr himself had slithered along and left behind the imprints of his scales. Carved ravens could be found almost anywhere you looked, their beaks pointing you in the right direction through small runes carved atop their outstretched wings had you found yourself lost.

Dallen preferred to assist in the development and construction of the caves within, and below, the mountain. Which was helpful for knowing each secret route that Ivaldr wanted to be made. Dallen drained their Sacredness slower than the Karls or Thralls, which gave him the ability to carve into the mountains longer. I preferred to work the crops, hunt for meat, and other hands-on busywork over grounding out new hallways, common areas, and caverns. Dallen was skilled with a chisel, creating artwork that spanned entire sections of stone. Had he not been born to the parents he had, I was sure that he would be known for his art.

The end of my hallway met a circular cavern, with hallways connecting in three different directions. It was easy to get used to the intricate beauty of the mountain, but I found it important to never normalize myself to it. I wanted to always appreciate it and never place myself in a position where I was not thankful for the way I felt so connected to the Gods. There were many common area caverns throughout the mountain, too many to count, with each having off splitting hallways of either three or nine.

These numbers were sacred to our people, though Sidirna as a whole had abandoned the knowledge of the Gods and Goddesses who had once walked our land. My father never permitted me to learn of the Gods, but that did not stop me. I would often, much to my tutor's displeasure, sneak into the restricted shelves of the library to find as many books as I could about the Gods. While there are many aspects to Sacredness, numbers were a direct connection to the Gods. I had learned of this through my grandmother, who was Thrall born. The knowledge continued to pass through the Thralls and

Karls through word of mouth. Something that the Alfrikr's of the past had never accounted for.

Three is a divine number that pays tribute to the three Norns, the three days Odinn laid dead after sacrificing himself to become a God, and the three roots of Yggdrasil.

Nine is a Sacred number that honors the nine days that Odinn hung on Yggdrasil. After, the Sacredness of runes were revealed to him. The number also stood for the nine realms that flowed from Yggdrasil and the nine steps Thor will take before falling dead during Ragnarök.

It is common knowledge that our distant Alfar ancestors had carved nine sets of three runes into their skin for nine generations before we were graced with the knowledge and powers of Sacredness. There were once two races in Sidirna; the Ljosalfar and the Dokkalfar. The Ljosalfar were light elves of soft, distinct beauty and kindness. While the Dokkalfar were their direct opposites, unappealing and evil. Through the many years, the two races intermingled throughout Sidirna to the point where one was not distinguishable to their ancestors.

Though, I'd heard once that distant lands still held archaic laws that prevented the intermingling.

Though, the lack of presence of the Gods could be indicative of their displeasure of our actions. The fact that the Alfrikr's held no respect towards the Gods had to be the reason Sidirna suffered as a whole. We were now born with the nine sets of three runes upon our skin, on our forearms. The runes were a mix from the Norns, each person being their mix. While most did not know much about the runes, I had heard from my mother that the Norns decided which runes we needed most. Though, the Karls and Thralls seemed to be losing their Sacredness, thus their connection with the Gods.

Some throughout the rebellion claimed that the Gods were

displeased with the lack of honor, strength, and loyalty. That the Karls and Thralls had become complacent, no longer were the most honorable, strongest, nor loyal in charge of the peoples. They claimed that the nobly bred, and their darker runes, were graced by Loki for being the most deceptive tricksters. I was not sure where my thoughts agreed, perhaps somewhere in the middle. We exist for the entertainment of the Gods, and maybe giving us Sacredness was not entertaining enough.

Living deep within a mountain surely was not.

Our Sacredness came from the runes, as though they were all little flasks that held the depths of our energy. Our strengths and weaknesses of Sacredness were found in the visibility of our runes that settled completely with maturity. While we all had access to the basics of fire, water, and ground Sacredness, each person's strengths were their own. Some could control the temperature of their water, such as creating ice or even boiling water, while some could barely control a spurt of water. We must first have direct access to the element, before being able to control it. We cannot summon fire if there are no flames nearby.

I am not incredibly powerful, but my reserves are vast. While I am skilled with fire and water, ground Sacredness is one that I rarely use. Fire and water Sacredness need less of my energy to control. Ground Sacredness is almost foreign to me as it requires my full attention. Though, not all are like that. Dallen is quite skilled with ground Sacredness, and his reserves seem to last as long as mine do with fire. Doran seems to have an ease of access through all three.

I was lost in my thoughts of the Gods, runes, and Sacredness during the walk to the council room. My feet had taken the path without any necessary thoughts, and I now found myself standing in the common cavern connected to the planning and political system of the rebellion. Another flare of pain shuttered down my body, the iciness causing a deep shiver. Nine hallways branched off, with only one entrance shining light out. A part of me briefly wondered if the boys would be here too, though I was doubtful. To get the full explanation of such a delicate situation, you must separate each person and piece it together through a woven explanation of what happened.

"Alfred?" Ivaldr's warm, deep baritone floated out of the entrance; his steps so silent I could barely make them out.

Nine years later and he still did not remember my name? Times like these made me want to bash Ivaldr's head in and take his seat of power. Power, that is all it was. Ivaldr knew I was stronger, so he took to petty words to push me below him. Had he been waiting in the shadows for my arrival? The top of his head came six inches below mine, though he was no means a small man, as he stood 6 '0 tall. I stood there silently, unsure of what to say as a small shiver wracked my body. *Was this a situation where I was looked at as a fellow member, or was I still on the outskirts, eternally different from all those that surrounded me?* As if there were not one point in my life where I fit right with anyone, besides Dallen and Doran. In the past, with Esmeren, though, that could never be rectified.

"Feeling better?" Ivaldr motioned me into the cavern, "You looked like Hel earlier." He padded after me with heavier footsteps, they almost seemed threatening.

Was this where I would die?

I could easily turn on my head and bash his head into the stone walls before he grabbed me.

"Better, yes." I hummed softly, stepping around the chair in front of his desk, waiting to sit until he sat, as was our custom.

Our roles should be reversed.

Ivaldr frowned at me as he slowly sunk into his chair.

"Although, I'm not feeling completely alright. It feels as if my body has flowed down Èlivàgar." I tacked on quietly, honestly.

Somewhere in the Distant Lands, a river was infused with Sacredness from Niflheim, the land of eternal ice, and is said to run along the border of our realm from theirs. Élivàgar flows from a well, Hvergelmir, where Ymir the ice giant was created, and where our lands were built by his corpse. Sacredness had built our lives, and Sacredness had destroyed mine. Were others feeling this way? Was it a chill that I had picked up, or was Ivaldr finally making a move to take me down? He was too petty and cowardly to do so, I decided. It had to have happened at the raid.

Ivaldr hummed a tense sound, his eyebrows furrowing, and his bottom lip coming to rest between his lips. He gnawed his lip between his teeth, tearing at the skin as he sat in silence. I shifted awkwardly as the ribbons of cold seemed to take hold of my ribs, twirling so it could touch between my bones.

"Start from the beginning, when you left with the others." Ivaldr spoke after what felt like an eternity of silence.

5

HAUNTINGS AND SOULS

THE MORNING OF THE RAID

I HAD SPARRED ENDLESSLY SINCE THE MOMENT I COULD WIELD A sword, but I had never once found myself truly participating in combat. It had been nine years since I'd found myself venturing further out than a few miles for hunting, and yet I was not filled with the slightest drop of enthusiasm that morning. A small puddle of dread had settled within my belly, as though an omen had been drunk down like an unsettling mead. For all my years here, this ninth had felt the hardest. I had spent many agonizing moments during those years before Ivaldr's hearth, pleading to play an active role within this rebellion.

Begging to branch off from the peaceful route that was getting us nowhere.

This winter would be the end of a cycle, a nine-year cycle, where food would be more scarce than usual. Through much deliberation, as in, *I had begged and pleaded,* and the elders had begun to voice their concerns. We were finally making a move. The winter stores for the Rikr and his inner circle of Jarls were kept in a discreet and small town, ten miles from the Mountain and twenty miles from the Rikr's Stronghold. Through our spies within the keep, mostly servants and a few unnamed

Jarls, we had learned of their plan to keep the stores far enough away that they hoped townsfolk would not raid them in desperation. It was another example of how the upper class cared little for the people.

Every able-bodied person was coming along to ensure that we were able to carry as much food back as we could. The warriors would start the journey first, after twenty minutes all others would start after us. Those who were not warriors would partner with others to pull wagons behind them, lead the horses, or fill their packs with as much as they could. The walk would take us warriors two hours, the others would take four to five hours. This allowed us enough time to secure the storage buildings, reducing the lives lost. Ivaldr had taken the credit for my plan, but I was willing to let it go to him. *They would never trust the idea coming from me.*

My shield was strapped to my back, and I felt like a meandering fool as I walked towards the crowd outside. Navigating throughout it was difficult, the edge of my shield kept clanking against others. There was a hum of excitement that seemed to radiate from the ground and through the air surrounding the crowd. I had finally pushed myself through the crowd far enough to find Dallen and Doran.

"I thought you weren't going to show, Riki!" Dallen exclaimed as he punched my arm lightly. His hair was braided back neatly against his scalp, much like everyone else's gathered around us. The wind blew softly, fluttering the pieces of his beard around.

"Aye, I'm not even late!"

"It must have taken ye a moment to squeeze into yer armor!" Dallen shouted as he reached a fist out to mock punch my stomach. While it has been years since I have worn my armor, I would not say that my stature has changed much in nine years. Though maybe I was kidding myself.

"You're one to speak, where are yours?" I replied, his gaze hardened as I looked him up and down.

Dallen's eyebrow suddenly quirked, and a goofy grin appeared on his face. It was then that I realized how much we had aged, how the last time we had gone on a trek together, he had glowed with his youthful agility. How much we both must have changed internally, and how much life we had squandered while sitting on our hands.

This rebellion was weak, but I would never be considered anything apart from someone who bore a resemblance to the old Rikr.

There was no point in rebelling against the rebellion; my other options were slim.

"I've just grown more muscular!" he claimed as he moved to flex his arm.

He had grown more, yes, but time will do that to you. Not that our sparring together went anywhere, though today could be counted as a singular moment deserving of the rigorous training we placed upon ourselves. I spent a lot of my time with Dallen, or alone. I still feared the judgment of others, and it felt suffocating as I stood in a crowd of people.

A horn sounded from somewhere up ahead, signally our departure would be soon. I dreaded the walk, but I was excited about finally taking a stand against my father. I could almost picture the way his face would twist as it took on an unimaginable shade of red. How he would splutter and spit as he tried to find the words to scream. A smile worked itself way onto my face as I imagined it all.

"Are you prepared?" Doran asked as we began to trail after the other warriors.

"As well as can be." I replied with a shrug.

"I could barely sleep last night, I was so excited!" Dallen practically hooted out as his steps held an undeniable bounce.

"I went by your caverns and you weren't there." Doran tutted out, elbowing his brother with a grin.

The hopeful feeling was infectious as we all trailed down the mountain's path. Laughter was had, food was shared, and I just knew that this day would be one that I remembered for the rest of my life.

How wrong I was then to think I'd be old and gray looking back on this day with joy.

THE TREK WAS LONG, and I felt as though I would fall where I was crouched. My shoulders ached from the extra weight, and the arches of my feet felt broken in two. We'd just reached the outskirts of where the grains are stored, and Ivaldr, Doran, and a few other high-ranking rebels stood huddled together whispering. Dallen sat beside me as I stretched my arms behind my back, placing my palms flat on the ground before falling far enough that my rump hit the ground.

"What do you think they're whispering about?" He asked as he nodded his head towards the men.

We both shared the same insignificant amount of animosity towards Doran for being accepted within the rebellion in a way neither of us were, which we would learn why in a few months from then. Doran had always been the more level-headed of us, the more passive, and Ivaldr had praised those qualities within him. Through the last nine years, his loyalty had never wavered from defending me, but I still felt resentful that he had been given a chance to speak while I was silenced.

Dallen and I had views that were considered too extreme for the rebellion. We viewed direct action as the best way to get what we wanted. I still held on to my hope that I would one day be accepted. Dallen had been formally excluded from all official talks. He could not even attend the open meetings that were held on each solstice, where all people were encouraged to share their thoughts and ideas.

One too many times he had publicly ridiculed the lack of anything achieved by the rebellion.

I admired his ability to cause a scene. My heart would hammer in my chest as if a tiny blacksmith were crafting a blade within my chest at the mere thought of public ridicule. Though I was no stranger to it, it happened whether I spoke out or not. Yet, Dallen had the courage to straighten his spine and hold his head up straight as he demanded attention and respect.

"Can't you just...hear your brother's thoughts?" I wasn't quite sure how it worked, and I'm not sure whether I'd ever truly understand it. I was once again thankful my soul had not been born to split into two bodies.

"It doesn't work that way, you should know that." Dallen shook his head, "It's simple, you know? I can speak into his mind. He can speak into mine. We can share memories, thoughts, and all that if we are really using the connection. It is not a steady link."

Was it that simple? I was never genuinely concerned about how their minds were interwoven. I knew they never liked to be apart for long, and I was often jealous of their connection.

I'd never really focused on the specifics of their connection, and I felt guilty for it. Not that I thought I would remember this for any future reference.

"Huh, well, have you asked him?" *It could not be that hard, could it?* I moved to scratch at my elbow, knocking off a bug in the process.

"Only a dozen times." Dallen sighed as he flopped completely onto the dirt.

His shirt rode up as he stretched his arms above his head, the deep black of his lower abdomen seemed to shine in the sunlight. I averted my gaze back to Doran, squinting as I tried to make out the movements of his mouth. It was a futile attempt to keep myself informed, but there was no doubt that he was going to shirk any responsibility of sharing information.

Time moved slowly as we sat upon the ground, laughter swirled around us, and Dallen had begun to ramble about his latest conquest. I had closed my eyes and only half-listened, as I knew that they would not be around long. I admired his ability to create connections with others.

"…and then she dug her nails so deep into my arse that I felt blood wash down my legs. I'm going to see her again once we return." His head was still tilted up towards the sky, eyes closed.

"You'll see who again?" Doran's voice lilted out, his steps silent as he approached. I jumped as I turned my head up to catch him fiddling with a knife above me.

"We will march soon," Doran added as Dallen began naming off names, unsure of the name of the last woman in his bed.

"What were you talking about?" I asked Doran, ignoring Dallen's ramble.

Doran's eyebrows turned downwards as he gave me a quizzical look. He did this often, staying silent to avoid answering directly. I knew he would avoid being honest, but I still believed in his ability to further the rebellion. He was just quiet by nature, the polar opposite to his brother. It must be some split-soul thing. Doran was no threat, but I often had to remind my cycling thoughts of that fact. Every once in a while I would get a tug to my intuition that there was something he was hiding. *That deep down he hated me as everyone else had.* Yet, I'd never felt that way about Dallen, and I knew they were the closest things to brothers I'd ever have.

"Get your arses up." Ivaldr shouted, my head whipping in his direction.

We all scrambled to our feet, not in unison at all. We were a thrown together crew, never having interacted all together enough to truly anticipate the movements of the ones next to us.

A sad excuse of a rebellion, one that was too passive to even run drills.

Thank the Gods that the Rikr had not forced his way into our mountain, for if he had, we would all perish.

"Together we will ensure our people are fed! Together, we will show the wicked Rikr that we are always watching! Together, we can..." Ivaldr had begun shouting, though the cheers had far outweighed his ability to project his voice.

Dallen bounced on his feet as we started off towards the man. This was our chance to make a real change. We would ensure our people were fed and would starve the Rikr to accomplish it.

"Ready?" Doran asked from my side, hovering close to my side.

I nodded in response, unsure of what exactly to say. I had been ready for a long time, and I had nearly gotten on my knees to beg Ivaldr to do this. Of course I was ready, and he had to have known that.

"A lot will change after this," Doran added softly, barely above a whisper. "Our people will be fed, and we will prosper."

Before I knew it, we were marching down, more so scrambling like little ants, towards the grain stores. I could feel in my bones that today would be a significant turning point in my life, though I had far underestimated just how significant it would be. Plans had already fallen through and many simply ran towards the closest buildings. Doran and Dallen had closed in on either side of me, but Doran directed our steps. It was complete and utter chaos all around us, so I didn't bother to ask him where we were going. It wasn't long before we entered a building near the outskirts of the small village. Doran was first to enter with his back straight, though his steps faltered as he saw two men already inside.

"Hello!" Dallen called out as he maneuvered around his brother, and began to grab bags of grain.

Time moved quickly as I began to help, and I was bent over hauling bags of grain into a wagon when I first heard the pounding, in-sync, footsteps of what could only be the guards. My back straightened quickly as I whipped my head towards the entrance of the building I was in. *May the Gods be in our favor, and may we all survive.* There were only a few of us in here, Doran and Dallen were near the entrance, Winser was to my left, and Hallok stood in the far corner. I felt the flair of adrenaline in my chest, the longing for a fight I had anticipated for the last nine years, and joy seemingly flowed down my arm as I readied myself.

Would this be the moment I could finally spill blood in the name of the rebellion?

Three distinct shadows fell onto the floor, steadily moving towards the doorway. It only took me a moment to drop the bag and pull my sword from the scabbard, the other men following my movements silently. This was it, the moment I would draw the blood of those loyal to the Rikr. One shadow broke off from the others, stepping inside first.

"Esmeren?" Dallen called out, feet away from her.

My heart stuttered in my chest as I recognized the deep black braids, as though I had just seen them yesterday and not nine years ago. She was not the first I had expected to draw blood from, but I welcomed it nonetheless. Retribution, that is what it would be. Anger flowed through me as I glared at the woman.

"Alfrikr." She softly called before dropping her sword and approaching me quickly.

Did she think me daft?

She must have envisioned me still as the young man full of hope, thinking he could change the way our people still suffered.

I kept my sword firmly in my hand as my previously betrothed stopped feet before me. There was a single moment where I wasn't sure how to react, but my anger won the battle quickly. Her betrayal stung harsh within my heart, feeling like it had when I first left. When she had chosen to stay behind, break our betrothal, and betray me. Esmeren meant nothing to me, but I could admit I often imagined the moment I would kill her for her betrayal.

Her red rimmed eyes welled with tears, highlighting the stunning green I once loved, as Esmeren came before me. I was not that young man anymore. The green was disorienting and angering now. I would not be captivated by her, nor would her emotions tug at my heart. The old Alfrikr had died that night along with my mother. Esmeren would not know what was coming for her, and I would happily end her. My left hand lurched towards her quickly, tangling in her hair. Esmeren's eyes widened as her chin tilted up, as though she expected me to press my mouth to hers.

What a foolish woman. I tugged down harshly, bringing her to her knees before me.

"Of all the people, It. Is. You?" I muttered as I tilted her head up to look at me. She struggled slightly, just enough to be irritating. "What are you doing here, little bird?" I asked as I dropped the tip of my sword to the dirt, leaning against it to peer into her eyes. It was once a term of endearment, a reference to when we were but children and a flock of ravens had come to roost near the castle. Esmeren was enchanted by the birds; always drifting to watch them, feed them, or speak softly with them.

"I-I..." She sucked in a large breath, a small but obvious attempt of steadying herself.

I loosened my grip in her hair by a fraction as I almost felt guilty. We'd grown up together, knowing that one day we would marry. There was barely a memory of my childhood that did not have Esmeren's laugh tinkling through it. Though, she had cut down that respect when she had refused to leave with us. She was always a touch too loyal to her parents. I hated how much they'd always loved her. Merelda had chosen us, though she had also received that love.

Esmeren was weak.

I did not care about her.

I would not give in to the turmoil within me.

"After you left," Esmeren began quietly. "My father refused to house me. My mother wouldn't look at me. They were disappointed because I didn't stay true to you, and my future position."

I quirked an eyebrow, encouraging her to continue. She had nine years to find me, and yet she still stayed within the perimeter of the stronghold. She had always been a dull girl, but I had hoped she would have grown since then. Though perhaps she was fated to end tonight. *I hoped I was fated to end her.*

"I joined the Rikr's Valkyrie section of the guard, thinking it would cleanse any bad between my parents and me."

My hand tightened in her hair as I narrowed my eyes towards her. It sounded like a ruse.

"Alfrikr! Let her go!" Doran yelled out, but he did not move. It was not often he raised his voice, and I was stunned as I stared at him.

"Take me with you; I could share information or help in some way. I need to get out of the stronghold."

This was a ploy, it had to be. I didn't trust a single word she had uttered. I didn't hear the footsteps, but my attention shot away from Doran at the sound of a voice clearing. I'd forgotten we weren't alone. Though I wasn't prepared to see another member of the guard. A sharp pang hit my chest, right at the center, as my gaze met a cold, dark, obsidian pair. I barely felt the shiver that wracked my body, but I felt all the air leave my lungs. My fingers twitched as my heart began to thud loudly.

Was it him? Could it be him?

He stood broad in the doorway as his shoulders nearly touched either side. His long black hair hung freely, aside from the handful of smaller braids decorated with shining jewelry. He was unforgettable, striking in a vicious way. My lungs froze as I tried to heave in a breath. The center of my chest began to burn hotly against the cold that consumed my body.

I'm not sure how long I stood there staring at him, long enough that he had made his way across the room. All I could focus on was the sharp, cold presence that came with him. The world around me faded away as fear and pain enveloped my senses. Shivers began to wrack through my body as it became hard to focus on anything but him.

My muscles felt frozen as my chest pulsed an unfamiliar beat.

Thump, thump, thump *sounded in time with his footsteps.*

Has time slowed down?

Was I about to die?

He stood before me now, and my eyes fluttered up to meet him again. There was probably a two-inch height difference between us, but he was far more broad than me. I wanted to react, to swing my blade up at him. I knew I would lose, but I couldn't force myself to move. I stood there, frozen as he wrenched Esmeren from my grasp, dragging her away without a single word. Strands of her hair stayed tangled between my fingers as I watched him drag her out. I shivered as a cold chill rushed down my spine. *Fear. I should have died.*

Slowly, my muscles tried to warm and I finally took in the surrounding room. Time had seemed to freeze, but it had continued on without me. Doran now stood to my left, Dallen to my right. Hallok and Winser had moved to the doorway, guarding it, most likely. Each held their own brand of fear on their faces.

"Alfrikr? Can you hear me?" Doran's voice tilted out anxiously as he moved a hand to touch my shoulder.

"What happened to him?" Winser asked while peering out of the doorway.

6

BITTER AND FROZEN

Ivaldr folded his hands under his chin on the ornate desk in front of him. It was some scrap of wood that he thrust into Dallen's hands with the demand of a **desk fit for a Rikr.** *Not that he was anywhere close to being a Rikr himself.* I wasn't sure exactly where he saw himself, but it was easy to see how drunk on power he had gotten through the years. If anything, Ivaldr was a passive, petty prick. The respect I'd once had for him faded after arriving at the mountain. He thought himself a God among men, but pretended he had more humility than that.

"What happened after that?" Ivaldr asked, tapping his fingers on his chin. It would be easy to reach across the desk and smash his face in.

"We trekked back." I said, "You were there for that part."

He sighed. "There was nothing said during that. Not even from Doran." He said, then dropped his hands from his chin. "Was it that difficult to inform me beforehand?" He asked.

I couldn't help the look of disbelief that adorned my face as I stared at the shiny-headed man. *What was I to tell him? That I didn't feel well as if he were my mother?* We sat for a moment in silence, me staring at the light reflecting off his head, and him staring intently at me as though he could force me to speak.

"Tell me again about him?" Ivaldr finally sputtered out idiotically. Why did people ask for a story if they did not listen?

I straightened my back in the chair, wiggling uncomfortably. "There was a moment that I felt frozen, the world continued on without me. I did not hear, I saw, but I did not move." His left eyebrow quivered before it rose slowly.

"He left with the girl?" Ivaldr said, "The one you were betrothed to, who is now betrothed to him?"

I felt the icy dread surround my chest, squirming its way into my soul. The bones in my body felt heavy, like they were weighed down by a sheet of ice. My head nodded, I had heard from Doran on the trek back that Loreth was now betrothed to Esmeren. Winser confirmed it, Hallok nodded, and Dallen grimaced.

We had all heard about the man, his reputation preceded him.

He was as soulless as one could be. I'd heard that he would do anything to get what he wanted, and the shiver that wracked my body was confirmation of that. *Had Loreth practiced blood Sacredness to free himself, work his way up the ranks, and then be betrothed to a rich Jarl's daughter?* I wasn't sure how else he could have worked his way into the rank he now relished in. It was obvious that he did what he wanted, so I wasn't sure why my father kept him around. The man killed first, asked questions later. A part of me had always thought he was a myth that mothers told to scare their children into not straying far from the mountain.

"You've given me a lot to think about, Alfred."

I wouldn't give him the satisfaction of seeing me succumb to his petty games. I nodded curtly as I brought myself to stand. My knees were weak, my chest ached, and my lungs felt full of icy dread.

"May the Gods be with you." I muttered as I turned to leave. If anything, I was the one who needed to think about what I had learned. To think about the way a chill shot through my body at the thought of him. I shivered as I closed the door behind me. *How long would I live with this?*

Doran stood in the common area, leaning against the wall to my right. He never strayed far from the man, but I was still surprised to see him lurking about.

"Alright there?" He asked me grimly.

I heaved a breath through the shiver that wracked my body, this was Loreth's fault. It had to be. Though, I wasn't certain exactly what the sickness inside of me was.

"I told him what I know," The lie came easily as I shrugged my shoulders. "I don't feel well."

I took in Doran's form, the way the torch on the wall cast shadows upon his face. He was dressed nicely, as he typically did. Doran was a passive man, but he was determined to still look the part of a Jarl's son. Dallen and I did not share the same sentiment, but it was fun to poke fun at Doran's fashion choices when he was not around.

My trousers and tunic were clean, but they had seen better days. The once dark gray trousers were worn in the knees. I typically wore them while working out in the fields. Today was usually the day I went out in the fields surrounding the mountain. There was a quaint village at the base, filled with Karls, who raised livestock and tended fields of crops. I was not paid for my work, but my work contributed to the community, and that was enough in itself.

"Are you feeling it still?" He questioned, motioning to his chest with his hand.

I nodded once, perhaps a little abruptly. *Thinking about it seemed to worsen it, only surpassed by thinking about Loreth himself.* A shiver wracked my body as the memory of his eyes haunted me again.

"I've got to get to the fields," I said. "We've got a lot of work to do, and winter is approaching fast."

"You're working the crops today?" Doran asked. "Are you well enough to do so?"

"If I don't work, I don't eat."

Doran frowned at me as if he had just learned of the rule. We were meant to work together, meant to support each other, and if you did not contribute you did not get the benefits. Though, perhaps he did not understand, as his work was mostly skulking about and gathering knowledge for Ivaldr.

"I'll see what I can do to change that."

"I don't want you to. The others will not see it the same as you do. I'm not one of them."

"You know that's not true, Alfrikr. You put yourself in that position because you feel guilty of your bloodline." Doran said.

My bloodline had always ruled Sidirna, and I knew that it was a line of wicked Rikr's. There was no good Rikr, and the people revered this notion. While I had never questioned our laws as a child, as a man I had a different perspective. Our borders were only open to the richest Jarls, and the Thralls in their service. The Thralls were left on the ships or killed so they did not share of their adventure to the Distant Lands. They were the only who went and traded goods that were not found here.

The Jarls then owned those goods, after a tax to the Rikr of course, and they regulated those goods to other Jarls or rich Karls at shops in large cities. It was a broken system meant to keep the poor starving and the rich with full bellies. Much would change when I was one day the Rikr of Sidirna.

In the Distant Lands, there were Svatalfar, Ljosalfar, and mixed bloods. All of Sidirna was mixed because of our closed borders.

The first ruler of Sidirna, Alfrikr the First, was a Svatalfar man who intended to keep the bloodline purely Svatalfarian. As time went on, there were plenty of Ljosalfarian and mixed wives to the subsequent Alfrikr's. The harsh and cruel laws of Alfrikr the First only got harsher and crueler. While the Karls had a range of rich to poor, they were under the control of the Rikr nonetheless. Bound by laws that kept them down, they never rose farther, only kept complacent.

It took me years to work through the inherent biases I had been raised to believe.

"It's been nine years, and I am still shunned," I replied. "They avoid me like I will taint the very air they breathe."

"Perhaps they avoid you because of the scowl on your face."

"I don't scowl!"

"Even your smile looks...mean." Doran said, matter-of-factly.

"May the Gods be with you, brother." I muttered as I turned on my heel and stalked out with heavy footsteps.

Doran was accepted within the ranks. He did not understand the way that Dallen and I were treated, instead he blamed our actions for our shunning. *I knew how they whispered. How they avoided me.* There was not much I could do to change their perception, though perhaps I was harsh with a scowl, but I was not my father.

Doran knew how I felt about my father, and for him to

insinuate that it was because I looked mean was ridiculous! *I did not look mean.* Sure, I wasn't a very sociable man, but that did not make me mean. I sighed, slowing my steps as I veered down another hallway.

There was not a single time that I really felt as though my father was happy about my presence. As a child, I talked too much, asked too many questions, and played with the Thrall children too much for his liking. When I hit teenage years, I learned the easiest way to exist would be to put on a mask of what he wanted. I was crueler. I treated the Thralls badly, even when not in his presence because I knew how fast talk got around the stronghold. *There was not a night that I did not sit in my room and feel grossly disgusted with myself.*

My mother understood the feeling, and it was then that we would meet and plan a better future. She was optimistic and always felt that I would take the crown and change Sidirna for all. She had come from a Thrall family, too beautiful to be left there, my father had claimed. Though, I knew that he had accidentally gotten a Thrall servant pregnant while forcing himself upon her. It was why he was so insistent on me not fathering a bastard. *We could not risk the crown going to a weak son, and I was lucky that I was not, or he would end my life.* I could lay with as many men as I wanted, but I was to be cautious and avoid women. I always found it odd how my runes had displayed my powers so vast.

How I had not looked the same as others who had come from a powerful father and a weak mother.

It was not common knowledge of where she had come from, this was something I did not learn until I was 12 years old. It had been used against me the first time by my father, as I kneeled before him, waiting for my lashing. I had been caught again playing with the Thrall children earlier that morning, and my fear festered throughout the day as I awaited my punishment that came at night. My father had berated me for his actions; insisting that my mother had done it on purpose.

He'd threatened many, killed many, and only left my mother alive so she could help with me as a babe. It only made me want to play with Thrall children more, but instead I treated them as lessers. There were many times I'd wished I was one instead of an heir. I was sure to have grown to be stronger, and not mean. I was not a mean man, but perhaps an angry one. The slight warmth in my body dropped considerably as I made my way out of the underground caverns, the worn path kicking up dust in the freezing breeze. Soon, I would need to go out and hunt. I needed a new fur lined cloak for the winter. We all knew what loomed ahead, but speaking about it could entice the God's into worsening it.

For we did exist solely for their amusement.

Every nine years, since the borders closed, we would be hit with a harsh winter. The cycles seemed to be getting worse, as though the land was angry we were here. Many died through these winters, and the spring that followed would be so wet that the crops could not flourish. Floods would overtake the fields. The following summer would reset the cycle, which I always found odd. There had to be a reason why the seasons where the dead were supposed to regrow would be so harsh.

My fingers spasmed and toes curled as a chill wracked my body. My eyes scanned my surroundings, I was not entirely certain he had not already found me. I knew he had promised to take us down, we were a threat to Sidirna, even if we did not do anything but exist. He could be hiding in the trees, waiting to strike me down as I walked. I shook the thoughts out of my head as I continued down the path.

I would not go down without a fight, and it was a dishonorable way to take down an enemy.

"Alf!" Winser called from behind me.

He was shorter than me, probably standing around 6'2. I turned to look at him as he hurried down the path. Winser had a mess of brown hair that never laid flat, yet he did not braid a single lock of it. With a wide set face and his round brown eyes far enough apart; he resembled a fish. While Winser was a simple-minded man and lacked power reserves, he made it up with brute strength. He can drink ale like it is water, and even though he had invited me plenty of times, I never felt he truly wanted me there. Doran said I was doubting myself, and that the brutish man did like me. I thought he was mistaken. I tried to smile at the man, but I found the feeling odd upon my face.

"Crops or livestock?" I asked.

"Aye, a little of both!" He replied, his steps now matching my own.

"Are the sheep prepared for winter?"

"As much as we can get them to be, I reckon we'll lose a few dozen," Winser said.

It was common to lose livestock in the winter through freezing temperatures, wolves, or lack of food. This winter was a different set of circumstances, though. We both knew that, even if Winser wasn't the most intelligent man I had come to know. He was a good and loyal man, I'd give him that.

"May Freyr look down upon us," I muttered.

Freyr was the God of harvests, abundance, health, wealth, and rain and sunshine. It was him that those of us who still looked to the God's worshiped during these times. He is the brother to Freyja, and was once one of the most revered God's aside from Odinn. I said another silent prayer, hoping the God's were still listening.

My father's mother had instilled the knowledge of the God's in me, which was furthered by my research while sneaking through the restricted tomes. My father hired tutors, but they taught me the ins and outs of running the Konungdomr. I would sneak away anytime I could, trying to learn more of those who could bless us. There was once that my grandmother told me that the Norns had visited her in a dream, and it was important that I learned about the Gods so that I stood a chance.

"Aye." Winser said simply, bobbing his head in a nod that was almost ridiculous.

I was unsure of what to say as we walked side by side, so I said nothing. Doran's words cycled in my mind as I tried to figure out what to say. *Was I the creator of my own shunning?*

"So," I finally said with a sigh. "The Cycle will start soon, yeah?"

"Aye." Winder said solemnly, shaking his head as we continued on.

"Nervous?" I wasn't sure how to respond when the man only responded with one word. Was this how it felt to speak with me?

"Aye, but we'll make it."

The cold within my chest seemed to awaken with a vengeance at the talk of the Cycle of Winter. It felt as if the winter had begun inside my body, and this sickness was created from the coldest winter to ever exist. My lungs ached as I drew in the crisp autumn air. The muscles in my hands began to ache as they shuddered and shook, each finger seeming to twitch to its tune.

"W-we have enough meat t-then?" I stuttered out as the cold enveloped my body.

Winser did not react to my sudden chill, but simply nodded his head. I slowed my steps as the cold began to envelope each bone within my body. Winser continued a step in front of me as he nodded his head again. I stumbled as my left knee suddenly went weak.

The sickness inside of me was an icy river carving its path through my body with a vengeance. Filling my lungs with air burned, but I pushed through it as I willed my body to move. I would fight through it. This sickness would not take me, as though I were a weak man.

I was Alfrikr and I would not be sick.

Three steps before we reached the closest field, a sharp pang hit my chest.

The breath left my lungs as my steps stuttered to a stop. Spasms overtook my hands up to my arms, and my knees wobbled as they felt too weak to hold my weight. My blood turned to ice in my veins as I wavered back and forth. Black dots began to crowd my vision, dancing around to the tune of an unfamiliar beat in my chest. Shivers wracked my body as I sank to my knees on the hard path.

Darkness enveloped my vision, and all I could think of were the dark obsidian eyes as I felt my head hit the ground.

7

SHIVERING AND TIMBERS

Darkness. Thick black darkness. My body felt loose and pain free as I floated within the nothingness. Whispers of sounds floated through the darkness; branches cracking, leaves crunching, and huffs of breath. Darkness consumed me in a way that settled any fears that lingered within me.

Breathing was simple and easy. Pain did not coat my bones. Warm. Safe.

I'd stay here forever if I could.

Would death be like this?

I would welcome the warm embrace of death if it meant that I would exist within this safety.

My head felt fuzzy as I opened my eyes, blinking slowly. *Where was I?* The edges of my vision blurred in and out. I blinked through the heavy darkness that flowed to cover the sight before me. Forest. I was in the forest. The leaves had turned, it was autumn. *Why was I here?*

The surrounding trees were familiar, I knew that much. My steps stumbled as a bolt of cold pain laced through my chest. **The sickness. The sickness was within me.** I stumbled to lean against the nearest tree, catching my breath as though I had been running. I could feel the faint feeling of the bark pressing into my shoulder, but the feeling faded in and out.

Pain. Cold, dark, and endless pain.

Safe. Warm, comforting, and eternal safety.

As if one moment I felt fully, followed by a feeling that reminded me of floating in warm water. *The forest.* I was in the forest. The sickness. *Sick. Sick. Sick.* I stared straight towards the small path that had been stamped down by forest creatures. Hunting? Winter. Fur. I needed fur? *Cold. Cold. Cold.*

There was a rustle behind me, but I could not turn my body to see what it was. I tried to flex my fingers, but it was as if I were not leading my body. My vision faded out for a brief second, going completely black, before it slowly came back. **I was floating again, lost in the warm body of water.** The rustle behind me sounded again, but my body did not turn. I knew I was in the forest near the mountain, I typically hunted in this area.

My thoughts were hazy, but returned to me as I leaned against the tree. I took a deep breath of the fresh air as the pain began to fade away. There was a distinct thumping within my chest, but the thought did not unsettle me. **The sickness must have gone to my brain.** I had to be out hunting, but I'd simply forgotten where I was going. I tried to move my arm, but it refused to move. *Rest.* I would need to rest if I wanted to hunt.

I had once lacked the skills of tracking, hunting, and butchering. I'd grown up privileged, without having to learn such skills. That was what we had Thralls for. It was embarrassing to admit that to Ivaldr when I had first arrived, but not as embarrassing as it was to be grouped with small children to learn. The practice bows were small, the targets low to the ground, and the giggles made my face heat with shame. *How I'd felt so grown then, barely a man, surrounded by children whose Sacredness hadn't even fully formed.* They moved small bursts of dirt around, covering my vision as I aimed at the straw stuffed deer.

With a deep breath, my body moved forward one step after the other, yet I was not controlling it. **The sickness.** *Did the sickness control me? Did the Gods laugh at me?* I hopped over a fallen tree; feeling the impact in my right leg as all of my weight landed harshly. *Where was I? What was I doing?* **I could not remember.** *Hunting? Was I hunting?*

The rustle behind me sounded again, followed by a pained grunt. I clutched the short sword in my hand. I felt the cold metal for a moment. **I was drifting now, my thoughts had trouble forming.** *Was I that sick? Has the sickness set in deeper?* My body stopped moving, my head began to turn, looking to the left. I tried again to move my arm, focusing as deep as I could on my fingers. Nothing.

"Almost there." I found myself grunting out. My voice came out throaty, deeper than usual. **I had not had to think to speak, and I did not know who I was speaking to.** *Where was I?*

"Are you sure this is the right way?" A feminine voice sounded from behind me. **It was familiar**, but I could not place who exactly it was. *Who was it? Where was I?*

"Stop talking." My throaty voice said again.

She huffed in response, and I felt the anger build within me. It was a feeling I knew well, but I was not ready for the level in which it consumed me. I wanted to inflict pain on either her or me. Rage filled me in a way that felt entirely foreign. I took a deep breath as I quickened my pace.

"By the Gods," I muttered as I clenched my fists. "Now is not the time."

My steps were quick and precise as I navigated through the thick brush. It was an odd feeling to experience the surrounding life, but not be able to control myself. My feet moved without a thought. I stepped over the roots, scanned the area, and moved almost silently through the brush.

My vision cut out again, and all I saw was black. **I was floating again, almost feeling the current drift my body.** I turned my head to the left, but all I saw was black. The darkness held me tightly as it wound its way around my body. *Confined. Stuck. I was not safe. Danger. Danger. My intuition screamed at me through the haze within my mind.*

I do not know how long I was within the darkness, only that it surrounded me completely. I was warm, but I did not feel safe.

Slowly, my vision trickled in again. I had somehow moved while in the pitch black. My body felt tight, wound up, but the feelings still pulsed in and out. I now stood before the river; the one that flowed near the base of the mountain. *This was where I washed. What was I doing?*

Hunting? This was not the direction where most game lingered. Why could I not move? **Fear.** *Fear enveloped my body.*

"We rest until nightfall." I found myself calling out, but again my voice did not sound like my own. It was masculine, but a deeper, scratchier feeling overtook my throat.

The haze in my mind did not lift as my body moved to kneel by the water. *This bank was familiar, but why was I here?* I tried to move my arms, but I could not move them. **My body felt cold, the pain in my sternum like a sheet of ice, much like it had since the raid.** Yet, this feeling was duller than I remembered, it pulsed in and out. My breath did not catch as it sliced through me.

Anger, regret, and sadness seemed to fight for control within me. I wasn't sure why I felt this way, but I knew that the thoughts threatened to control my every move. **I wanted to rage, but almost as if I wanted to rage at myself. Was the sickness going to kill me?**

A tremble threatened to slide down my body, but somehow I suppressed it. I felt fully now. I could feel the wind on my face, blowing my hair through the breeze. I ran a hand through the locks to untangle it before I pulled it back into a bun at the top of my head. Darkness threatened to take my vision as I heaved breaths through the pain.

I kneeled and began to drag my fingers through the dirt at the bank. With a single finger, I carved the algiz rune into the mud. My boots were much tighter on my feet than I preferred. I tried to look around, but my head would not move. Odd, I felt odd. My hands moved to rinse the mud from them before cupping water. **My hands did not look like my hands. They were thicker, more muscular.**

Where was I?

What was I doing?

Why did I feel so dazed?

I took a hearty gulp of the water, feeling droplets trickle down my beard. *Tired. I was so tired.* I wanted to rest, but I knew that I would not. Fear trickled through me. I wasn't sure what the fear was from, but I knew that it was important.

"Can't we just go in now?" The feminine voice called out from somewhere behind me.

My body leaned towards the water, quickly plunging my face into the cold stream. The shock of it did not fully reach me. It was pulsing again. A moment of shocking cold followed by a moment of dull coolness. As though I were going through the motions, but not truly living. *Was I dead? This was not Valhalla.*

As my face emerged from the water, I made eye contact with the two black orbs that haunted me. I could not open my mouth to scream. My vision went out again, rushing me into the darkness.

COLD. *All I felt was cold.* I could hear a rushing sound faintly in the distance. *I must have fallen asleep at the river.* The river felt important, though I was unable to remember why. I tried to pry my eyes open, but my muscles were too weak. The rushing was getting louder, along with the buzz of a bee nearby. The haze in my mind seemed to press down harder, my thoughts unable to form completely.

"Alf?" I heard a garbled voice faintly say, they must be around the bend. *Wasn't I with a woman? Wait, why would there be a woman? The river. What happened at the river? It's difficult to hear over the swift current. Why was I at the river? I couldn't remember.* I groaned as I finally opened my eyes, trying to blink away the fuzziness of my vision. The sleep I had felt more refreshing than a full night's rest.

Where was I? The river. Was I at the river?

Above me was the sky, cloudy and grey, and the fish-like face of Winser. His beard nearly touched my nose as he leaned over me, eyebrows furrowed together. My nose wrinkled as I smelt the stale ale waft over my face, his breathing coming out heavily. *Wait. Winser?*

Why was Winser at the river?

"Alright there?" He boomed loudly, the sudden pang in my head from his voice made me nauseous. The buzz was gone now, along with the sounds of the river. *Where was I? I thought I was at the river.*

I slowly sat up, nearly heaving up the contents of my stomach in the process. My head was soaked in a layer of sweat; a single bead falling from my brow into my eye. I blinked the burn away. *Where was I? I was not at the river.* Yet, I had flashes of memory of kneeling at the river. My body felt heavy as I heaved a breath through the steady pulse of cold pain.

I was sitting in the middle of the main path, where I had just been walking with Winser. *Not the river. Why did the river feel important?* My stomach churned as I tilted my head back. *This was it. I was losing my mind, the curse was consuming me.*

I tried to shake out the grogginess, "Yes?" I hesitantly replied. My gaze hit the expanse of forest straight ahead, it was still a ten-minute walk to the river. I wasn't going to the river, I was going to work the fields. Fall harvest was coming, the carrots were ready to be pulled. A shiver wracked my body as my chest tightened.

The curse.

"We was walking," Winser slowly enunciated, as though I was a small child. "Then…BOOM! You were on the ground next to me."

"What?"

"You fell," Winser held his hand out to me. "Your eyes rolled back. You sure you're alright?"

"Yes." I did not feel alright.

"I think ya should go to Merelda." Winser's hand grabbed my own, squeezing as he heaved me off the ground.

My legs trembled beneath me, knees barely holding my weight. "How long did I lay there?"

He tilted his head side to side, as if he was not sure of himself. "Yan-a-bumfit?"

"Uh?" I shook my head, *what did he say?*

"Yan-a-bumfit." Winser firmly nodded. He was a dull brute through and through, I'd never understand how he'd once been a Jarl. I'd never known him as a child, but I had heard about his family's successful village. They traded in sheep, which was why he played a big part in our livestock at the mountain.

"Counting?" I was sure he had to be joking, but the haze in my mind left me feeling outright confused.

"Sheep." He quipped with a small frown. "Yan, tyan, tethera, methera…"

I stopped listening as I turned myself back towards the crops. I'd have to be content not knowing. I'd be slower today, but I could not afford to lose my spot in the meal lines. Each day, we were given a meal token based on our accomplishments. These tokens were handed out by high-ranking rebels who called themselves Tyr's Enforcers.

Tyr is the God of justice, law, and war. I once read a tome about Tyr, huddled in the back of the dark library. Tyr had helped the other Gods to bind Fenrir, a giant wolf, as a display of trust. The other Gods didn't untie Fenrir, so the giant wolf bites off Tyr's hand. Tyr nullified the deception of the other Gods because he had allowed Fenrir to take his hand. Though, Tyr's Enforcers would not know war if it came and smacked them upon the head. I could only assume they liked the bit about law and justice. Meal tokens were a tradable item; I often saved them in a chest beside my mat. *Yet, I would rather not be weak.* I wanted to work the field as I had intended, get my token, and add it to my collection. I could hunt for meat myself, cook it at the fire in my cavern, and not have to talk to others.

I took a deep breath as I steadied myself to continue walking. My legs were still weak, my head was jumbled, and my muscles felt frigid. I wiggled the fingers on my right hand, looking down at the seamless movements. My left hand was sluggish.

"Wrong way." Winser slung his arm around my middle, catching me as I stumbled forward.

When I was a child, there was a great snow that fell because of the nine-year cycle. I remember standing by the window in the tower, waiting for my tutor to come. I'd been learning about trade then, though I had found it incredibly dull. I'd rushed out as soon as the quill was set down, running as fast as I could to see the fat flakes. I'd not stopped for a thicker coat, nor had I thought about grabbing one. This would be the first cycle winter I would remember; I'd been born in the middle of one. I had to see how it differed for myself. My thin tunic and trousers did nothing for me, I felt as though I had plunged into a frozen lake naked.

Yet, I still stood in the middle of the courtyard, palms out to catch the flakes.

I don't know how long I stayed out there, but I do remember the lashings I got for it.

"You could have caught a chill!" My father yelled, spittle hitting my face. I did not flinch, for I had learned that lesson the year before.

"Yes, father." I'd said meekly, earning myself another. I tried to hold back a shiver, my clothes were still wet from the snow.

"My heir will not be weak!" More spittle hit my face. "I will not have my only heir weak, it will only make me appear weak."

I'd gotten lashings for getting ill before. We, with Alfrikr blood, were to always appear strong. *We were not to be weakened by things such as fevers or snotty noses. We were superior.* I kneeled there for I don't know how long, just that the coldness had seeped under my skin. Later that night, I screamed as my Thrall nanny pushed me into the tub. The water had felt like fire, but I still slept shivering that night. **The chill had attached to my bones.**

I felt like that now, as I hobbled weakly to the entrance to the caverns. Winser stayed silent as he held my weight. I could see the odd look on his face from the sides of my eyes. It could have been a pity, but I think he saw me as weak. My heart only raced slightly at that revelation, followed by the dreadful feeling of knowing my father still affected me. While people knew he was wicked, they did not seem to know he was also wicked towards me. There was not a time when I had looked up to him, like others do with their fathers. He was not a God on our land to me, but I had seen plenty of young boys regard their father in this way.

"Almost there." Winser grumbled out.

A shock shot through my body, and the burst of energy caused me to bolt upright. Almost there. Almost there. Almost there. I'd heard that. I'd said that. Had I dreamed that? The forest, the darkness, and the river.

Loreth's eyes becoming my own.

8

TOADS AND CHORUSES

THE HEALERS QUARTERS WERE BUILT TOWARDS THE FRONT OF Ymir's Mountain; the cavern system continued deep beyond them. I'd been to them a few times, but I mostly waved to Merelda as I passed by. There was something about being visible by all entering that was unsettling. *Did they think I was weak as I sat there?* Those types of thoughts circled in my head plenty, whether it was an old man with a cough or a young child with a scraped knee.

Alfrikr's did not succumb to such feelings, which made me a poor Alfrikr. Weakness was saved for people who were lesser than me, but I'd come to realize we were all weak in our ways. Yet, my father's words still cut deep into my being. Appearing weak made my stomach churn and my heart race. *How could I be consumed by such opposing feelings?*

I did not mean to look at others in such a way, and I often fought to fight against the voice of my father who rattled in my brain. *Weak, weak, weak. They were all weak, and so was I. I was a stain upon the legacy. I would never be as powerful, strong, and revered.* Yet, I would rather not be remembered for the hatefulness that those before me were known for. I fought to be kind, and if kindness was weakness, then I would happily be a weak man.

It did little to settle the thrum of terror as I sat stewing in my weakness.

"Alf?" Merelda's voice rang out as she stepped into the hallway, shuffling to where I sat awaiting my turn.

"Merelda," I said with a nod, trying to keep the shake from my voice. Weak. I was weak.

"He fell right down!" Winser boomed. "Then his eyes did this!" He rolled his eyes back into his head, only the whites showing.

The man was a little dramatic if you asked me.

"It wasn't that bad!"

"Aye, don't listen to him. It was that bad." Winser countered. "He did it for yan-a-bumfit."

"Fast or slow?" Merelda asked him like she knew what it meant. My face scrunched up as I tried to decipher Winser's words.

"Slow."

"Come in, Alf." Merelda motioned towards the entryway, pulling back the thick buckskin curtain.

I waved Winser off as I pulled myself up to stand. I already looked weak, but I wouldn't put on a show for everyone to see. They already looked at me like I was responsible for my father's actions. I couldn't handle them adding a dash of pity to their glares. *May the Gods let me be weak, and let them look away.*

"What's it mean?" I asked quietly, trailing behind her.

"There's something wrong with you, and it's good you came in."

"No, no. His words? Yams?" I tried to keep my voice hushed as we turned into the caverns, keeping my eyes to the ground.

"Sixteen minutes," She turned her head over her shoulder to frown at me. "You work sheep and don't know how to count them?"

"I know how to count them!" I exasperatedly answered, throwing my hands out.

Counting was simple. It was something all children learned regardless of their status. What Winser had said was not counting, and just because I did not understand didn't mean that I couldn't count.

That man was odd.

"Hmm?" Merelda hummed out. Though, it almost sounded like a laugh.

"I just butcher them or deliver babies." I admitted quietly.

"Lambs, Alf. They're called lambs." I could hear the roll of her eyes in her voice.

"Yeah, yeah." I waved my hands, brushing off her specifics.

We stopped at an entrance halfway down the hall that radiated the smell of incense. My nose scrunched as I breathed in the thick sage and pine air. It smelled like a poorly made soup, or the pits of my arms after sparring. *Another reason why I never came here.* It smelled.

"Hilda will be in shortly," Merelda stepped into the room, I reluctantly followed. "She's with someone now."

I sat on the stone table she motioned to, one that looked well-worn and old. I knew Hilda would reprimand me if I didn't listen to Merelda. The old woman had taken Merelda under her wing when we had first arrived. She was one of the few rebellion members who did not treat me differently. *Part of me wished she shunned me as the others did.*

The last time I'd seen her, in line for an evening meal, she had swatted my arse so hard I yelped in front of everyone. "Let this old woman eat first." She had demanded, her voice so hoarse that it almost made my own throat hurt. *It was an embarrassing moment that I often thought about late at night.*

"Hilda?" I groaned out, letting my head fall backwards.

"What happened, Alfrikr?"

"She's just… Embarrassing."

"You know what I mean, Riki." She hummed out, crossing her arms as she stared at me with a frown.

"I…" I tried to breathe as my chest tightened into a dreadful iceberg. I would rather not admit what I saw. *What had happened? I didn't even know what happened, but I knew I was cursed.* "I don't know"

"You just suddenly collapsed?" She quirked an eyebrow, like she did not believe me.

I did not blame her, not one bit. I would not have believed myself either, and I knew she could see through any lie that curled off my tongue. We'd known each other long enough, but I hoped her ever-so-optimistic attitude would kick in.

"Yes?"

She hummed a short sound, narrowing her eyes in my direction. I had to come up with something fast, I knew she would keep pestering until she was satisfied. I could admit to the chills, the sharp cold in my chest, and the weakness in my limbs.

Any talk of Loreth and the river would stay with me.

No one could ever know.

"I felt cold," I finally said. I pointed a single finger to the middle of my chest. "It hurts, but it feels cold like ice. I keep shivering even when I'm by the fire. My body feels weak."

She nodded at me to continue, and her silence made me feel uneasy. It would be easy to be caught in a lie, but if I stuck to the bare bones of what happened, I might be believed.

"It started after the raid, the coldness set in. I thought I was just tired, but my body still feels weak. It was like I blinked, and suddenly, I was on the ground." I only hoped that I sounded truthful enough that she wouldn't pry for more.

"I'm sure it's just a sickness you picked up."

"Aye." I nodded with a grimace.

"How have you been?" I asked sheepishly.

I hadn't seen her much when I had been preparing for the raid. Merelda had become like a sister to me since we'd all left together that night. *Though, she'd changed much since settling down with Doran.*

"It's been busy. You were lucky that you did not get attacked by those guards who showed up."

"Did… Did Doran tell you?"

"He said she looked healthy." Her brows furrowed as her teeth clutched her bottom lip.

Esmeren was a sensitive topic for the both of us in vastly different ways. I was still angry all these years later. My boyish anger had melted and fused into a furnace of anger which had slowly gone out over the years. Esmeren had been my first lover, the girl I had shared my dreams with, and the one I had envisioned marrying. Merelda held her sister in her mind with sadness. She was ever optimistic that one day her sister would come to us. All would be well, we just had to wait for her.

Sit on our hands and wait, just as the rebellion functioned.

"Alfrikr?" Hilda's parched voice sounded from the doorway.

My eyes shot over to her wrinkled face, she had to have been a hundred years old. Hilda survived out of spite, I was sure of it. The top of her head only reached my armpits, but I was certain she could knock me on my ass. Her hair was sheared on one side, with the other in a braid long enough to reach her knees. She was a frail woman as her smock hung off her like it was 3 sizes too big. Merelda shot to her feet, halfway to the doorway before Hilda had the chance to hobble in. I shivered as a cold chill came over my body, followed by the fear of weakness. She'd not seemed that afraid, but the way she looked at Hilda made me nervous.

"Let's talk out here." She said softly, her head turning to smile tensely at me before ushering Hilda out.

My stomach churned as I watched them with heads bent, whispering. *They knew something I did not know.* Something that Merelda would know would unsettle me. I slowly eased myself from the table, I would not be kept in the dark about my demise.

I may be a weak man, but I am not a fool.

"I'm SICK, I know!" I bit out harshly, leaning against the doorway. "Just tell me what you know."

Hilda stood strong, glaring into my eyes as Merelda cowered next to her. She was weak, as she'd always been. Weaker than I was, evidently. I turned my gaze from hers to Hilda's, matching the intensity in her eyes.

"If the boy knows," Hilda sighed. "Go fetch Froggy."

Froggy? Why the Hel did they need that old fool? The most he knew was—blood Sacredness. He knew of blood Sacredness. My body suddenly felt weak as I stumbled into the doorway. Sick, I was sick.

How sick was I?

"Yes, Hilda" Merelda turned on her heels and skittered down the hallway.

"Get back on the table, boy."

I did as she said in a daze, one that was almost drunkenly stumbling. Perhaps I listened to her because I was honoring her and not because I feared what was to come. Hilda was not a foolish woman, she'd gathered much knowledge in her years. She was old enough to be my grandmother twice over, I'd assume. If I were as daft as Dallen, I'd ask her age. I knew to never ask that of an old woman, especially not the crotchety old woman that stood before me.

"Who?" It was all she said, the word sounded so dry that it made me thirsty.

"Alfrikr?" I answered, unsure of what she was saying.

"Who did this to ye, boy!" She grumbled in response, her hand shooting up to smack me.

I admittedly flinched in response. That only made her smile widely as she lowered her hand.

"I don't know." I schooled my expression as the chill grasped my chest.

It radiated out from behind my ribs, stealing my breath as it threaded between my ribs. A harsh breath wheezed out as I collapsed against the wall behind the table. My shoulder screamed in pain where it hit the wall, but the pain was nowhere near what had enveloped my chest. *I was dying. I had to be dying.* She tutted as she reached into one of the pouches sewn into her ill-fitting smock. Faster than I thought she could move, she threw a handful of dried pine needles in my face. I jolted, sputtering as they invaded my open mouth. *What the Hel. What was wrong with this woman?*

By the time I opened my eyes, she was digging into another pouch for something else. My eyes widened as I stared at her, half expecting another assault.

"Uh, Hilda?" I picked a pine needle off the front of my tunic. They littered the table, floor, and my body. My tongue tasted like I'd drug my tongue along the branch of the tree.

"What's that for?" I used my nails to scrape my tongue, but the taste lingered.

"Did that help?" Hilda asked, a tad too aggressive for her, having just thrown pine needles at me.

"Help?!"

"Your breath smells rancid."

I brought my hand to cup around my mouth and nose. I'd cleaned my teeth before going to see Ivaldr that morning. All I smelled was pine. *It must have helped then.*

"Yer breath smells of…" She put a hand on her hip, tilting her head towards me. "Death right as the soul departs from the body."

My heart seemed to plummet to the ground as I registered what exactly she had said. *The vision of Loreth at the river suddenly made more sense.* **My soul had somehow drifted into his, likely caused by the sickness.** *We had fused as one for a moment, and the thought of the complexity of the blood Sacredness to achieve that made me nauseous.* **It likely had required a sacrifice, if not more than one.** I'd heard Froggy speak of blood Sacredness before, but I had thought him the last of his line. The last to use such means to get what they wanted. He may have been a foolish, odd man, but he knew much about the old ways.

As if summoned by my thoughts, the old man hobbled into the doorway, with Merelda trailing behind.

"What's that smell?!" He exclaimed, loud enough that I was sure the entire mountain had heard it. My face flushed with embarrassment as I looked down at the ground. *By the Gods had this day gone in a different direction quickly.*

"Pine needles?" I muttered as I looked up to meet his eyes.

He gave me a look at my reply, as though I was the dullest man he had ever seen. Froggy shook his head three times before using his fingers to plug his nose.

*The two fingers were deep enough in his nose that
I was sure he could feel his brain.*

"Did he die and come back to life?" His usual toad-like voice sounded even more like the creature.

Die? Was that what had happened at the river?

"He passed out," Merelda murmured. Froggy looked at her the same way he had looked at me. He waved her off with his hand, turning towards Hilda.

"He says he started to feel cold after the raid," Hilda paused to clear her throat, the sound nearly made me gag. *I prayed to the Gods to never grow old in such a way.*

"Right in his chest, radiating down, and into his very bones. He shivered three times in the last minute, and his reflexes are extremely delayed." Hilda finished with another gurgle of phlegm. *Shivered? I didn't remember shivering.* Perhaps, she was seeing things. She was older than Hel herself. Hilda was right about my reflexes, though. Any other time, I would have covered my face or closed my mouth before being pelted by pine needles.

"Hold out your arm." Froggy croaked out, making a hurrying motion as I held my arm out towards him. He hobbled over three steps, pausing for three beats, and then three more steps. He was superstitious, always moving in sets of three or nine. He tugged at the rusty knife at his belt, making me flinch as he brought it up to my arm. Froggy was slow, making me clench my teeth and body.

"Woah! What're—"

"Yer cursed, boy." Froggy grumbled out.

My thoughts seemed to cease as he carved a straight line down my inner arm, from elbow to wrist. Partially over my runes. I watched as blood ran down, my 9 runes seemed to jolt within my skin at the intrusion. I do not think it was a regular blade.

Cursed.

Cursed.

Cursed.

I was cursed?

My body shuddered and shook as I tried to make sense of what he had said. Yet, I found myself simply staring at the blood as it ran through my runes. *The Gods. They knew. The Norns wove this fate for me.* The first rune on my arm was barely visible as blood covered the entirety of raidho, the rune for journey and transformation. Dagaz came the second, meaning day, dawn, or new beginnings. Eihwaz was clear from blood, the third on my arm, and represented the yew tree, transformative energies, and the cycle of nature.

The fourth rune was algiz; elk, protection, and the strength of the Gods. Hagalaz came fifth for hail; a disruptive and uncontrollable change. The blood began to flow over the sixth, tiwaz, the rune for victory, honor, and sacrifice. My last three runes were the same, which was not common, isa. Isa stood for stillness and ice.

I always wondered why the Gods had chosen three of the same runes to bless my arm.

I understood it now that a freeze had settled over my chest. As my breath stuttered to a frozen stop in my lungs. How my body felt as though I'd rolled around in the snow as life was beat out of me. Froggy dug his finger into the shallow cut, dragging it down the line. I shuttered as the pain ripped through my arm. Blood Sacredness, Froggy now had my blood for his wicked Sacredness. *Yet, the feeling did not entirely feel wrong.* A large part of me had hoped he would be able to reverse whatever effects the curse had on me.

However, I couldn't hold back the gag as he brought the finger to his mouth, rubbing the blood along his upper and lower gums.

"Hmmm." He smacked his lips three times. "It tastes like something I've never tasted before."

"What's that supposed to mean?" My voice sounded smaller than I wanted it to be. "The Hel, you mean I'm cursed?"

"Somehow," He stuck the finger in his mouth again, scraping the blood from beneath his nail with his teeth. "You picked up a complicated curse. A big part of it has to do with your soul, I can taste that much."

My soul. My soul. My soul.

Had I lost it entirely? I needed to look at my eyes.

"Ye feel it in yer chest, huh?" Hilda rasped out.

"Right here." I pointed directly in the middle, causing Froggy to gasp.

"You've got a soul curse," He let out a croak-like sound, I had to assume he was nervous. "Let me take some of your blood with me. I need more time to taste the smaller notes in it."

Did I want to give Froggy my blood? *No.* **I did not know what he would do with it.** *What other choice did I have, though?* **I was destined to die whether he had my blood.** *There was a chance he could figure out what I was cursed with, maybe able to reverse the effects.*

I nodded my head slowly.

"I need more!" Froggy bit out.

I nodded without hesitation. I needed to spend some time offering the Gods. *Perhaps one of them would take pity on me, instead of watching me die painfully for pleasure. Cursed. I was cursed. My soul. My soul. Not my soul. I couldn't lose my soul.* I kept my arm held out as Froggy cut two more identical lines in my arm, knowing there would be no scar over my runes, but would be around them. Hilda held out a wooden bowl that looked older than her, my nose scrunched at the thought of how filthy the bowl was. The red blood streamed down my arm, enough to make me feel dizzy. The ache in my chest faded as my blood ran out.

Would simply draining my blood take the curse away? Could I get my soul back? I did not know enough about souls to know.

Hilda and Froggy chatted as I sat there watching the three streams collide into one that flowed from my middle finger into the bowl. Their conversation was a mix of croaking, rasping, and phlegm cleared. Had I not been in the position I was, I might have laughed at how funny it sounded.

A chorus of toads, that was what I would remember this as.

9

OLD FRIENDS AND NEW FIENDS

MY EYES MUST HAVE DRIFTED CLOSED WHILE FROGGY AND HILDA had collected my blood. I was disoriented as soon as my eyes opened, my head felt heavy, and my arm burned. I shut my eyes again, the spinning sensation was too much. The ache in my chest had dulled, breathing felt a bit easier. I laid on the stone table for a moment longer, gathering my wits about me. The last few days were more living than I had done in the past nine years. This was probably what the bears felt like after sleeping for the winter. A long period of nothing, followed by frantic days trying to get their bearings on what had changed.

Cursed. There was a curse inside of me right now.

"Fuckin' cursed." I muttered out as I closed my eyes. A dark laugh began to echo through my mind as I laid there.

If my mother were here, she would know exactly what to do or say. She was a Goddess in my eyes. It was known that the Gods and Goddesses once walked our world, Odinn especially. He walked through our world disguised as a regular man, interacting with us on a personal level. It had been many years since one could claim to have seen him, especially since our borders had closed. Though, there was an instinctual part of me that knew the God's still watched us. I could only hope that my mother had been accepted into their halls, peering down at me from the top of Yggdrasil.

I still thought she was a Goddess, though perhaps it was the child in me that saw her as other-worldly. A familiar lullaby cycled through my head, one that I wasn't sure where I knew it from.

Was it the lullaby my grandmother used to hum to me?

I opened my eyes a second time as I heard the scuffle of footsteps coming down the hallway. I didn't know how long I'd been in the healers caverns, it was after midday when I had gone to work the fields. My rest had been unsatisfactory in the sense that it could have been fifteen minutes or eight hours. I could not tell the difference. The steps had halted outside the doorway, and I pushed myself up enough to see who it was.

"Alfrikr," Ivaldr's voice was laced with a pity that burned through my body. "I came as soon as I heard."

I raised a single eyebrow at him. *I had no idea what to say to that.*

"Are you feeling well?" He asked, stepping into the room.

What a poor question, one that I was not sure how to answer. On one hand, the pain in my chest was dull enough that I could breathe without icicles forming in my lungs. On the other hand, the simple movement of sitting up had me feeling like I had jumped on the back of a horse who only knew how to buck and run in tight circles. I settled on nodding my head three times. If it worked for Froggy, it would have to work for me.

"Great!" He clapped his hands as he nodded furiously. "I have something to show you."

"Show me?" My throat felt dry as I choked the words out. *Is this how Hilda felt?*

"I'd tell you about it now," Ivaldr looked behind him before finishing. "I'm not sure what ears are nearby."

Had Froggy already figured out the curse? Was I to be cured this soon? ***Another laugh filtered into my mind, one that made me feel uneasy.***

"I understand." My throat burned at the simple words.

I pushed myself up further, no longer resting on my elbows. My stomach lurched as I sat upright and acid flowed up my throat. Moving my legs was harder, but I was determined not to show any weakness with Ivaldr here. I slid off the stone table, my bare feet hitting the cold stone.

"Here," Ivaldr softly said, the same tone he would use with the small children who circled him in common areas.

He held my boots in one hand, still far enough away that I had to stand to reach. I stood shakily, my knees wobbly with my full weight. One step, two steps, three steps. I tried to snatch the boots, but my arms moved so slow that it was embarrassing. I turned, moving to the small chair along the wall before slowly sitting myself down. *My mind cackled at the weakness in my body, and I wanted to bang my head against the wall until it shut up.* My face flared as I shakily laced my boots, I could feel how red my face had to have been. *Weak, I was weak. Alfrikr's were not meant to be weak.*

That knowledge settled deep in my gut.

"How far?" I grumbled, barely anything but a growl.

"The bottom." Ivaldr's voice was still soft. He tilted his head as he looked down on me. My face flared hotter.

MY BODY COOPERATED MORE with each step that I took. We walked in silence, which was better than small talk. Yet, my mind continued to hum that lullaby. I knew that six levels down were restricted to Tyr's Enforcers and other high-ranking rebels. Dallen had worked on the project, which meant I knew the cells were held down here. My mind raced with thoughts as we turned from the last common room, the hallway before us was a slope downwards. The air felt colder down here, but no colder than the ache in my bones. Torches lined the hallway in groups of three, switching sides of the walls after the third. A sharp pain lanced through my chest, almost stealing my vision, before it settled down again.

Cursed. I was cursed.

"Ivaldr?" Doran's voice rang from behind us. "A word before you take Alfrikr down?"

My brows furrowed as I moved to rest against the wall, watching Ivaldr and Doran turn down a different hallway. Doran hadn't even looked at me, which felt unsettling in itself. *We were supposed to be friends, to the point where we felt like brothers.* We'd never been as close as Dallen and I were, but I'd have expected something. I let out a sigh as I let my head fall against the wall. My sheared head did nothing to protect from the chill radiating out of the stones. Merelda was sure to have already informed him of my fate. *Cursed, I was cursed.* The silence this far down was almost deafening, and I could hear the crackle of my breath in my lungs.

The chill was returning.

I ran a hand against the top of my head, using my nails to lightly scratch at the faint scruff that was growing back already. It would be a long time before my hair would grow out how I preferred it; long enough to cover the tips of my ears. There was something about the wind hitting the small, delicate, point that I could not stand. The winter was worse, and I knew that soon I would have to hunt for fur to make a hat and cloak. *Cursed, I couldn't think about being cursed.* I needed to think of something else. I began to hum the lullaby aloud, the one that had cycled my thoughts earlier. I tapped my toe on the floor, the steady thunk reverberating against the walls.

What the Hel was taking so long?

The longer I stood waiting, the more disrespected I felt. Doran had not come to check on me in the healer's caverns, but had obviously known I was with Ivaldr. *He had deliberately ignored me when he should have been concerned with my health.* The ache in my chest flared colder as hot anger began to radiate through my body. Doran was supposed to be my brother. *We had grown up together, and left the stronghold together. We ate together every day at least once.*

Yet, he could not spare me a single glance?

My eyes shot towards the hallway they had walked down. It was well lit, and I could barely make out the door at the end of it. If I was quiet enough, I could listen at the door for what was so important that I had been left alone in a restricted access area. The same area that I had longed to be in, longed to be included, was now looked upon in contempt. There was nothing special about it, and I felt a fool for all the times I wished to be down here with the people who seemed influential. There was once a time when I was indispensable, even if it was to Alfrikr the Wicked, I missed it.

How I longed to be influential again. I wanted to be revered in the ways Ivaldr was.

I took a single step towards the hallway before taking two more steps quickly. My legs felt stronger now, though still nowhere near where they should be. *Doran had pulled Ivaldr in for what? To talk about me? To tell him, I was a weak link in the rebellion and I should be shunned and cast out? I'd never felt more betrayed than I had at this moment.* I had seen the little ways that Doran had changed, how he had pulled back from Dallen, Merelda, and I because he had new friends. How he controlled Merelda as though he were her keeper. The looks he gave me when he thought I wasn't looking. Yet, it wasn't until this moment that I had truly noticed how deep his loyalties went to the rebellion, and not to me.

I shook my head, trying to displace my anger. Maybe Doran was not betraying me. It had to be nothing, right? Something else came up, and he was probably so focused on his task that he forgot to check on me. Dallen had not come either, and Merelda was only there because she was a healer. I wasn't even sure if Merelda had known that my curse had been confirmed.

She had not come into the room with Froggy, only lingering in the doorway before leaving. Though that was most likely because I had already let my anger get the best of me. I was working on it, but I did not have a lot to show for nine years of work.

Anger, I needed to focus on anger and not the curse.

I had been born angry, my mother had told me this whenever I had an outburst as a child. "Ye just have an angry soul, my dear." She'd whisper as the Thralls would clean up the remnants of my outbursts. "The fight in you will settle. You'll use it for good." How wrong she was.

The Norns had woven my thread with bursts of red, she'd said.

I hoped she could not see me at this moment. That the hall she looked down from did not show her my face. She would be disappointed in my weakness, my anger, and my curse. If she heard my thoughts, she would shake her head at the absurdity of them all. Doran was my friend. *He was my brother.* He would not betray me nor suggest that I be shunned.

I hope.

I could not help the groan that slipped out as I moved back to lean against the wall. I should have told Ivaldr that I needed more time to rest. *But that would have been weak. Weaker than I already was.* It was then that my resentment of Ivaldr began to burrow deeper. There was no way that I did not look the way I felt. He had to have known the toll the curse had taken on my body. I would not have been surprised if Winser himself had knocked on Ivaldr's door to share the news of me collapsing. Ivaldr would be the new Rikr when we took power; *why wouldn't he be joyed at my demise?* I would hold the powers of the crown, but he would lead our people. Doran could be pleading my case right now, begging Ivaldr to not shun me. I braced my back against the wall, steadily sliding myself until my butt hit the floor. *I might as well get comfortable.*

My stomach growled as I brought my left knee up towards my chest. After this, I would find Finnian and get enough stew in my body that my stomach ached. Tonight was the feast; the blot was held to thank the Gods for their mercy in allowing us to live through the raid and commend the ones who did not. At least, that was how I had viewed it in my head. The other rebels would see it as a feast, maybe say thanks to Odinn, and then go back to their lives. I knew the Gods were still with us, even if we had not seen or heard from them in so long.

The Gods knew I was cursed. Had the Gods done this to me?

It felt like an eternity before the door at the end of the hall opened. Only Ivaldr stepped out, slamming it closed behind him. I'd never seen him act like that. I wonder if he forgot I was in here. Dallen and I had a theory that Ivaldr was more aggressive than he let on. Kindred spirits recognize each other.

My intuition prickled and my anger sung to his, much like it did with Dallen's.

"Ivaldr?" His steps faltered, going from heavy to soft as he approached me. The smile on his face did not reach his eyes.

"Apologies!" He held a hand out to help me up. "Doran

noticed a discrepancy in the number of grains we counted before leaving the stores and after we had returned."

"Too much or too little?"

"Oh, don't you worry about that!" He wiped his hand off on his trousers, like touching me was something gross. My anger flared as I resisted the urge to spit on him. If my hand was so disgusting, I'm sure my spit was worse.

"You have something to show me?"

"Someone, actually." He waved me first down the hallway.

Him behind me made me feel uneasy, my gut intuition was screaming, but I went anyway.

"Oh?"

"You'll see. I think you will be pleasantly surprised," He whistled three sharp bursts, and I jumped as the stone to my left slid open to reveal a separate hallway. *Where were we going? Why was there a hidden hallway?*

"In here?" I asked, cringing as I heard how dull I sounded. Ivaldr hummed a positive, so I turned into the darkness on my left. *Dallen had not told me of this secret. Had he known about it?*

My back straightened as I felt the warmth of runic wards, likely blood Sacredness, cast over my body. I was well versed in the runes, and the ways to utilize them. Though, I did not know how to practice blood Sacredness. My father's stronghold was full of protections such as these. I felt the protection of Algiz the strongest. It was meant to keep something in. *Was I the something?* I slowed my steps as I awaited my doom. *To turn and run would show fear, which meant weakness, and I was not going to be weak as I approached death.* I braced myself as I expected to be attacked. No wonder Ivaldr wanted to walk behind me. I kept my exterior as relaxed as I could, continuing down the barely lit hallway.

My mind flashed back to the man I'd seen as a boy, the first rebellion member.

I would take this death as easily as he had.

With honor, grace, and acceptance. We were approaching a common cavern now, and I could smell the wafting scent of piss and shit. *Where the Hel was I?* My steps slowed as I reached up to cover my nose with the collar of my tunic. I almost coughed as the scent of pine overtook my senses. I guess Hilda throwing pine needles at me was worth it if it covered the smell I was getting into.

"Almost there." Ivaldr said curtly, his voice muffled. I hated those words now because my thoughts threatened to drift towards Loreth. *The curse.*

"What the fuck smells so bad?"

"The cells," Ivaldr moved around me, now side by side with me. "Are down here. It's where we question those who arrive from the Wicked Stronghold."

My father's stronghold? I'd never met someone who claimed to be from there, though I knew they had to exist if we were getting information from spies.

"Oh." Was all I could say as we stepped into the round room.

Crates littered the floor, strewn out in ways that I could only assume that people had slept on them. The walls were dripping liquid that, I hoped, was water and not sewage from the levels above. It smelled like sewage. *Yet, somewhere deep inside my mind, it reminded me of the night I'd left. How we'd huddled around crates as I begged them to come with me. In the* corner was a woman with a mess of tangled hair, from what I could tell of the back of her head. She was curled tightly in a ball, her face nearly touching the wall.

I turned to look at Ivaldr, raising a single eyebrow as I tilted my head towards the woman. "What is this?" I whispered, not sure if the woman was sleeping or dead.

"Your betrothed has arrived." Ivaldr whispered, the wickedness in his voice an almost direct mimicry of my father's. My heart stuttered in my chest as I took in her form, but stayed where I was. I should have focused on Ivaldr's voice more then, but it would be years before I began to see what I had missed.

"Esmeren?" I called out, cringing as a rat skittered over the crate nearest her feet.

She jolted at my voice, turning her head to look at me before shuffling to stand. Both of her ankles and wrists were shackled with a thick metal cuff and short chain. *What the Hel's was happening?* I shook my head, as if I would awake from this moment. Blood and bruises marred her once smooth and pristine skin, and her arm hung limply like it had been broken. My eyes trailed her body, taking in the obvious aftermath of torture. *Why would Ivaldr torture her?* I thought he was all about peaceful methods of obtaining justice.

"Alfrikr," The clanking of chains made my ears ring as her feet shuffled near me. "I-I..." I made no move to get closer to her, but I did feel a twinge of pity sprout into my years of anger. *She was nine years too late.*

"What are you doing here?" I bit out gruffly, taking a step back as she approached me.

"I've finally come to join you, Alfrikr." She'd never called me Alf or Riki like the others did.

Years after leaving, while sitting alone in my cavern in this same mountain, I would realize it was because she was attracted to my title and not me as a person.

"Him? Or have you come for the rebellion?" Ivaldr bit out.

She tilted her head as she shuffled to a stop a few feet from Ivaldr, who now leaned against a crate with a grin on his face. *He was enjoying this.*

"Both. Loreth cast me out of the stronghold. He beat me before dragging me to the river near here." Her voice was soft, gentle, and honest.

"He brought you here?" *Why would he bring his betrothed to the same rebellion he vowed to eradicate? It didn't make sense.*

"He wants me to spy." She shuffled closer to me. "To gather information so he can cut you all down and dance in your guts."

"And you're…" I didn't know what to say. I didn't understand why I was here. Ivaldr had never allowed me to know anything of the rebellion, but now I was privy to such knowledge. "You're what? Telling us all this like we should trust you?"

"I want to tell you because I hate Loreth and I wish to take him down." She stood right before me now, close enough that I could reach out and touch her. My fingers wiggled as I controlled my urge to drag her to her knees and tell me the truth. *I didn't believe her.*

"You want to double-cross him?" Would anyone be so daft to believe her?

"And I need you to help me. Doran has already petitioned

Ivaldr for permission to house me under for a trial, to prove I'm honest." My gaze shifted to Ivaldr, who only nodded once.

"I don't trust you." I bit out harshly, taking a step away from her. "I don't want you here." Tears welled in her eyes as she looked up at me like a dog begging for scraps.

"I swear, Alfrikr." She shuffled closer again. "I was wrong all of those years ago. I should have left with you. I swear I'll make it up to you."

"There's no need. We are not betrothed anymore, and we never will be again. Do what you want to do. I just want no part in it."

"That's where we require you," Ivaldr called out as he pushed himself off the crate, walking towards us.

"Me? For what?"

"Esmeren needs to convince Loreth that she has infiltrated us and gotten close to you." Ivaldr now stood beside Esmeren, placing a hand on her shoulder.

"I would rather not spend a single fucking second with her." I bit out, shaking my head three times.

"You said you wanted an active role, Alfrikr." Ivaldr tilted his head at me. "So take it. Complete this, and we'll see where you can advance."

Ivaldr had me by the neck and he knew it. I'd spent years begging for more to do. Working with Esmeren would hurt, and I did not want to go through that. She had been my first, but I had many women after her. *She was not special anymore. Esmeren had betrayed me.* I did not want the role if it meant interacting with her.

If I didn't take this chance, I was destined to stay at the bottom of the ranks forever. If I advanced in the ranks, I might be able to make some actual changes. I would rather not take this chance.

I could find another way to move up.

IO

FEASTING AND FEELINGS

I FELT RENEWED AS A BURST OF ENERGY FLOWED THROUGH MY body, followed by the dread of sickening anxiety. *Esmeren was here.* She was in the mountain, joining the rebellion, and brought a considerable opportunity for me. Yet, I didn't feel that stirring in my heart nor the tingling in my stomach. *I felt dread and mistrust. What we had when we were younger had shriveled up and died.*

> There was once a time that I would have been happy to spend the rest of my life with her.

But as I looked back on it, nine years later, there was nothing but contempt and disappointment. *Esmeren had to be lying, there was no chance that she had suddenly changed her mind.* Nine years was a long time, but too long of a time to suddenly decide she wanted to rebel. The walk back to my cavern was filled with thoughts about Esmeren. There wasn't a time in my life that I did not know her. We had grown up in the stronghold, every child there was bound to know each other. I used to know her better than anyone, and I knew she was lying. *About what? I was not sure.*

I did not think she was here to make amends, but I would keep a close eye on her as I worked with her. I needed to do this to advance in rank. Yet, I still didn't trust that she was here to help us. She was going to learn the hard way that she did not know me anymore. I would be the cause of her downfall. The last time I saw her still hurt, as it had for years, the look on her face as she watched us sneak out of the only home we had known. *She had made her choices and I knew there was no reason to look back.* We had separate lives, and I don't think we could ever go back to what we were.

I would be the last look on her face as she died, but not as I had once thought when we were young.

It wouldn't be while we were old and gray ruling the kingdom together. It would be while she was on her knees before me and spilling the truth of her wicked plan.

I didn't want to go back to what we were. She may have been my first and I thought would once be my only, but the years that had passed since then there had been many after her. Laying with another was not frowned upon, nor did it matter who you laid with. Not all of Sidirna was this way. My father had encouraged me to remain celibate with anyone who could carry a child because of the risk of a bastard child.

There was a freedom here that made the lack of progress a little less irritating.

I weaved my way down the hallways, as my mind cycled through the happenings of the day. It had been a brutal day, nearly as brutal as the raid. Lack of sleep, food, water, and rest had taken its toll. Yet, my body did not feel as run ragged as I had expected it would, and for this, I was thankful. The emotions of seeing Esmeren lingered through my mind, body, and soul. *Which was apparently the burst I needed to make it to my bed.*

I shut the curtain behind me as I stepped inside my home, taking in a deep breath of the familiar scent.

My nose crinkled as piss and shit still seemed to linger in my nostrils, sullying the better scents. My fire had gone out at some point, my stuff all appeared untouched, and my blankets were still kicked to the end of my cot. Ivaldr hadn't found anything, at least I hoped he had not. Deep in the chest under my bed were a few books on the Gods. I wouldn't be reprimanded for having them, but I wanted to keep them to myself. All books that entered the rebellion were supposed to go to the library, but there was no system that kept them organized nor who had the books. It was a free for all, and that was how I got the books in the first place.

At the bottom of a stack near a puddle on the floor, not anywhere a book should be.

I went through the motions without thinking, much like I had before this day from Hel had scrambled my brain. I lit a fire, changed my clothes, rinsed the sweat from my body with my washbasin, and moved to sit on the ground near my fire. I hung my head as I took in the warmth as much as I could. The ache in my chest pulsed, but it gave no relief. It was as if I had a second heartbeat completely made of pain. My arm was wrapped, but it burned and stung with every movement. With a heavy sigh, I cautiously unwrapped the bandage on my arm. *Gone.*

The marks were gone, but the pain remained.

Blood Sacredness? Has Froggy done something to me?

I'd intended to get food, but the thought of going out into the common areas was enough to quell my hunger. The curse was sure to be common knowledge by now. Yet, I wondered how many knew of Esmeren. *How long would she stay in the squaller? How would I deal with her arrival?*

Cursed. I'm cursed.

I was immersed in my pain, both mentally and physically, so when a hand dropped on my shoulder I almost lurched into the fire. "What the Hel!" I yelled as I tilted my head up to see who had snuck in.

"Riki," Dallen purred out with a smirk. "I sat with you after Froggy and Hilda left. I had to go talk with Ivaldr, and couldn't stay." His smirk had dropped, showing the concerned look on his face. *Great. More pity.*

"He showed you?"

"Showed me?" Dallen's brow raised as he moved to sit beside me.

"Esmeren? She's down at the bottom of the mountain, chained up." I shrugged my shoulders, like it was a common occurrence for someone to be chained up down there. Someone we had both once adored.

"She's what?!" His whole body jolted with shock, eyebrows furrowing as he tilted his head slightly.

The fire in the pit flared, casting his skin in an orange haze. He reached a hand up, running his hand over his sheared head, and tugging on the tip of his pointed ear. He dropped his hand quickly, instead moving to pinch and prick the skin of his hands. It was a nervous tick he'd had since he was a child, tugging on his ear or picking at his palms as if it would reset his emotions.

"What did Ivaldr tell you?" I turned back towards the fire, gazing into the flames.

"He told me she was here," Dallen's voice was flat as he spoke. "That she wanted to redeem herself. He said that Doran was going to sponsor her, keep an eye on her or something.

That you were going to work with her, but that I was not to pry about why you were working with her."

"Yeah," I shrugged my shoulders, unsure of what to say. "Doran probably has to if he wants to stay in Merelda's good graces." She was her sister, after all. "I don't know what to think about her being here… I don't want to work with her."

"You don't trust her?" His voice dropped, barely above a whisper. I wonder if he felt Doran nearby, some twin thing I didn't understand.

"Of course not," I whispered back, turning to look at him. "How convenient is it that she shows back up right after I'm cursed? Cursed by her new lover?"

Dallen nodded his head. Tilting it for a moment as he gazed at me. *It was all too much. It was so much that for once my brain could not focus on a singular thought.*

"What can we do about it? They won't believe us, and I couldn't even petition against it." Dallen wasn't allowed to attend any meetings, and I was on my last chance. Ivaldr did not like anyone speaking out against him.

"We wait." I held my pinky out to him, a once childhood promise that had lingered into adulthood. Dallen curled his pinky around my own. "We watch, listen, and wait. She will slip up eventually."

"I'll act as if I believe her," Dallen whispered as he tightened his pinky around my own. "You keep her at a distance, I know how your heart is involved." I dropped his pinky with a sigh.

"My heart is not involved." I rolled my eyes, looking back at the flames curling around the logs. "It hasn't been for a long time. I don't think it ever will be. She betrayed us."

"You still need to be careful," Dallen nudged me with his

shoulder. "If her breasts have grown since we last saw her, I might struggle too."

I huffed out a laugh, shaking my head. "I didn't look."

"Well," Dallen reached a hand towards the fire, swirling the flames around his fingers. "I'm taking a break from women anyway. That one I was telling you about, the nails one?" I hummed in agreement, vaguely remembering his detailed recounting of their time.

"She has a husband, right?" Dallen said loudly, as if he only had two volumes. Whispering barely above a breath or shouting. "Well, her husband and I really get along." He nudged me again. "So we're testing out how all three of us…" Dallen trailed off, turning his head towards the curtain.

We both heard the pitter-patter of steps, one set heavy and one set light. I looked back to Dallen, exchanging a nod before turning to watch the curtain.

"Dallen? Alf?" Merelda's voice rang out as she pulled the curtain open.

She was wearing a red dress that hugged her curves graciously, the belt around her waist holding a single drinking horn. Doran stood behind her stoically, his red tunic and brown trousers pristine. *What a beautiful couple*, I thought sarcastically.

"The feast will begin soon," Merelda said softly as she came to stand near the fire, Doran trailing behind her. "Are you well enough to come? I can bring you a bowl of stew, if not." The pity in her voice made me cringe, how weak did she think I was?

"I think I can make it," I reluctantly said.

Finnian's stew was best while it was piping hot, and I needed a little normalcy in my life today. *I would not stay long, I knew that.* Merelda nodded as she reached out, the back of her hand settling on my forehead. She pulled it off before holding it towards the fire. She must feel the shivers I have been fighting against.

They threatened to overtake my body, but I would not give in. The curse could not have me.

"You're freezing, Alf." She said quietly, her gaze full of concern.

I was weak. I broke eye contact with her, unable to face her wide eyes. I should be thankful that she cared enough about me to be concerned, but I could not find it in myself to truly see it that way. All I saw was the weakness that I once had beat out of me. It made me want to beat anyone who looked at me with that gleam in their eyes. *I was a weak fool, and I would be fine. The curse will be drained from my body, whether through death or blood Sacredness.*

"Umm," Doran said quietly. "Esmeren will be there."

Already? Ivaldr was allowing her into the common areas too quickly. It was suspicious, and I wasn't sure about the trust that was easily handed to her. It would be easy for her to slip a poison into the barrel of mead, close the entrances and burn us all, or to simply crack Ivaldr's neck while he was well intoxicated.

"She will!" Dallen exclaimed. I knew he said he would play along, but I wasn't prepared for how convincing he was already. *Was he this false with me? How was I to know he was truly on my side about Esmeren? It could be a ploy, much like he was doing to his brother now.*

"I gave Ivaldr a dress for her," Merelda said excitedly, her pity towards me gone now. "I can't wait to see her! I knew she would come back to us!"

I had nothing nice to say, so I said nothing whatsoever. I had never believed in the optimistic line of thoughts that

Merelda held, and I still did not believe that Esmeren was here for good.

The three of them chatted as we walked towards the main cavern, I was sure they'd cleared out the tables for this feast. There would be standing room mostly, and the ache in my bones protested that thought. I was a few steps behind the three of them, something that had never bothered me until this moment. *I felt out of odds with my only friends, like I did not belong with them anymore.*

A shiver wracked my body as we turned a corner, *was it always this cold in here?*

It had to be winter approaching, *not the curse.* I crossed my arms over my chest, hoping to gain some semblance of warmth. The clash of music, voices, and laughter had started to drift down the hall. *All were about to see how weak I truly was. Was it too late to turn around and go back? Would they all whisper about my fate?* I groaned inwardly as another burst of pain wracked my lungs. My head felt dull, a fuzzy, cold sensation enveloping my very thoughts.

My bones ached to the core, as if that spongey bit in the middle had frozen solid.

"Coming, Alf?" Merelda called out from ahead of me. I hadn't realized I'd stopped walking.

I picked up the pace as I stepped out into the open space. The ceiling was high above me, the natural rock formations had been carved into images of the Gods. I sent a nod to Freyr, as I always did while in here. The curved walls were carved intricately with images of battles, people laughing around fires, and a large map of the cavern system. All the carvings lined the circular space like one continuous page from a giant's book.

Groups of people were littered all around the cavern, barely enough space to stand without another bumping shoulders. Merelda and Doran had their heads bent in conversation, and Dallen had already rushed over to the line at Finnian's stew pots. With a shiver, I made my way over to stand near Dallen. *With this many people in here, I should be sweating with warmth.* However, my lungs felt as if they had filled with icicles. My bones felt like they were coated in a frosty layer. I was sure that if I continued to feel this cold, I would begin to resemble Ymir, the ice giant. *Would my skin and hair turn as blue as the ice giant had once been?*

"We're in luck!" Dallen called above the noise, stepping aside to allow me room beside him. Our bodies touched from our shoulders to our feet, and the heat that came from his body felt like I had been doused in flames. I arched my eyebrow in response to him, tilting my head away to look at him. "Finnian used venison this time around!"

I much preferred elk or reindeer, as the texture of deer meat reminded me of wet and crumbled parchment. Though, this was not something I had shared with others, for they thought my preferences were odd. I nodded my head three times, and *by the Gods I felt as weird as Froggy.* We were halfway through the line when the edges of my vision began to be littered with black dots.

"Dallen?" I tried to raise my voice above the crowd, but I wasn't sure that my mouth had even moved. With a single intake of breath, sharp and cold, the dots had faded. *I was okay, I had to be okay. I'm sure it was from lack of sleep and food, not the curse.*

"Huh?" Dallen had succeeded in raising his voice, had I actually said it aloud?

"What're your plans for the feast?" I settled on shouting back at him as a tune began to spread through my mind. The surrounding sounds almost drowned out the lullaby. This feast was not planned well, I thought. It should have been outside where we could mingle without the echo upon echoes of our voices.

"Well," He took a step forward as the line moved. "Asher and Kraka are over by the fire, I'll head there. Looks like Siv is there too."

I understood what he was implying, but I had not seen Siv since she threw me out of her cavern. I had not meant to stay so long speaking with her, but she had strict rules about men overstaying their welcome. As she put it, she got what she needed and no longer needed my company. *It did not offend me at all, and it worked out for my preferences as well.* I would rather not form any attachments, I'd done so once and it had burned me.

Now that same woman would be here tonight, and I hoped she did not seek me out.

"We'll go there." I shouted above the crowd. Dallen nodded in response, taking another step closer.

My stomach rumbled as the scent of food wafted towards me. I hope we were not too late for a roll, Finnian's wife made decent bread. The line seemed to move slower as the ache in my chest grew stronger; it once again pulsed like it had a beat of its own. I glanced towards the fire, hoping to catch Siv's eye. *I knew she would not wait for me, and I wanted to be the one in her cavern tonight.* She made no look in my direction, so I took a moment to appreciate her beauty. Her hair was a shade of copper I could never find the words to describe, almost glowing from the light of the fire. Her hair was thick, long, and contained many small braids that wrapped around my fist beautifully. Siv's creamy skin was mottled by freckles almost the same hue as her hair, making her even more so, too beautiful for me.

After what had felt like an eternity, I had finally gotten to the front of the line. Finnian thrust the bowl into my hands, the sides slopping over onto my hands. There was no roll, but I did not feel too discouraged as the scent of stew enveloped my senses. I was in a cold and starved daze as I followed Dallen, weaving through the crowds until we were sat at the fire. Siv nestled into my side immediately, plucking a carrot out of my steaming bowl.

"Riki." Siv said in greeting before turning back to Kraka and resuming her conversation.

I took my first bite, almost moaning at how good it tasted. I must have underestimated my hunger. I practically inhaled my food, tipping the bowl to ensure I got all the contents. I set the bowl by my feet by the time Dallen had gotten halfway through his bowl. The warmth of the stew in my belly seemed to settle my chill, if only slightly. It was then that I strung my arm along Siv's shoulders, dazedly, trying to follow the conversation.

"No," Kraka said with a slight frown. "I always start with stretching, and then I get into the movements with my sword."

"Do you stretch after?" Siv asked, leaning her head back onto my shoulder. I shivered at her touch, the warmth of her skin felt a little too hot, but it was a nice reprieve.

"Of course, it helps balance out your muscles so you're not as sore the day after." I nodded my head as I agreed with Kraka. She was a short, thick woman who could almost beat me in swordplay. I hadn't directly sparred with her, but I had watched her skill grow over the years. Her hair was sheared short, but speckles of brown had begun to sprout.

"Hmm," Siv pursed her lips. "Every single time?"

Kraka burst out a laugh as she shook her head at Siv, "What is your routine, Alfrikr?"

"Run, stretch, sword work, spar, and stretch again." I replied with a shrug. It was a simple routine for me before breakfast most days. Though I hoped my body would comply tomorrow morning, *perhaps skipping one more day would not be awful.*

"No wonder you are built like that." Kraka replied, Siv nodded as she turned toward me.

Her hand drifted up my thigh slowly, curving towards my hardening cock. She then snatched the hem of my shirt and pulled it clear up to my neck. "Keep it up," Siv purred as her other hand went to trail my stomach. I was not as toned as some men, but the muscles became more defined as I flexed them under her touch. Showing off was not something I usually did, but Siv's touch made me want her to see me worth much more than I was. **A laugh sounded in my mind as I flexed beneath her touch.** *It was embarrassing, and I wasn't sure why I had done it.* Yet, I kept them firm as she explored my body. She let my tunic drop, but kept her hand under it.

"You're so cold," She circled my navel. "It feels so refreshing, I'm burning alive with this heat!" She must not have heard of the curse, and I would not be the one to tell her.

"Hey, Riki!" Dallen called out from his spot next to Asher, across the fire.

Asher was tall and thin, with hair as black as a raven's wing. He didn't say much, but when he did, it was always something smart. I liked him, but I wasn't sure he felt the same about me. *I wonder if he could solve the chill inside of me.*

"Yeah?" I replied as Siv tweaked my nipple, causing my voice to inflate almost embarrassingly.

"Talk the girls into coming with Asher and me to the river, will you?" Dallen smiled widely at me, it was a weird smile. The kind of smile he would wear when he knew he was bringing trouble with him. "Ash and I are going to go grab enough mead for the night!" He glanced briefly behind me before looking back at me, repeating the movement several times. I nodded before turning back towards Siv and Kraka.

"Does he not realize we can hear him either?" Siv laughed as she shook her head, sliding her hand down my chest. She gave my cock a light squeeze before pulling away from me. Yes, I thought, she would be welcoming me tonight.

"He's not the brightest, but we love him anyway, right?" Kraka added as she gathered her jacket from the ground next to her.

I stood first, extending my hand down to Siv. As she stood before me, my eyes drifted above her head. Right to where Ivaldr and Esmeren stood in line for Finnian's stew. *That was why Dallen wanted to go. He must have seen them arrive.*

Siv's fingers curled with my own as she moved to stand by my side, following where I had been looking.

II

WARM BODIES AND COLD BONES

"THAT'S HER, ISN'T IT?" SIV ASKED ABRASIVELY. THE JEALOUSY was something new. It was an odd feeling to see the usually carefree woman smile so freely. There had been times when she had invited women with us, but I agreed that Esmeren was different from most women. The sight of her was unwelcome as dread began to fill my gut. *Why was she here?*

"Unfortunately." I replied, squeezing her hand gently.

The lullaby in my mind hummed louder, angrier almost. The same tune that once comforted me kept returning to my mind, but I only felt *uneasy*. It was dark, guttural, and off-key. I maneuvered us around the bench we had been sitting on, an intricately carved piece of wood that held traces of Dallen's Sacredness signature. I felt the small wisps of his energy float down my arms as they moved to settle on the wood again. *He must have made this before coming to get me.*

"Alfrikr!" Esmeren's voice rang out, a stark difference to the lull of Siv's husky voice. *Had I really once found that voice to be pleasing?* Siv's grip tightened on my own as we watched Esmeren weave through the crowd towards us.

"Fuck," I muttered as Esmeren got closer. *Could I turn my back to hers and walk away? I probably could have had we not looked at her for longer than three seconds, but especially not as Ivaldr trailed after her. Did they not want their stew?*

Go back to the line, I wanted to yell.

"Her ears are uneven, and her hair is dull." Siv mumbled as she pressed closer into my side. *Was this for my benefit or her own? I did not know.* I hummed a small chuckle, looking down at the Goddess on my arm.

"Her voice is squeaky too," I whispered as I tucked hair behind Siv's ear, ghosting a kiss on the point.

"Ivaldr, Esmeren." I said in greeting, nodding my head to each of them. *Did Ivaldr truly think I would be friendly enough with Esmeren? How had she wormed her way into this mountain so easily?*

"Where are you off to?" Ivaldr asked, his whimsical voice held no accusation, but I felt the intent behind it. *He wanted me to stay.*

"Did you need me for something?" I drawled out with a false smile. He had never asked that of me, and I had retreated from feasts plenty of times with a woman on my arm. *It was suspicious, all of this was suspicious.*

"I had hoped you would be around to show Esmeren around. Doran is engaged with writing an account of our victory feast and cannot properly introduce her to everyone." Ivaldr replied cheerily, ignoring the aggression in my tone.

"She's not my ward." I practically growled at Ivaldr. Esmeren cringed slightly, pulling her bottom lip in between her teeth. "Her sister is here somewhere, drop her off with her kin." Siv squeezed my hand twice, a deliberate attempt to calm me down, as my mind chuckled in response.

"Oh, yes," Ivaldr replied quickly. "Esmeren had just hoped to catch up with you while you showed her around."

She could speak for herself, could she not? Though perhaps I was used to strong women, and now that I looked upon my past,

I realized how weak she had always been.

"We're off to fuck, I'm not desiring two women tonight." I shrugged, glancing over at Esmeren as her face began to heat. **A deep and angry feeling began to fill my bones as my mind growled.** *Was she truly here to deceive us but still could not handle vulgarity? How had she handled being a Rikr's Valkyrie because those were some of the most vulgar people I had ever met?*

EXHAUSTION CREEPED through me as I reclined on the river bank with Siv, Kraka, Asher, and Dallen. The horn of mead braced in between my bent knees shook as my legs shivered. We'd built a small fire, but it was as if my body did not feel the warmth. There was a chill to the air, one that foretold the winter that was fast approaching, and *one that seemed to sing to the sickness inside of me.* The leaves had begun to fall off the trees, with the crisp and distinct smell that signaled the end of the season. This would be the last time we would sit out here, but I could not find it within me to savor the moment. I was uneasy with thoughts of the sickness, Esmeren, and my purpose in this life. It all felt too much, and I wished to turn my mind off if only for a moment.

The lullaby continued to the point where I felt as if I were losing my mind. It would not stop. Over and over and over.

"I have to ask," Kraka finally said, her head leaning on Dallen's shoulder. "Who was that woman with Ivaldr?"

My body tensed as I blew out a deep breath. *Where to begin?*

"It's a long tale..." Dallen softly said as our eyes met. I did not know Kraka and Asher well, but I trusted Dallen's sense of a person's honor. Dallen nodded to me, "Not many babies are born within the stronghold."

"It's a planned event," I added. "For if the mother is to die in childbirth, there should be one available to feed the babes. Much like her mother did for Dallen and Doran."

"Esmeren was born the same year as us; right in between Riki and us." Doran added. A cold pulsed through my chest, almost taking the breath from my lungs. Siv stirred next to me, looking up with a raised brow.

"We were set to be betrothed because she had been born before the boys, had they come first I could have had a vastly different future. They both would have been betrothed to me, and me to them."

I was thankful that had not happened, even if I saw the two of them as my closest friends. There were rumors that my father had almost ordered Esmeren to be killed, thinking that having three rulers would be better than two. Even if the other two were mostly for show. He had a fixation on appearing unified, which is why he let Esmeren live. Her parents were well liked, and he had known what the repercussions would be.

"We grew up together knowing this," I continued. "There were no others but her for me. Until she stayed when we left." I finished with a shrug.

Was I leaving a lot out? *Yes, of course.* Talking about it was difficult, and I wasn't keen on appearing weak to so many at once. I was already attempting not to shake from the chill that seemed to have settled into my bones. *From my head to my toes, I was cold.*

"So, she's why you won't marry Siv?" Asher asked, his quiet voice barely loud enough to hear.

"Umm," I felt my cheeks heat at the thought. I believed that Siv did not want anything more, which is why we worked. It was easy. We entertained each other, but led our lives separately. *Had I misjudged what she had said?*

"I don't do titles. You know that, Ash." Siv's tired voice rang out from where she was curled against my side.

The silence that settled after she spoke was almost enough to make me get up and leave. *It was awkward, and I hated being the source of the tension.* **The lullaby in my mind did not soothe me as I soaked in the uneasy tone that refused to leave.**

"Honest or bjoda?" Dallen asked, straightening his back as he turned to look at everyone.

"Idiotic, childish games." The voice within my mind seemed to growl.

The look on his face meant there was no use in saying no. Honest or bjoda was a game we played when we were children, and then drinking around a fire, much like this as teenagers. It was a simple game, but Dallen loved to push past limits. If you chose honest, you were to answer any question asked of you truthfully. In turn, bjoda was an old term that once meant you were to do something, but in a bad sense. It was a test of honor, strength, or stupidity.

The last bjoda that Dallen gave me was to run naked through the cavern hallways, hollering about a spider chasing me.

"You first," Kraka said with a grin.

"Bjoda!" Dallen yelled, raising his horn of mead towards the sky. *This night would be long, and I knew I would regret it in the morning.* I was already feeling half dead, my chest ached with a cold chill, and my eyes were having trouble staying open. The pulse in my chest was enough to keep me awake, not letting my body settle long enough to feel comfort.

The lullaby continued to drive me mad.

"Hmm," Kraka tapped a single finger to her chin. "Close your eyes, spin in nine circles, and then jump over the fire."

"That's all?" Dallen's grin was instant as he jumped up off the ground, closing his eyes tightly. He began to spin quickly, in tight circles, the smile never leaving his face.

"Nine!" Kraka screeched through her laughter.

When he was done, he opened his eyes slowly, but I knew he would do just fine. I sucked in a sharp breath as a sudden pang of frozen pain radiated through my body. Dots started to filter into my vision, the edges threatening to take away all of my vision.

The humming stopped. If only for a moment, then began again louder.

"Go! Go! Go!" The other three yelled as Dallen ran closer to the water, slightly off pace and wobbly.

He took off towards the fire, and I hesitated slightly. At the last second, he dropped the flames low, and leaped over the pit. The pain slowly filtered away, being replaced with a sense of eyes watching me. I looked around the others, minus Siv, but they were all watching Dallen. *It was an odd sensation, like an intuitive part of me had woken open.*

Someone was watching.

"What!" Kraka hollered as she pointed a finger at him. "You can't use Sacredness on the flames!"

Dallen walked around the fire, back to her side. He pressed a soft kiss on her cheek as he sat down. "You never said that," He wiggled his eyebrows at her with a grin, before turning towards us. "Honest or bjoda, Siv!"

"Mmm," She sleepily sat up, still leaning against my side. "Honest."

I tried to shake off the feeling of eyes on the back of my head, but the urge to turn around was strong. I took three deep breaths in an attempt to focus on what was in front of me. *Something was wrong, but I couldn't figure it out. It was all too much, and the dread began to suffocate me.*

The humming threatened to consume my entire being, but the pain had faded. *It was a terrible exchange. I almost missed the cold pain.*

"Boo!" Kraka called from across the fire, smiling at her friend fondly.

"Why don't you do titles?" Dallen asked, like he had any right to inquire. He had been the same way until two days ago, drifting here and there to get his needs met. Many of us were like that here, each for their reasons.

"I see no need for a man to always be around. If I ever settle down, it will be with a woman." She shrugged lightly, bringing a hand up to brush her stray hairs out of her face. "Men have that thing where they claim to want to take care of a woman, but it almost always ends up with the woman taking care of the man..."

"Pathetic company." The voice growled through my inner ears. I tensed as I tried to control my breathing.

Something was wrong.

"Picking up his dirty clothes, making every meal, reminding him to wash his ass, and practically becoming a mother to him. I want an equal. I can find that with a woman, I just haven't found the one I will settle with."

"Praise to Freyja!" Kraka yelled, raising her horn to the sky. Siv giggled before raising her own.

"Riki is great," Siv continued like I was not there. "But he is not quite my equal. Though I do appreciate how well he respects me."

I pressed a kiss to the top of her head as foreign anger enveloped me. I did respect Siv, and I appreciated how easy it was with her. Yet, even I knew that we were not meant to live our lives together. The Norns would decide our fate, we were just along for the experience.

"Ash," Siv called out. "Honest or bjoda?"

"Umm," Asher wiggled, obviously uncomfortable at being the center of all of our attention. "Bjoda?" He hesitantly said.

"Show everyone the tattoo on your butt cheek!" She hollered, pointing her horn of mead towards Asher. His face had turned a deep red, glowing off the orange of the fire. I almost felt bad for him, but I was also sure that he did not really like me.

Asher stood slowly, untangling Dallen's arm from his own. He turned slowly to face away from the fire. Did I look away? I did not want to actually see the man's arse, but I was a little curious as to what he had tattooed there. He pulled his trousers down, his tunic still covered the offending region. Slowly, he pulled his tunic up to reveal the pale globes.

On his right cheek was a black outline of a tree, *which was odd*, but not as bad as I had assumed it would be.

THE HUMMING *in my mind had slowed down as I stood in the doorway.* I would rather not be presumptive in thinking she would invite me in. I had learned that the hard way many moons ago, and now I always stood at the entrance before being invited in. She was picking up the articles of clothing that littered the floor, apologizing for the mess. *Not that I was really concerned with how she kept her living space.*

Though I had found it a little comical that she did not want a man because of the very problem she seemed to have.

"Alright," Siv finally said as she dumped an armload of fabrics onto the floor beside her chest of overflowing clothes. I assumed the chest was clean, but knowing Siv, it could go either way. "Come in."

"You know I watched you clean it up, you could have just left it there."

"Get on the bed, and shut up" She snipped at me.

I may be a fool, but I was not such a fool that I did not listen to her. I pulled the tunic over my head first, the fabric getting momentarily stuck on the roughness of my head. My trousers came next, and I flopped onto the bed in just my breeches. Siv's mattress was nicer than mine, she must have gotten it from a village. While mine was a hard lump stuffed with moss and hay, hers felt like how I'd assume clouds felt to lay upon.

Siv stood at the end of the bed, gazing down at me. "You know the rules."

No talking, no touching without her asking me to, and if she doesn't finish first, I can never come back. I knew them well, even if I did not fully understand them. I nodded my head. She smiled at me before untying the knot that held her cloak around her shoulders. I took a moment to trail her body with my eyes, she was a beautiful woman who could do much better than me.

Not that I was complaining.

Siv slipped her arms out of the sleeves and let the dress pool around her feet. The pale expanse of her skin glowed in the fire light, making her look like a Goddess before me. Her pink nipples stood at points. My eyes drifted lower past her freckled stomach, and to the curly patch of copper hair covering her cunt. My cock hardened quickly enough that it ached painfully. I slipped my hand under my breeches, giving my cock a hard squeeze that brought me no relief. I couldn't help the moan that fell from my lips as my eyes trailed back up her body. *Nothing underneath? I had sat beside her all night with nothing more than a few layers between us?*

I pulled my hand from my cock before facing my palm towards the fire, urging the flames to grow taller and brighter. She had a tendency to prefer more light when we laid together. Siv smiled softly at me before she crawled onto the bed, placing her thighs on either side of my hips.

"You'll make a woman very happy one day."

I grunted in response, for currently there was no other woman on my mind than the one on top of me, and I knew better than to speak. She tilted her head slightly before speaking again.

"Hands on my hips."

They practically flew up to her hips at her direction, the bones digging into my palms as I held them tightly. She leaned down, her nipples dragging along my chest, and pressed her mouth to my neck. *I ached to be inside of her, for her to allow me to worship her body as she deserved for allowing a plain-looking man like myself to bring her pleasure.* My hips jutted up at the wet feel of her tongue sliding against the skin of my neck, my covered cock pressing against her bare core.

I wiggled my body enough to loosen her soft thighs grip on my hips, pressing my cock harder against her. *I was pushing the limit of no touching, but I knew it was more so regarding my hands.* I was rewarded as she moaned softly against my neck. The mixture of air hitting my neck and the sound of her pleasure sent a shiver of pleasure down my spine, and a moan left my lips.

I tightened my grip on her hips, slowly taking over her soft and slow rhythm to replace it with a hard and slow rhythm. Siv ground herself down roughly on me as she nuzzled into my neck, her breasts pressing hard against my chest. Her slow movements were almost enough to drive me insane, the steady leak of my pre-seed soaking the fabric of my breeches.

The humming stopped, anger filled me. I could not focus on the anger long with her body above mine. A growl sounded, but I pushed it away.

I ached to run my hands down her back, to urge her on, and find more relief. We laid there for a moment; my hands on her hips, her face pressed into my neck, and my covered cock rubbing against the wet folds of her pussy.

I could finish from this alone, make a mess of myself like an inexperienced man. Though I'd done it plenty before, and Siv had claimed she loved it. I still felt embarrassed, but I knew she thrived on being so attractive that I could come before entering her. She sighed softly, almost sounding tired. *I wanted to ask if she was sure she was up for it, but her rules prevented me from speaking.* My body somehow relaxed under hers, despite my cock being painfully hard and trapped under a layer of fabric. The fabric was stuck to my cock from the combined wetness from her pussy and the leaking head of my cock as we ground against each other.

"Hands off." Siv whispered.

My hands fell to the mattress, the soft thunk of them heard above our ragged breaths. My cock twitched as she lifted herself off my chest, missing the feel of her body against my own. Her soft freckled skin glowed from the fire behind her and my mouth parted as I took in the woman. *If I were an artist, I'd paint this very moment and hang it on the wall to see every day.* Her braided hair hung down her back, except for a few smaller braids around her face. Her cheeks were a soft pink, her pink bottom lip was between her teeth, a patch of flushed skin was pink above her breasts, and her soft pink nipples were pointing straight out. *I'd title the painting Pink.*

Without a word, Siv shimmied her legs up my body until her knees were placed on either side of my head. *I could die here right now, and Valhalla would not be as pleasing as the feast I was about to partake in.*

I groaned as she lowered herself, her glistening pussy rubbing against my mouth and chin. She was a Goddess, more than I deserved, and I felt honored to be in this position. I felt my cock drip onto my stomach, bobbing in anticipation. I was caught up in the view of her above me, but it did not take me long to part my mouth and run my tongue through her folds.

Siv squirmed as my tongue circled the bundle of nerves, her tufts of hair tickling my nose slightly. I moved my attention to her hole, lapping at it slowly. Siv ground down against me, whimpering as she tried to urge me on.

"Faster," She moaned out as she dropped her weight further into me.

I hummed a small laugh against her pussy; she may be in control, but I knew she enjoyed being toyed with. She was musky, warm, and delicious. My member ached as I lapped up her juices, I wanted to pull her down and feel her tightness around me. She was loud as she ground against my exploring tongue. My cock pulsed as I leisurely lapped up her juices, *I wouldn't last long and I knew it.*

The pressure built with each sound that fell from her mouth, her taste on my tongue, and the way her thighs tightened around my face.

I resisted the urge to grab onto her hips and pull her fully onto my face, and instead focused my attention on pulling her clit into my mouth. She moaned above me, tensing as I sucked harshly before sliding my tongue back down to her hole. The pressure that enveloped my cock was almost too much as I dragged my tongue through her folds, moaning softly as I felt her drip onto my chin. I kept up my pace of exploring her pussy with my tongue, lightly probing her entrance with my tongue, before moving up to circle her clit lightly.

I gave her a few sucks, trying to keep her guessing on what my next move would be. *I loved the way she squirmed above me; I wanted her to use me until she got exactly what she needed.* I knew there was no turning back from the throbbing, and I moaned against her, urging her on to finish first.

"More, please, more!" She moaned out as she ground her hips down in a circle.

I slowly brought one hand to her thigh, sliding my hand up gently to give her the chance to push me away. *If she were to send me away after finishing her, I'd still come crawling back the next time just for the chance to taste her.* I took her resounding moan as a positive, and moved both hands just as slow to her hips. With a groan, I pulled her further against me and picked up my pace.

My tongue flicked over her clit; left, suck, right, up, circle, down. I kept the pace steady as my hands tightened on her hips, moving her back and forth to ride my face. Siv's legs were quivering on either side of my face. My cock felt ready to explode with each sound that came out of her mouth. I picked up the pace of my tongue, urging her on with a moan.

She ground herself hard against my face, cutting off my breath, but that did not stop me from devouring her. I held her hips down as I gave her clit a hard suck, arching my neck so I could blow out through my nose the breath I had been holding. Her moan was loud and long as her body stiffened, the sound going straight to my cock.

A shiver wracked Siv's body as she slumped over, her head

hitting the wall in the process. I couldn't help the groan that forced its way out of my mouth as the head of my cock throbbed in relief as I followed her. *Bliss, pure bliss, consumed my entire being.*

She moved from my face slightly, giving me room to breathe as I felt my come pooling in my belly button. I brought my hand down, squeezing the last dregs of my seed from the head, closing my eyes with a sigh. *It would take me a few moments to be ready again, but I hoped she would allow me to stay.*

"This is why you're my favorite," Siv whispered as she shimmied herself down to snuggle into my side. "You are always so responsive. I don't even have to touch you, and you'll finish for me." I huffed out a laugh as I wiped my hand on my thigh before moving it to pull her closer to me.

"Any other man would be embarrassed," I whispered back.

"You're not like any other man, Riki."

"Yeah, yeah, yeah" I muttered, running my fingers up and down her back softly.

There was no buildup for the pain that encompassed my entire body, but as if I had just been dipped into the icy waters of Elivagar head first. My muscles tensed as a pained grunt forced its way out.

My vision went black as the cold chill took over my senses.

12

CONFUSION AND PAIN

Cold. **All I felt were the waves of cold enveloping my body in a steady rhythm.** I tried to open my eyes, but all I saw was the same swirling black that I saw behind my closed eyelids. *I've died and gone to Valhalla. It is too cold to be in Valhalla. The curse. The curse had killed me.*

My body felt no pain, *but the cold sensation felt comforting in a way.* It pulsed and flowed out of my chest like the beat of a heart, but it did not match the rhythm of my own. *Where am I? What is happening?* **My thoughts were jumbled, and my body did not react.**

I tried to flex my fingers and wiggle my toes, but all I felt was the dull thud of cold radiating out of my bones. ***It was the chill that had flowed out of Loreth's eyes and carved an aching chill into my chest.*** I could hear the thudding of my heartbeat in my ears, competing steadily against the pulsing chill.

Was this where my soul was to stay forever? No longer inside the cage of bones and beside my heart. There was a sound in the distance that I could almost hear, a rhythmic guttural sound that faded in and out.

*Was that...a **raven**? Was I alive, or was I lying dead in Odin's hall with Huginn and Muninn cawing above me?* I had heard once as a child that Huginn would search your thoughts, while Muninn searched your memories. This was how it would be decided if Odinn was to allow you into Valhalla.

I have died. I died. I died.

I am dead.

I heard the guttural **kraa kraa kraa** again; like I was by an open window, and it had swooped by. Opening my eyes was a fruitless endeavor; all I saw was darkness. I could not tell if time was passing, just the steady beat of radiating chills.

My heartbeat thudded faster in my ears as the weight of reality settled low in my gut. *This was the end.* I had not achieved anything in my life. Where I had hoped to be at this age was not anywhere close to what I had become.

As a boy, I often sat and thought about what I would do with the crown upon my head, the same one that still sat upon my father's head. That thin strip of gold was the most mundane piece of jewelry my father owned, but it held the most power. Sacredness had been placed upon the crown many years ago; complex blood Sacredness that only responded to those with the original bloodline. It was how the previous Rikr's ensured that Sidirna would continue to be protected, though I was not sure what was protected besides the Rikr himself. The layers of Sacredness would hold until there was no one left with our blood, and the protective barrier around Sidirna would stay intact.

The barrier ensured that only those who were proclaimed could pass through, which was something I had always wanted to do. I'd seen the barriers frequently while I was growing up; the stronghold was not far from the cliffs that separated us from the ocean. *Yet, I was dead, never having seen the barriers again. I died having done nothing.*

Dead. Dead. Dead.

The barriers were as tall as you could look; like someone had placed a protective bubble over Sidirna. *I longed to see them once more.* They glowed similarly to the suds on my tunic as I washed it by the river, or like the haze of a rainbow in the distance. My grandfather had told me that the Gods had lent us spare pieces of the Bifrost to protect Sidirna. *I'm not sure whether I truly believe that.*

I tried to move my fingers again, using all of my force to force my fingers into a fist as the **kraa** of the raven sounded once more. *I needed to break out of this, this could not be my end. I was not ready to die when I had barely been living.* My hopes for my future could still be achieved; I would see my father's head roll as I brought the axe down. Ivaldr was a cowardly man and a piss poor leader.

I was a fool to have followed him for as long as I have.

Dead. Dead. Dead.

I will break out of this darkness. I will enact my revenge. I will lead Sidirna. I will ensure my people are free. I will line up every Jarl who served my father faithfully, and I will drive my sword into their shriveled, hateful heart.

I will not die. I will not die. I will not die.

I will do anything to ensure that my bloodline does not end with me; I will raise my son to be an honorable, courageous, and fair Rikr. I felt my smallest finger twitch as I continued to try to force my body to cooperate. **This will not be my end.** I will not allow the Gods to pull me from this realm before I have shoved the Norn's dreadful fate for me up their asses.

My chest seized as a burst of freezing pain overtook my entire body. I felt my fingers move then, but not in the way I had hoped. They shuddered and shook as the pain continued to seize my body.

I wrenched my eyes open and saw fleeting bursts of scenery before me.

A river, trees, fire, children playing, and the fresh mound of a grave.

My stomach churned in nausea as the pain continued to overtake my body. **A river, trees, fire, children playing, and the fresh mound of a grave.**

A river, trees, fire, children playing, and the fresh mound of a grave.

A river, trees, fire, children playing, and the fresh mound of a grave.

A river, trees, fire, children playing, and the fresh mound of a grave.

My vision blurred into focus, and nausea churned in my gut. There was a strange hue to everything, but I almost recognized the interior of the room. I was standing in the doorway, with my hand clenched around the wood of the frame. My nails were digging into the wood, but I could not feel the prick of pain that I would expect to feel. The pain had subsided, but the cold still overtook my body.

I stumbled slightly as I took a step forward, my shoulder bashing into the wood with a thunk. **Where was I? Where had I been?** I tried to rack my brain for the information as a chill shuddered its way through my body. My grip on the frame loosened, and I only slightly felt the grain dragging along my palm as I attempted to straighten my shoulders.

I shook my head, trying to get the odd haze out of my vision. I staggered another step without a thought; all I knew was that I had to break out of this so I could get the crown.

The crown...the crown that Alfrikr the Wretched had placed upon his unruly brow. One he did not deserve to wear.

He did not care for the people like I cared for the people.

Another step brought me closer to the mattress, steadier this time. I will recover. **I would beat the curse.** My body seemed to move on its own as I made my way across the room. Slowly moving to sit on the edge of the bed. I reached a hand down to untie the laces of my boots, and it was then that I had realized that it was not my hand.

It was not my boot, nor my bed.

Where was I? Who was I? Dead? Alive?

Could I move this body?

I tested out moving my hand, but my fingers did not move. I was not dead, and that was a good sign. Though I did not know where my body was; I knew that my body was not strewn before Odinn for judgment. I heard the **kraa** of a raven again, and looked towards the source of the sound. In the corner of the room stood an ornate cage with a large black raven pecking at the bars.

"Knock it off," The deep gravel of my voice rang out from my body-his body. I kicked off my boots, groaning as I moved to lay flat on the mattress.

Did he know I was here? That I was seeing from his eyes as if they were my own. **Were they my eyes now?** I tried to move my fingers again, hoping that I could control him as if he were me.

Could I speak?

I tried to shout, but it was much like thinking. If I took a breath, I wasn't sure. I shouted again, **a full force battle cry.** I needed to get out of his head, and back into my body. **I needed to live, and live for myself. What I thought was living was simply existing.**

"What the fuck?!" His deep, gravely voice exclaimed, sitting himself straight up. *It sounded similar to the voice within my head.*

So, he heard me? I did not know what was happening. *Would I return to my body?*

I stayed silent, though I was unsure if my thoughts were staying within my mind. When Froggy had said I was cursed in my soul; *was this what he meant? Was I cursed to exist without a body, forever lingering in darkness?*

I laid back down, or he laid back down. I needed to create a separation between us; between our souls.

I am Alfrikr. I am Alfrikr. I am Alfrikr.

He settled onto the bed, and I felt the scratch of his fingers on his chin. *My chin? Our chin?* He twisted the hairs of his beard around his fingers, curling and uncurling as he stared at the ceiling. I tried to move his body again, any movement would settle the fear that had latched itself onto me. **My soul, my body, and my purpose in this life did not belong to him. I will curse the Norns themselves for this. I will not lie down and admit defeat; the curse will be broken, and I will return to my body.**

I will do more within the rebellion.

I will see my father's head roll.

My vision went black as I felt the moment he fell asleep. An odd sensation enveloped me, almost as if I were falling off a cliff. My arms wanted to flail as if I could flap my arms and fly myself to safety. Instead of hitting the ground below me, my vision shifted to a hazy view of a large oak tree at the top of a hill. Before me was a small village that had seen better days. A woman stood nearby, her dark hair braided down her back, scrubbing a white linen in a washbasin.

Was this his dream?

Had I drifted somewhere else?

I quickly looked down, relieved to see my body. My sword hung low around my hips, and I could feel the weight of my shield on my back. My boots were the same worn out ones that Dallen poked fun at. The trousers and tunic were the ones I'd traded for just before the raid. My feldr was lined with the bear I had hunted three winters ago. I cautiously brought my hand up to feel my hair—still sheered. The woman before me did not turn to look at me, though I was sure I looked like a fool standing there examining myself.

Where was I?

I cautiously walked towards the center of the town, my gaze catching on the tree in the distance again. **I needed to get there, though I was unsure why.** I could feel the sharp tang of my intuition guiding me. I always thought that intuition was the God's or the Norn's way of guiding a person towards their fate; the strands had been woven, I knew that I would find myself in the situations destined for me regardless of my actions.

The homes surrounding me were more huts than houses, as I stared at them more intently. The shutters on the house, behind the woman, were barely hanging on. Everything was faded and dull. People milled around me, chattering in a language I almost did not understand. It was similar to my own, but almost like my ears were not picking up exactly what they were saying. **The tree, I needed to get to the tree.** *Though, I was not exactly sure why.*

It was not until I was halfway through the town that I noticed my body felt warm. The chills that had engulfed me seemed to be faded here…**wherever here was.** I brought a hand up to my chest and pressed my fingers into the bones until it hurt. The pain had receded. *Was I dead, or had my soul simply left my body?* I never thought this kind of thing was possible. Froggy had known it was my soul that was cursed, *was this part of the curse?* He was well-versed in blood Sacredness. If he had known it was my soul, it must be something that can be affected by blood Sacredness.

I jolted backwards as a man with a cart pulled by a horse almost trampled me.

The tree… There was something about the tree that felt important. I could tell from here that it was an oak tree; it was broad, with limbs full of red and orange leaves. Much like the trees were by the river last night. **I hoped I was not dead,** *but I very well could be.* A trickle of nervousness flowed through me as I weighed where exactly I was. *Could the curse have given my soul to him? Would I be able to exist within my body again?* I could only hope that this would pass, much like the last time I found myself within Loreth's mind. My steps halted as I reached the end of the stone pathway; the lush grass hill before me.

The pull in my gut told me to keep going. I *needed to get to the tree for something, and it was important.*

Yet, I still stood there. *Would this be my end? Was I walking on a path to inevitably end up within some God's hall? How was I to know that I was alive?*

I had no answer. I could let this fear fill me and do nothing, much like I have been doing for the last nine years. I had been filled with the fear of what others thought about me, how they **judged** me, how they **mistrusted** me, and it led to me doing *nothing*. I had run from the fear of my father finding out my betrayal; **only to do nothing.**

The first step onto the grass was a turning point…one that would change my life for **good.**

If only I could let go of the fear that consumed me. It was only moments ago that I swore I would change the way I had been living life, and this was my first step.

If I find myself dead when I reach the top of this hill, I will not cower in fear. I will not look the other way, I will not be weak.

The thought of being weak made me shutter. My father had instilled it in me that I was to never be weak. *Yet, I spent years being weak within the mountain.*

I did not fight for a better rank.

I let people whisper behind my back.

I was halfway up the hill now. **If this was the hill that I died on… at least it was beautiful.**

I heaved a breath as I tried to veer my thoughts away from how weak I had become in the past nine years. *How I had let such a foolish man lead me into a life of nothing.* I wished to go back to the energetic, rule breaking, rebellious boy I had been at 18. Yet, here I was at 27; cursed, stuck within the mind of my enemy, and with no achievements towards improving Sidirna.

Where had I gone wrong?

Why am I not panicking more about being in this hazy new reality?

I shook my head, trying to dispel the barrage of thoughts within my head. I needed to focus on the task before me, not on how disappointed I was with myself.

My steps crested the top of the hill as I looked around. There was nothing but hills and land before me; the village at my back. The trunk of the tree was the thickest I had ever seen.

This tree had to have been around long enough that the Gods had walked the land and rested beneath it.

There was nothing at the tree.

I had built up some idea that this tree was a path of fate I had to walk; that something important would happen. Yet, I stood here and nothing happened. The wind blew, the leaves rustled, and I stood there *idiotically*. I huffed a laugh, shaking my head before walking and sitting down against it. I leaned back against the trunk, staring down at the village below. I'd always wanted to see a village like this; one that held the people of my kingdom. I'd never been allowed to travel like the other kids at my father's stronghold.

I sat there watching the specks of people mill around the town. Such a simple and easy life, yet I had been living the same way. Anger coursed through me as I closed my eyes. *Was this where I existed now?* I wanted to scream, to cry, to stomp my foot like a child, and go back to my measly existence.

If I just did not think about it, did it not matter?

Could I ignore the ever pressing feeling of disappointment in myself? I groaned, bringing my palms up to press into the sockets of my eyes.

I had gone from a simple life to an insane life in the matter of a single breath. I went from working the fields, fucking a good-looking woman, and eating meals with friends to this.

Stuck in the mind of a man who wanted me dead.

A man that I had only heard tortuous stories about, who I had *feared* like the rest of Sidirna did.

I was **cursed**; I knew that. I knew I needed to change my life around. I needed to find my way back and then fight. I needed the rebellion to take it seriously. We weren't supposed to be sitting around braiding daisy chains and raising livestock.

We were meant to be taking over a kingdom and fighting oppression.

Before I could react, I was flying to the ground with a hand wrapped around my throat. I scrambled to pry the hand away, and opened my eyes to meet the harsh obsidian eyes that started it all.

Loreth's hand tightened, cutting off my air-supply quickly. He was here. **He had cursed me.**

"Alfrikr," He growled down at me, shoving his knee between my legs harshly as he held me down. I grabbed his wrist, trying to shove it away from me. "Why are you here?" Loreth whispered venomously.

I struggled beneath him as my lungs began to burn. **This was not how I would die.** My right hand searched the ground around me for something to strike him with. *There was nothing.* I moved my hand to his hip, searching for the hilt of his sword, as he loosened his grip on my throat. He still held me down with the weight of his body, eyes narrowing as he glared down at me. *I would have happily died on this hill minutes ago.* **But not now that Loreth would be the one to end me.**

I cursed the Gods for their joke; I would live.

I hacked out a short cough, gasping for air as Loreth pinned me down. I wiggled beneath him as if I could worm my way out of his hold. I needed to practice hand-to-hand combat, it was embarrassing how easily Loreth held me down. *How I floundered like a turtle on its back.*

He shoved me down into the dirt harder, "Why are you here!?" Loreth shouted in my face.

I flinched as the specks of his spittle hit my face, still attempting to squirm out of his hold. **What an idiotic question to ask.** *Did he not know what was happening? Did his body not quiver and shake with the pain of the bone chilling cold? Do I play dumb?* I stared at him, quirking an eyebrow as I weighed my options.

"Loreth," I finally snarled out. "I should kill you for what you did to me."

My left hand was still pushing against his hip, but I eased off slightly to try to move it up to his face. I could go for his eyes in this position; gouge them out before ending him.

"Kind of difficult to do that while you're beneath me," He growled out, moving his hand to grab my wrist. He slammed my arm into the ground with a laugh. I grunted in pain, which only seemed to make the laugh louder.

"Why did you curse me?" I grunted out as I tried to pull my wrist out of his grip. It was a weak attempt, but I did not stop.

"Curse you?" He asked mockingly, tightening his grip. I stilled as I met his eyes. *Anxiety flared in my gut as I thought of the way they had haunted me in the short days since the raid. He had to know what he did. It had to have been him.*

"Where are we?"

"You don't know your kingdom?" His voice mocked me again, sending a flare of anger down my spine.

I struggled again, shoving my hips up to try to knock him off. Loreth grunted as he shifted his weight, shoving his knee further into my cock. I winced as the pain shot through me and caught the breath in my lungs.

"Get the fuck off me!"

"Do you think if I kill you here," He leaned closer to my face, his grimace almost resembling a smile. "That your body will die? I'm sure that poor red-headed whore is already crying because you aren't waking up."

The events of the night rushed back as his words settled in. I had been in Siv's cavern, moments away from fucking her. *How did he know Siv was there?* My mouth fell open as I stared up at him.

"Nothing to say?" Loreth threw his head back with a laugh. "Oh, you poor idiot. I almost feel bad for you."

"I..." I took a deep breath, trying to find courage within myself. "I don't know who you're talking about."

"I've tortured many men," His grip on my wrist tightened as he looked back down at me. He stretched my arm further above my head, grunting as he pressed more of his weight down. "But none have been as stupid as you. You can't control your ugly face; lying there gaping up at me like you want me to stuff my cock in." He tilted his head, as if weighing if he would truly try it.

My face heated as my cock twitched at his words. *I wanted to bash my face in, or rip my cock off, for reacting to the man.*

"What did you do to me?" I hated how weak my voice came out, how my body had begun to shake beneath him. ***I hated Loreth, but I hated myself even more for the tent in my trousers. I did not want to fuck him; his closeness just confused my body.***

"Oh right," Loreth pressed his knee further into my crotch.

My hips jutted up on their own accord, my hard cock dragging against his thick thigh. **Fuck, I hated the man.** Loreth was a cruel, sick, brute of a man. **Why would my body betray me like this?**

"You'd finished before even making it into her pussy. What a sad and desperate heir." I struggled beneath him again, face flaring in embarrassment.

If I could punish my cock, I'd have its head for the way it leaked at his words. The shame that filled my gut was almost unbearable. He'd been in my head, and I had not even known. *How long had he watched me?*

"What did you do to me?" I asked him again, glaring as I tried to shove him off. "You know, your little curse lets me into your head too. I can share anything I want with Ivaldr and always be one step ahead of you."

He stilled above me, eyes going wide. His grip loosened fractionally, not enough for me to slip away from him. His thigh was still pressed against my crotch, painfully pressing into my weeping cock. *It was from thinking about Siv. It had to be.*

"You're lying." Loreth growled out.

"Am I?"

"Stupid boy, It's not a curse," He tilted his head as he looked down at me. "It's a…"

My chest tightened with the familiar cold pain as my vision faded black.

I3

REGRET AND MEAT

My eyes shot open as my body shuddered, but I could not see as I gasped for air. The ache in my chest pulsed in a cold fury as it threatened to overtake my body. Warm hands touched my shoulders, shaking me gently. **Loreth. Loreth had me. He was going to kill me.** I flinched before heaving my body upwards, my arms wrapping around the body atop me. I heaved myself over them, pinning them down as I brought my hand to their neck. The darkness in my vision began to fade around the edges, but I could not see fully.

I would not let him kill me.

This would not be my end.

"Alfrikr!" Siv yelled beneath me, scrambling to push my hand off her neck.

Shit. Shit. Shit. It was not Loreth.

"Oh Gods, I'm so sorry!" I mumbled out as I flung myself off her, moving quickly to plant my feet on the floor. My body felt too cold after the warmth I had been feeling. I felt a snowstorm within me, one that threatened to consume me.

"What the Hel happened?" She questioned, moving to cover herself with her bed furs. "Your eyes rolled back into your head like a Seidr! Then you started shaking and got freezing cold. The fire went out!"

She looked at me in fear, like the curse was contagious. It was odd that I'd looked like a Seidr, those who practiced an old Sacredness to get glimpses of the future from the Norns. Was what I saw the future, or was it a dream? I did not think it could be the future because Loreth had mentioned Siv, and what we had just done. Something was wrong. *The curse was wrong.*

Am I to die?

"Hello?!" She screeched as she leaned forward to smack my stomach.

"I-I don't know? How long was I like that?"

"Only a few moments? I don't know! What the Hel happened!" She pulled her bottom lip between her teeth before continuing. "I think it's best if you go. I don't think you're well..."

I nodded my head solemnly. Without a word, I dressed myself, giving her a small wave as I left. The depth of reality sunk deep in my gut as another shock of icy pain radiated through my body. My body moved without a thought back towards my cavern, utterly consumed by what had just happened. The cold that had consumed me had slowly turned tolerable; as if I were a regular temperature again. I was exhausted. I'd overrun my body. It had been days since I'd gotten a good rest.

The dream was just a manifestation of my fears—that Loreth had cursed me.

I was hesitant to accept that it was Loreth who had fixed his attention on me. *Why had he cursed me? Why me? I'd heard plenty about the man. I wanted to be nowhere within his mind. He was a sick, cruel man who held no morals. He had no honor.* My body tensed as I turned the corner, ducking my head as a rowdy group of boys ambled past me. *I missed those days.*

When the only bad thing in my life was waking up after drinking far too much ale.

I brought a hand up to my chest, rubbing the center harshly. The pain was not the same as it had been before; it felt deeper now. As if it had latched itself onto my bones. I cringed at the thought of the curse sinking through my skin, fat, and muscles until it settled into my bones. The mental image was similar to watching a pork hock simmering in a pot of spiced water. Loreth had begun to tell me something about the curse, what was it he had said? *That it was not a curse? Not that I could trust the word of the dishonorable man.*

I did not want to think about it, but the disgust simmered in my gut.

Loreth had threatened my mouth with his cock, and ***my body had somehow found pleasure within that***. I didn't understand how or why. When I thought of Loreth now, I only thought of how pleasant it would be to hear the crack of his bones as my fist pummeled his face. Or how much joy I would have as I slid my blade into his chest cavity and watched him bleed out. **His suffering was one I would relish in.** At the last second, I took the sharp left that led to the front of the cavern system. There was a map of Sidirna there; I wanted to find the hills that I had seen. **He'd said my kingdom. He meant we were somewhere that existed.** I needed to know where so that I could find him and separate his head from his body.

I would not think of his cock. I would not think of his body over mine. How his thighs flexed. The veins in his arms as he held my throat. Dishonorable thoughts. I would not think of them.

I would not succumb to the wills of my cock.

My body was sluggish and slow as I meandered my way through the twists and turns. The slow incline of the paths steadily stole the breath from my lungs. I felt the pulsing cold within my chest settle deeper with each step I took. I was unsettled by how quickly Loreth had snuck up and disarmed me. I'd spent the last nine years honing my skills; or so I thought I did. I sparred most mornings, I went for runs, and I worked the fields.

Loreth was only a few inches taller than me, but I had to admit that he was far broader than me. The muscles that strained as he held me down. *I appreciated his form, his physique. I did not want to fuck the man, nor did I want him to fuck me. I* needed to work harder if I wanted to kill him. Train harder than I had been and hone in my abilities. *I would not think about his cock, and if its size was anything comparable to the size of the man.*

When I was stuck in the darkness, drifting into nothing, I had made myself a promise. Yet, it all felt fuzzy as I tried to recall what I had sworn to myself. I knew that I needed to work harder on becoming accepted within the rebellion and influence our future actions. That was a goal I had floundered lately and would be the first thing that had to change. I'd dreamt up such a beautiful future when I began dealing secrets to Ivaldr. **How I would come into power and I would be backed by the very people my father had hated; the ones he had oppressed.**

It all felt so easy then.

I knew now that I hadn't the first clue about running Sidirna. Taxes, laws, feeding the people, and all of that which went into being the Rikr was foreign to me. My father had wanted to wait to teach me those things until I had come of age, no use in teaching an heir if you didn't know he would survive, is what he would say. My mother would tell me it was because he viewed me as a threat. Did my father view Loreth as a threat? Was the man doing his bidding? I'd learned how to be ruthless from my father, though. It'd been many years since

I'd acted that way, but I knew it still simmered inside of me. I knew how to sneak a poison into a drink, how to get information out of an unwilling man, and much more. I could use those skills to advance here; something that had always felt wrong to do.

Yet, as my steps rounded the last corner, I knew it would be what I did.

I knew that I would have to do things that went against my morals, my honor, if I wanted to take Loreth and my father down and seize the crown.

Ivaldr would very soon find me useful, and the people here would learn to bow before me. I would need to think this through. Meticulously plan exactly how I was to quickly turn the people against him. **This curse had made me a changed man; it had given me a purpose, and for that, I was thankful.** I was beginning to feel cold. Not as cold as before, but still cold. I stepped up to the large map, worrying my lip between my teeth as I flitted my gaze throughout it. There were hills in the east, but I knew none of those were as green as the ones I had seen. The midlands were flat, and we were in the south— the only area of Sidirna that I knew well. My only option was the west of Sidirna. I dragged my finger across the terrains, thankful that Dallen had created such a realistic map.

Tommerhamm, Vikhamm, and Ravenheim were the only towns listed. Tommerhamm seemed to be in the middle of a forest, Vikhamm was a port town, and Ravenheim was a mountainous area. The halls on the map held no towns, but I knew that there must be something deep within those forests. Exactly what I was searching for. Loreth had a raven, and we met in Ravenheim? **That felt like the Norns.** I knew 9 years ago that the west was poor, low populated, and held nothing worthwhile. At least, that's what my father had always said.

Their port was small and rarely used, but Vikhamm was where all Varangian Guardsmen went to train. The area was low-populated and poor enough that no one commented on the bodies that were thrown into the rivers. The Varangian Guardsmen were brutal. I stared at the map for a moment, wondering the importance of Ravenheim and why I had seen Loreth there. **What did the raven mean? Why did the man have one?** *Was he touched by the Gods?* I dropped my hand that had been on the map to my chin, worrying the hairs of my beard between my fingers. I would find him, but it would take time.

"Planning on leaving?" Ivaldr's voice rang out. My body was sluggish to turn, and the pain in my chest was still steady.

"No," I replied, a small frown appearing on my face. "Just contemplating how hard this winter will be for the people further from cities."

"Ah, yes," His snidely voice responded. "It is a cycle winter. The east will be hit the worst. They're used to the sun beating down, and hardly any crops grow there. We will flourish here, they should have come to join us."

"Is it too late to help them?" I asked, turning to look at the map again. *Where was Esmeren?* There was something amiss, but I could not tell what. The pulls at my intuition urged me to placate him. To begin the plan now.

"Unfortunately." Ivaldr took a step closer, standing at my side. "Why the sudden interest?" A pulse of cold shivered its way out of my chest and dragged through my body. I grimaced as I tried to will the feeling away without shivering.

"I'm going on ten years," My unsteady voice made me cringe. *Weak,* **but I needed him to view me as such.** "A lot to think about, a lot more I wished to have done."

Ivaldr hummed in reply, making me want to grab his head

and bash it against the stone map. **It was his fault that I was at such a low station, but I would play nice with the petty fool.**

"They did not like her." He finally said.

"Who?"

"Esmeren, of course." He tutted softly as he adjusted his tunic. "I had hoped they would be welcoming, as they have been with you."

I held in the scoff and retort that were at the tip of my tongue. They had not welcomed me, but they knew I would win in a fight. Ivaldr tilted his palm down and crafted a poorly made, stone stool. A useless display of Sacredness, though it was probably some petty way to remind me how important he was. **It did not work.**

"Oh?" I hoped he would spill details, I'd known the man long enough to understand how he worked. **I had to feign interest, but not enough that it spooked him.**

"Aye," He said, his voice teetering on a solemn tone. "I had thought to find you curled up with Siv. Did she change her mind after your boasting?"

I willed the snarl away as I resisted sending my fist into his face.

"She did not want more than one round, and she doesn't accept overnight guests." A little lie could go a long way.

I didn't want him to know the truth of the curse. As I stood there, it had shot out bursts of cold pain. I wanted to double over or perhaps cry a little. Yet, I knew that showing that kind of weakness was not an option. *He already knew too much of my fate.*

"I've heard that about her," Ivaldr crossed his legs, staring up at me. "I've sent Esmeren to a cave next to mine. It's guarded, but I have full faith that she will win over the rest of our people."

He'd already known how I felt about the woman. A zap of cold shot through my body; this curse would kill me. It would be difficult to change his mind, but if I wanted to make it into his inner circle, he would have to believe that I was on his side.

"Why do they distrust her?" I asked, hoping my dull question would make him view me as an idiot. There were many people who would spill their innermost secrets if they thought the person was not a threat.

"For the same reason you do." Ivaldr replied, eyeing me wearily. I shrugged my shoulders before moving to lean my body against the wall.

"I'd like to believe her," I furrowed my eyebrows, hoping that he would see me as a conflicted man. **I was not conflicted, and I did not trust her.** My toes began to feel numb from the cold, slowly making its way up my legs. "I just haven't spent enough time with her, I think." He eyed me up and down, and I could tell he was suspicious.

I said my goodnights, and drifted back to my cavern, lost in thought. I would need to plan this out better; Ivaldr could not suspect that I was after his position as head of the rebellion.

The real question would be whether I kept him alive.

Sleep did not come easily, nor did it stick around. I tossed and turned throughout the night, afraid that the curse would send me to Loreth or him to me. I didn't know what was happening, but I knew it was bad. It was hours past dawn by the time I heaved myself out of my bed and made my way to the training caverns. A morning meal could wait. I was thankful they were near my cavern, as I still felt sluggish. The pain had come and gone in waves; no rhyme or reason to it. The cold had only gotten worse, and I missed the moment of warmth that I had felt while dreaming in Siv's cavern.

I was stone-cold now; a rock that had been thrown upon an ice coated lake.

I looked around the sparring area, hoping to see Dallen. Though I knew it was fruitless as he was always in and out before dawn broke. I'd not had the energy to move that early, and my body still felt off. There were men around me that I knew were Tyr's enforcers, though I did not know their names. The tallest one of the bunch was currently pummeling a younger, and smaller man. *If I were smart, I'd turn around and come back tomorrow.*

I knew I was foolish as I called out, "Enough!"

The man froze with his fist still in the air and turned to face me. "The lonely heir wishes for a fight?" He called out with a manic grin.

I was a fool. The man stood to his full height, at least four inches above my 6'6. He was broad enough to look as if he were half giant. I flattened my expression, giving the man a cool shrug. My chest ached, my bones ached, and my muscles were seized in cold pain. I was a God's damned fool. I couldn't even focus on his insult as I made my way to the circle. Pausing to admire the intricate carvings of ash tree branches that interlocked to create a large enough circle for sparring.

Would this be where I died? This could very well be where I took my last breath, but I was thankful for the surrounding beauty. If only for a moment.

"Your name?" I asked, holding out my arm for a handshake.

His large hand engulfed my forearm as we shook three times. "Meat." His deep voice replied. I tilted my head and raised my eyebrow as I released his arm. His runes were dark, signifying that he had decent stores of Sacredness. *Big, powerful, and able to kill me. I was a fool.* **At least he was not Loreth.**

"Meat?" There was no possible way his parents had named him that. I thought Alfrikr was a terrible name, but I have finally found a worse one. He threw his head back with a laugh, roaring in a way that was not necessary. ***Perhaps death would be a mercy, if only to get away from his guffawing.***

"I am called Meat or Herald. Whichever you prefer." He said between laughs. I shook my head, taking three steps backwards. "No Sacredness." Meat added, copying my motion.

I rolled my shoulders back, trying to ease the ache. A flare of cold pain had been working its way through my body since I had arrived, but it suddenly clutched my chest as I took my stance. My body jerked forward slightly as it felt like a freezing wind had blown between my ribs.

"Final words before you go to Valhalla?" Meat, Herald, called out. I rolled my eyes with a scoff. I was sure that I could best him in a duel; he was slower because of his mass and favored his left knee.

"May the Gods be entertained!" I called back to him.

He lunged forward just as I was expecting. I sidestepped him with a small chuckle and continued moving. My chest ached in the cold, but I pushed it away. **Death would come for me, but I hoped I'd go out with honor.**

"You're just as filthy as that whore, Esmeren." Meat grunted out as he turned to face me.

His method of enraging me was poor, but I didn't figure his brain held many thoughts. He kicked his leg out, aiming towards my knee. I brought my foot up to slam against his own. He grunted at the impact, hopping away from me.

"How does it feel to be the heir of nothing?" He taunted again, swinging a meaty fist towards my face.

My arms shot up to cover and clenched my teeth at the impact. The spot he hit felt like it had shattered, but I knew it did not. A sharp cold suddenly came over my arms, spasming as I tried to keep them held up.

The brute of a man took that opportunity to slam his fist into my gut, immediately sucking away any breath that I had.

I groaned as my body began to double over, "That all you got?" I taunted back at the man.

I was a fool, and I knew it. He took that opportunity to jump and slam me to the ground with his hands on my shoulders. My eyes fluttered open and closed as I stared up at him.

"**Pathetic.**" He spit out, his voice sounding eerily similar to Loreth's. I shook my head, trying to dislodge the haze.

"I heard you're cursed," Herald said as he pressed down on my chest, the cold ache flaring under his touch. "Is it true?"

"No." I bit out, trying to shift my weight to throw him off me.

When that did not work, I brought my knee up to hit him in his lower back. He huffed out a breath, shifting his weight to hold me down with one hand. His other came up, preparing to slam into my face. I rolled my body as hard as I could, it was futile as the weight of him mixed with the curse draining my strength took over. I took the hit with a smile and a laugh, much like I used to when I wanted to taunt my father.

Herald hit me again, harder this time. It brought tears to my eyes and made my teeth feel loose in my mouth. I groaned as the curse seemed to wind up from my chest, straight to the source of my new pain. It latched onto it with a vengeance; like it had slid into the pain and twisted until it was frozen. He pushed himself from me, which surprised me. He held out his hand for me and I took it as he pulled me up off the ground.

"Tell me about Esmeren, and I won't pummel you into blood and dust." He grumbled out, clearly unhappy to not have the chance. I spit out a mouth full of blood before shrugging.

"I don't trust her," I replied. "If that's what you're asking."

He nodded his head, pursing his lips like he was deep in thought. *Was he on Ivaldr's side?*

"I do think we should give her a chance. Let her prove that she is with us. Everyone deserves that." I added, amazed at how quick I had found the neutral words. "Though, she should be watched closely. Her loyalty should be tested."

I used the sleeve of my tunic to wipe the blood from my mouth. My muscles screamed, and the cold pain enveloped my body. I felt the edges of my vision darken and used whatever energy I had left to excuse myself. I pushed against the blackness seeping into my vision. **I would not let it take me. My body may be weak, but my mind is strong.**

"You should have killed him, you weak fool." A deep voice clambered through my thoughts.

I stopped in my tracks. *What the Hel was that.* "What?" I found myself whispering.

I turned in a circle, not seeing anyone in the hallway. I shook my head before making my way towards my cavern. *It was not Loreth. I would know if he were in my mind.* I'm sure it was nothing, but I still had the feeling I was being watched. The cold within my body seeped to slowly seep out, leaving me warm by the time I reached the washbasin in my room. I stripped off my clothes carelessly, letting them drop on the floor wherever I flung them. My cheek and mouth ached, but the bleeding seemed to have slowed down. I cupped my hands, bringing water to my lips, and swishing it around before spitting it into my piss bucket.

"*Disgusting.*" The deep voice reverberated through my mind again.

Insane, I was going insane. I heaved out a sigh, shaking my head. The embers of my fire still smoldered, and I held a hand out to stoke the flames. I was not cold, but I needed the light to see better. My breath caught as a sudden realization hit me as hard as Meat had slammed his fist into my gut.

Loreth was in my head. The voice was Loreth.

"Get out." I whispered, unsure if anyone passing by my cavern could hear me.

"**Why would I do that when I'm having so much fun with your pain?**" His laugh was loud inside my head.

"I'm going to kill you."

"*Ah,*" Loreth chuckled again. "**You couldn't even if you had the chance.**"

A part of me knew he was right, but my pride screamed in protest. When I was feeling better, I would track him down. **He would beg before me, and I would laugh in his face.**

"Are you sure about that?" I questioned.

"**Yes,**" he replied. "**I just saw you lose to a man named Meat.**"

"How do you know it wasn't on purpose?" I exclaimed, forgetting to lower my voice. Loreth laughed again, the sound sending a shiver down my spine. "You're not the only one playing games, Loreth No Name." I added pettily.

"**What was the game? How quickly can you wound your pride?**"

There was a part of me that wondered if this was truly happening. Was there some part of the curse that connected our minds, like Dallen and Doran's? Loreth was not my brother, I was certain of that. My father was incredibly careful with his mistresses; the crown needed to remain the firstborn sons.

"When I find you," I finally said. "I'm going to take my time with ending your pathetic life."

"You are a weakling," Loreth responded with a laugh. **"You would not stand a chance. I would pin you beneath me before you'd taken a breath."** I knew he was right, and I knew that I needed to work on my training.

I would spend the coming winter honing my skills, and Loreth would soon regret cursing me.

"Not if I find your body while you're stuck in my head." I countered, immediately regretting it. *I was playing a risky game, taunting the man, and my emotions were getting the better of me.* Had Loreth not already thought of it; he would plan it now.

"First you'd have to find me."

"In Ravenheim?" I taunted; hoping I was correct.

"Who told you!?" He harshly spit out. I could almost feel the anger that consumed him. As if it had become a steady stream of feelings beside my own.

"Tell me of the curse, and I'll tell you." I taunted with a grin he could not see.

The shock of the cold coming back was enough to bring me to my knees, crashing down on the stone floor with a pained yelp. I stayed there for a moment, heaving breaths loud in the quiet.

Fuck.

Did that mean he was gone? Or was he quickening the pace of killing me with his curse?

14

PISS AND FLOWERS

Confusion swirled through me in a way that rivaled the cold which had overtaken my body. I'd stayed there for far too long, my knees aching horribly, as I tried to process what had just happened. I could almost excuse it as a moment of insanity; *that I had just lost touch with the world I resided in.* However, it was obvious that the cold curse had created a bridge between Loreth and I. He had spoken to me within my mind, and I worried that his cruel mind could read my very thoughts. **I would need to figure out how it worked.** There had to be a way to protect myself from the man who could spy on me from within my mind.

When I was a child, I'd often wondered what it would be like to share my life with someone in such a way that they knew my very thoughts. Some sort of all consuming connection, much like I'd seen the way loving couples finished each other's sentences. The thought of that now made my insides curl within themselves in shame. The worry remained that Loreth would be able to listen to me think as though he were a silent reader of a story of my life; something that I would be ashamed for others to hear. *The way they would hear me whinging and moaning about like as if I truly had it hard.* As though I had not been born in a place of privilege and still went to bed with a full belly every night. Those thoughts that eerily sounded like my father's voice swirling within my mind. The ones that I kept locked down within my mind; *how* ashamed I was to have not completed anything worthwhile in my measly existence.

How, if I were to die today, I would only be known as the Lonely Heir of Sidirna who ran away to shovel horse shit until he died.

Knowledge needed to be found, and I knew who exactly would know; Doran and Dallen. There was a part of me that cringed at the thought of them knowing exactly what had happened, and I attributed that to a gut feeling within me. I would follow my intuition because it could be the Norns guiding me in the right direction. That little tug in my gut had never led me astray. Doran and Dallen were never separated long or their souls would call out to the other half, I knew that much. There were many times that I could have gained knowledge about them, but I had never thought it to be that important. They were simply the way they were, and I knew how much the both of them detested being equated as one being. Dallen would answer any question I had about it if I phrased them in a way that did not raise his suspicions. Doran would be harder to approach as the opposite of his brother. Dallen was a talk first, think later type of man.

Doran's brain worked overtime to take in every bit of information before he considered answering.

I was not as quick as I once was as I changed my clothes, and headed towards Dallen's cavern. I tried to disregard the flowing pain, though it was not as simple as that. My left knee ached with a frigid pain, one that caused my leg to drag slightly with each step. I hated feeling, looking, or being perceived as weak. I was the heir to Sidirna and yet, even as I tried as hard as I could, my leg would not move as it had once moved.

I could only hope that it was because of falling onto the stone floor and not the curse that flowed through my body.

I held no ill will towards those with weaknesses they could not help, and I often went out of my way to make their lives easier. I just did not want to be weak myself, and it was not something that I could easily come to terms with.

As he regularly did to me, I threw back Dallen's curtain without announcing myself. I took three heavy steps inside, fighting the smile that fought to be seen.

"What the Hel!" Dallen shouted as he whipped around to look at me from where he sat by his fire, a book in his lap. "Oh, it's you."

"Nice to see you too, brother." I replied as I stepped further inside, taking a few short steps to his side.

"I heard what happened." Dallen said, a slight mock to his voice. *My mind went blank for a moment as fear shot through me. How had he heard about Loreth already? I'd not told anyone, and Siv had not made it known that she knew what happened.* His eyebrows furrowed as I maneuvered myself to sit beside him, my body slow and sluggish to respond. I winced as I bent my knee, quickly deciding to straighten it instead.

"Aye, he fucked ycr knee too, did he?" He slurred out, the mead evident on his breath.

Meat-Herald! He was talking about the sparring I had done with that brute. I nodded my head in response, as I was unsure what to say. I had gotten my arse handed to me in more ways than one today.

"Ye went after the biggest man here, ye fool!" He grabbed the pitcher from beside him, offering it in my direction. With a nod full of misguided trust as I hoped to chase away my feelings, I took a large gulp. The reaction was immediate. I sputtered and choked as my body tried to reject the offending liquid; **it tasted like piss—no, flowers that had floated in a puddle of piss as the sun beat down on the hottest day of summer.**

"Who the Hel made that?" I coughed out, handing it back. My body shivered as I gagged, wiping my mouth with the back of my hand.

"I'm trying something new, a hobby of sorts." Dallen twirled his hand in front of him, as if to make his point stronger.

"Well, you should find a new one." I coughed out, nudging his shoulder with my own. "I was surprised to not find your bed occupied?" It was common within the confines of the mountain to love freely; something that did not happen elsewhere in Sidirna. I had always thought it great how freeing it felt not to hold shame here for having multiple partners, though it was not often that I branched out myself. I'd thought that Dallen had fallen into a steady relationship with Kraka and Asher, and had expected them to be curled into his bed.

"Aye," He responded solemnly. I didn't push him for more, but instead sat in silence with him for several long moments. "There's something seriously wrong with me, Riki." I raised my eyebrow at him, nodding as if I understood what he was talking about.

"I've, and you got to believe me because I tried not to," Dallen took a deep breath that worried me. Had he somehow caught the curse from me? Had I unknowingly cursed my best friend? "I've developed a connection with someone, er—someone's, and I'm scared." I huffed out a laugh as I nudged his shoulder with my own, certain that he was joking.

"That's all I'll say," He sighed dramatically. "I've got a lot to think about, and sorry, but you're the last person I'd ever discuss my love life with." We sat in another uncomfortable silence that lasted entirely too long, passing the pitcher of mead back and forth. There was no ill will towards his reluctancy to elaborate on Kraka and Asher with me; *I was not known for my amazing relationships. Nor any at all.*

"Do you know where Doran is?" I finally asked.

"No, Why?" He gave me an odd look as he turned almost completely to look at me.

"I thought you could do that with your twin connection?" I shrugged my shoulders as I gestured with one finger from my head to his.

Dallen groaned in response before snatching his pitcher from my hands and taking another swig. "It doesn't work that way. As I've told ye many, many times, ye dull fool."

I pretended to take a moment to think, furrowing my brows as if I were truly a dull fool. "Well, how does it, then?" I asked as I motioned for the pitcher, gagging as I took another swig. Mead was mead, I suppose.

"If I focus really hard," Dallen hiccuped. "I can talk in his mind, but only if he lets me in." *It sounded similar to what I was experiencing with Loreth, so similar that fear slithered into my veins.*

"Lets you in?" I tilted my head, continuing to play a fool. I'd known that the curse had affected my soul, but I had not realized it would be similar enough to the same things that those with a split soul dealt with. *Had Loreth split my soul?*

"Think of a…" Dallen brought his hand up to his chin, twirling the short hairs as he thought. "Bridge with a gate." He finally settled on. "When there's something I need to tell him, I go to the gate and knock. If he answers me, then we meet at the middle of the bridge, and I can talk to him."

"So, you can see him?" I raised an eyebrow as I set the pitcher of mead down, giving him my full attention.

He shook his head with a frown. "I can hear him like I hear my thoughts."

"Y'know," My vision swirled as I turned my head towards the fire. The mead had settled into my gut and I almost felt carefree. "I don't ask because I don't want you to think that I think that you think…" I paused for a moment, glaring at the fire. What was I trying to say?

"What?" Dallen asked in a deadpan voice, edging the pitcher of mead away from me.

"I think…"

"Is it your first time?" He quipped with a laugh, taking a hearty gulp of mead.

"My first time?" I turned to look at him with a frown. "Well, you know that story. You were there?"

Confusion swirled through my thoughts as I tried to process what Dallen was talking about. He'd been there the first time I'd fucked a woman because he'd stood guard by the door to listen for anyone coming. My father was insistent about no bastards, which meant that I was meant to be chaste until marriage. Esmeren had been quiet and still, though I had only lasted mere moments. I had worried that Dallen would poke fun at that, but there was not a time that he had ever mentioned it again.

"I think ye have had enough, Riki." Dallen patted my shoulder, pity shining through the tone of his voice.

"Aye," I nodded my head quick enough that the mead filling my stomach threatened to bubble into my throat. I tried to remember what it was that I had been concerned about, and why I had come to Dallen, but my mind came up blank. I shivered as a cold touch seemed to slide down the line of my spine.

Scooting closer to the fire did not help, and it was then that I remembered.

"Do ye ever worry about Doran spying into your mind?"

"What's with all of these questions about me and him? You've never cared before." Dallen's voice got angrier as he spoke, spitting out the last sentence almost cruelly.

"No," The word ended in a hiccup, and my stomach sloshed as I shook my head. "I never wanted you to think that I saw the two of you as one person." He didn't respond. The breath in my lungs started to feel colder, as if I were breathing air straight from a pile of snow. "Ye remember when we were kids and how mad ye would get when my father would call you guys one whole person? Like there was something wrong with you?" I felt the slur in my voice as my tongue felt frozen solid.

I shivered again, running my hands up and down my arms.

"Or when he would say Doran was the good half, and I was the evil?" He huffed out, sadness clear in his voice.

I nodded in agreement and turned to give him a smile. "I never pushed you to tell me because it doesn't really matter to me," I took a deep breath through the pain that began to pulse in my chest. "You're just my best friend, my brother, and your brother is merely that whiney little brother I never wished to have." I said with a laugh, cringing slightly as the pain squeezed my chest tighter. The effects of the mead seemed to recede as the pain grew; as if they were battling inside my body for who would control me.

I could almost feel the touch of warmth and cold

swirling around each other in a mad dash to see which would take up more space.

"Aye, he is pretty whiney." Dallen nodded with a smile. "He was just complaining earlier today about how ye haven't told him about the curse, and how he had to hear more about it from Mer." I knew she would tell him, but the thought of it still stung a bit. I reached for the pitcher and took another long swig. *I wanted that feeling of confusion back. I'd wanted no one to know about my affliction.*

I sighed heavily through my nose. "There's not much to say." I shrugged and reached a hand out to twirl the flames of the fire around my fingers. We sat in an uncomfortable silence as I played with the fire, much like a child who had just come into magic would sneak off to do.

"It's..." I finally said as a wave of dread fell over me. "It's not good." I shrugged again, unsure of what else to say. *How was I to admit that there was a bridge in my mind that had no gate? Could I admit that Loreth had slithered his way into my mind whenever he pleased?*

"Fine," Dallen said with a dramatic sigh. "I'll tell you." I whipped my head towards him, narrowing my eyes. "Kraka and Asher want me to move in with them, and I freaked out and ran away." He dropped his head into his hands with a groan, rubbing at his face furiously. The ache in my chest was starting to grow stronger. It pulsed erratically, flaring its reach of cold pain further every few beats.

"You're scared?" I internally cringed as I heard how soft and meek my voice came out. As if I were scared, while asking him if he was scared.

"Obviously, you dull fool!" His hands dropped back into

his lap with a thud. I pursed my lips as I thought of what to say. As quickly as the pain had surged in my chest, it had dulled considerably. It now slowly branched itself out throughout my chest, latching a deep chill onto every bone it could reach.

"You like them?" I finally settled on saying, giving him an encouraging nod through my pain. He nodded his head in response.

"Okay," I shifted myself, trying to ease the discomfort in my body. "Is their cavern not big enough for all of your things?"

"It would be simple to make it bigger." Dallen practically whispered. "But, it's not my things that worry me."

"Then what is it?"

"Do you…" He sighed and looked away from me. "Do you ever hear your father's voice in your head? Like when you really want to do something but… You just hear him telling you all the reasons why you shouldn't?" Dallen admitted with his voice full of shame. I nodded my head with a grimace. *If there was any person in this world who understood, it was me.*

"Every single day." I admitted quietly.

"I just think about how he had told us that we needed to always stick together. That we would marry the same woman and live our lives together because we were only half without the other."

It was as if the Norns themselves had guided me to Dallen's cavern tonight to reassure him that he was his own person. The odds were very slim that I would have come to have this conversation about him and his brother on any other day, except that twist of intuition that had guided me here. I had never viewed them as the same; if anything, I liked Dallen better than Doran because of how easy it was to interact with him. Doran was always a stick in the mud as a child, and he grew up to be a log in the bog.

"You know," I said quietly. "I've always felt pity for you because you're stuck with such a boring sod of a brother."

"What a poor time for me to arrive." Doran's voice rang out from behind us. The both of us jumped and turned in sync to see the intruder. What a poor time indeed.

"I heard you coming, you oaf." I called out in greeting, putting on my best fake smile as I nudged Dallen. I could only hope that he knew I was honest when I had admitted how I felt about Doran.

"A get-together without me?" Doran asked in the weak, whiney tone of voice that reminded me of him as a child.

While Dallen and I would be running around the stronghold causing havoc, Doran would be set by the window hemming clothes with the women. He'd always been frail and sickly as a child, which meant that he was left out of much of our romping around. Doran had grown to be a strong man; I could admit that his strength now rivaled his own. Yet, he still acted as if he were the frail boy who always complained that we spent too much time without him. I always secretly felt that we'd spent too much time with him. *His calm demeanor had to be a farce.*

"Have you come to drown your worries in mead as well?" Dallen dramatically sighed with a perfectly timed change of conversation.

"I've just come from Riki's cavern," Doran took a seat beside his brother, daintily folding his legs as if he were afraid of getting his trousers dirty. "I just wanted to see how you were doing." I grunted in response with a slight shrug of one shoulder. Dallen waved his hand dramatically, as if he were shoo-ing me away.

"Enough about him. I've got more important problems, Dor!" Dallen practically shouted.

"Do go on, brother." Doran moved his attention from me, though I could swear that he was still examining my every move as he always did. I straightened my spine slightly, shifting my weight so that I no longer hunched into the pain that blossomed in my chest. The pulse was dull now, but I found myself shivering from the ribbons of cold that wound through my ribs.

"Asher and Kraka want me to move in with them." Dallen said simply. His body tensed as he gazed at his brother for a reaction. Doran's face did not change, nor did his body. He sat there still for a moment, as if he were cycling through things to say.

"That's a little quick to settle down." Doran finally said as he brushed off his pant leg.

"That's my worry!"

I jumped at how loud he had shouted, not prepared for the sudden outburst. "I think it would be good for you." I countered, leaning forward to snatch the pitcher of mead back. I took a small sip before continuing, "Life is short. You deserve to do the things that make you happy. If it doesn't work out, then you leave. Simple."

Neither of the twins responded, though they stared at each other. I could not see Dallen's face but based on the way Doran's eyebrows furrowed, I knew they were speaking to each other through their connection. *Would I one day have ease of access to Loreth's mind?* The thought made me shiver with dread. Loreth was a cruel man, and I eagerly awaited the day that I watched the life drain from his body. I turned my attention back to the fire as the feeling of rejection seemed to slowly drift into me. I'd never felt this way before; but perhaps I had never noticed the times that they had been communicating in such a way that only they understood what was being said.

Thinking about the curse was the last thing I wanted to do. Yet, I could not stop the line of thoughts from invading my mind. I'd somehow heard Loreth in my mind and met him in what had felt like a dream. Loreth had access to my mind, and my body seemed to be getting worse and worse. *I was almost worried that he was slowly draining the life from my body.* Another chill seemed to seep into my body, flowing down my spine as if I had just submerged myself in cold water. *How long would I be able to ignore what was wrong with me?* It had not felt entirely impossible before, but hearing Loreth's voice had changed that.

Did I truly want to live with such a cruel man haunting my mind?

Would he slither his way into my dreams as I had done to him?

Each question that thundered through my mind seemed to settle the curse; as if simply thinking about the man eased the pain. Dallen's groan snapped me out of my thoughts with a jolt. I turned to look at the nearly identical men, noticing how Doran had braided the top of his hair back in a neater way than it had been before.

"Alright there, Riki?" Dallen asked as he stretched himself out, much like a cat would.

"I could ask you the same." I retorted with a single raised brow.

"It has been solved." Doran cut in, the usual soft tone of his voice had hardened considerably. I gave them a shrug and a small nod. It was not my problem, but the curtness had unsettled me.

"How is Merelda?" A change of subject would be good.

Though I was reluctant to know more about Esmeren, I'd need to know more if I'd wanted to follow my plan.

"She's well, thank you." Doran replied, with his voice a nasally but regal tone. He was too proper; something was amiss.

"She still spending her nights with Esmeren?" Dallen bitterly replied. Doran nodded in response, not offering more than that. We sat for a moment in silence that was thick enough I could barely breathe through it.

"Well," I shifted to heave my body off the ground. "I've got to head back. Things to do, and stuff." I muttered out, looking for any excuse to get out of there. Dallen turned his back to his brother, and gave me a nasty look. I smiled in response, clapping his shoulder as I passed, and nodding to Doran.

"Alfrikr," Doran called out as I pulled the curtain to leave. "Ivaldr wants to see you." My head nodded in response as I tried to figure out why he had not told me that right away. Doran had always been odd, but his behavior since I'd been cursed seemed to thrust a deep unease in my gut. Intuition told me to keep an eye on him, but my mind reasoned that he would never turn against me.

Though Dallen and I had been closer, Doran was still a good friend. I'd found him odd, unnecessarily fancy, and a bit of a know-it-all, but he was still like a brother to me. I shook my head as I veered towards my cavern.

If Ivaldr wanted to see me, then he could come find me. **I would not come running like a lamb to his slaughter.**

15

THINKING AND LIVING

LIFE HAD BEEN EASIER LESS THAN A WEEK BEFORE; IT WAS peaceful, calm, and steady. Every single day had been the same; **I had not realized how I had fallen into such a steady routine of simply existing until my life had taken a sharp and drastic turn.** When I had first arrived at the mountain, there was an air about everything that had felt exciting and new. There was the expectation that I would be changing lives, taking control of Sidirna, and leading our people to better lives. The first time I had realized that the rebellion was not what I had imagined it to be had been a few weeks after arriving.

Now, I was cursed. Cursed with my enemy in my head. Cursed to fall into his head. Cursed with a cold pain that radiated throughout my entire being.

There was a process when arriving at the mountain that every new member went through. We had all spent the first few days being interrogated and confined in a cavern. It was a crude cavern, but not as disgusting as the one I had seen Esmeren in, with nothing but a fire pit and a few bed rolls on the floor. Merelda had cried the entire time, Doran had consoled her, and Dallen had almost lost his mind from the lack of room to expel his energy. I remember sitting on my bedroll and thinking; much like I had done in my cavern on my bed then.

Years ago, I had sat there and thought about all I had to offer the rebellion. How great I could be for the cause, the changes we could make, and how it wouldn't be too long before I was sitting on the throne in power. The concept of the rebellion had been something of great power, and I now saw exactly how my young mind had overlooked countless things. There was once a time that I had thought that Ivaldr was a great man who had accomplished a lot, based on the anger that my father had held about the uprising. How he had ranted and raved about how the weak fools had thought they could overtake him and secure the crown for themselves.

The many he had put to death for even the slightest whisper of a doubt that they were in the rebellion.

All of these years later, I wished I had left at the first inkling that things were not as they seemed. The moment had been such a shock that I still remembered the way my breath had quickened, and my heart had dropped into my gut. His face as he told me that I was not allowed to ever join Tyr's Enforcers. Ivaldr felt my views were too outlandish. Where I had once thought we would be storming the stronghold was the opposite of what Ivaldr had planned. Though, I wasn't exactly sure what he had planned for anything these days. There was a time when I knew a fair amount of what was going on, but the channels of information tightened incredibly once we had found the spies within our ranks.

Ivaldr had pulled me into his office all of those years ago, right after I had gotten the very cavern that I still lived in. "Tell me about your plan for removing your father from power." He had said as he leaned against a poorly constructed desk. I remember the desk groaning under his weight, and the flush of his face as I failed at hiding a snicker. His face had dropped into a look of horror as I had detailed exactly what my plan had been.

"I'd take the Jarls out first; starting from those furthest from the stronghold and ending with those within the walls. They would be the only ones to fight the change." I'd said proudly. "From there, it would be easy to take control of the guard. Most of them are Karls and Thralls anyway."

Ivaldr's face had gone blank at that, and I remembered being confused as I continued. "If I take over his forces, he cannot fight me. It would be simple to walk up to him and drive a sword into his guts. The hardest part would be taking out the Jarls; it would have to be a planned event with many people." Ivaldr had squeaked like a mouse at that, and I remembered feeling concerned then. I had no idea that he was so against violence, but it was obvious by the fear that showed through his eyes.

"While others would be across Sidirna taking care of the Jarls, I would be in the stronghold. Once my father is dead, the crown will fall to me."

There was a large and uncomfortable silence after that. It had felt like an eternity before Ivaldr had gone on a tirade about how that was a horrible plan. How I was never to speak of it again, and how he was sure that he could not trust me within his upper ranks. **I'd felt such anger then.** One that I was sure would never fade from my being, yet over the years it had, in fact, *faded almost completely.* **As I thought of the all-consuming anger, it seemed to be stoked back to life inside of me.**

I felt used, manipulated, and taken for granted.

The years of my early 20s had been wasted on nothing more than existing.

I'd tended to crops, fed animals, and scooped their shit. Ate my meals, I talked to my friends, and the rebellion had done nothing substantial. Our numbers had grown considerably in the past nine years, but it was as if the spark of an uprising had dulled until it no longer shone. Such time had been wasted on nothing but existing. That seed that had been planted within me had begun to bloom again. **The anger had been stoked as I thought I was going to die in that all-consuming darkness, and now I sat in my cavern and I thought.** There was not much else to do but think, and I knew that I would get tired of my own company quickly.

I hated to be alone because it was next to impossible to turn my mind off. *It drifted, fluttered, and soared through anything, everything, and nothing.* As I festered in my anger, the seed of fear began to sprout. I knew that I was not taking the curse seriously enough, and there was only so long that I could sit around and avoid thinking about it. Froggy and Hilda had confirmed that I was cursed to my soul. Doran and Dallen had confirmed that there was some sort of connection between Loreth and I; though they did not know they had confirmed that. **Now it was up to me to figure out how I would get rid of the curse, and I knew that I would have to kill Loreth before he killed me.**

I'd had no idea where to start, and I'd need to take time to plan.

I would need to think it through completely and not fall back into my pattern of doing nothing. *I worried about my abilities and if I could truly accomplish something so large on my own.* It would make the most sense to bring someone in on my plan, but there was a twinge in my gut about how foolish that could become if it all backfired. Dallen would be the one I would choose—he was already suspicious of Esmeren's motives here. Doran could be a great help because of his station in the rebellion, but I feared his ability to keep it from Merelda. There would need to be some kind of push and pull to lure Ivaldr into a false sense of security; like I was the spider, and he was the fly that had flown into my web.

I needed to reach deep inside myself to find the younger Alfrikr before he had been dulled and domesticated. **The Alfrikr, who was feral and rebellious; who could play games with minds and words until he got what he wanted.** *I hadn't realized how I had lost that part of myself until I was faced with figuring out where he had gone.* There was a time when I had been the perfect heir for my father. I'd been cruel, ruthless, and would have one day become exactly how Loreth was. While I was thankful that I had not gone down that path, I knew that I needed to use those bits and pieces of who I used to be.

This curse may have changed my life, but **I couldn't help but feel thankful that it had snapped me out of the dull life I had been living.** The pain was as horrid as knowing that Loreth could enter my mind whenever he pleased, but I felt at peace knowing that I would soon find myself back on track to change Sidirna for the better. Ivaldr may be a fool, but he has fooled me well enough for the last nine years. I did not know what that made me, but I wasn't willing to admit it if I did. **However, it worked in my favor that Ivaldr thought that he had me under his control.**

If I could gain his trust, I could join the Enforcer's ranks. From there, I could turn his people against him. I knew that many of the elders were upset because of Ivaldr's lack of planning for the Cycle Winter. What I didn't know was if anyone within the rebellion was as upset at the lack of progress as I was. There had to be a group of them somewhere, it did not make sense if it were only Dallen and I who had our reservations about this pathetic rebellion. *I worried about how I would bring that up to people, as there were not many who, I felt, would trust me.*

How many of the people here had joined and thought there would be real change?

> Only for them to find out that the only change was a localized change. We were living peacefully, well-fed, well-fucked, and there was not much to complain about. It felt as if the rebellion had thought we'd won because we were living well.
> As if the suffering of those around us was irrelevant because we were okay.
> I was just as guilty as the rest of them.
> The change was only if you were able to leave and come to the mountain.

That still left hundreds, if not thousands, of people suffering within Sidirna. It would be wise to begin to stoke those doubts within the rebellion, but I feared that they would not be taken well coming from me. There were plenty of people who did not like me because of who I was, now I needed to show them that I was nothing like my father. I needed to go out of my way, and not just shy away from that attention. I hated thinking as much as I loved it. That young Alfrikr still lived inside of me. **I would wake him up, and we would work together to make real change.**

When I was a child, my father had once told me a story about his father, Alfrikr the Ferocious. It was a rare thing to hear about him from my father. He'd always held some sort of resentment towards the man, but he equally praised him.

"Sit down, son" My father had told me as he sat straight-backed in the chair behind his desk. He had seemed so big and strong to me then, and I remembered thinking how much I wanted to grow up to be like him. He'd woven a tale about how his father had made an agreement once with the leader of an uprising.

"He'd walked to the man's door, and knocked." My father had said. He told me how he'd gone with his father, how horrible and disgusting the longhouse was, and how before they left they had given the man money.

"...and the rebellion had gone away." My father had said smugly, leaning back into his chair with a grin.

It sounded so simple, "But what about the other people who followed the leader?" I asked him.

He'd laughed a full belly laugh, one that was even rarer than him talking of his father. "He'd killed them all! And then the leader!"

I remember sitting there confused. *Why would he give him money if he was going to kill him?* It had made more sense to me, as a child, to simply kill the pests and be done with it. Pride had shone in my father's eyes when I had confessed that, and so he had elaborated. My grandfather had lured the man into a false sense of security. He had paid him, gotten the information he needed, and then eradicated them. There was a lesson in that, one that I would use now as an adult, but in a very different way.

I would lure the leader of the rebellion into a false sense of security, and then I would take his place. *The thought had almost felt wrong at first—as if I were becoming too much like my father and grandfather.* I'd sat there and weighed it in my mind for ages.

The difference, I had decided, was that I was going to do it for the right reasons.

IVALDR HAD FOUND me at breakfast the next morning; hungover and shivering in pain from the curse. "Alfrikr," He said as he took a seat next to me on the bench. "I've been looking for you. I thought Dallen would have told you that."

"Oh? Have you?" I replied with a mouthful of mushy gruel. My chest constricted as I swallowed my mouthful, and it took everything in me to not heave it back up. The pain radiated and pulsed as if it had a mind of its own. I could feel the cold ribbon of pain slithered between each of my ribs and sunk deep into my bones. Ivaldr had given me a look; one that I couldn't quite decipher if he was suspicious or concerned about me.

"Have you thought about working with Esmeren?" He asked me, as if I had not already answered him before. I shrugged as I took another bite, using it as an excuse to refrain from answering. **I would rather not work with her, but I knew that I would need to figure out a way to get closer to Ivaldr.** I would have to find a different way to lure him in because I knew there was no conceivable way I could act as if I wanted to be around Esmeren.

"Did I not already give you an answer?" I countered, unable to keep the frustration from my voice.

"I hoped you would have talked about it with Doran and changed your mind. I know how much his woman wants her sister to be here. His woman was very vocal about it with me."

"Merelda's not property," I retorted, narrowing my eyes at

him slightly. "She's not 'his woman,' they are together, but she is not property." I'd spent enough time with Siv to understand the importance of phrasing when talking about women. **They were not lesser, and when men referred to women as such, it was important that I used my privilege as a man.**

Ivaldr waved me off, dismissing what I had said entirely, before he quickly stood. "Think about it." He snapped before stalking off. I knew that I had just affected my ability to have Ivaldr consumed by a false sense of trust in me; I had learned a lot from the brief encounter.

Ivaldr did not like to appear foolish, dull, or unimportant. He was an egotistical fool, as I'd already known. It meant that it would be easy to stroke his ego until he developed a large enough head that he did not even think about what I might be doing behind his back. It would take time to develop a plan that did not include Esmeren, which would be the hardest part. **I might have to give in, but I would try everything before I entertained that thought.**

"So, you are capable of learning!" Siv said cheerily as she took the place Ivaldr had just left. I took another bite, raising my eyebrow. "I didn't know you'd listened to me," She added as she set her bowl on her legs. "I always thought you just nodded and grunted at the right times."

"Eavesdropping, are we?" I retorted with a mock frown. Siv laughed as she gave her gruel an aggressive stir, most likely trying to separate the large chunks that tended to stick together.

"He's taken an interest in you since the raid; I'm just curious."

"Aye," I said through a mouthful. "He finally thinks I'm useful, and would like me to bend over and spread my cheeks so he can properly fuck me over."

Siv laughed so hard that she began to choke on her meal. I reached over and smacked my hand against her back with a laugh.

"I forget how funny you can be." Siv giggled as she leaned against my side. I was thankful that she had not brought up what happened yet, and I hoped that we continued to act as if nothing had happened. "How are you feeling?" She asked, dropping her voice to a whisper.

I wasn't sure how to respond, and settled on a grunt and a shrug. The pain in my chest continued to pulse and twist my insides until they ached with a bone deep chill. It was enough to make my handshake as I lifted the spoon to my mouth, but I had settled on ignoring it. Loreth had not entered my mind during the night; which I had been thankful for. **There was not much else to do but continue through the pain, but I had noticed how my body seemed to respond slower.**

"That bad?" Siv asked with pity lined in her voice.

"I'm cold," I replied quietly. "My chest hurts a lot, and I'm so cold that it feels as if I've jumped into a frozen river."

Siv leaned her head on my shoulder with a sigh. "Do you know what it is yet?"

"I've got to track Froggy down today to see if he's learned anything." I leaned my head against hers, slouching to make up for the height difference. I had hoped the decrepit fool would track me down.

"Do you want me to come with you?" She asked through a mouthful of food, the words slurring to the point they were almost impossible to decipher. I sighed heavily, not wanting to offend her, but not wanting her to hear anything about the curse.

"I think I want to do this alone."

She nodded her head against my shoulder, and resumed

eating in silence. *Siv was a good woman, one that was much too good for me. I still didn't understand what she had once seen in me,* **but I was thankful for it nonetheless.** It was easy with her in a way that I had never fully appreciated until that moment. She took life as it came, and she made sure that it always met her on her terms.

"Are you prepared for the Cycle Winter?" I asked her, breaking the silence, so I wouldn't be lost in my thoughts. She huffed a small laugh as she nodded her head.

"Yes, father." She mocked.

"I'm not asking because I don't think you're capable of preparing for yourself. I'm just worried it's not being taken as seriously as it should be." It seemed like the only ones who worried were the elders, Dallen, and me. The last Cycle Winter had killed many, though I had been too young to truly see how horrible it was.

The cold was unlike anything I had ever experienced, though the curse swirling in my chest was a close rival.

"If it takes me, then it was meant to be. I put my trust in the Norns, not men."

I gave the top of her head a kiss as I moved to stand. My views on the Norns were nothing positive these days, and they were one of the last things I wanted to think about right now.

"Want the rest?" I asked her, offering the half-empty bowl to her. She accepted it with a sound that could only be described as a growl, using her spoon to scrape the contents into her bowl.

"Stay safe, Riki. I worry about you, more so now than usual. Weird things are brewing, and the Norns are unhappy. All of us women can feel it." Siv said, through another mouthful of gruel.

I gave her a smile and a nod. I was used to the odd things

she would say, though I couldn't help the fear I felt trickle in with her statement. *My intuition had never guided me wrong, but I had felt how different those pulls to my guts had been lately.*

I knew that tracking down Froggy would be next to impossible, but I set off to find him anyway. He'd had my blood for long enough that I was beginning to feel suspicious. Blood Sacredness was the one thing that I would always trust the odd man about. Though I could not trust him with my blood for too long lest he get bored and decide to curse me. **Though, I was already cursed with not much else to lose.**

The walk to Froggy's cavern was longer than I had remembered it being. My knees ached all the way down to the heels of my feet with every step that I took. The pulsing in my chest had rapidly increased, beating my chest with an ice-cold chill. It felt as though the pain from my chest had leaked out and surrounded my entire body with a layer of painful frost. *If bones could combust, I was sure that mine were close to.* My hands shook more than they ever had, and I couldn't help but stop in an empty hallway and slide to the ground.

I leaned my head against the stone wall, shivering as another burst of pain radiated out. Each breath I took seemed to get colder and colder until my lungs felt frozen solid. I squeezed my eyes shut as my body seemed to shake and convulse on its accord. I wasn't aware I was screaming until I felt the distinct burn in my throat, I couldn't hear my voice over the thumping pain in my ears. My hands moved to clutch and claw at my chest, as if I could rip the pain from my body. As the pain grew, my hatred for Loreth grew faster. *All I could see with my closed eyes were those soulless pits staring at me.*

I'm not sure how long I laid on the stone floor; heaving breaths between my screams as I was consumed by the pain.

Slowly, the pain had begun to recede, though it lingered deep within my bones. **I would kill him for what he did to me.** I would watch as Loreth's life drained from his body, and then **I would piss on his grave.** My breaths were shallow as I struggled to pull in the air that felt ice-cold. The pain still fluttered angrily in my chest by the time I was able to pry open my eyes, only for them to flutter shut on their own. I felt my body slump down the wall as I was no longer able to move a muscle.

"*Fool.*" An indistinguishable voice seemed to echo within my mind. "*Breathe, you dull fool!*"

I tried to pull in another breath, but it felt as if my lungs seized as the ice entrapped them completely. There was no peace to be found throughout this deathly chill that enveloped my body. Each bone ached as it was ensnared by the chill. While the pain had lessened, my body seemed to give up the fight.

"O**pen your eyes, Alfrikr.**" The layered voice boomed again, startling me from the darkness I was coming close to accepting. "**It is not your time yet.**"

My eyelids felt as if they were too heavy to open, my muscles seemed to shiver, and I could feel my shuddering shallow breaths. The air was not enough to satisfy, but it was enough to make me ache for another breath. If this was death, it was not the peaceful end that I had thought it was. The painful pulse inside my chest seemed to beat faster; as if there were a tiny drum beside my heart being beat by a tiny warrior. It thumped in such an off-putting way that fear began to slither through me.

"**Open your eyes!**" The voices shouted, louder than I had ever thought imaginable. Each beat of the words caused an avalanche of pain that cascaded down my spine. I tried to pry my eyes open again, unsure why I was listening to the voice, but in too much pain to care.

One hum began to flitter through my mind.

A second hum joined in on a song I'd never heard before, but felt familiar.

Three distinct hums flowed through my mind as I sucked in a large breath.

The pulsing drum pounded faster and harder inside my chest; thumping through the pain until all I could feel was the vibration through my body. Pain had seemingly leaked out of my chest in a slow, steady, ice-cold stream as the harmonizing humming overtook my body.

"**He lived.**" The first voice whispered.

"**He lives.**" The second replied.

"**He will live.**" The third added.

16

WOLVES AND FROGS

THE SURROUNDING DARKNESS SWIRLED AS IT CARESSED MY BODY. I held no feelings while I drifted through the eery nothingness. From head to toe I was covered by the smooth, warm, ribbons of nothing. I floated and drifted as if I were a ship upon warm waters. As if I had flowed into the lives of my ancestors who had first sailed in their drakkar, only to land in our realm.

There was no way to tell if my eyes were open or closed, but I felt oddly certain they were open. The Gods were with me, or perhaps I was with them. My mother looked upon me fondly, I could feel her spirit caressing my hair. **Safe. I was safe. The curse could not find me here.**

I will live. I will live. I will live. I chanted to myself as time seemed to no longer exist. The darkness consumed me, or perhaps I consumed it. I let it flow within me, or it decided to take me over. **Warmth. How I'd missed the warmth.**

I was drifting, floating, and existing within its warmth.

The war drum continued to pulse through my chest in a steady beat, but the pain had left entirely.

Thump, thump, thump it went as I felt the steady movement of floating.

I felt comforted and safe; as if I were being held and rocked by my mother after a night terror as a child. As though, I sat upon my grandmother's knee as she hummed me a song. I was not entirely sure if I was alive, but I knew I was safe. I couldn't remember why I knew that I would live; the seed of assurance had sprouted within me. It had been declared that I would live, and I would accomplish my dreams.

I was protected and divine; nothing would come for me here.

As if I had simply blinked my eyes, I found myself on the back of a horse as it trotted through the bright and flourishing hills. My eyes struggled to adjust to the severity of the sun's brightness; I relished the warmth as it hit my skin. *Where was I?* My hands tightened on the leads as I looked down at the ornate gloves I wore. I had not seen them in many years; they were something I had left behind when leaving the stronghold. *Where was I?* My hands had not touched such finery since leaving, and I took a moment to appreciate it. My gaze moved to the horse's mane; an earthy brown to match its earthy body.

A trickle of fear began to flow through my body; *where was I?*

I looked around me, trying to recognize the scenery before me as I pulled the horse to a slow trot. Hills, flowers, trees, and the blue sky above me. *Where was I?* It was not autumn, but felt like the late spring or early summer. My clothes were well tailored, my boots fit snuggly, and my arms looked like my own. *Where was I?* A part of me longed to find a body of water so that I could check my face. The curse had affected me in such drastic ways that I almost felt safer in this landscape versus constantly worrying if Loreth was seeing through my eyes. *Where was I?* **I knew I was not dead, and I knew I would live.**

I repeated it within my head thrice for good measure.

I carried on and allowed the horse to lead me, for I had no idea where I was. I tried to reign in the panic that threatened to consume me, but it was as if it could not take root within my body. I had been trained for this; trained to enter into any situation with the air and confidence of a Rikr. **I was safe, divine, and protected.** The birds chirped in time with the pulse in my chest. **I am not scared. I will live. This will fade.** I repeated to myself as I urged the horse down the path until it began to trot.

I am safe. I am divine. I am protected. The Gods look at me with favor.

Kraa, kraa, kraa.

I heard the raven in the distance, though it sounded as if it came from every direction. I could almost remember why the sound was so familiar, but the thought was so fleeting that I couldn't be concerned. The horse trotted down the path as I took in the surrounding scenery. **I was safe, divine, and protected.** *Where was I?* We were approaching the woods, but I could not remember seeing them in the distance before. *Had they been there? Where was I?*

We were ten paces away when the horse stopped, not willing to be urged any further. *Further, I needed to go further.* There was something in the woods for me, but I was unable to remember what. ***A grave. Her grave. It was in the woods.*** *Where was I?* My movements were fluid as I dropped myself off the horse, giving him a pat on the neck as I passed.

"Good boy." I murmured as I continued past him.

Kraa. Kraa. Kraa. The raven called to me.

A-woo, a wolf responded from behind me.

Safe, divine, and protected.

I spun on my heels, facing where I heard the wolf call. Where the horse had once stood, there was now a large white wolf. He stood nearly as tall as the horse and was mottled with mangy spots along his too thin body. Where his eyes were meant to be, there were two pits of swirling grey fog.

He would not harm me. He could not harm me.

I felt a harsh lack of fear as I stared at the wild creature before me. **Where was I? Why was I not afraid?** The wolf had an energy surrounding him. I'd assume that in the flesh, the God's power felt the same. I took a step backwards as he showed his teeth and snarled at me. He advanced three steps closer, growling low in his chest.

"I will live." I told the wolf;

as if I spoke to wolves often.

"The grave," The wolf seemed to respond, his voice nothing but a guttural growl that I understood. "Stay away from her grave."

Pain enveloped my cheek as my eyes shot open with a shout.

"There ye are!" Froggy shouted as he leaned forward and practically touched his nose to mine. "I thought we lost ye for a minute there, Lonely Heir."

I blinked at him, confused as my body stayed frozen in place. The pain that had overtaken my body had faded, though the pulse still thumped steadily. **The wolf? Where was the wolf?** I turned my head to the side, brushing Froggy's forehead with the movement, and took in my surroundings.

"Where am I?" My voice scratched out as the pain flared in my throat from screaming. *Had I just seen Fenrir in the flesh, or had it been some sort of twisted dream?*

"A few hallways from me cavern," Froggy replied as he heaved his decrepit body away from me. "C'mon then." Every bone in his body seemed to crack and pop as he pushed himself up to stand.

My muscles were slow to respond as I maneuvered myself up to stand—my joints screaming in protest. "What happened?" I tried to stretch out my back, but yelped as pain shot through my chest.

"Dunno." Froggy shrugged his shoulders as he began to hobble down the hall. "I's just comin' back from meal when I found ye; eyes rolled back and shiverin' on the ground. Hollerin' and screaming."

I didn't respond as I walked beside him, thankful that he walked at such a leisurely pace. Pain had slowly replaced the warmth I had felt in the darkness. My body shivered as the cold settled into my bones. **I couldn't tell him what I saw, even if I thought he may hold the answers. The curse was mine to suffer through, and I lacked trust in the man.** It was an odd situation to be in; one that I was unsure how to act, so I simply did not. I did not say a word, and neither did he as I followed him the short walk to his cavern.

I attempted to focus on ways I could figure out what had happened without admitting how deep the curse lay within my mind. *Was it a message from the Gods?* I doubted it because they had abandoned us long ago. A part of me longed for that connection, but I was not honorable or strong enough to deserve it. It felt real in the dream.

Especially as I remembered the way my fine clothes felt compared to the scratchy tunic I was currently wearing.

He pulled back the ratty cloth that covered his doorway and tilted his hand out to build the flames of his fire. With his other hand, he directed the water from a pitcher into a cup. He displayed his magic so simply, but in such an intricate way as he entered his cavern. For a moment, I was struck by the thought that it was dishonorable and wasteful—but Froggy was closer to the Gods than anyone I had ever met.

"Is it not dishonorable to waste your magic in such ways?" I asked simply, trying to keep any emotion from my voice. I was mostly curious, but I knew it could be perceived as judgement.

Froggy waved me off with a single hand, and a grunt. He moved to sit on the bed that was so close to the fire that it almost made me nervous he'd burn himself alive. "You young kids don't know how to speak with the Gods; how do you know if it is dishonorable?" He croaked out angrily.

"Uhh," I scratched the back of my neck nervously as I stepped further into the cavern. "It's what we're taught?"

"And ye believe everything yer father told ya?" He retorted with a snort.

I was afraid to think of his point any further, but I understood the point he was making. I remembered as a child being so blown away by how many people my grandmother's age used magic as if it were meant to be used constantly. I had always grown up knowing from my father that we were to sparingly use it lest we anger the Gods. Yet, I remember those cold mornings as a young child with my grandmother. How she had told stories of how magic was meant to be honored and used, but it was greedy, weak kings who wanted the people weaker than them.

"There can be no uprising against oppression if the Rikr is always the strongest." She had said as I sat by her feet at the fire.

"Well, no?" I finally said. Froggy sat and stared at me for an uncomfortably long moment with a large grin on his face. He shook his head before letting out a gurgle sound that I could only assume was a laugh.

"When you speak with Freyr does he tell ye to not use the magic yer blessed with?" Froggy tutted softly as he grabbed his glass of water. *I did not know how he knew I spoke with the Gods, and it made me uncomfortable that he knew. It was not some-*

thing that I told anyone—including Dallen, Doran, and Merelda. I'd always felt superstitious and odd after making an offering to the God Freyr. *What if I was talking to nothing because he did not hear me?*

"How did you know?" I asked quietly, moving to sit beside his fire. It was not often that I made it out of the mountain and up to the altar I built, but I found the time whenever I could. Even as a child, I had felt a strong connection to Freyr, though part of it had been fostered and encouraged by my grandmother. My mother's mother was an old, decrepit Thrall-born woman; much like Froggy. It was odd how my grandmothers from both sides seemed to get along because of their old beliefs.

"I smell it." He said, taking a deep inhale through his nose as he leaned in my direction. "Fate, Freyr, divinity, and death." Froggy added in a hushed whisper.

I shivered as his words sunk in; his mention of divinity made my stomach churn. *How had he known that if he was not truly a fate worker?* I'd always assumed he was simply an odd, crazy old man. I'd never put much stock into his abilities, yet I knew he practiced blood Sacredness.

"What do you know of the curse?" I changed the subject. The unease of him knowing of my practices and details of the dream was too much to continue the conversation. I'd originally come here to find out what he knew about the curse, not what he knew about my offerings to the Gods.

"Aye, I figured you'd come around about that."

"And?" I asked as irritation lined my voice. I did not have time for games; I'd just played enough of them in that odd dream. One that I would have to dissect the second I was alone. *Not that I thought Froggy could read my mind;* the fear was still there regardless.

"And what?" He responded as he shuffled through his bag before pulling out a long pipe. I stared at him with my mouth slack, unsure what to say without reacting in anger. He examined the intricately carved wood as he tilted it upside down and smacked his hand against it. Burnt bits of herbs fluttered onto his lap and the floor.

"What have you learned?" I said between gritted teeth.

"About?" He piled the dried green herbs into the pipe, pressing them down with the knuckle of his middle finger. **I wanted to snatch it out of his hands and throw it across the room.** I knew he was trying to rile me up, that much was obvious. I couldn't figure out if he knew what was going on with the curse, or if he knew nothing.

"By the Gods!" I groaned out as I clenched my hands. *I would not hit him. I did not hit elders. He was just a decrepit old man.* I chanted to myself as I took a deep breath. "Stop pissin' around the bush and just tell me, ye old coot."

"Beatin'." He said simply as he brought the pipe up to his lips. He used his free hand to bring a long ribbon of fire to him and began to burn the herbs within the pipe. With a deep breath in, he let the flames sizzle back into the fire, and then exhaled a cloud of smoke in my direction.

"What?" I said with my eyebrows furrowed as I tried to figure out what he meant. **Beating what!** I wanted to scream.

"It's beatin' around the bush, not pissin'!" Froggy laughed as he inhaled again, only slightly choking on the smoke in his lungs. **An urge to reach out and smack the pipe out of his hands flared in me, but I resisted it.** I glared at Froggy as he took another inhale of his herbs. As much as I thought he knew something, I equally thought he was avoiding the fact he knew nothing.

"It's getting worse," I confessed as I held my face in my

hands. I would rather not confess anything about the curse, but I hoped that Froggy would see that it was not something to joke around about. "I've passed out again. Same as the last time, but I don't feel as worse when I woke up."

He made a noncommittal sound, and I dropped my hands to look over at Froggy. The old man's hair was braided back, the stark white of his hair reminded me of the wolf in an odd way. His clothes hung off his thin frame in a way that almost made him look three times smaller. Had the dream been my mind simply making things up? The correlations were too similar to ignore; though Froggy still had his eyes.

I cleared my throat before speaking again, the scent of his herbs making my throat dry and my nose began to run. "It starts with this pain in my chest...one that feels cold. I don't know how else to explain it." I shrugged my shoulders with a sigh. "It's as if there's a..." I brought a hand up to rub the spot on my chest as I searched for the words.

"There's this beat, like a pulse, that is always there. Every so often, I feel alright. Occasionally, it thunders in my chest and I feel a chill all the way to my bones."

Froggy hummed in response as he exhaled a cloud of smoke towards me. It almost felt disrespectful, but I wasn't going to call him out on it. "In the middle? Where ye soul is?" He asked.

"Here." I pointed to the center of my chest, right at the bottom of my breastbone. Froggy nodded his head, but said nothing. His face was dull, impassive, and calm as he stared at me. "The chills go all through my body, not just my chest." I added, hoping he would say something.

"So," he began with a heavy breath. "Ye got bone chills, pain, and ye pass out?" I nodded my head. "I've got yer blood over there, but all I can tell is that someone used blood Sacredness on yer soul."

I had known that was likely what had happened, but the news still hit hard. "How do I get rid of it?" I asked, my voice a pathetic whisper.

"Get rid of yer whole soul or suffer." Froggy said simply, as if it were an easy decision. I did not truly know how one lost their soul, but based on Froggy's own eyes, he knew. My father had not always held blue soulless eyes, but over time the copper flecks faded completely.

"How do I—erm—get rid of my soul?" I asked hesitantly. I knew it was not something I truly wanted to do, but if it meant the curse was gone, I might think about it. Our souls were what gave us our empathy, morals, and joy. *Soulless people were as close to evil as one could get.*

"Practice enough blood Sacredness and the Gods will do it for ye." Froggy took another deep inhale off his pipe as the features on his face twisted slightly. He'd never made that face before, and I wasn't sure what it meant. I could only assume that it was a deep sadness, or regret.

"Is that how…?" I gestured towards my eyes and then his. He nodded solemnly as he exhaled his smoke away from me. I would rather not push the old man for more answers, but I wanted to know exactly what he meant.

"I had a life partner," Froggy sadly said, his voice a croak I'd never heard before. "They were the light of my life, my calm within the storm, and I never wanted to live a day without them." I nodded my head as if I understood such an all-consuming love. "We'd married when we were young Thralls and bounced between many Jarls' homes during those years. They were such a troublemaker; my perfect match."

"They got real sick one Cycle Winter. We were only 33, and

I did whatever I could to beg the Gods to bring them back to me. I found an old book on blood Sacredness in the attic of a Jarls house many years before that. I tried every spell in it to bring them back to me." Froggy's voice had taken on a deeper, sadder tone.

"I'm sorry." I replied, unsure of how to truly respond in this type of situation. He was older now, at least fifty years above 33, and yet it still seemed to consume him.

"Aye," Froggy shrugged his shoulders. "The Gods did not take to it well. Loki took pity on me, I think." I'd heard that he'd been in Loki's favor, but I had not truly believed it then. It was not an easy thing to be seen by the Gods after they abandoned us.

Though, I found myself wondering lately if they had abandoned us or if we had abandoned them.

"Do you speak with Loki often?" I felt dull asking, as if my lack of knowledge was something to be ashamed of. I'd learned a lot from my grandmother, but there was only so much I remembered from when I was a child. When we would sit by the fire in the hearth early in the morning, before my studies, she would tell me stories.

My favorite story had been about how the God Thor had once dressed as the Goddess Freyja to get his hammer back. Loki had also shape-shifted into a woman servant and gone along with him. I remember howling with laughter as she'd tried to shush me. I now realized she had been trying to protect us from getting caught, but back then I had thought she was just a mean old woman.

"Do you speak with Freyr often?" He asked with a snort,

shaking his head. He brought his hands up to his hair and began to take his braids out. Each bead fell to the floor with a soft clank, the sound reminding me of a spoon hitting the side of a horn of mead.

"I attempt to. I'm not sure whether he listens." I admitted, feeling suddenly vulnerable. I knew that Froggy was considered an old fool for his belief that the Gods were still interested in us, but I could not deny that I had felt a connection with Freyr. "I've got an altar. I try to bring him offerings when I can, but I'm not sure whether it's enough."

Froggy nodded his head, but did not respond. I suddenly felt a wash of shame and embarrassment wash over me. *I did not know the man well, but here I was admitting things to him that were not commonly talked about.* There were many within the rebellion who did not know many of the Gods; only knowing Odinn or Tyr because they were mentioned infrequently, but enough to know their names.

"My grandmother was a Thrall who taught me all she knew of the old ways." I admitted quietly. Though I had felt embarrassed and dumb, I hoped that Froggy would understand why I asked about his connection with the trickster God. *I was not asking so that I could barter this information or use it to poke fun at the old man.* I was simply curious about things I did not understand fully.

"We exist for their entertainment," Froggy quietly replied. "I feel the most connected with Loki when I'm doing things I know would entertain him."

"Aye," I agreed. "Sometimes when the sun shines down on me while I'm working in the fields, I swear I feel the touch of Freyr's magic within it."

"Ye would've made a good king." Froggy said solemnly as

he set his pipe on the floor, beside his bed. "Now get out. I've got to rest."

I wasn't sure what Froggy meant when he said I would've made a good king, and I wasn't sure I wanted to know. I was still the heir to Sidirna, and the crown would be mine once my father died. I closed the old man's curtain behind me as I stepped into the hallway. It felt as if it were a confession, or as if it were some kind of omen. He had not told me about the curse, but I had an unsettling feeling that the curse would be the end of me.

Could I truly go through with losing my soul to get rid of the curse? I wasn't sure how that would change me. My soul was the one thing in this world that was mine and mine alone. It was not something that could be stolen, bartered, nor changed. **My soul could be lost, but it would never be another's**. I sighed heavily as I limped down the hallway, my bones aching with every step.

There was much to do, and I wasn't sure where to start. *Did I focus on myself and the curse? Or Sidirna? Or the rebellion?* **I wanted to bash my head into the wall until I could think no more.** I was overcome with such a sickly feeling as I tried to weigh the decisions I now had. There would be much to think about, and I was tired of thinking. It felt as if all I did was think these days.

I spent the walk back to my cavern thinking as the pain in my chest settled into an uncomfortable rhythm of cold, aching pain. It was only midday, but my mind and body felt as exhausted as I felt during the harvest. I'd awoken hoping for answers, but had instead found myself with more questions. The most pressing question was if the dream I had meant anything.

The last time I had gone unconscious, I had entered Loreth's mind and then dreamt alongside him. I'd walked through the town, sat by the tree, and he had found me. This time I had been alone until the wolf had shown up, but I had heard the raven calling as though it were the one in Loreth's bedroom. The wolf weighed the heaviest on me. *The way its sickly body had towered above mine as it bared its teeth at me.* I had felt no fear then, but as I remembered the way it looked, I felt the fear overtake my heart.

It had spoken about her grave, but I did not know who she was. I pulled the curtain of my cavern aside, groaning as I saw Ivaldr sprawled upon my bed.

"Ivaldr." I tried to say politely, though I could hear the bite to my tone.

"Alfrikr!" He responded cheerfully, moving to sit with his legs over the side. "I wanted to finish the conversation we had started during breakfast." I narrowed my eyes at him, knowing that he had been the one to end the conversation. **He was a petty, foolish, and insecure man who only solidified my view of him by the way he now disrespected my personal space.**

"No." I said simply, closing the curtain behind me. I turned my back to him as I walked to my box of clothes, hoping that the disrespect was obvious. I knew that I would need to play nice with him, but **I was already at my limit of playing nice today.** I pulled my shirt over my head and tossed it into my dirty pile.

"No?" Ivaldr asked as if he had never heard the word before. "I don't think you understand how this works. I am the leader." He added bitterly.

Ivaldr reminded me of a child, especially now. Trying to pull rank to get what he wanted; *much like I did as a child with all the Thrall-born children.*

"You asked me if I thought about it at all," I replied as I shoved my pants down, showing my bare ass to him. "And I'm telling you I haven't. Not sure what status has to do with that." I took my time as I pulled my sleep clothes on, hoping that the man would feel disrespected. He had come into my space, it only made sense that he be ready to see my ass.

"Well," Ivaldr said curtly, his voice sounding closer to the exit. "Think about it."

I should have killed Ivaldr then, he'd become a part of my everyday life soon after this, and I grow to regret allowing him to live.

I turned enough to watch him storm through the curtain, and aggressively close it behind him. I couldn't help the smile that formed on my face, nor could I help the laugh that bubbled out. **I had forgotten how fun it was to get on the nerves of others.** I made my way to my bed, my vision darkening as I pulled the covers down.

The edges of my vision had gone fuzzy by the time I laid down completely, and fear thrummed in my chest.

"*Foolish boy.*" Loreth's voice rang out before pain enveloped my chest completely.

"Go away." I grunted out. I did not have the energy for this, and I was sure Loreth knew it.

"*Or what? Will you show me your ass too?*" He laughed out, his voice fading away as my vision went black.

17

WEAK AND PATHETIC

"ALFRIKR…" A VOICE WHISPERED BESIDE MY EAR AS I JOLTED OUT of bed into the darkness with a shout. **My body worked on instinct as I grabbed Loreth by the neck and dug my nails into the soft flesh.** His neck was thinner than I expected, but I thought nothing more of it as I squeezed. **He would meet his end by my hand, and I would laugh as life left his body.**

"Woah! It's me!" Dallen grunted out, his hands scrambling and scratching my own as I held him by the neck. *Dallen, not Loreth.* My hand was quick to move as I mumbled an apology, not quite sure why I'd reacted that way. "Are you alright?" He asked, taking a step away from me with a frown.

"Aye," I responded simply, as I adjusted to being awake. The last I'd remembered was Loreth laughing as the darkness had overtaken me. *Was this real? Was Loreth still lurking within the confines of my mind?* "Was just having a dream. You startled me, that's all." I quickly added.

"Oh…" Dallen moved to sit beside me on the bed as he rubbed the base of his neck with a grimace. "Do you… Want to talk about it?" He asked, almost painfully. I shook my head with a groan; it was too early for this.

"I was erm—fighting-a-bear." I mumbled quickly, hoping he wouldn't press for details I did not have. Dallen let out a laugh that echoed through my cavern as the tension seemed to evaporate.

"Tell me more!" He said as he continued to chuckle as if it were the funniest thing he had ever heard. Dallen was usually quick to change my moods around, but I felt the anger lingering beneath my skin. **I felt violated and spied upon by Loreth, and it was a feeling that was not quick to leave.** My chest ached as I pushed myself from the bed and walked to my fire pit.

"Oh, c'mon!" Dallen urged as he laid back on my bed, giggles still coming out.

"Piss off!" I called in return, grabbing my flint and steel. I could feel the curse winding and weaving through my body. It left such a stark, cold residue that ached as it settled into the very marrow of my being. "What're ye here for anyway?"

"Oh!" Dallen replied, giggling one more time. "I just wanted to check on you. Last night was a blur, but I remember you stopping by and looking all sad." My brows furrowed as I struck the flint for the third time, finally using my magic to urge the small flame to take. I hadn't realized that my face had given so much away, but I had a healthy amount to drink and was not entirely surprised.

"I should be asking you the same," I added a few small logs to the fire. "Did you decide?" It wasn't that I did not want to talk about it, *it was more so that I was afraid to ask too many questions regarding his connection with Doran.* There was a tug in my intuition as I thought about how their souls connected them, but I pushed it away.

"No," Dallen hummed out solemnly, the giggles gone now. "Dor says I shouldn't get involved with them, let alone move in with them."

"What does he know about these things? He's been stuck to Merelda's side since we were kids." I retorted, shaking my head as I moved back to the bed. I shoved Dallen over and settled down, pulling my furs over my lap. I shivered as the chill seemed to latch harder onto my chest, bringing a surge of pain into the center.

"Aye, but what do we know?" He nudged me with a small sigh. "Speaking of..." It was almost as if I knew exactly where he was going with that, and *I knew I did not want to go that direction.*

"Don't even start." I muttered, looking away from his frowning face.

"Have you heard anything new about Esmeren?" He asked anyway, his voice almost too quiet to hear.

"Ivaldr came around last night, asking me to work with her again." I shrugged, moving to fiddle with the edge of the fur over my lap.

"I don't trust her. There's this part of me screaming that she's up to no good." Dallen whispered back.

In time, I would learn the truth, and I now wished I could go back and scream the truth at my idiotic self.

"You can sense it too?" Whenever I thought of Esmeren, which was often, I could feel that same distrust of her intentions. There was something happening, but I just didn't know what. "I would rather not work with her, and I think Doran knows more than I do. Has he told you anything?"

Dallen shook his head before responding, "Only that I should talk you into doing it. I told him I would, but I'm not. I think you should keep telling them no."

"It just makes no sense," I shivered as another jolt of pain shot through my body. "Why would she wait ten years, and why does it line up to me being cursed?"

"Aye," Dallen shifted himself to sit, moving to lean against the wall. "Do ye think she has to do with it? The curse?"

"She was betrothed to Loreth. Loreth cursed me. She showed up at the mountain. They didn't do an impressive job at covering their tracks." I shrugged, picking at the blanket again. It all lined up perfectly, which continued to build my suspicions towards her.

The Esmeren I knew was dead, and there was no way I would willingly be around this new version of her.

"Merelda said that Loreth used to beat on her. That he got real mad when she was caught talking to you, beat her down badly, and dragged her to the mountain. I don't believe it, though." Dallen replied as he moved to smack my hands away from the blanket. "Stop doing that before you pluck out all the hairs." I smacked his hands back before settling them under the blanket. It was a terrible habit, but one that I could not control.

"She was pretty bruised when I saw her—the night she showed up here, but…" I trailed off as the memory of drifting into Loreth's mind came back to me. *Loreth had been walking with a woman, not dragging one.* She must have come willingly, which didn't align with what she was saying. *There was no way that I could prove that without putting the connection between Loreth and I.*

"But what?" Dallen urged, his whole body perking up as he leaned closer to me.

"But I can't let go of how I was cursed, and then she appeared at Ymir's Mountain. I think she knows more than she's letting on." Another jolt of pain overtook my chest as my breath stuttered to a stop. It ebbed and flowed through my body as darkness began to flutter through my vision.

"Alfrikr?" Dallen's concerned voice filtered through my

ears in such a distorted way that I could barely understand him.

Flashes of images overtook my vision as I felt myself begin to shake.

A river flowed quickly, trees swaying in the wind, and children played in the trees near the fresh mound of a grave.

Over and over those images flashed within my mind as the sounds of my own screaming faded in and out.

The river suddenly turned red; as if blood had begun to flow instead of water.

The trees turned black as a fire overtook the forest.

The children wore scraps of clothes as they hacked and coughed.

The dirt around the grave shuttered as shook as a single hand burst out.

All I felt was pain as the images flitted back and forth between happy and horrifying. My chest felt as though it were made completely of ice. Each breath seemed to rattle and crack through the frost that coated my lungs. If I could feel my hands and feet, I was sure they would be black with death from the cold that consumed me. I don't know how long I screamed and shook as the flashing images encapsulated my mind. **Pain was a friend of mine now, but it was a horrible friend who tortured me.**

One that lured me into a false sense of security when my body felt as if it were my own again, only to take me harder the next time.

All I could do was endure the pain and wish for death. It

was not an honorable thought to have, and I knew I did not truly wish to walk the halls of a God. *Yet, I was consumed with wishing it would all end, so I would no longer feel the pain inside of me.*

"Riki! Alfrikr!" Dallen's voice seemed to trickle into my mind as the images left my mind completely. All I saw was darkness, a thick black darkness where I couldn't tell whether my eyes were closed or not. *It was not safe, I did not feel divine, and I was not protected.* "Can you hear me?!"

I wanted to respond, but it was as if the pain had stolen my voice completely. I was no longer screaming, but my throat felt dry and scratchy as I tried to swallow. The drool in my mouth seemed to trickle slowly down my throat as my muscles refused to move. I felt my body cough and choke; there was nothing I could do.

"**<u>It's not your time yet.</u>**" A myriad of voices seemed to whisper inside my mind.

I felt the cold recede from my bones as quickly as it had settled into them. A gasping breath heaved into my chest as my eyes flew open. Dallen kneeled above me, from where I now lay on the hard stone floor. There was a faint and subdued pulse in my chest, but nothing close to the pain I had just experienced. My head pulsed with a harsher pain and my muscles seemed to ache as if I had just sparred for hours without rest.

"Riki?" Dallen whispered as he reached his hand out to lay it on my chest. I felt him press against me harder, as if he were searching for the beat of my heart. I swallowed roughly, hoping to coat my dry throat with enough so I could speak.

"Hello?" I finally rasped out, trying my best to smile at the man.

His face was contorted in such horror; one I had never seen before but would see again in the near future.

Dallen heaved in a breath as he removed his hand from my chest and leaned back on his heels. "What..." He shook his head, running a hand over his head. "What the fuck happened?"

I sat in silence, trying to figure out exactly what I could tell him. He *knew of the curse, but he obviously was not aware of the effects of it because I had kept that information from him—and everyone.* I laid there and focused on the steady beat of my heart and the responding pulse of the curse.

"I..." I started before a cough overtook me. I hacked so hard that I felt the bile from my stomach bubbling up my throat.

By the time I had finished coughing and opened my eyes, Dallen had a cup of water in my face. My body was slow and achy as I pushed myself up to sit. I took a large gulp, and then another. I still had no idea what I was going to tell him. I couldn't tell him what I saw, in case that dredged up the idea of being connected to Loreth.

I heaved in another breath, "I wish I knew." I finally settled on.

"Is it... that curse?" He hesitantly asked. I nodded in response, taking another drink of the water. "Y-your body?" He tilted his head and took a shaky breath. "You got...cold? And then...you stopped breathing." A shaky breath rattled him, almost sounding like a sob. "Your-your..." Dallen reached his hand out again, pressing against my chest. "Your heart stopped. I couldn't feel it?" He almost seemed to yell, as if the panic of the situation was settling in again.

"It did?" I asked gruffly, my throat still burning in pain.

Dallen nodded his head as he removed his hand from my chest. "I-I-I didn't know what to do? I just…shoved you off the bed and shook you around. You-you were so cold?" Dallen shivered, reaching out again to press against my chest.

"You need to see the healers." Doran's voice called from the entrance of my cavern. A piercing ache tore through my neck as I turned to look at him—*how long had he been there?* I shook my head in response, making no move to get up.

"I'm alright." I said, though it felt as if I were still trying to convince myself of that. My entire body ached as I sat there. I shivered as the images I had seen seemed to flash to the front of my brain again. *Something was happening, but I wasn't sure what it was.*

"You just died! Right here! And came back!" Dallen yelled as he pushed himself to stand. He began to pace back and forth in front of me. His hands moved quickly as he picked at the palm of his left hand.

"Alfrikr…" Doran said gently, his voice jolting me into the memory of his father's voice the day my mother had died.

As we grew older, we all began to look more and more like our fathers. Doran had the same prestigious and gentle expressions as his father, Dallen flew into a rage as quickly as his father, and I was jolted with shock whenever I saw my reflection. I *was thinner than my father was, but my reflection is how I remember my father when I was a child.*

"I'd just seen Froggy," I admitted with a shrug. "No point in going back. It's just a curse, I'll be fine."

"Stop it!" Dallen smacked his head with both hands, pacing

faster. "You can't die. You just can't! We-we have to do something!"

"There's nothing to be done, brother." I heaved my body off the floor, swaying as I kneeled before him. "This curse will not take me; I will not allow it."

Doran still stood at the entry of my cavern, as if he were afraid to catch what I had. His face was ever-so-regal as his eyes flitted between Dallen's erratic pacing and my *pathetically weak kneeling*.

"You will go." He finally said. His voice was impassive, cold, and almost distant. It was a harsh difference from the pity that had lined it before.

"No."

"Then they will come here." With that, he turned on his heel, his cloak fluttering as he briskly left. I turned to look at Dallen, who still paced back and forth while he alternated between clenching his fists or picking at his palms.

"Dal," I groaned as I tried to lift myself to stand. "Look at me? I'm alright." He did not turn to look, but only continued to pace. It felt like an eternity before his head shot towards me and I saw the panic held on his face.

"Did you hear them?" Dallen's voice was quiet and shaky, something I had never heard from him. His reaction caused a panic to cascade down my spine; *what had he experienced while I was consumed by the pain and visions?*

"Hear what?"

Dallen stopped pacing quickly and shuffled towards me. He kneeled, leaning close to my face to whisper-yell, "The Gods? The Gods? Did you hear them!?" I froze as he stared deep into my eyes; *as if he could see the soul within me.*

"What do you mean?" I whispered back.

"There was this... this mumble?" He leaned closer, his face

mere breaths away from my own. "When you were screaming, it was a… feeling? This feeling that took over the air in the room with power. Such great power. I could hardly breathe. I heard voices whispering, but they didn't speak our language and they were too quiet. Did you hear them?"

I sat for a moment as I tried to understand what he was speaking of. *There were no voices of Gods, nor was there power. There was death, destruction, and sickness.* **Yet, I did hear something—or someone—tell me that it was not my time.** *Could it have been the Gods? Were they so amused by my curse that they spared my life so they could laugh at my pain some more?*

"I-I…" I tried to respond, but the words would not form. I shook my head, my nose brushing against Dallen's with the movement. The Gods had left us; they would not have spared me. "Perhaps you were just hearing things?" I finally said. Dallen jolted away from me with his face lined in betrayal; his eyes narrowed, and his lips thinned as he stared at me.

"What. What happened?" He said sternly; his eyes narrowing with each sound that left his mouth.

I stared at him as I fought the urge to glare back. **I could easily reach out and grab him by the neck; as I had when he first arrived.** *How dare he speak to me like that? I am meant to be his king and he will be my jarl; he does not make demands of me.* My heart skidded to stop as those thoughts swirled within my head; *I sounded like my father.*

"Darkness and pain." I finally said, leaning back to rest on the heels of my feet. "I felt the cold pain in my chest build until it took away my vision. I felt my body shiver and shake, but I couldn't hear or see anything."

"And?"

I shrugged. "I woke up on the floor, and the pain lessened."

Dallen stared at me for a moment, and I could practically

see the thoughts that swirled in his head. He did not believe me, but he wanted to. *I had not witnessed what he had, nor did he witness what I had. We were stuck at an impasse of sorts; where he had been honest, and I continued to lie.*

"What did you feel?" He asked, moving to place his hand on my chest again.

"Huh?" I moved away from him as a feeling of awkwardness began to creep up from his need to touch my chest.

"The power, did you feel the power?"

I sat for a moment as I thought about what he said, but I had not felt the power of anything except pain. *The pain had chewed me up and spat me out.* I finally shook my head. "Just pain. The worst pain I've ever felt."

"I felt the Gods. I heard them." Dallen mumbled as he shook his head, picking at the skin on the palm of his hand. "I know I did. You have to believe me!"

I had a choice to make, one that felt incredibly important. *If I were honest, I would tell him that I believed him; if I lied, I would tell him he was crazy.* **There was a pull to my intuition; one that felt unlike any I had ever felt before.**

"You can't tell anyone. I don't trust anyone but you..." I said with a grimace. "There's more to the curse than we know, and I think this proves it."

Hurried footsteps began to echo down the hallway outside my cavern, with unintelligible whispers following. Dallen gave me a curt nod as he shot to his feet, taking a few steps away from me. I pulled myself to stand with a deep groan as the muscles in my body ached in displeasure. The pulse in my chest was still there; it was nothing compared to the pain I had just gone through. I turned towards the doorway just as the curtain flung open to reveal Hilda, Ivaldr, and Doran.

"Dallen!" Hilda exclaimed as she shuffled into my living space. "Ye say he died?"

I groaned inwardly as she shuffled in my direction, her hands sifting through the pouches on her smock. **I feared being assaulted with pine needles more than I detested the number of people in my space.**

"Aye," Dallen said solemnly, the shake lingering in his voice. "He started to scream and shake. Then his body went still and when I felt him, he was as cold as ice."

"So, he was simply cold?" Ivaldr interrupted; his voice holding a smug indifference. It was as if he found this whole thing entertaining—*as if my suffering were a good tale.*

"I wasn't done." Dallen responded bitterly. "His heart didn't thump in his chest. I shoved him off the bed and tried to shake him awake, but when I put my ear to his chest it was so cold and so quiet."

Hilda's face seemed to get more pale as each syllable left his mouth. She looked so gaunt and small as hobbled closer to me, her hands shivering and shaking as she let them rest midair.

"Yet he stands before me right now?" Ivaldr muttered from the doorway. He did not come closer, but I could feel his eyes peering into my being.

"Aye," Doran said as he walked to stand beside his brother with his back straight and gait smooth. "I trust that my brother believes he experienced what he claimed to. He is an honorable man; not a liar."

There was a moment of silence after that; though it took me a moment to understand what he meant. **Doran did not believe Dallen, but he did think that Dallen thought that is what had happened.** There was no way to determine if my heart had truly stopped beating, but there was a part of me that **knew he spoke the whole truth.**

Hilda stood before me now, her hands grappling through her pockets. "Go sit down, Alfrikr." She said quietly, almost solemnly.

I nodded my head and moved my aching and slow body to my bed. Each bone in my body felt as if it had been crushed, and my muscles ached as though they had been left out to freeze. I was closer to eye-level with Hilda as I sat on the bed; the decrepit woman standing between my legs.

She pulled a single smooth stone from her pocket and brought it up to gently press into the center of my forehead. The stone almost felt warm, though I was sure it was because I was freezing cold. I felt incredibly uncomfortable when she began to rub the rock in slow circles around my face; her eyes were closed, and she mouthed words as though she were singing a song.

I peered past her shoulder to meet Dallen's eyes in hopes that he would provide some comedic moment as he usually did.

Dallen stood with his shoulders hunched, picking at the skin of his palms. He did not look my way, but I could see the panic still looming on his face. *Had he truly heard the Gods?* A shiver wracked through my body as the pulse of pain in my chest sent out another wave of cold pain. I looked towards the doorway, where Ivaldr and Doran now stood with their heads bent together as they whispered. Time seemed to drag on as I sat there with a rock being rubbed all over my face; over the bridge of my nose, down a cheekbone, across my chin, up my cheekbone, and across my forehead.

"Boy," Hilda suddenly said, pausing with the rock in the middle of my nose. "What happened?"

"I got cold and a sharp pain in my chest. Then I woke up with Dallen above me."

"No," She said softly, barely above a whisper. "What truly happened? There's something wrong with your soul. It reeks of the Norns, they're unhappy."

"I-I…" My shoulders shrugged as I tried to find the words to say. I needed to lie, but I wasn't quite sure what to say. "I don't know. Pain…there was a lot of pain and darkness."

Hilda hummed softly before abruptly removing the stone from my face. She tossed it into her pocket before digging around in a different pocket. She pulled out a single sprig of pine, and I felt my body recoil. **I hate pine trees now.**

"Keep this with you, always."

I nodded, grabbing the vile and *smelly* twig.

"Do not tell anyone what you experienced. Not me. Not Froggy. Not your friends." Hilda spit out, barely audible. She stepped away, turning her back to me. "His body is fine. His heart beats. His body is cold, but not concerning… I don't know. I will speak with Froggy." She said matter-of-factly.

It was a harsh and stark difference to the bitter and mean woman I had been expecting. *Her tone concerned me, though I wasn't exactly sure why.*

"I came here for nothing, then? Will he live?" Ivaldr grumbled. "Have you changed your mind yet, Alfred?"

"About what?" I wanted to walk across the room and slam his head into the floor. It wasn't clear to me why Doran had grabbed him, but he must have been really concerned.

"Playing your little games still, I see." Doran's quiet voice shakily mumbled. "Just work with Esmeren. She's here to help."

"He-He's okay?" Dallen's anxious voice rang out above his brothers, effectively cutting him off.

"Aye, for now." Hilda quietly replied, making her way towards the doorway. "Stay close, and stay in bed." She added before leaving as quickly as her old body would move.

Ivaldr slithered out behind her like the little snake he was, Doran following him like a small child.

It was only Dallen and I again; though the air was thick with tension. I wasn't sure what to think about what had just happened, though I knew that it hadn't been anything good. *My soul? Something was wrong with my soul,* and then she just walked out of here like she had told me I simply had the sniffles.

"Well, that was pathetic," A deep voice rang out and seemed to echo within my mind. ***"Even your leader does not care for you; only what you can provide."*** I did not respond as I continued to watch Dallen pace.

"Poor lonely heir," Loreth laughed out. ***"Only having the company of weak, pathetic people."***

18

RISKS AND SPYING

IT WAS EVENING BY THE TIME I'D BEGUN TO FEEL BETTER. I was still nowhere close to feeling like I had before the curse, and I was certain I never would again. There was a moment, days ago when dreaming of Loreth, that I had felt **warm** again. The ache had faded into a dull feeling, and my muscles only faintly ached. I'd decided after Dallen had left, while lying in bed gazing at the ceiling for hours, that I would head out before dinner to hunt. Winter was fast approaching, the leaves were turning, *and I still needed new furs.*

More so, I wanted space away from everyone, *as selfish as it felt.* I required time to plan exactly how I would act with Ivaldr and Esmeren. **I needed to decide what I would share about the curse.** Not only that, but I needed time in my sanctuary, the woods, to connect with the Gods and myself. *I'd ask for guidance, but I did not expect a response.* I slung my pack of hastily packed supplies, doused my fire, and headed out while I knew everyone would be occupied with their meals. The note I left had explained, but I did not expect anyone to seek me out tonight. I was certain that in the morning the boys and Merelda would find it.

I was known to miss evening meals, but it was rare that I missed a morning one. Dallen was sure to seek me out before that. He'd spent almost an hour staring at me before he'd left. I stepped off the main pathway to head towards the river to fill my water skins. The sun had begun its descent, though it was not incredibly dark yet. I sighed heavily, slowing my steps now that I was fully covered by the surrounding trees. This winter would be Hel, but there were far more cold things that weighed on my mind.

The curse was difficult to track, based on the hours I'd spent trying to find a pattern.

It came and went as it pleased, which made hiding it difficult.

There were many who knew already of my fate based on the questioning looks I'd gotten. It would make sense for Tyr's Enforcers to know; they were a higher station than most. Merelda and Hilda knew the most, but whatever Merelda knew, Doran would know. Whatever Doran knew, Dallen would know. Hilda could not keep a secret to save her life. *Which meant that anyone could know.* I was certain that she would keep her worry about the Norns to herself. There was no way to know for sure. Dallen might tell others of the power and Gods, but there were not many who would believe him.

I would have to admit to the pain and cold. **I would keep the connection to Loreth to myself.** It would not be hard unless I was caught talking aloud to him. I would have to be careful with what I let him see, but I knew I could use it to my advantage. I crouched down beside the river and began to fill the first skin. The water felt the same as my body; which could not be a good sign. It was late autumn, and that meant the river would be colder at night. I did not shy from the cold water and instead dipped the entirety of my hand into it. *Interesting.*

By the time I'd filled the three skins, the sun had completely fallen. The moon was not bright; I had weeks until she would be full. The trek up the mountain would be difficult in this light, but the fattest bears could be found there during this time. They would be having their great sleep soon, and would be angrier than usual, so I'd brought my sword and bow. I could use my Sacredness to help trap a bear, but I knew the Gods would frown upon that. *Sacredness was meant to help us, not carry us.* Using our physical and mental strength was the honorable thing to do. If a task was easily completed through labor, then it was not necessary to use Sacredness. The Gods had blessed us with Sacredness, and we would honor their blessings. It was why we worked the fields by hand rather than encourage growth through Sacredness. It would be wasteful and dishonorable to waste Sacredness on something we could do ourselves.

Though, perhaps I was a hypocrite because I often used my own to stoke the flames in my cavern.

Sacredness was dwindling in the Karl and Thrall lines, and we didn't know why. They once had power that rivaled the Jarls and Rikr, yet as the years passed the Gods had slowly pulled back their blessings. There were theories that circled regularly about why, how, and whom to blame. It was not something I had thought deeply of, which I was ashamed of. I'd spent too long ignoring that I was one day going to rule over Sidirna. There was much about myself that needed to change; I could only hope that I accomplished that before the curse sucked the rest of my life-force. I veered from the well-worn trail and angled myself towards my favorite hunting spot. There was a clearing halfway up the mountain with a section of the river that flowed through it. I had found it to be peaceful, and I considered it to be my own.

Near one of the trees furthest from the river was a shrine I had set up to Freyr.

It was not common practice to leave offerings to the Gods anymore; something that my father's mother had taught me as a child. It was important to give thanks, but never expect anything you ask to be heard nor granted. *It was something that I kept to myself, lest I am considered as odd as Froggy was.* It was mine, and mine alone. The walk there would take a few hours, but it was a necessary sacrifice to my already ailing body. I could only hope that my call would be answered, but I did not hold an expectation. *The Gods give, and the Gods take.* I could only hope that they would take pity on me; the one thing in this world that I hated the most—below Loreth, of course. Just the thought of the man made my heckles rise and anger churn in my icy chest.

This was his fault, and he would pay for what he had done to me.

I WAS A SHAKY, sweaty, and freezing cold man by the time I had reached my clearing. My pack felt at least nine times heavier, and I had debated stashing it away many times. What used to be a relaxing, albeit hard, trek had become my own personal punishment. I sank to my knees as soon as my feet hit the luscious grass before me. Offering to Freyr would have to wait until I could breathe through the icicles lodged in my lungs. I heaved another breath, tears prickling my eyes as the pain shot through me again. *Currently, I want to die more than I wanted anything.*

No, I couldn't think like that.

I needed to plot, plan, and change. I needed to rework myself until I was Alfrikr, leader of the rebellion, and heir to Sidirna. Alfrikr, who was adored by his people, and graciously helped all within his borders. **Alfrikr, who opened the borders and encouraged travel throughout our world.**

I moved to lay myself on the ground, gazing up at the stars as I choked through each breath. **I felt no pain. I felt no pain. I felt no pain.** I chanted to myself as I focused on the brightest star in the sky. I had to figure out a list of things I had to accomplish, and how long I would give myself. Though, *I truly had no idea where to start;* **I only knew where I wanted to end.** The wind blew through the trees and shook a few orange and yellow leaves down. The cycle winter would be here soon, and I still needed fur to make a new feldr cloak. The end of winter would be how long I gave myself, I concluded. The Gods must have sent me a message, and I hoped they looked upon me with favor. I dragged a hand down my face as I groaned. My breathing had not returned to normal, and it felt like I had laid there for an eternity already.

I needed to get close with Ivaldr; that would be where I would start, and **I would accomplish it by the end of winter.** First, I needed to get his attention. I needed him to look at me and wonder if I could be of help to him—**Esmeren!** He had asked me to watch her and go with her while she met with Loreth. If I could convince him that I was serious about the task; that I had changed and was willing to forgive a woman who had scorned me ages ago, maybe I could gain more of his trust. *It would come at a cost; the people within the mountain did not like her.* Yet, a part of me wondered if I could catch her in a lie to reveal the truth. **I did not trust her,** and I still believed that she had come to the mountain for a different purpose than the one she had claimed.

That is where I would gain Ivaldr's trust.

I would have to gain the trust of the people if I were to take his title from him. I would need to turn them over to my side, and I had the perfect opportunity this coming winter. There were many disgruntled elders who felt that Ivaldr had not taken the threat of the Cycle Winter seriously enough. That he had not planned nor prepared adequately. **I could play with that and form their resentment into my weapon.** There were many who would listen to the elders. If they had nominated me to take Ivaldr's place, I could gain the respect of many others. I would find resistance and difficulty within Tyr's Enforcers. They were all so far up Ivaldr's ass that they could see out of his eyes. Yet, I was sure that I could gain their respect slowly but surely while also gaining trust with Ivaldr.

I sucked in another deep breath, shuddering in pain as the cold surged through my chest. Smaller, shallower breaths seemed to work better with the pain. I massaged the middle of my chest, where the pain originated, with both hands. I felt no pain, I reminded myself solemnly. There was only so much that one could convince themselves of a lie. *I was afraid that this lie was too large for me to believe. I could only hope that I survived the night and felt well enough before dawn to seek a bear.* Before I could do any of that, I needed to make my initial offering to Freyr. I had also intended to give him a majority of the meat and organs that I got. I would keep the fur and perhaps the skull. I would need to bury the skull deep, though; let it sit until next winter and retrieve it.

The more I kept my brain occupied; the less I felt the pain.

There was a skittering in the woods nearby, and I turned my head to attempt to investigate. The pattern sounded small

—*not a threat.* The act of turning my head sent a wave of dizziness through my vision, and I tried to blink through it. *How long would I suffer with this?* I could only hope that through killing Loreth, I would cut the connection of blood Sacredness. I rolled onto my stomach, slowly pulling myself up onto my knees. My vision tilted and spun, but I pushed myself through it until I could crawl myself to my pack. I had brought a skin of mead and a helping of pork for my offering, things I knew he would enjoy. With my offerings safely tucked into my arm, I dragged myself to the hollow tree on my knees. By the time I made it, my eyes were watering from pain and my chest had been seized with a pain so deep that I could barely breathe shallowly.

"Freyr," I began, closing my eyes. "Ingvi-Freyr, I call upon you with an offer. Take this mead and pork in good faith that I will return with better." I dropped the items into the base of the hollow, hearing them thunk on the ground. "I ask that you look upon me to grant me with better health, though I do not expect an answer nor an action. I am at your disposal." I heaved a breath, opening my eyes. My vision darkened around the edges. I sucked in a too large and painful breath as I felt my body begin to fall before it all went black.

I heard the steady drawl of a familiar voice, but it was difficult to understand what was being said. My gut sank as I knew exactly where I was. **I needed to figure out a way to push myself back into my mind.** I tried to pry my eyes open, knowing that I had done it before, but not quite remembering how. The last time, I had tried to move my body, but I knew now that it was futile.

"Loreth…have you discovered…with the…" I heard a familiar voice say, the words cutting in and out. *Jarl Danr, it had to be him.* I would recognize his voice anywhere. **This could be**

my chance to spy on Loreth. My eyes shot open with my sudden burst of energy and I found myself, or rather Loreth, sitting in my father's war council room.

"Why would I tell you that?" Loreth's gravely voice spit out as he leaned back into the chair. I could feel the hardback of the chair digging into his shoulder as if it were my own. Loreth uncrossed his arms, looking down as he adjusted the neck ties of the rough black tunic on his body.

"You forget your place." Jarl Danr spit back, slamming his fist on the table. Loreth chuckled darkly, moving to lean his elbows on the table. I felt the spark of joy within him as the other Jarls tensed.

I felt the pulse of cold pain within my chest, but I could not determine whether it was **his** or *mine*.

"It is you who forgets yours," His voice rang out menacingly. "I will squash you like the sniveling little worm you are." Loreth slammed a single fist upon the table; *it was as if my hand stung from the pain.* "You are not the snake you think you are." He added as he leaned back into his chair.

His head turned towards my father, *who held a look of a pride I had never seen before.* He had aged since I last saw him; grey peppered his beard, his forehead wrinkled deeper, and **I was filled with the urge to leap up and shove my sword through his gut.** I felt the same way about Loreth. It was challenging to admit I was *jealous* of the pride my father held for the man.

"Now, now." My father chastised as he turned to look at Jarl Danr with a smug smile.

Loreth relaxed considerably, but the tension still filled the room. I felt another pulse of pain, though it had dulled incredibly. Loreth stilled suddenly and clutched the arms of the chair. I felt his nails dig into the finished wood, scraping back a layer with ease. *Had he noticed my presence? I had not noticed when he had invaded my mind, but I had been incredibly distracted that night.*

"I was simply inquiring," Jarl Danr responded. "It is my right to know what is happening. My sons are there as well."

"Perhaps," Loreth's voice rang out. I was surprised my father had let Jarl Danr respond when it was clearly directed towards him. "If you go three nights without visiting the brothel, and spilling all you know to a whore… I'll tell you." The room chuckled as Jarl Danr's face turned deep red. Loreth turned towards my father, nodding his head once, and pushed himself away from the table.

"Unlike you lot," My father said. "Loreth has important things to do."

I hated Loreth even more, I decided. The cruel brute had slithered his way into my father's council, held his respect, and was obviously trusted above the other Jarls. **Loreth No Name had somehow managed to do what I had never done, and I was the heir. Then the fucker had gone and cursed me?** I would end him.

I would no longer be Alfrikr the Forgotten Heir or Alfrikr the Lonely Heir.

I would rise from this curse and destroy them all.

The halls were not the same as I remembered as Loreth leisurely strolled through them. *They were dreary,* as I remembered. *Cold, gilded, and tacky.* Paintings of my father still hung proudly framed in gold, but every painting of my mother had been removed. I was surprised to see childhood paintings of myself; and even more amazed as Loreth stood in front of a *current painting of me.*

How had my father commissioned this? He had not seen me for ten years; I could only assume that he had spies within the rebellion. How would I tell the others without divulging how I knew?

"What an ugly son of a whore." Loreth laughed, reaching a hand out to shift the frame so it hung off center. **If only I could take control of his body and smash his head into the wall until he died.** He took three steps down the hall and stopped again. I felt the smugness radiating through him as he turned to look at the wall. A portrait of Loreth hung there, with his cruel, harsh features on full display. His hair hung down to his chest, stark black against the royal grey of his tunic. His black, soulless eyes did not hold the same level of hatred as they did in real life. At the bottom of the painting was a stone carved with "_Loreth No Name. Head of the Varangian Guard_."

Loreth laughed to himself as he headed back down the hallway, twisting and turning until he was at a door. I recognized the interior as soon as he stepped in; the raven Kraa-ing in greeting. He didn't say a word as he walked to his bed and grabbed the bedsheet. I couldn't help but wonder what the man was doing as he flung it over the cage. The raven let out a few guttural sounds and clicked its beak before it settled. Loreth moved to stand in front of the ornate mirror, hands moving up to the ties at the collar of his tunic.

"Alfrikr," Loreth's voice growled out. "If you're going to spy on me," He unlaced the top of his tunic, pulling it over his head. "Then I'll give you something worthwhile."

Loreth's gaze moved down his body in the mirror, giving me full access to his bare chest. _I willed my body to not respond, but I couldn't tell what was my lust and what was his._ Perhaps he was right; I would not best him in a battle right now. Loreth was giving me an advantage that he did not realize I would have. I **would study the way his body moved to find his weaknesses.**

There was an odd bind-rune carved into the center of Loreth's chest, but his eyes did not linger long enough for me to study it. His body was broad and muscular in a way that I had never seen before. I would look small beside him, despite being a large man myself. I needed to train hard this winter if I wanted to take him down by the spring. His muscles were double my own. It almost looked unnatural, in a way, like he was carved from stone in the image of a God. He moved to look at his face in the mirror; it looked as if I were standing across from him.

Lust flew through my body as I stared at the man, or as he stared at himself.

"I know you're in there." Loreth taunted as his hands moved to his belt buckle. It was an odd sensation to feel the leather of the belt as if I were touching it myself. *I wanted to close my eyes and look away, but there was no way for me to.*

"Come out, come out, wherever you are!" Loreth taunted again, trying to get a rise out of me. I did not say a word as I watched him move to shuck his boots off. They were different from the ones with laces. *I didn't know how that would help me, but I would store that information.*

"I can feel you, Alfrikr." He said, tilting his head as he pushed his trousers to the ground with a thwack and ting of his sword. "Do you enjoy spying?" He looked down at his cock as he gripped it. The sensation was as if I were gripping my cock, yet not at the same time. Our cocks looked to be the same length, but he was far thicker. He stroked himself leisurely as he stood there gazing at his body.

I should not enjoy this, but I was. **The Gods were the only ones who could judge me for this.** *As I would tell no others.*

Loreth's hair was pulled up into a half knot on top of his head, with the small silver piercing on his left ear on full display. He'd kept his Thrall mark? I tried to keep my attention away from the sensation of Loreth stroking his cock. Yet, I failed miserably as he twisted his hand around the head of his cock, smearing his pre-seed around.

We both moaned at once. The sound seemed to encourage him, and he brought his gaze down to his cock.

I felt a churning of *disgust* in my gut, but I couldn't help but **push it away** as Loreth sped up his strokes. The pressure of his grip on his cock was unlike anything I had ever felt, and I moaned again as he moved to cup his balls. He massaged them roughly; something I had never experienced before. Loreth moved in a steady rhythm, tightening his grip with each stroke of his aching cock.

I wanted to speed him up; I wanted to feel how he felt as he finished. He was rougher than I was, but I felt the thrill of it deep within myself.

"You like this, don't you?" Loreth grunted out as he squeezed rougher. "I hope you think about this," His strokes became erratic as I felt the pressure building up. "While you're dying at my feet. Begging for me to spare you."

Loreth squeezed the head of his cock roughly, sending sparks of fire racing down my spine. I was close, or he was close. I was not sure, all I knew is that **I needed release. The man who had sworn to kill me, the man I had sworn to kill, had made me feel a thrill I had never felt before.** I wanted to finish; I would not beg for him to spare me, but *I would beg for him to finish.*

"Hurry up, you sick fuck." I half moaned, hoping I didn't sound as eager as I felt. That seemed to encourage him, his pace quickening to a pace I had never reached before. His grip was firm as he moved to focus his attention on the head of his cock. I moaned again as the pressure built closer to release. His toes curled as we chased the high that came with a release. He grunted deeply, slowing his strokes as he came in long ropes on the mirror.

I let another moan slip as I floated on the feeling; almost forgetting that I was not in my body.

Loreth made no move to clean himself up. He stood there, his chest heaving, and stared at himself with furrowed eyebrows. He was an average looking man; not beautiful, but not handsome. *I wanted him, in some sick way.* As the high began to fade, disgust began to settle deep within myself. I could feel Loreth's own smug happiness.

What had I just done? Why did I enjoy that?

"Next time," Loreth's deep voice spoke quietly, almost menacingly. "I'll have you on your knees before me. I'll fill your throat with my seed before I slit it." He promised, and *I believed him.* I didn't know what to say, so I said nothing whatsoever. "You'd be so eager, wouldn't you?"

I wanted to say no. I wanted to scream at him, bash his face in, slowly torture him to death, and laugh as he begged for mercy. Yet, I couldn't find it within myself to respond. There was a part of me that was excited about his threat, as if I could feel my cock pulsing in delight. **I began to develop a newfound hatred in Loreth that stemmed from my reaction to his words.**

"Fuck you." I finally settled on.

Though, I was sure that I sounded pathetic as he laughed deeply at my response. **Loreth was a sick, cruel man. He would pay for what he did to me.** From the curse to the way he made my own body betray my mind. **Loreth would never touch me in the way he had touched himself.** *No matter how badly my cock ached for it.* It was simply a body's reaction.

Anyone would react that way. Lust had consumed me, one that I could not fight.

"Your internal battle amuses me." Loreth said as he turned from the mirror. "I can feel the battling emotions. The hatred mixed with the longing." He laughed as he grabbed a rag, squeezing the last drops of seed from his head. "Is it hatred for me? Or hatred for yourself because of how badly you want it?"

"I'll never want your cock. You're a sick, cruel, evil man."

Why did the thought of his cock make my own twitch? Why did I know that if he pried my mouth open, I would take it willingly?

"Is that so, Alfrikr? I can taste the dishonesty in your words. I can feel the swirling emotions in your gut." He tossed the rag onto the floor and made his way to the cage.

I stayed quiet as he pulled the sheet away, flinging it back onto the bed. He was right, and he knew he was right. I didn't understand where this feeling came from. I'd been consumed by such hatred for him only moments before, drifting into his mind. *How could I want someone that I hated? It was as unnatural as the curse that raged through my body.*

The world around me tilted and swirled as he laid himself down on his bed. I could feel how relaxed he was, how confident he felt at that moment. I wished I could take control of his body. If I could, **I would kill him in such a way that he would never walk the halls of any God. He did not deserve anything but pain and torment for eternity.** *It had to be the curse that made me feel like I wanted him.*

Everything went black as Loreth closed his eyes.

19

BEARS AND GODS

THE GROUND WAS COLD AND HARD BENEATH ME, AND I OPENED my eyes to the darkness of night. I sucked in a deep breath and turned my head to find the moon. What had felt like an eternity inside Loreth's mind had only lasted a few minutes—*just like the last time?* My chest was tight, but the cold pain that had overtaken me had faded into a warm pulse. This was not the first time that drifting into Loreth's mind had melted the ice within me, and I was hesitant to call it anything but a coincidence. I moved to sit with a groan as my muscles ached from lying on the ground, jolting as a cold spot on my breeches came into contact with my cock.

What the fuck? My stomach churned as everything came rushing into my mind with the force of a great river.

Seeing my father was not as troubling as what came after. Disgust fell through my body in waves. *Not only had I enjoyed it, I'd filled my pants with seed during it.* I could still picture the way Loreth had stood in the mirror with full confidence. *The way his muscles rippled and the vein in his arm popped out as he fisted his cock.* I shook my head, bringing my hands up to push into my eyes. *What was wrong with me? How could I hate someone as much as I admired his body?* I couldn't say that I wouldn't enjoy doing it again because deep inside myself I knew that *I would think of that moment once more.* **In the dark of my cavern, with no one there to witness the thoughts swarming my mind.**

I brought a hand up to smack the side of my head; I was

disgusted and ashamed with myself. **Loreth was a man who could not be redeemed.** His ways were not honorable, and the curse upon my soul was a prime example of that. I'd heard about the man he had skinned and left for the rebellion to find. Once, I'd heard whispers about how he had held a condemnation for my father in the town beside the stronghold. He'd held a man's head under the water in a trough, letting him up for a few gasps of air, and kept going until the man died. I'd hated Loreth since the first time I had ever heard of him.

I would not be swayed by a single moment; *no matter how appealing he looked naked.* I would do to him what he had done to others, I decided. **Not only that, but I would not give him the luxury of a quick death as I had imagined before.**

The cold from the ground began to leech into my clothes, and a shiver wracked my body. I couldn't risk a fire if I wanted to catch a bear, and *I desperately needed to wash myself in the river.* I hadn't brought any clothes with me, so I was unsure how I would clean my trousers. I dragged both hands down my face with a loud groan, just as I heard a loud crashing in the forest nearby. I said a quick thanks to Freyr before hopping to my feet and grabbing my sword and bow. My body was quick to respond, quicker than I had anticipated, and I almost toppled over as I leaned down to grab them.

I stopped to listen, turning my head towards the sound of the bear. I would have to be quiet and quick or the bear would get the upper hand. I weighed each weapon in my hand before setting the bow back down. I needed to work off some of the feelings that were consuming me and dispel Loreth from my mind. I could hear the bear traipsing through the woods, most likely heading towards the river to fish. I had a few options, climbing a tree and jumping down with my sword hitting his neck seemed to be the best option. I would have to run like Hel afterward, until he bled out.

I listened again, trying to determine his path, before taking off for the trees to the left of me.

I made quick work of shimmying up, thankful that the curse had receded from my body. *I was not sure that I would have been able to do this had the curse still wracked my body.* The sun had just begun to crest over the horizon as the large brown bear came into sight. His fat body lumbered slowly as he crushed any bush on his way, stopping to sniff them for food as he passed. I cursed internally as I saw the two yearling cubs in the distance behind her; she was a mother bear. The cubs were big enough that the logical part of me knew they would survive without their mother.

Yet, the part of me that had lost his mother too soon could not reconcile taking the mother from her cubs.

We were all creatures, after all. I sighed as I shimmied myself higher, putting my weight on a thick limb. It was a cycle winter; one that would be worse than usual, and I needed fur for a winter feldr cloak. *Was this a test from the Gods?* Was I meant to choose one way or the other to determine if they would lift my curse? The bears were close enough that I could smell their stench, but not so close that I would miss my opportunity. I was unsure if the cubs would attack; I had already made up my mind.

I would spare her, and send her with blessings in hopes that she too would survive this winter.

BY THE TIME I returned to the mountain, the curse had come back with a vengeance. My chest felt full of ice, with my lungs taking the brunt of the pain. It felt similar to stepping from the warmth of a home to the brutal, frozen winter air. *I couldn't help but wonder if the Gods would have taken the curse away. I should have taken the life of that bear,* I chastised myself as I stumbled my way to my cavern. As much as I wanted to curl into my bedding, I knew that I had to wash myself of the *evidence* of what Loreth and I had done. I felt the anger rise within me; having moved from feeling disgusted to my hatred doubling. **Loreth knew what he was doing,** but I couldn't exactly figure out why he had decided that was what he wanted to do while I was in his head.

I was almost certain that it had been some form of *torture* that his *sick, cruel mind* had decided on. He *had me completely under his control, but part of me wondered if it had been some form of payback.* He had mentioned Siv when I had seen him in the first dream I had drifted into, now that I thought of it. Fatigue settled deep into my body as the movements of taking off my clothes felt ten times as difficult. *At this moment, I almost wished I would have fought the bear and lost.*

Fuck the Gods, draining the curse from my body. I didn't have it in me to fight anymore. I would die before the curse was lifted, and I knew it.

I thought it would be so easy—taking the crown from my father and ruling Sidirna. Yet, I sat here, completely *weak and foolish.* I had accomplished nothing in the nine years that I have lived comfortably in Ymir's Mountain. *I was part of a rebellion that did absolutely nothing rebellious. An uprising that just sunk into the dirt.*

While I've been sitting around scratching my balls and filling my belly, the people of Sidirna are starving, oppressed, and dying.

I wanted to slam my head into the stone wall until I felt the pain of realizing I was a weak fool flowed out of my blood.

While I was doing nothing, Loreth came out of nowhere and rose in station.

He was well-respected by my father, honored even. Loreth was the head of the Varangian Guard, which was not an easy position to take and hold. I had known countless heads during my childhood, and none were allowed to speak over my father in the way I witnessed Loreth do. *Though, I would not put it past the man to curse my father into thinking he was a God among men.* I had spent so many years disconnected from the reality of Sidirna, and it was now that it all came tumbling upon me. All the while, I felt **angry** and *disgusted* for having had a sexual moment with the man who swore to kill me.

I scrubbed my groin harder at the thought, even though I knew the man had not actually touched my body.

Thinking about the moment was not the right choice, as my cock began to harden. *I'd cut it off if that meant I'd never find release with Loreth again.* I lifted my hand and used my magic to cool the water in the basin to almost freezing before dipping my cock in. I yelped at the shock of my poor decision. I dug through my bin of clothes and pulled out last winter's feldr cloak, my warmest trousers, and my thickest tunic. The cold of the water was nothing compared to the chill that wracked through my body.

This curse would be the death of me, and there was much I needed to complete still.

The thought of making my way out of my cavern to see others made my heart race. I would rather not be seen by everyone while I was *weak*, **but I was to stop playing the part of the fool**, then I needed to get off my arse. **I'd planned while in the woods, and I would have to start somewhere**. *I just wish it wasn't tonight that I was going to start.* I did give myself the entire winter to usurp Ivaldr and lead the rebellion towards true action. I would have enough time that I didn't need to start today. **The decision was made for me as I heard a voice clearing from my entry.**

"Alfrikr." Ivaldr greeted me, as I turned my naked body towards him. *Perhaps it was a display of dominance to leave my cock hanging free, much like Loreth had done to me.* I would rather not admit that I understood his game better now.

"Ivaldr." I nodded as I set the pile of clothes on my bed, taking out the trousers and sliding my legs into them.

"I didn't know whether you'd be back yet or not. Doran told me you'd gone hunting." He stated. I was unsure of what his purpose was, but it felt as if he were trying to draw information out of me. As if he wanted to confirm my whereabouts. I grunted in response, sliding my tunic over my head. "I'd like you to change your mind."

"On what?" I replied, fastening the feldr around my shoulders.

"Helping Esmeren convince Loreth that she had gotten close to you in here," Ivaldr made his way into my cavern as if it were his own. Taking a seat at my empty fire pit.

"I don't trust her." I replied with a shrug.

"What if we tested her?"

"How?" This felt as if it were a test for me, in a way. As though Ivaldr were setting me up to do his bidding. *Had Dallen told Doran?* Though, I guess Ivaldr was doing that in a way, but he did not know that I planned to take his position of power from under him.

"She's staying under guard near my cavern." Ivaldr tilted his head back and forth slowly, as though he were deliberating something within himself. I wondered if this was something that went against everything he stood for—*peace, health, and safety.* "What if you were to sneak in tonight and offer to let her out?"

"I don't think I could make that believable," I lied. If I could make Ivaldr think that I respected him, then I could do this. "I'm sure she knows how much I hate her." I thought for a moment before adding, "I could torture her? I'm sure she wouldn't lie then."

Ivaldr sucked in a large breath, his displeasure clear on his face. I'd never been one for torture, but this seemed a necessary evil.

"How could you suggest something like that!?" He practically yelled.

It seemed a bit of an overreaction, but I shrugged in response. Ivaldr couldn't be so foolish that he did not believe in any sort of action. *Wars were not won through sitting around and doing nothing—much like the rebellion had been doing.*

There would be no change in oppression if we just sat around complaining about how much we hated being oppressed.

"We will stick with what I have suggested." He said firmly. "If I find out you have hurt her at all; you will be forced to leave and fend for yourself during the winter."

A flash of pain jolted through my chest that caused my body to spasm. I brought a hand up to rub the center of my chest as if burned with a cold pain.

"Shake?" I asked as I held out my arm, making no move to step closer to him.

If he were to enter my space, then he would have to come to me. Ivaldr pushed himself off the chair and nodded towards me. His hand felt like fire as he clutched my forearm and shook. *Would the touch of others always feel so warm?* I would rather not think of the curse, but it overtook me often enough that I couldn't help but wonder. Ivaldr left without another word, making his way out of my cavern with his head held high.

I was sure that the man thought that he had won me over. That I had changed my stance on this because I was an obedient, low-ranking member of his rebellion. **I wondered if he would look back on this interaction and know that he had been played as I sat in his chair and led us to victory.** If I let him live, that is. There was a part of me that was unsure whether I would see to his death or not. If I were to take him out now, there would be chaos as the ranking members fought for his chair.

I could only assume that Doran would take his place.

While Doran was close enough to be a brother to me, I knew that he held similar ideas as Ivaldr did. He would never lead us to taking over Sidirna, either. He was not weak, but instead too peaceful to find it necessary to take things with brute force. Though, perhaps that was a bit foolish of him. Doran and I had drifted apart a lot in these last few years. I held a lot of resentment for his rise in station, and he disagreed with my feelings on what the rebellion should be accomplishing. I knew that it was inevitable that we would drift closer again now that I had agreed to work with Esmeren because of his relationship with her sister.

I SPENT the afternoon lounging in bed, but I now found myself standing in line for the evening meal. The main cavern was bustling with activity, as it was every meal time, but it was rare that I arrived during the busiest times. **I would need to start making my presence more known. I could not hide away any longer if I wanted to one day lead these people.** I would no longer be known as "Alfrikr the Lonely Heir" and it would take a lot of effort to do so. I gave a smile to the man in front of me as he turned to look over his shoulder.

"Hey!" I said, trying my best to sound pleasant. He gave me an odd look before turning around, and I glared at the back of his head.

"Alfrikr!" I heard Dallen's voice ring out from near the front of the line; he was always early for meals. I gave him a small wave back as he flailed his arms above my head trying to get my attention. He waved his hand towards me, beckoning to join him further ahead. I would normally do so regardless of the way those around me felt. Yet, I found myself shaking my head as I stayed where I was. **I would need these people to respect me.** Dallen gave me an exasperated look before turning back around to say something to Asher, who stood beside him.

"Where were ya?" Dallen asked as he jogged closer to me,

sneering at the grumbles from the man behind me. "It's not like I'm really skipping the line." He bit out before turning his attention back towards me.

"Hunting." I responded with a shrug. I didn't need to explain any further; it was the simplest version of the events of last night.

"What'd ya get?"

"Not a damn thing," I responded with a shrug. "I'd expected to see some bears out there, but I only saw a few deer and plenty of birds."

"Why didn't you get a deer?" He accused me, as it was one of his favorite meats. I shrugged, pursing my lips as I tried to find an excuse that wasn't the truth. *The curse had bogged me down after climbing out of that tree, and there was no way I would have been able to carry one home.*

"I was just out for fur. I need a new feldr if I want to survive the winter."

Dallen gave me an odd look like he couldn't understand why I wouldn't get meat while I was out, but he didn't question me. "Gunther had some nice ones in his shop yesterday," We took three steps forward as the line moved. "If you got the coin or goods for it, you might be in luck." I'd have to stop by after my meal, but before I went to Esmeren.

Speaking of her, "Have you seen Esmeren again?" I asked out of curiosity.

"No," Dallen frowned as he looked away from me to stare into the crowds of people. "Merelda went to see her this morning during morning meal. I haven't heard how that's gone yet. Mer and Dor are convinced that she's here for good. I still don't believe it."

"I don't either," I responded with a sigh. "Things are

changing around here, and I'm not sure if it's the way we want it to."

I knew that Dallen could be helpful because he held similar ideals as me. **Yet, there was a significant part of me that wanted this to be something I had done on my own, and couldn't trust how deep the twin connection went between them.** They were two halves of one soul. The soul curse between Loreth and I gave us a connection between our minds, much like Dallen and Doran.

"Aye," Dallen agreed solemnly. "I've heard from Merelda that Hilda is furious with how the Cycle of Winter has not been taken seriously. I think Ivaldr only agreed to the raid because of that."

I nodded my agreement with a frown. The winter weighed heavily on me too. *We'd have enough food for the bare essentials, I hoped.* The grain stores brought a significant haul, but no one but Ivaldr and his croon of Enforcers knew the exact amount.

"Have you reinforced the entrances?"

"Not as much as needed. He still thinks we don't know where they all are. Just the main ones, but I was planning on sneaking down there tonight and adding extra to the doors and surrounding walls." Dallen was skilled in ground magic, and I knew it would be simple for him to thicken what was needed.

"I worry about those in the lower levels," I frowned before continuing. "The ground will be colder down there, and they're far from the main area's fire pits."

The man behind us scoffed loudly, clearly listening to our conversation. I turned to look at him, attempting to school my expression. "Did ye have something to add?" Dallen quipped, his frustration clear in his tone.

"The winter won't be bad," The man spit out. "Ivaldr has

prepared as much as required. You noble fools are worrying about nothing because you've always had more than you needed."

I grabbed Dallen before he lunged towards the man, quickly pulling him towards where Asher and Kraka stood.

"Can you believe people can be that dull?" I pondered as we sidled up beside the two. Asher gave me a warm smile before reaching out and pulling Dallen closer. I was sure that he could see the fight that was brewing in Dallen, and I gave him a nod of appreciation.

"He's foolish!" Dallen practically shouted as he still fought to stare the man down. "We've struggled every winter; especially since we've been here!" He grumbled out, still not settling down.

"You have to remember how they view us," I stepped into Dallen's line of sight, cutting him off from his stare-down. "We'll always be considered the enemy. We just have to work on changing their minds."

"You sound like Dor." He muttered in response, shoulders sagging as he leaned into Asher's side.

"What was that all about?" Kraka finally asked, peering around me to look at the man. I shot her a look, hoping that Dallen's anger wouldn't come surging back.

"That poor fool isn't worried about the Cycle of Winter, and he thinks Dallen and I are noble fools." I shrugged, shaking my head at the thought. I could recognize that I had grown up in privilege with a full belly every night, a warm bed, and anything I could have wanted. Yet, it was not a happy and jovial childhood, and I had spent the last nine years living exactly as the rest of Sidirna lived. **My name did not hold the weight it once had, and I would do my best to change that.**

The line moved quickly now that we were at the front, and I took my place near the fire across from the others. Siv was not here this time, which I was glad for. I rested the bowl full of stew on my legs so I could dip the rock-hard roll in. Whoever made this today was a piss poor cook; the apples and carrots were hard, and it had a watery, milky color to the broth. I cringed as I took another bite and hoped that closing my eyes would make it taste better.

It did not. I gagged as I spit out the roll into the soup. "What the Hel is this?!" Dallen hollered from across the fire. *If this were what we would be eating this winter, then we were all sure to die.* I didn't have much in my stores for food, but I could see what kind of dried meats Gunther had in his shop. With my belly painfully empty, I dumped the contents in the food pit and dropped my wooden bowl in the dirty pile before heading towards Gunther's shop.

The hallways were crowded with people on their way to an evening meal. I felt pity for them, as they would soon find out how someone could turn piss and shit into stew. Gunther's shop was not far from the main cavern, where we all ate. I walked into the entrance, half expecting it to be full of people, but it was eerily empty.

"Gunther?" I called out as I took another step inside, looking around the packed shelves for the small man. I didn't see him, but decided to keep browsing. He had a full stock of dried meats, furs, spices, and weapons. No one knew where he got them all from, but it was easier to not ask.

I loaded my arms with three different furs, one brown bear and two elk, before moving over to the section of meat. There wasn't much fish, but he had a good selection of red meats that I picked and chose from.

"Ye weren't gonna leave without payin' were ya boy?"

Gunther's voice rang out from behind me. I startled and almost dropped them all as I turned to face him.

"You know me better than that, you old coot!" I replied, looking down to give him a grin that he returned. I wasn't sure that the man really liked me as a person, but he undeniably did love my coin and trades.

"Aye, I didn't recognize ya without yer hair!" The man practically shouted. I was certain he had some old Dwarven blood in him because he looked exactly as they did in the old history books; short and plump with red-tinted long hair with a matching beard that tried to hide his rosy red cheeks.

"What've you got in the back?" I knew better than to beat around the bush with Gunther, lest I wish to lose all of my coin on simple things. He kept a plethora of valuable things under protection that he only sold through trade. No coin was enough.

"Wouldn't you like to know, baldy!" He turned on his heel and headed towards the back of his cavern, where a small alcove held the items.

"I would," I huffed a laugh. "That's why I'm asking."

"Yer gonna wanna put them furs back." He replied giddily. "Where ye found 'em ye menace!"

He hadn't turned to look at me, and somehow knew that I had shuffled my arms to drop them on the nearest shelf. I practically ran to put them away, and did run to return to him. He stood at the entrance of the alcove with three different furs over his arms. The first one that stood out was a stark white elk pelt; a rare find that would cost me, but I would take it. The other two were bear pelts; one black and one a reddish brown. The cost of these would be high; I knew Gunther loved to deal in information.

"What'll it take?" I asked, breathlessly stepping forward to run my hand across all three furs.

"The curse, the woman, and Loreth." Gunther whispered as he took a step further into the alcove. I figured he would want to know at least two of them, but was surprised that he knew Loreth was connected.

"I was cursed after the raid," I solemnly said back, my voice a hushed whisper. "It's leaked into my bones. Some kind of cursed frozen chill overtakes my body constantly. I don't feel warm, and I might die." I truthfully confessed. He would know as much, I knew Hilda often traded with the man.

Gunther nodded, a deep scowl on his face. "Ye can't reverse it?"

I shrugged in response.

"The woman is the daughter of a Jarl. We were betrothed, but she chose to stay when I left. I don't trust her, but I'm willing to try. She was always a weak girl who went along with whatever anyone else wanted, not much of a leader." Gunther nodded furiously, so I continued. "Her name is Esmeren. Her sister is Merelda." I shrugged, not knowing what else to tell him.

"She a threat?" He asked.

"I wouldn't call her a threat, but you might get some good information out of her if she ever makes it down here." That seemed to excite him, and he waved his hands, encouraging me on.

"Now Loreth!" Gunther whispered.

"I don't know much, but I'll tell you what I do know." I lied with a frown. *I wasn't about to tell him what his cock looked like.* Nor was I going to tell him how the curse connected us. "He's cruel, bitter, and highly respected by the Wretched. Head of the Varangian Guard. He's the one who skinned and hung up that man last winter. He swore to take down the rebellion, and I believe him."

Gunther gasped, covering his mouth with his plump hand. "Take the meat too," He whispered. "Tell me if he's the one who cursed you."

I nodded my head three times as I took the outstretched pelts.

"May the Gods be with you." Gunther called out as I turned my back to him.

"You as well."

20

PLANS AND DECISIONS

Dread loomed over me as I sat in my cavern eating dried meat by the fire. The curse pulsed steadily in my chest, with the frozen core hurting the worst. *There were times that I wanted to scream from the pain that wracked through me,* **but I couldn't help but feel appreciation for having those reactions beat out of me.** The years that I had spent being shaped and formed by my father's fists had given me a tolerance like no other. My body felt drained and tired, but my mind felt alive and full. There was much to accomplish, and yet, I felt no dread overtake me as I thought of facing Esmeren.

She would be the key to gaining some sort of trust with Ivaldr.

Somehow, I found myself dreading giving up the normalcy that I had become dependent on. *There would no longer be lazing about or working the fields once I had the rebellion under my control.* Those responsibilities I had never learned would loom over my head, and I cursed my father for not allowing me to take an active role in learning how to run the kingdom. It made little sense to me as a teenager. **Wouldn't he rather have me learn sooner?** Yet, my mother had once told me that he was worried I would kill him and take the crown if I knew too much. For a while, I was unable to socialize with the Jarls because he feared they would turn me against him.

Though my father turned me against him just fine by himself. His fears when I was a child had come true, except he had been the one to plant them within me. It was nearing the time I would need to head out and enact the poorly made plan. I held no faith that Esmeren would believe me, and I hated Ivaldr a little more for not giving me a solid time or plan.

Would the guards be aware of what I was doing?

I could only assume that they would not because that is the way my luck fell. *The Gods gave and took as they pleased.* It would make sense for them to turn this lack of planning towards more amusement for them. It had been years since I had snuck around, but I could only hope that it was a skill that I had not lost. My hands shook as another chill shuddered through my body. The curse seemed to worsen at night, though there was still no pattern. I'd need to start my feldr sooner rather than later if the cold of the curse continued to overtake my body. It would be easier to use my feldr from the last three winters; I would need to replace the fur and mend any holes to make it usable.

The furs I got from Gunther would be essential in the coming months. **I looked forward to seeing myself draped in such a regal, clean, and soft feldr**. Though, I was unsure when I would find the time to sew such a garment. My grandmother, from my mother's side, had made sure that I knew how to sew my clothes. It was as though she had looked into the smoke of a fire one day and decided it to be so. It would make sense that the Gods would talk to her, but I was unsure as a child why it would be important. I could see now, as an adult, why it was a necessary skill to have.

My mind ran wild with thoughts as I stared into the fire. I had lost track of time completely, but could only assume that it was late enough for me to head out. Ivaldr's cavern was far from my own, and my body was already weak from the effects of the curse. It hurt, but I was able to breathe through the pain now. I'd felt that moment of reprieve while still in the woods, though it felt as if I had wasted it by sitting in a tree. I should have stayed and recovered from passing out instead of heading into the woods. *I felt like an idiot, but it had been good for me to figure out my next steps.*

With a heavy sigh, I held my hand out to urge the flames to smolder. I'd wasted energy in building the fire, and I knew it. The warmth would not seep into my bones as much as I longed for it to. There would be no warmth for me unless I was drifting in the darkness in between my soul and Loreth's. My steps were slow as I dragged myself out of the comfort of my cavern. **The truth was that I had signed up for this, but I still felt disgruntled at having to leave at such a time.** The mountain had settled in for the night, and silence seemed to echo through the halls. The air was almost as cold as my body as I got closer to where Esmeren was staying.

Ivaldr had not told me which cavern she was staying in, and I could only hope that I did not run into an Enforcer. A pulse of pain flared again and sent me collapsing against the wall. I could feel the ribbons of cold weaving between my ribs and clutching my bones. Breathing hurt, but holding my breath seemed to be worse. I don't know how long I stood there on shaky knees with a hand clutching the center of my chest. I could barely feel my nails as they dug into my skin; the cold had numbed the outside of my body as pain overtook the inside. The pain had been a deep pulsing throughout the day, and I wished it would go back to that. Tears formed in my squeezed shut eyes as I stood there, consumed by the pain.

I would live, I would beat the curse, I would rule over

Sidirna, and I would kill Loreth. I chanted in my mind over and over.

Though a part of me wanted to die at that moment. The looming dread of knowing something was wrong with my soul seemed to suffocate me. As long as I stayed busy, **I could pretend I didn't know.** The pain left my body as quick as it had entered it, and I fell to my knees on the stone floor. I sat back on the heels of my feet and hung my head. Breathing felt easier, though it was still cold. I heaved breaths in and out; my lungs still did not feel as if they were filling completely. My body continued to shiver as I sat there, trying to regain my composure. I took a deep breath through the icy pain, holding it as long as I could, and focused on the feeling in my chest.

One by one my ribs seemed to ache less, but cold pain lingered in my bones.

I was reminded again of the time as a boy that I had caught a chill to my bones, the very same feeling that wracked my body now. In and out, I breathed as I kneeled on the floor, thankful that no one had witnessed my moment of weakness. *Though my body may be weak,* **my mind was not.** The thought did not dispel the disgust that overtook me as my father's words echoed throughout my brain. It was difficult to bring my body to stand, but even more so to make the first step. One after another, I made my way down the hallways until I hit the entrance of Ivaldr's caverns.

I hid in the shadows of the entryway, focusing my attention on the surrounding sounds. Nothing but the rattle of my breath—perfect. I risked a glance around the corner; nine doorways, with the one furthest from me guarded. The concept of guarding didn't fit the situation as he was slumped in his chair, head against the stone wall, and sleeping. To my detriment, he was a quiet sleeper. It would have been easier to time my steps to his snores. I hobbled around the corner, cautiously sticking to the wall for support. My body ached all the way down to my bones with each step rattling from my heels into my jaw.

I could make it. I was not weak. I would use what little strength I had remaining to do this.

My body shuddered as I took another step towards my new fate. The thought of what I still had to accomplish felt dreadful. There was much to do while I was still unsure of the effects of the curse on my soul. *Would I wake up one day with no soul remaining? Would loreth enter my mind and never leave—or me to his mind?* I was halfway across the room by the count of the guard's ninth breath. A good number that could be a sign from the Gods, though perhaps I was a little superstitious. Dallen had claimed to feel their presence, and I couldn't help but feel hopeful that the Gods were with me. I had made my offering to Freyr, now I would wait and see if he would take pity on me. I would persevere, and **I would choke the life out of Loreth over and over until his body couldn't take it anymore.**

One day, I will laugh as I watch him suffer beneath me.

Pain flowed through my body in a short burst that threatened my vision, making me blink the black away furiously. *Was it a sign that Loreth was in my mind?* I could only hope that it was not. Another nine breaths had me two doorways away, with six more bringing me right to her door. I was cautious as I brought my hand towards the handle; cringing at the creak of the latch. I paused and held a lung full of icy breath. His breath altered slightly, but the guard's body didn't stir. I flung the door open wide enough for me to squeeze through as quickly as I could. If you opened a squeaky door fast, it was less likely to make a loud sound. That was one positive thing I had learned as I spied on my father's Jarls.

I closed the door behind me just as quickly, slowing considerably to latch it. Esmeren jolted from where she lay on the bed as I eased the latch fully closed behind me. I brought a single finger up to my lips in hopes to keep her quiet, part for show and part because I was unsure if the guard knew what I was here to do. There was an unsettling feeling in my gut, one that was equally intuition as it was anxiety. *Something was wrong, yet I wasn't sure what it was.*

"Alf?" She called out, voice confused, as she slung her legs over the side of the bed. "What are you doing?" Esmeren added loudly.

I was slow as I hobbled towards her. Partly to keep my steps quiet, but mostly because of the shiver inducing pain that wracked my body. "Shhh!" I urged her. "They don't know I'm here. I had to see you."

She gave me an odd look as she tilted her head. The look itself almost gave her away; **she was hiding something.** Though I wasn't sure what exactly it was. "I don't... understand?" She timidly asked.

"I can get you out of here."

"What do you mean?" Esmeren moved to stand, taking a step closer to me.

"I know why you're really here..." I put my hand on her shoulder, giving it a slight squeeze. "You're here to spy for Loreth, and make Ivaldr think you're betraying Loreth. You have no plans to betray Loreth."

"I-I-I..." Esmeren stepped back quickly; her eyes widening

as she stared up at me. Her mouth hung open slightly, and it was suddenly aware of just how much she had aged in the past nine years.

Esmeren was no longer the quiet mouse-like girl I had grown up with, and I had no idea what kind of woman she had grown to be.

"We have to hurry!" I snapped at her, looking around the room. "Do you have things to pack?"

"I-I can't go, Alfrikr." She stuttered out. "Loreth will kill my mother and father! He threatened to torture them if I was found out! Has he already spoken with you?" **I knew she was lying,** and I relished in the feeling for a moment. Ivaldr, Doran, and Merelda were **wrong.**

"So," I couldn't help but chuckle. "You're not here because you are going to betray Loreth?" Her face contorted as she took in what I said, and her eyes narrowed at me. *It was almost startling to see her look at me that way, and not with love and admiration as I was used to.*

We stared at each other; eyes locked and neither moving. Esmeren was here to provide information to Loreth, and I had easily sussed her out. She huffed out a small breath before finally looking away. My knees wobbled as I stood, and the dreadful pit of weakness opened up in my gut. *My body felt weaker and weaker as we stood in silence.*

"You're here to spy, then? Truly spy on the rebellion?"

"Ivaldr can't know this, Alfrikr." She spit out, her voice losing whatever anxiety it had just contained. "I wasn't planning on telling Loreth anything. I'm going to betray him. I can't risk my parent's lives."

I stared at her for a moment as I was unsure of what to say. The edges of my vision began to fade as the darkness threatened to overtake me. She had flipped so easily, but the tugging was back in my gut. **I knew she was not here because she believed in the cause.** *Yet, I also knew that Loreth had probably threatened their lives.* **I was not eased into submission, and I knew she would most likely double-cross us to share information with Loreth.** Another pang of icy pain radiated through my chest as I stood there.

"Gone to see your old lover, have you?" Loreth's voice rang out within my mind.

I heaved a breath in as the cold pain began to fade away. *This was the worst possible time for him to be preying upon my mind and spying on my life.* If Esmeren was being honest, he would kill her parents for this. I pursed my lips as I tried to decide what to do next. Saying anything more could implicate her, and while I felt no pity for her, *I held some for her parents.*

"Goodbye, Esmeren." I said softly as I turned and strode towards the door. My muscles had relaxed, but still did not feel quite right.

"Alfrikr! Wait! You must not tell anyone!" Esmeren cried out, but she did not move to follow me.

"Not going to put on a show for me?" Loreth's laugh echoed through my head as I pulled the door open. *"Not to worry; it's nothing I haven't seen before. She's not a very animated lover, is she?"*

Loreth was wrong if he thought that I still cared for what Esmeren did, or rather who she fucked. **There was nothing left inside of me for her besides contempt.** Those feelings had faded and been lost years ago. I snuck past the guard, whose mouth was now wide open as he continued to sleep. **Useless oaf of an enforcer.**

"Nothing to say?" Loreth asked with another eerie chuckle.

"Go away." I whispered, unwilling to wake up the guard behind me. I looked around me, hoping to find somewhere to hide away until Loreth left my mind. **I didn't want him to know the interior of the cavern more than he already probably did.** I slipped out of Ivaldr's cavern and took a left into the dark hallway.

"Go away!" Loreth mocked, his voice raising several octaves.

I let out an exasperated groan as I shook my head. *Childish. The man who was feared throughout Sidirna because of how badly he tortured, maimed, and killed people just mocked me like children do.* "What do you want from me?" I whispered, hoping that no one was around to hear. *The last thing I needed was to be seen whispering to myself.*

"What have you got?"

There was no use in responding to his immature responses, so I stayed silent. I veered down a hallway that would take me to the opposite side of the mountain from my caverns, hoping that Loreth didn't pay too much attention as I walked. The pulse in my chest had dulled to a small thud that I could hardly feel as it almost aligned with each step I took. My body felt rejuvenated and fresh as I moved, almost as I had before the curse. Loreth being in my mind was poor timing, and I was angry that he had the opportunity to do so.

How was it that he was able to change the entire course of my life in one day? I didn't understand why he chose me to curse; what did he gain from it? When I die, the crown goes to no one. My father doesn't have any other heirs, that I know of, and it seems irrationally idiotic to curse the only heir. **There had to be more to it.** Something that I didn't understand yet. *Unless the curse would not kill me, and Loreth did it as a way to control me?* He was inside my mind right now, and there was nothing I could do to change it.

Violated. **I felt violated and angry as I walked down the dark hallways as Loreth hummed an annoying tune in my head.** I wanted to violate him back. I wanted him to feel a fraction of what I felt at this moment. *A part of me felt as if I were imagining it all and had gone insane.* I couldn't understand how Loreth could enter my mind, nor how I could just as easily fall into his mind. *It was the curse, I knew that, but how had he done it?*

Shame lingered as I thought of the last time I had entered his mind. *The way he had gripped his cock. The way his veins bulged in his arm as he dragged the palm of his hand over the head. How I had awoken with my pants stained with evidence of how much I had enjoyed it. How I had tried to forget the image, but it was as if he were burned into my mind.* **The urge to bash my head into the wall hit me as I thought of how Loreth had stood in the mirror; powerful, strong, and confident.** *All the things I wished to be, but usually found in a bedmate instead.*

My cock began to stir in my pants at my shameful and dishonorable thoughts of my enemy. *The man who had cursed me, tortured people for fun, and spent his spare time doing the bidding of my wretched father.* The most feared man in all of Sidirna—even above my father. *Yet, I could easily slide my hand into my trousers and pleasure myself at the thought of his naked form. The sounds he made as he found his release. The aggression and roughness as he stroked his cock.*

I tried to be casual as I reached down to adjust my cock in hopes that Loreth wouldn't notice. It was embarrassing and shameful to be having these thoughts, and I didn't know where they had suddenly come from. *His humming didn't stop; the tune almost sounded like an old lullaby my grandmother would sing to me when I was a child.* A part of me wanted to hum along as if I were listening to a tune and not the man who cursed me inside my head. It was familiar. *The same lullaby that I had stuck in my head recently, but I would rather not think about it more.*

I couldn't understand the feelings that flowed through me as I continued to listen to the man hum. **I hated him with every fiber of my being. I was planning how to get stronger, more powerful, so I could kill him with my bare hands.** Loreth had brought death and destruction wherever he went; his name brought a type of fear that could hardly be fought against. Loreth was a dishonorable man who could not be redeemed. He had used blood Sacredness to curse me, and he had most likely sacrificed someone for it.

Yet, there was this small part of me that was fascinated by him and his very existence. How he had worked his way out of Thrall-hood until he was the rightmost hand to the king. *How the muscles in his stomach tightened as ropes of seed shot out of him.* The way that Loreth held enough confidence to do what he wanted, regardless of the repercussions. *Loreth would have made a great man had he not gone such a violent and bloody route.* He obviously had a drive about him that could not be rivaled. **Still, I would kill him, as there was no redemption for him.** My shameful thoughts were a product of lack of company lately.

I still found myself veering to the right as taking the path towards the unoccupied, and unfinished caverns. The ones that sat waiting until more people came to join us in Ymir's mountain. Loreth's humming seemed to get louder as my heart picked up rapidly. I turned into the first cavern off the hallway, relishing in the darkness for a moment. **I would do what Loreth had done to me, I'd suddenly decided. He would feel as violated as I had.** *No one would find me here; no one would see what I was about to do.* Loreth continued to hum as

I shoved my trousers to my ankles, and fisted my half-hard member.

"Am I supposed to be impressed?" Loreth droned out, almost making me jump at the harsh difference from his calm humming.

My eyes did not take long to adjust to the darkness of the cavern. I felt a thrill wash through me as I stroked my cock slowly, keeping my gaze on the movements of my hand. It was not light, there was no mirror, but I knew that Loreth could see enough through my eyes. *My cock twitched at the thought of the man watching me as I had watched him. This was a sick game that we were playing, one that I was sure to regret after I was done. I couldn't be bothered to focus on that for long while I slowly stroked my cock.*

My hand moved up slowly and down quickly; my grip tightening as I neared the head. My mind moved back to the memory of Loreth in the mirror. The way he had roughly fucked his hand without a single worry that I had been watching him. How deeply satisfying it had felt to feel his cock as if it were my own. It only felt right to repay the favor. I leisurely stroked my cock as thoughts of Loreth filled my mind.

"Pathetic." Loreth grunted out, his voice deep and guttural.

My grip tightened around my now fully erected cock as I heard him speak. *I wanted him to keep talking, for his voice to fill my head as I kept stroking my cock.* I could only imagine how it would feel to have his breath against my ear as he spoke. How he would push me roughly to the ground and take what he wanted. How it would feel to be beneath him, his thick thighs squeezing my hips. I shivered as a flash of pleasure ran down my spine. Pressure had begun to build, and I squeezed my cock, trying to fight off the urge to quicken my pace.

He may be the man I swore to kill, but just knowing that he was watching me was enough to make my hips buck harder into my hand. My pace was slow and steady as I continued to stroke my cock. If I stroked myself any faster, I would be finished. I moved my thumb to the head to smear my pre-seed, but it was not enough. I brought my other hand up and cupped it as I spat into it before smearing it around my cock.

"You're wasting your spit. It'd look better running down your chin as I fucked your mouth, Lonely Heir."

I grunted in response as his words sent a flash of thrill down my spine. I could almost picture myself on my knees before Loreth. My pace quickened at the thought. With his cock in my mouth as he fucked it as hard as he had fisted his cock. I gripped my cock harder as I fought the urge to close my eyes and imagine it fully. The way my nose would bury itself into his hairs as he filled my throat with his cum. I moaned as I felt the pressure building and my balls tighten.

"You're always fast, aren't you?" Loreth said as I felt the pressure hit the point of no return. A deep moan echoed with my own as I rushed over the edge; spilling my seed onto the floor. I took a heaving breath as I tried to regulate my breathing as the pleasure continued to flow through my body. I could only hope that Loreth woke up from wherever he was with his trousers full of cum, as I had.

A flash of darkness came over my vision as my chest suddenly exploded in an all-consuming pain. I stumbled, almost falling over, as my pants were around my ankles still. "Fuck!" My knees hit the hard stone before me with a thunk that echoed through the empty cavern. I sat there for a moment, trying to breathe through the icy pain that flowed directly into my bones. *Tears began to fall from my eyes as I kneeled on the floor.*

Loreth was the reason I was like this, and he would die for it. The curse brought forth a pain that was unlike anything I had ever experienced before. I shivered as another round of pain overtook me. There was no way to tell how long I kneeled on the floor, but it was long enough that my legs had begun to go numb. My body was slow and heavy as I pulled myself up to stand. I leaned over with shaking hands and pulled my trousers up.

What had I done?

I took an unstable breath as the shame settled deep within me.

21

GRUEL AND RATS

THE NIGHT HAD GONE BY IN A FLURRY OF TOSSING AND TURNING. The fear of falling into a dream with Loreth outweighed any need I had for rest. My body ached, and I felt exhausted as I stood in line for my morning meal. *The surrounding crowd seemed too loud, the fires too bright, and I just wanted to go back to my cavern.* I did not have the resources to mingle today, which affected my plans entirely. However, I required food if I wanted the energy to take over the rebellion and kill Loreth. I stepped forward in the line as thoughts of Loreth drifted into my mind. I felt an inkling of shame at what I had done, but only for the fact that he was my enemy. *He was the man I swore to kill, but there was this inartistic need inside of me that wanted to find pleasure from his body.*

The first time he had pulled out his cock, I had felt the overflowing pressure of shame and disgust, but those feelings had faded. **Why could I not find pleasure in a man who was so dishonorable and unredeemable? Loreth had confidence about him that I would do good to watch and learn. He had taken what he wanted, and had no shame in doing so.** Though, a part of me grappled to understand how these emotions had flipped so suddenly. I sighed and ran my hand down my face as I neared the front of the line.

The pulse in my chest had slowly built itself up to an almost unbearable pain during the night. I needed to learn more about the curse, and my only source of information would be Loreth—*unless Esmeren had knowledge of the curse. I* knew that Ivaldr would be slinking around looking for me, and I dreaded having that conversation. I may have relented, done what he requested me to do, but *I was dreading having to put on a mask to lure him into a false sense of security.* **I needed to be specific in my words, body language, and choices from now on.** If I made a move too quickly, he would get suspicious that something was amiss. I took the final step in line, bringing myself to the stone counter where Finnian stood.

"Alfrikr." He nodded at me as he scooped a helping of what looked like slop into the wooden bowl.

"May the Gods be with you." I mumbled as I accepted the outstretched bowl, snagging a spoon as I veered to the left.

This winter would be rough if this is what we are served before the hard months come. *I thought we had gotten enough grain, but fear still churned within me as I looked at my slop.* Decisions. I had many decisions to make right now, and I wasn't sure my brain had enough power to properly make them. I could retreat to my cavern, eat in silence, and then return my bowl at the next meal. **Though, staying and finding a spot would most likely further my plans and begin my ascent within the rebellion.** I needed more people on my side, and to accomplish that I needed to create some sort of connection with them. I sighed heavily as I stood there, looking around the hall for at least one familiar face.

Looking back now, I was sure that the Gods had created this moment. It had all lined up a little too perfectly for it to have been a simple happenstance. Each of the men I sat with that day would soon become critical to this tale.

There was a distinct separation of little groups that had formed within the rebellion; which was obvious during meal times. There was extra seating at each table, but *it was an unspoken rule to only sit with those who were within your group.* **Much would change when I was leading these people, especially how there was a lacking cohesive identity.** *We may all have been part of the rebellion, but beyond that, there was no camaraderie. We were not a cohesive group that could rip the Jarls from power.* I was too late to have caught Dallen, Doran, or Merelda. I could hope that Siv was here somewhere, but I knew it was too early to see her.

Slowly, my eyes scanned the room until they stopped on the decrepit, old fool.

Froggy sat near the back of the hall, surrounded by other elders. I sent a quick thanks up to the Gods for they must have been here guiding me. Winter was fast approaching, and I knew how angry many elders were over the lack of preparation. **It was time to start creating connections and stoking the flames of their anger. Ivaldr would no longer hold the position he did not deserve.** Each step I took towards the group of elders solidified the plan to urge the elders to act upon their anger. I knew I would be looked at oddly as I sat and ate with the people who were deemed odd because of their beliefs in the Gods. *I could only hope that a part of Froggy was eased by my admission in his cavern.*

"May I?" I asked as I gestured towards the open seat beside the man. He looked up, eyes narrowing as he took me in. Froggy took three deep inhales through his nose, leaning closer to me with each sniff. *I resisted the urge to lean away and keep my face free from the judgment I felt coursing through me.* As odd as it was, a part of me believed in his strong belief of the

Gods and knew that there was a greater purpose for his oddities.

Froggy nodded his head once, leaning back into his chair. "I heard, but I did not believe until now." He croaked out.

I pursed my lips as I set my bowl on the thick wooden table. Hilda must have spread around what she had learned. "Aye?"

"Yer soul is... different. Different from the last I saw ye. Hilda was right."

I wasn't sure what to say, so I simply nodded in response. **The less I thought about my soul, the better I would feel.** There was an unease that settled within me as my thoughts began to drift towards the topic. Without knowing anything about souls, it was difficult to gauge how bad the news was.

"Who're ye?" An old, plump man said from across the table. His hair was thinning considerably, but what was left of it hung to almost his shoulders. His beady black eyes seemed to stare into my very soul as he slurped the gruel from his spoon.

"Alfrikr."

His body jolted backwards as he fumbled his spoon back into the bowl. "What do you want?" His voice seemed to shake, but only slightly. I sighed heavily as I looked down at my bowl.

"To eat my meal?" I finally responded. *There it was. The way that people changed once they found out who I was. How they would go straight to the idea that I was just like my father, though I suppose I was a little like him,* **as I really sat here for another reason.** Froggy laughed beside me, which did wonders to break the silence that had settled over the table. There were three other men, besides Froggy and the plump man. All at different ages that looked ancient, but each with different looks on their faces. One man continued to eat in silence; his cloudy white eyes straight ahead as he spooned the gruel into his mouth. He was the cleanest of them, and the one who seemed to care the least that I was there.

Next to him was a man with a sour expression, and *if looks could kill, I would be dead where I sat.* His long grey hair and beard were tucked under his tunic, and he was quite muscular for being so old. Next to Froggy sat a man with a shiny bald head, his bowl lifted to his mouth as he scraped the dregs of his gruel into his mouth.

"Yer here for a reason." The blind man said, his voice a pleasant drawl that reminded me of my grandmother.

"Aye," I agreed. "I must confess…" I set my spoon back in the bowl. "This Cycle Winter will be hard, and I'm seeking knowledge to best prepare myself. I worry that things are not prepared enough, and I've heard that you all agree." The words spilled out of my mouth as if they came from the Gods themselves. **There was no thought, and it was easier than I thought because it was the full truth. Though, they did not need to know how I planned to use them to create more strife within the walls of Ymir's mountain.**

"So, ye are a smart lad." The man at the end of the table said condescendingly. His beady eyes flitted back and forth between me and Froggy, as though he were looking for confirmation from him, and not me. Froggy gave the man a small nod, one that was almost so small I did not see it, though he repeated it thrice.

"Occasionally, but not always." I joked, hoping to ease some of the tension.

"He's Gnar." Froggy said, pointing towards the man at the end of the table. "Pthun, Ipsra, and Jerrick." He pointed from the blind man, to the muscular angry looking man, and finally to the bald man beside him. I nodded at each of the men before looking back down at my bowl.

"This Cycle Winter," Pthun began from across the table. "Will be unlike one you have ever experienced, Alfrikr…" His tone was eery as his head turned slowly in my direction. "You will know the way. You will do what must be done."

I felt a shiver crawl down my spine; one that was unlike the curse riddled ones that typically wracked my body. I nodded in response before realizing he could not see me. Ipsra let out a snort, an angry sort of sound that reminded me of a bull. He was bullish in appearance too, so the sound was fitting.

"What do ye have prepared?" Jerrick asked, his voice a scratchy snarl.

"Erm," I cleared my throat as I set my spoon down. "New and thicker furs for a feldr. A small stash of dried meat." I shrugged my shoulders, unsure of how else to answer. "I'm not sure where else to get food, as Ivaldr keeps it locked up. I don't think there's enough anyway."

"That's all?" Froggy laughed out.

I nodded as the heat of embarrassment began to heat my face. "I've been a little distracted lately…with the curse…" I mumbled.

"Many will die; do not be one of them." Pthun's gentle drawl responded, his gaze now straight ahead of him. I shivered again as the pulse seemed to ignite with a fury. "You will doom us all if you do." **Thump, thump, thump** it sounded as it pushed its frozen pain between my ribs.

"What…what more can I do? Not just for myself, but for others?" I asked, my voice taking on a weak shake. I *knew it was too late for us, and that many would die. This was the harsh reality of Ivaldr's foolishness. Though, a part of me hoped that there was some way to circumvent many of those deaths.*

Ipsra snorted again. "There is no way. Winter is only days away; I can feel it in me bones, boy." He grunted out roughly.

I sighed heavily, shaking my head. "How could Ivaldr be so foolish?" I half groaned as I spoke. "I spent months tracking him down and urging him to prepare more. It was a pain in the arse to even get him to agree to raid the grain stores."

Froggy huffed out a small chuckle, "I think we had a larger part in that, lonely heir. I swore to curse him with blood Sacredness, though it was bad luck because it was ye who ended up with a curse."

I glanced over at him, narrowing my eyes slightly. *I knew it was unlikely that he had been the one to curse me, but this information was startling.* Jerrick laughed as he caught the look on my face, and Froggy's cheeks seemed to heat up. *Has Froggy been the reason for the curse?*

"What more is there to do but wait?" Jerrick's nasally voice rang out. "We shall commit their souls to the Gods, and hope that they spare enough of us to continue on." I nodded in agreement, taking a mouthful of my now cold gruel.

I ate in silence as the old men bickered and spoke around me, unsure of my next steps. **I had planted the seeds of my agreement, and it would be foolish to press them harder.** Spending time waiting would be the hardest part, but I could only hope to catch the men at more meals.

They held a weight about them that was not found elsewhere, even if they were an odd bunch.

The elder women held more of a weight, but I knew it would be more difficult to find a place beside them.

The women were smarter and more attuned to the games I

was about to play. I could risk my hand in getting them to join in, but it would take even more time to gain their trust. Hilda would be a good way to get closer to them, and I could make an excuse to go visit her. Yet, there was a part of me that did not want to even approach her. Her startling statements about my soul were haunting enough. *I did not need her to elaborate on what was wrong with me.*

"What say ye, Alfrikr?" Froggy croaked out from beside me.

"Huh?"

"Do ye think Ivaldr will survive the winter?"

I huffed out a small laugh. "Aye, unfortunately. He may be a foolish man, but he is the one with access to whatever he requires. He'll fatten himself up while we starve, much like my father did."

There was a sudden tension that overtook the group as I mentioned my father.

It was as if, for a moment, they had forgotten that I had once lived with such great privilege while they all suffered and starved. It was a misstep on my part, but I could only hope to come back from it.

"I spent my last Cycle Winter at the stronghold," I admitted. "There was this feeling in the air, one unlike anything I had ever felt. I was caught smuggling food to the Thralls, so my rations were cut to match theirs." I shrugged as I set my empty bowl back onto the table.

"Were ye now?" Gnar sputtered out, his voice still holding an odd shake.

I nodded my head in response, tilting it slightly as I

thought back to that winter. "If he thought it would make me change, he was mistaken. It only made me despise his treatment of our people more, and I often split my rations with a Thrall named Cor."

"Ye knew Cor?" Pthun asked quickly.

"Yes, he was the one who brought me into the rebellion."

"Aye, he was to marry my granddaughter once. Before a Jarl bought him." Pthun responded, his voice going from joyous to sad in the span of a few words.

"He died with honor," I said softly as the memories of that day seemed to trickle back. "Valhalla awaited him kindly."

I SAID my goodbyes soon after, and was on my way to my cavern when Ivaldr found me. I now walked behind him silently as we weaved through the hallways towards his section of caverns. I knew he would want to know about Esmeren, but *I was ashamed to admit that I had left rather hastily.* There was not a way to truly explain why I had suddenly left, nor why I had not gotten further information out of her. **I would have to hope that he only saw me as a brash man who didn't know how to get information out of someone.**

My cock twitched in my pants as I thought of the aftermath; *how Loreth's voice had sounded in my head as I had fisted my cock.* I was quick to adjust myself, unwilling to allow Ivaldr to see the tent that was growing in my pants. It was an unsettling feeling as I acknowledged that I felt such a deep arousal about the man I would one day kill. **Though he had cursed me and might succeed in killing me first, I still accepted how our mutual hatred fueled my desires.** *Even if it* *churned my gut with shame, I could picture myself on my knees before him.*

We veered down the last hallway before entering the main cavern of Ivaldr's rooms, and I was surprised to see Esmeren lounging on a bench near the fire. Her dark hair was braided back neatly, and she now wore a clean dress that looked too impressive to be within this mountain. She jolted as we entered, the book almost falling out of her hands.

"Alfrikr!" Esmeren called out, as if we had not just seen each other the night before. I raised an eyebrow at her, tilting my head, confused, as she rushed to stand. She was before me in only moments, grinning like I was the best thing she had ever seen. I felt my cock deflate suddenly as I stared down into her mousey face.

A rat, actually. Esmeren was more like a rat.

"Esmeren." I greeted, my voice unable to keep the disdain from flowing out.

"Ah!" Ivaldr exclaimed, clapping his hands. "Good! You're out here!"

Esmeren turned towards him, giving him a smile as a blush began to fill her cheeks. "I'm so happy that Alfrikr has agreed!"

"Wait—" I exclaimed, the shock surging within me to nearly rival the way the curse took over my body. "What? I've not agreed to anything!"

She turned on her heel, frowning with her bottom lip extended in almost a child-like way. I glared in response. **I had not agreed, nor had Ivaldr asked me.** I had thought I was coming to meet him about what I had learned. The most I had done was agree to speak with him. **Was he that dull, or was I** being manipulated to agree? Perhaps it was a mix of the two.

"Yes, yes." Ivaldr waved his hand, brushing me off. "You'll agree. You had your little test, learned that she's going to help us, and now you'll work with us." He said plainly. I grimaced and ran a hand down my face. **This was not how I believed my plan would go. I had hoped to string him along a little longer, and then finally relent when I had him where I wanted him.**

I could walk away now, but that would put me behind the rough schedule I had created for myself. There was no telling how he would react, and I could only hope that by agreeing now that he would feel a touch more at ease with me. I would take him down by the end of winter, I knew that for sure. **I needed to get closer to him, and this would be the only way to do so.**

"What..." I sighed, rubbing my temples with the tips of knuckles. "What does it entail?" I finally asked.

Esmeren let out a squeal that sounded much like the rat that she was. I cringed as the noise pierced my ears, once again glad that I had not ended up marrying her. Ivaldr clapped his hands together again before motioning towards his office.

"Follow me," he said with a wide grin. "We can talk in here!"

I groaned inwardly as I followed behind the pair, trying to gather myself internally. **I hated both of them for different reasons,** but if I wanted to overthrow Ivaldr's leadership, then I would need to learn to play nice. Each step seemed to solidify the part of me that channeled the younger Alfrikr inside of me. **I would play their games, but they would be playing mine as well.** Though, soon I needed little work to urge them on, and they would do my bidding without me asking. I opted for the seat nearest to the fire, as the chill within my bones seemed to be rising again. I suppressed the shiver inside of me the best that I could, though a small shiver still shuddered down my body.

"So…" I said, keeping the bored expression on my face. "What does it entail?" I asked again.

"We'll spend time together." Esmeren said as she bounced over to lean against Ivaldr's desk, directly in front of me. Her knees almost brushed my own as she settled against the ornate wood. I resisted the urge to recoil away from her. **Did she think we were still betrothed?** Though I could not help the curl to my lip as I stared at her. I could only hope that Esmeren didn't try to start something with me. **I would rather have my cock shrivel up and fall off than lay with her again.**

"Then you'll come with me when I go to meet with Loreth in the spring. That's when I'll share everything I've learned, except it will all be lies!" She laughed too loudly at the end, and I felt the tug at my intuition. **She was up to something, but I couldn't determine what exactly.** Esmeren was a rat…a spy that had infiltrated our ranks to further Loreth's bidding. **She had already admitted it, and I was unable to see why we would all believe that she planned to double-cross Loreth.**

I did not believe a word that she said, and I found it odd that Ivaldr had suddenly known the thing she had begged me not to tell him the night before. *It all felt…fake as I sat in that chair.* As if this were all some sort of dream that made little sense. *Did she think I was that dull?* **Was Ivaldr really that dull?** I knew the answer to both questions, but I fought to keep my expression blank. I forced out a small smile, leaning back as I looked up at her.

"What if I would rather not spend time with you?" I said, flowering my voice to a cocky drawl. **I would need to agree to work with her, but I knew it would be equally suspicious if I**

suddenly relented. Channeling younger Alfrikr was easier than I had thought, and I felt the coursing false confidence in my veins.

One day, Esmeren and Ivaldr would both kneel before me and beg for their lives as I spat in their faces.

"Erm…" Esmeren turned her head to look at Ivaldr, who only arched a brow in response. "Well," She huffed out. "That doesn't fit the plan."

"What plan?" I asked, leaning back into the chair and widening my legs. *My exterior was calm, but my innards were a scrambled mess of pain and nervousness.*

"For tricking Loreth?" She answered quietly, as if she were unsure of the answer herself.

"We know there are spies here," Ivaldr droned out, his voice an octave too nasally to truly enjoy listening to his foolish speech. "They have to see you with her if Loreth is to believe she is following his plan."

I nodded my head in response, taking a moment to gather my thoughts. **It made sense, in some sort of odd way.** I knew that there were spies because of the portrait my father had in his halls of me. Though, I wasn't sure how many nor where they were. *If Ivaldr knew about them, why was he not doing anything about it?*

"So, we what? Eat a few meals together?"

"Yes!" Esmeren exclaimed, clapping her hands together excitedly. The disdain was challenging to hold in as I watched her practically shake in excitement. It was annoying—plain and simple. **Her entire being annoyed me, and I dreaded**

spending any time with her. Where there was once an undying love now lay a hateful remorse. *I would never get those years that I wasted with her back, though a part of me wondered what I ever saw in her.*

"That is all?" I raised my eyebrow as I asked, not willing to fully believe that it was that simple.

"Perhaps a few outings here and there. Just be seen with her in a friendly way." Ivaldr smoothed his beard as he spoke, though it did little to tame his unruly thin beard.

The sharp pain in my chest continued to grow as I sat, and I could only assume that it would lead to another encounter with Loreth. With a heavy sigh, I nodded my head. "If I agree, I want a bigger role in the rebellion. I won't do your bidding blindly." I confessed.

I couldn't help but notice how Ivaldr narrowed his eyes at me for a half second before his face twisted into a smile. He nodded his head as though he agreed with me. Esmeren made a sound that could only be described as a rat caught by the tail as she leaped off the desk and tumbled into my lap. **With a grunt, and a hidden urge to shove her off, I wrapped my arms around her.** Her arms wound around my neck as she buried her face into the side of my neck, much like she used to when we were younger.

"Thank you! Thank you!" She whispered, her lips dragging against the skin of my neck with each word. I shivered as a jolt of sharp, cold pain overtook my entire chest. I tried to heave in a breath, but my lungs felt frozen solid. Esmeren was quick to scramble out of my lap as the pain overtook me, my body flushing with a frozen cold, and a shiver overtaking my ability to move.

"Alfrikr?" Esmeren and Ivaldr said at once, their voices harmonizing together as if it were a song.

"I… I…should go." My voice stuttered out as my tongue felt frozen. I stumbled up, bracing myself on the arms of the chair. My vision went in and out as I stood there, swaying slightly.

"You should lay down!" Esmeren shrieked, her squeaky-rat like voice piercing my eardrums.

"No."

Ivaldr was slow to respond, and my vision faded in and out as he made his way around the desk. I took a deep breath, holding it through the pain, and let go of the chair. My body swayed slightly as my muscles seemed to go weak in time with the pulsing pain.

"Sit down!" Esmeren shrieked. I shook my head as I forced myself to take a step towards the door. Ivaldr grabbed Esmeren's arm as I passed, holding her in place as she tried to rush towards me.

"Let him go." He mumbled to her, loud enough that I could hear.

I was in a daze as my vision filtered in and out in time with the cold shock that pulsed rapidly in my chest. I wasn't sure how long I walked before I began to use the stone wall for support. Each step felt harder than the last, and my breath seemed harder and harder to catch. *All I could focus on was the ice-cold pain and the fact that if I were to die, I wanted it to be within the confines of my cavern.* I would not die at the feet of another, especially not Ivaldr or Esmeren.

My body shivered and shook as I stumbled through hallways with only small flashes of my surroundings. Left turn, right turn, straight before I finally pulled back my curtain. I made it one step, two steps, three steps before everything went black.

22

CINNAMON AND CEDAR

I SLOWLY PRIED MY EYES OPEN AS THE FAMILIAR FEELING OF drifting in the endless void came over me. My body felt nearly refreshed, lacking the distinct pulse I had gotten used to. I stared out into the never-ending black that surrounded me, turning my head as if I would suddenly see. **Dark. Warm. Safe. I was safe. I am safe.**

I was protected. I am protected.

I was warm. I am warm.

Faint touches began to wrap around my middle, as if I were being tied by soft-silken ropes. *One,* **two,** *three* times they spun around my body. Down my arms, across my legs. *Safe. Safe. Safe.* Calm began to seep into my bones through those wisps that swirled and covered my body in a cocoon. *Protected. Safe. Calm. Safe. Safe. Calm.*

Where was I? The thought drifted away before I could focus on it. *Thinking? Was I thinking? Safe. Safe. Safe.*

Warmth spread over my body, a feeling that I had missed since the onslaught of the curse. *Warm. Safe. Warm.* I longed to stay here, where I was warm and safe. *Darkness. Darkness all around me.* **Warm. Warmth cursing through my veins.** *Calm. Calmness deep in my bones.* **Safe. Safe. Protected.**

The Gods. *The Gods would protect me. They would save me.* **The curse.** *The curse.* **The curse.** *Cold.* **Cold. Cold.** *Pain.* **Pain. Pain.**

Threes. God's blessed number. **Threes of everything, threes** *of all.*

Waves crashing against a shore began to filter into the darkness. *A beach? My father's stronghold. The barrier.* **Water. Water. Water. Three. Three. Three.**

They were harsh, and loud as I continued to drift, disrupting the warmth I found in the silent darkness. *Cold.* **Cold.** *Cold.* Specks of water hit my body as the waves thundered down. **Cold.** *Cold.* Cold. The cold water began to slosh at my feet suddenly. *Cold.* Cold. **Cold.** Three breaths in of salty air, three breaths out. *Three. Three.* **Three.**

Where was I? *Where? Where?* **Where?**

Who was I? *Who? Who?* **Who?**

Cold. Cold. Cold. Three. Three. Three.

I sucked in a large breath as the world brightened around me, flashing the beach behind my father's stronghold into my vision. I looked down to find my body, thankful that it was there. ***Where was I?*** I wore the clothes that I once owned, many years ago, while I still lived within the stronghold. Shiny, clean, and expensive boots. A pristine and soft tunic tucked into clean and thick trousers. My short-sword that I had left behind was strapped to my hip, and my bag clinked with coins as I shifted my stance.

Where was I? Why was I here? **Did Loreth linger somewhere in the distance?** *Waiting for his chance to take me down?* **Could he kill me in this strange reality?** *I didn't want to know.*

One *breath,* **two** *breath,* **three** *breaths.* **Look. Look. Look.**

I could see the barrier from where I stood, the one that kept us locked inside the borders of Sidirna. It spanned from deep under the waters up to as far as I could see. **Deep. Deep. Deep.**

The barrier shone against the dark clouds that covered the sky, and I could see the reflective rainbows shining deep under the thunderous waves. I wanted to tear it down, but I had no idea how I could do so. Leaving Sidirna sounded nice, but I would need to stay and lead our people. **Run. Run. Run.**

I started off down the beach, walking in the direction that seemed to call to me. *It was odd, all of this was odd.* **Odd. Odd. Odd.** I didn't know where I was, but I knew that I still lived.

There was a tug to my gut as I walked, urging me to continue forward. The waves still crashed to my right, soaking my side with the spray that flew off. **Splash. Splash. Splash.**

I folded my arms over my chest as the chill of the wind began to seep into me, it was such a different feeling than the curse. Yet, cold all the same. **Cold. Cold. Cold.**

The sand beneath my feet seemed to give with each step, leaving clean indentations of each step that I took. Loreth would find me easily like this. **Run. Run. Run.**

My mind felt hazier than usual, as if the darkness had seeped inside of me only to make thinking harder. I felt my surroundings, but anything more than observing felt harder. **One** step, **two** steps, **three** steps. **Three felt important,** *but I couldn't remember why.*

Three. Three. Three.

Through the haze in the distance, there was a dark shadow moving towards me. **Faster. Faster. Faster.** I wanted to **run**, but instead my feet came to a *stop.*

Loreth. **Loreth. Loreth.** *I had to find Loreth.* Though, I couldn't remember why, but my gut forced me towards the shadow again. **One** step, **two** step, **three** steps.

Three. Three. Three.

"Alfrikr! Come out, come out, from wherever you are!" The shadow called out, his voice a gruff shout.

Loreth. Loreth. Loreth.

My feet continued to move without a single thought until I stood mere feet away from the shadow. A powerful wave of heat burned through my body as soon as my eyes met those deep, soulless eyes. The haze lifted as I felt my heart begin to pound erratically within my chest. Loreth stood before me with a snarl-like grin on his face.

"You listen well. What a good boy you are." Loreth said in a condescending tone.

"How do you keep doing this?" I said between gritted teeth as the flames inside of me burned hotter.

I felt the urge to throw my fist into his face just as my cock twitched at his words.

"Hmm?" He arched his brow.

I waved my arms around as I gestured around the beach. "This? Entering my mind? Making dreams?"

"So, you dream of me often?" Another snarl-like grin appeared on his face as he stared at me.

I wasn't sure if Loreth was trying to be intimidating, or if his smile truly looked so...*menacing?* I knew there was not much that I could do in this situation, much like when he entered my mind. *I wasn't completely sure if I could kill him—either in this dream land or through brute strength.*

I needed to be **stronger**. *Stronger. Stronger. Stronger.*

"Yes, you always look so pitiful as you take your last breath." I snarked back, trying to keep the flush from my face at his insinuations.

"Is that so?" Loreth drawled out, his voice seeming to drop an octave lower as a grin slowly appeared on his face.

Talking to Loreth was like talking to the wind, I spoke but got nothing to respond to. A flare of burning pain flared in my chest, and I gasped as my hand flew to cover it. What had once been ice-cold, was now hot. A scream began to form as the ribbons of hot pain wound through my ribs.

"What's wrong with you?"

My knees wobbled beneath me before I sunk into sand on them. Each one of my ribs felt as though fire consumed them, my lungs felt full of scorching flames, and the center of my chest felt as though a hot dagger was piercing it. A loud groan escaped my lips as I hung my head, breathing through the pain the best I could.

The curse had come for me in a new way, one that almost made me miss the cold.

Loreth was silent as he approached me, but a deep tug in me senses his closeness. I tilted my head up just as he stood before me, towering over me in such a powerful way. He was barely taller than me when we stood near each other, but while I was on my knees he looked like a giant. My body shuddered as another dose of fiery pain shot through my chest, and *I was reminded of the thought I had recently had.*

Now I knew how it felt to be on my knees before Loreth, and I wasn't sure how I felt about it. Pain enveloped my body in such a way that thinking with my cock was *nearly* impossible. Flames swirled inside of me, weaving through my ribs before they clutched my heart.

"Finally dying?"

I shook my head in response, knowing that my voice would sound *weak*. A gust of wind blew Loreth's hair, almost making him look attractive. We stared at each other for what felt like an eternity. His onyx black eyes held no emotion, **no soul**, and they filled me with a *fear* I couldn't explain. It was a moment I'd never forget; me on my knees shaking as pain overtook my body, and Loreth standing over me with an air of **strength** and **confidence**.

"If you wanted to suck my cock, all you had to do was ask. No need for the dramatics, Lonely Heir." He ended with a laugh, one that caused a shudder to tear through my body.

The burning flare in my chest pulsed rapidly as it sent more hot pain into my body. The center of my chest burned the hottest as the pain radiated from that centermost location. I gasped as Loreth's hand shot out, landing on the top of my head. As soon as the fiery pain had overtaken me, it was gone. His hand covered most of my head, and I felt my cock awaken at his touch.

With one hand on my head, Loreth used the other to hurriedly unbuckle his trousers. I heaved in a breath, trying to steady my breathing as my body recovered from the burning beating it had just taken. Loreth's hand was steady, while mine shook in my lap. I wasn't sure how I felt as my emotions battled inside of me. I wanted this, but he was my enemy.

I wanted his cock in my mouth, **but *I also wanted to watch him die at my feet.***

My eyes shifted from his crotch to his face, where I met his soulless eyes. We said nothing as we stared at each other with understanding. With a grunt, Loreth shoved the material down. I couldn't help but lick my lips as I took in the view before me; black hair that curled around the base of his thickness, a thick vein that pulsed, and finally, where a bead of liquid pooled at the head. My mouth watered in anticipation as my cock began to quickly and painfully harden. I resisted the urge to shove my hand into my trousers, knowing that I would not last long.

"Open" He said gruffly as he smacked my lips with the

head of his cock. A small moan escaped me at the feeling of the soft head. I may have *detested* the idea that he was **stronger** than me, but the thought of him overpowering me was just as attractive. The fingers of his other hand dug into my scalp as he pulled me towards him. There was no thought behind my jaw dropping as I willingly leaned closer. "Good boy." Loreth grunted out as he directed his cock into my mouth.

Loreth wasn't slow, nor was he gentle, as his cock roughly invaded my mouth. My jaw began to ache at how far I had it stretched open, and I knew that the ache would only grow worse. His musky scent consumed me as I tried to drop my jaw further, hollowing my cheeks instead. His cock filled my mouth entirely, and I struggled to sweep my tongue around to explore him.

I moaned around his length as it neared the back of my throat. Loreth may be an unredeemable man, but his cock was certainly his best quality. A sharp pain shot through my jaw, my cock twitching at the pain. I took a deep breath through my nose, taking in his cinnamon and cedar aroma, as he shoved his cock further into my mouth. I wouldn't last long, but I knew it would be a powerful finish. A moan slipped out as I gagged around his cock, his head pressing into the back of my throat.

"Deeper." Loreth's voice commanded, his tone filled with authority. I was sure it was the voice he used when he commanded the guard, and that thought made my hips buck as I gave him an eager suck. My balls were already tightening as I tried to blow my load early.

I wasn't sure if his entire length would fit in my mouth, but I still pushed forward until it hit the back of my throat. I buried my nose deep into his musk filled hairs and moaned at the scent. I was sure the Norns were laughing at me for how much I longed to smell him always. The taste of his pre-seed began to fill my mouth, causing a deep moan to grumble through me. I was close to finishing already, and he had not even fucked my mouth properly. Loreth tasted better than he smelled, and he smelled incredibly good.

Loreth held his cock deep in my throat as I gagged and swallowed around the thick head. Tears leaked out of my eyes, and I resisted the urge to fist my cock as I choked on him. I was already close, and I knew one touch would end me. Darkness started to blot my vision, and it was the best feeling I had ever experienced. A small surge of disgust ran through me as I accepted the idea that *I was eagerly and happily sucking the cock of the man who had cursed me.*

He was fast as he pulled his cock back, allowing me less than a second to breathe before he slammed it back in. I moaned deep in my chest as he held his cock as far as it would go. Loreth growled in response, his nails digging deeper into my scalp. My vision blurred, my eyes fluttering closed as darkness threatened to overtake my vision. My cock twitched and bobbed in my trousers, and I ached to touch myself. *I wanted Loreth's thick hands wrapped around my cock as he fucked me. I ached to feel his thickness inside of me,* and the thought shamed me to admit.

Loreth growled out another moan as he slowly pulled his cock out of my mouth. I blinked through the tears as I heaved in breaths. His cock bobbed where it rested against my lips. How could such an evil man be so appealing? I swiped my tongue out and collected the pre-seed and spit that coated my lips. I eagerly opened my mouth and took the head of his cock back into my mouth. Loreth's moan only encouraged me to suck harder, swirling my tongue around his leaking head. He was quick to thrust himself until he was fully seated inside my mouth again.

Loreth held his cock deep in my throat, his nails seeming to dig even harder into my head. My cock ached as I felt the pressure almost building until I burst. My vision began to blur and darken, and I let out a weak moan. He pulled his cock back again, letting me heave in two breaths before pushing himself back in. I gagged harshly as he began to fuck my mouth. His strokes were steady, but rough as he pounded the back of my throat.

I moaned around his cock as I tried to suck harder. My jaw and neck ached from the position, but *I didn't want this to end too soon.* I felt as my pre-seed leaked from my cock and began to soak my trousers. I would **one day kill the man,** but for now, *I was happy to suck him off.* Perhaps I would fuck him too before that day came.

"Fuck." Loreth moaned out as he began to guide my head, still pumping into my mouth.

Tears streamed down my face as I sucked his cock eagerly. My vision began to darken again, and I felt my cock bob eagerly as I struggled to breathe. His cinnamon and cedar scent consumed me as each breath took it in. My hands began to tingle as darkness threaded to overtake my vision completely. A spark of euphoria shot down my spine as I felt myself tumbling closer and closer to completion.

"Look at you," Loreth grunted out, quickening his pace. "The heir of Sidirna on his knees before me, taking my cock like the good little bitch that he is."

My balls tightened, and I moaned deeply as the pressure exploded inside of me. My brain went hazy as I filled my trousers with my seed.

"Pathetic." Loreth moaned out. His pace quickened until it

was almost unbearable. I moaned in response, as my body slackened to the point where it was difficult to keep myself upright. My vision faded in and out, almost in sync with his thrusts. With a final guttural moan, he filled my mouth with his salty seed. I gagged as the thick liquid began to pour down my throat and into my mouth.

He was slow to pull his cock out, and I groaned in relief as I was finally able to close my aching jaw. "Swallow." He commanded, his voice causing a shiver to run down my spine. I pried my eyes open, staring deep into his soulless pits as I gagged through a swallow. My jaw flared in pain as I opened my mouth before sticking my tongue out. I heaved breaths in and out as I stared up at him, not trusting my body to move.

Loreth hummed softly to himself as he leaned down to pull his trousers up. *It was the same lullaby tune that he had hummed inside of my head.* I could barely think as I kneeled on the cold sand, still trying to catch my breath. Shame and disgust threatened to overtake me as I came down from my high. *I had just sucked Loreth's cock and liked it.*

No, I loved it. I would do it again and again until the day came that I watched him die a slow and painful death.

THE START OF WINTER

23

DAWN AND PARCHMENT

MY BODY ACHED AS MY EYES STRUGGLED TO OPEN, THE STONE floor cold beneath my body. The ceiling spun above me as I dazedly blinked. **Loreth.** *I had sucked Loreth's cock and liked it.* I huffed out a groan, bringing my hands up to press into the sockets of my eyes. Shame and disgust filled me as memories of what happened assaulted my mind. Yet, my cock twitched in my trousers as the memory of his scent. Cinnamon and cedar would forever be tainted. I was sore as I moved to stand, but thankful that my jaw did not hold the soreness it would have if it had not been a dream.

Was it a dream? I wasn't entirely sure, seeing as my trousers were filled with the evidence. *I briefly wondered if Loreth had awoken with dried seed plastered to his skin and clothes.* I shook the thought of the man away as dread began to fill my veins. *What was wrong with me? How could I long to kill someone just as much as I wanted to lay with him? It was abhorrent, dishonorable, and unredeemable. Loreth had killed many, tortured innocent people, and cursed me!* **Yet, a part of me longed for the next dream that he invaded.** I continued to berate myself as I cleaned myself up, burying the evidence deep under the pile of dirty clothes.

The thought of food was not appealing, yet I knew that I would need to go to the hall. **My plans could not wait, just because I was filled with such self-hatred.** It should have filled me with renewed energy. Given me another motive to enact my plans so that I could be the one to tear Loreth down. Unfortunately for me, it did not work out that way. *I only* *wanted to hide away in my cavern until thoughts of Loreth no longer consumed me.* The walk to the hall was short, and I was glad to see the group of grouchy old men in the same place as yesterday. I was lucky to have awoken at the right time, as there were no others in the line for the morning meal.

Finnian's wife stood at the counter, though I wasn't sure I ever knew her name. I would have to ask Dallen if he knew it. She gave me a tense smile as I approached, and I knew it was because of who I was. *Horrible name, horrible lineage, and I was a horrible person.*

"Yer loud friend already ate." She said tersely.

"Aye," I responded as I took the bowl from her outstretched hands. "He does love an early meal." I mumbled, unsure of how else to respond. *Dull, I was a dull man.*

"Tried for seconds, he did." She added with a humph.

"May the Gods be with you." I mumbled in response as I turned to leave. Was I that **horrible** at conversations, as I had no idea what to say to that either? *Dull and horrible.*

"And you, you'll need them this winter."

I wasn't sure what that meant either, and **I wanted to bash my head into the wall as I tried to figure it out.** *Was it because I was cursed?* I was sure that everyone knew, but I did not need their pity. It could have been because it was a Cycle Winter, but I doubted that.

"Back for more?" Pthun greeted me as I sank beside him. I wasn't sure how he knew it was me.

"I fear you lot are the only ones left with sense." I muttered in response as the *dread* of interacting with others settled into the pit of my stomach.

"The Cycle has begun, poor boy. We are all doomed." Ipsra grunted out. His voice was rough, and his face was contorted into a menacing scowl.

"Has it now?"

"Aye," Jerrick's nasal lined voice made me cringe, only slightly. "The grass was lined with frost during my morning walk."

"Ye go on walks in the morning?" Froggy croaked out.

These men were an odd bunch, but I could appreciate how they had allowed me to sit with them as if I were one of them. Though, perhaps I was as odd as them.

I spooned a mouthful of gruel into my mouth as I watched the two men bicker.

"You know this!" Jerrick slammed his spoon into his bowl. "You come with me all the time!"

"On night walks. I walk with you at night." Froggy's eyebrows furrowed as he spoke through a mouthful of gruel.

"I don't go on night walks! I walk at dawn!"

"How can it be dawn if the sun has not yet risen?" Froggy countered, bits of gruel fell from his mouth and onto his beard.

"It rises during the walk!" Jerrick's voice only got more nasally as he yelled, and I wanted to cover my ears. **How could a man have such an awful voice?** *If I were him, I would never speak again.*

"Oh, shut up, would ya?" Ipsra growled out. He pointed his sloshing spoon between the old men, flinging gruel in the process. I grunted out in agreement as I flinched away from the flying food.

"Night." Froggy muttered under his breath, barely audible. Pthun chuckled, but Jerrick did not seem to hear him.

In the back of my mind, I knew that I would need to find

Dallen soon. We usually didn't go long without speaking, and it had felt like an eternity since I had seen him last. I hoped that his problems were settled so that I could truly discuss what I was to do with Esmeren with him. I knew that Ivaldr and her would expect me to be seen with her soon, though I was unsure how it would affect my plans. I feared that I would not be able to get as close to the right people if they believed me to be a traitor as they did her. There were many within the rebellion who still viewed me as such, and it was evident in the way that they treated me. I sighed heavily as I scraped the last of my gruel onto my spoon.

"Something troubling you?" Pthun asked gently, his elbow nudging my side softly.

"Just my worries for the winter." I half lied. It was true that this winter I would need to get a lot done, but Pthun did not need to know that.

"There's not much else to be done, Alfrikr." He said quietly. "We must band together and help where we can. But we cannot fix what we cannot control."

I grunted in response, unsure of how to respond. I felt dull and slow this morning, and it was not until then that I noticed that the curse did not pulse through my chest. **I did not feel cold, nor did I feel hot. I felt normal.** I'd finally gotten a moment of relief from the curse. I had been so consumed with my thoughts that I had not noticed. *Dull. I was a dull and horrible man.*

"What say you, Lonely Heir?" Froggy croaked out. I jolted as I looked up at him.

"About?"

"Does the moon shine at dawn?" Jerrick asked as he leaned forward, his eyes narrowing as he stared at me. ***Great, I was to be the decider in some decrepit old man spat.***

"Depends on the cycle." I answered with a shrug, hoping it was sufficient.

"Aha!" Froggy shouted. He did a shuffle as he sat, an odd movement that almost resembled a dance.

Ipsra groaned out a growl from where he sat, clearly annoyed at it all. "Bunch'a children." He muttered as he shook his head. "May the Gods be with you." He added as he slowly pushed himself up to stand.

He left his bowl and spoon at his spot, and I made a mental note to bring it with me when I left. There was a pull at my intuition as I watched the man shuffle away. *I knew he would be important, but I wasn't quite sure why.*

I would soon know exactly why I'd felt that way, but it would be near the middle of winter when I found out why.

"And you!" I shouted after him, longing to leave as well. Ipsra turned slightly, nodding his head at me. His face held no expression in a way that reminded me of Loreth. *The thought of Loreth reminded me of what I had done, and shame and disgust shuddered through my body.*

"Grumpy old fool!" Froggy shouted at the man. Ipsra continued on, not turning to give any inclination that he had heard the decrepit fool.

"It will snow soon." Pthun said, his voice a steady drawl. He brought one hand into the air as he spoke, spinning his wrist in circles.

Pthun's hands were thin, with gnarled knuckles that looked to be thrice the size they should be. His fingers moved rapidly, as if he were using his Sacredness. His wrist circled slowly in a rhythm of threes. I was transfixed on the movements as I thought of how the number three seemed to haunt me. During that dream, at the beach, I had been consumed with the urge to do everything thrice.

"Let us hope that the fool Ivaldr does not plan a feast to celebrate. He will doom us all if he does." Pthun muttered as his other hand moved to join. Both hands spun in sync, but the fingers of each moved differently.

"You feel it?" Froggy whispered in a hushed croak.

"That I do. Deeply and thoroughly." Pthun responded.

Jerrick let out a squeak of a sound as he scrambled to collect his bowl and spoon. His movements were slow, shaky, and held the weight of his age as he tried to move quickly. The man did not say a word as he slowly rose to stand, and shuffled away.

"He gets nervous." Froggy commented, pointing one decrepit hand in the direction of the man. "Thinks he's going to die soon, but he's been sayin' that for years now."

I nodded in response, understanding exactly how that felt. This winter would be hard, but I had a feeling that this curse would be harder. Though, it had not latched itself back into my bones yet. I was hesitant to believe that it had gone away completely, but instead feared that it slumbered deep inside of me. **I couldn't wait to kill Loreth, and I hoped that freed me from it.** *I wasn't sure what I would do if not.*

"May the Gods be with you." I said as I stood, collecting my bowl and spoon. I snagged Ipsra's on my way past, and nodded at Froggy. Neither of the men said anything as I left, and it almost felt like an omen.

THE WALK to Dallen's cavern was quick, though I was not surprised that the man was not there. There was no telling where he was. I could wait for him in his cavern, but that felt like wasting time. Time that felt suddenly stretched too thin as the Cycle of Winter was fast approaching. *There was much to do, and I dreaded every minute of it.* My priority right now needed to be tracking down my best friend and making sure he knew why I was about to be seen with Esmeren. I knew myself well enough to know that keeping myself occupied would distract me from thoughts of **Loreth.** Yet, my mind had already drifted back to him as I closed Dallen's curtain behind me. It was an odd feeling as I continued to justify and lie to myself. *Loreth had to be good for something, right?*

He had *cursed* me, and that gave me every right to think of him **however I pleased.** Whether I imagined him **dying** or I imagined him *thrusting in and out of me.* A groan slipped out of me as I turned the corner, and stomped down the hallway. I wanted to hate him, and I did hate him. Every fiber of my being hated the man, but I couldn't deny that I wanted him on such an **animalistic** level. It was an urge that soared through me, much like hunger. It pained me to admit that *I looked forward to the next time I saw him, to admit that I would fist my cock at the next opportunity to remember how he overpowered me.*

I stopped and paused in the middle of a common cavern near the training hall. A familiar **thump, thump, thump** had begun to pulse inside my chest. Though, it lacked the distinct frozen chill that usually wove its way through my body. *The curse was returning.* I wanted to scream and claw at my chest in hopes to tear the dastardly thing from my chest. **Fuck.** *Fuck, fuck!* I didn't have time for this, and I hadn't had enough relief from the pain I knew was going to settle deep within me. No longer did the animalistic need to fuck Loreth course through my veins, as it was replaced with the animalistic urge to **tear his heart from his chest.** My hands began to shake as I stood, resisting the urge to pound them into my skull.

"Good day," someone spoke from behind me. I spun on my heel quickly, and huffed out a breath as I took in the woman before me.

"G'day." I muttered in response. I racked my brain as I tried to figure out who she was, or if I even had seen her before. Seeing as there was a lack of structure within the rebellion, it wasn't odd to come across someone I'd never met.

"**Are you lost?**" She asked as she brushed the brown curls that had fallen in her face.

"No." *What an odd thing to ask?* There were directions carved into the walls that ensured no one would get lost. *Did she think I didn't know that?*

"**You look lost.**" Her eyebrows furrowed as she frowned at me. I couldn't help the expression on my face as confusion and anger began to build.

"How does one look lost?" I bit out, placing a hand on my hip as I stared down at her. She was short, thin, and her clothes were threadbare. Her hood was slung over her head, and it hung so low that her face was hardly visible. *The woman had to be new here, and I knew she most likely had no clue who I was.*

She gestured at me with a single finger that traced up and down my body before she shrugged. "Like that."

"I-I... What?!" I sputtered out, shaking my head as I began to turn away from her. My feet were fast as I shuffled away, the pulse in my chest thumping alongside my heartbeat.

Odd, it was odd. I couldn't help but feel that there was something suspicious going on. *People didn't talk to me,* especially not in such an offhanded kind of way. There was a possibility that she didn't know who I was, but I assumed that **she was a** spy. **Had Loreth sent her? Could Loreth connect to her mind in the same way he did mine.**

If I could go back, I'd spend more time thinking about who I'd talked to that day.

"**<u>Alfrikr</u>**," The woman said, breaking me from my thoughts. "**<u>Winter is fast approaching. You must survive the winter.</u>**"

A sense of great power washed over me as I turned to face the woman again, only to find her *fading away.* My jaw slackened as I watched her form slowly fade out of existence. *What the Hel?* I shook my head, rubbed my eyes, and continued to stare at the spot in which she had just stood.

"Hello?" I whispered cautiously, peering around the room.

It was impossible. There was no logical way that she could have…*disappeared? Faded away? I didn't understand, and it unsettled me.* Her appearances did not align with any Goddess I could think of, but there had been a powerful presence? My steps were quiet and quick as I half-ran to where she once stood.

Nothing but a scrap of parchment remained, *the same one I had crumpled and thrown in the library.* A bind rune; **algiz, gebo, and dagaz.** I didn't know what it meant, but it now felt a lot more important than it had the last time I'd seen it. I'd seen it before, but I couldn't remember where. My hands shook as I folded it neatly, and shoved it into the pouch at my hip. *What the Hel? I hadn't imagined it, or had I? Was the curse taking my mind from me as well?* There was no way I would tell anyone about this, but a part of me wanted to confide in someone to find out if I had gone insane. *Was I as odd and foolish as the old* *men I ate with? Did I look the same as Pthun had this morning with his odd hand movements?*

"Alfrikr?" Ivaldr's voice rang out from behind me.

I straightened my back as I turned, plastering a false smile on my face. *How the Hel had he found me in a random common cavern?*

"Ivaldr!" I greeted, my tone laced with a false nicety that made me want to gag. "I was just on my way to the training caverns."

"Aye, I was just looking for you there. I was about to head to your cavern next." He tutted out. His eyes narrowed for a half moment as he examined me. I pushed my shoulders out in response, standing as tall as I could. **Two could play at this game, and I was certain to be the winner.** I knew he was a petty and foolish man. One that would puff his chest more so that he felt bigger than me. **This time I would not succumb to his whims.**

"Feeling better, are you?" His question was long and drawn out, as he did exactly as I had guessed. Ivaldr's back could straighten no more, so he walked himself to one of the benches against the wall.

"Aye, it was just a one-off." I stayed where I stood, not willing to sit next to the man. While I knew Ivaldr felt as though he were more important, **it was him who now had to look up at me to meet my eyes.**

"Is that so?" He hummed out, twisting the hairs of his patchy beard. "Tomorrow morning, you will go out with Esmeren."

"Okay." I responded with a simple shrug. Ivaldr's face contorted as he sat silent for a moment, as though he had expected me to argue. I knew there was little point in arguing. **I needed to lure the man into a false sense of security by the**

end of winter. The winter that I needed to survive. *I shivered at the thought of the strange woman.*

"You'll eat a morning meal together, and go for a walk outside." He nodded as he spoke, as though it were a great plan.

"Okay."

"That's all?" He sputtered out, almost cringing back. "I thought you'd have more…oomph?"

I couldn't help the smile that formed on my face as I congratulated myself for knowing exactly how his thoughts formed. **I knew that he was a simple, foolish man.** Yet, I was almost amazed at how easy it was to guess his next move. Perhaps my years within the rebellion helped me understand him better. I heard the sound of footsteps shuffling nearby, and I turned my head to peer at each hallway. *Each of the three entries were dark, and I couldn't tell which one the sounds came from.*

"I am a man of my word, and I gave you my word. I will work with her, on my honor."

Ivaldr hummed softly to himself, his fingers working the hairs faster. *It was an ugly sight, one that made me second guess my habit of fiddling with the hair on my face.* The shuffling sounded again, and I whipped my head in the direction. *Someone was listening in on us.* I peered at the entryway the closest to where Ivaldr sat, slightly to my right. There was no movement, but I couldn't be certain with how dark it was. I sucked in a deep breath as the pulse began to thunder louder within my chest. The curse was settling back in. I had to find Dallen, and this was wasting my time.

There was no telling how long I had before the

curse hit the point of no return, one of those dreams with Loreth.

I also needed to head to the library to find out more about this bind rune. I needed to figure out whom I had seen, and why she had come to me.

"Very well," he finally said. "Why don't you take a walk with me so we may discuss this more?" He asked in a way that gave me no choice but to agree. Another shuffle sounded from my right, and I thought *I caught a glimpse of something moving.* **I wanted to bash Ivaldr's head in.** I could do it, and be quick about it. Yet, I knew that it would do nothing to ensure the people would follow me. Plus, whoever was lurking around the corner would witness it. **So, instead of bashing his head in,** *I nodded in agreement. The Gods were laughing at me, I was sure of it. They were bound to know what I had planned, but instead I would be stuck with Ivaldr.*

"Where to?" I asked as he pushed himself to stand.

"Towards my cavern?" Ivaldr called out, a little too loudly for my comfort. *He knew someone was listening, and I was sure he knew that I was aware.*

I pursed my lips, nodding in response. That was the opposite direction in which I needed to go, and I could only hope to find Dallen before the end of the day. It also took us away from whoever spied on us. **Ivaldr was a fool by how easily he implicated himself.**

"What else is there to discuss?" It was difficult to keep my voice calm, and kind. I wanted to snap, and deep breaths did nothing to help calm the storm within me. *It was a familiar feeling, but one I had not felt for anyone besides Loreth in quite some time.*

"How are you feeling?" Ivaldr asked with a hum.

*I should have bashed his head in then and there.
If I could go back, I would have done it then and
there. Then I would have turned around and grabbed
the man who lurked in the shadows and shook him
until he told me the truth.*

"Alfrikr? Ivaldr?" Doran's voice rang out from behind us as he entered the common cavern. I'd wished it had been his twin, but a familiar face was welcome.

"Doran!" I called out, the chipper tone of my voice almost made me cringe. *It was too much, I needed to tone it down with him.* Doran knew me better than Ivaldr, and I knew that he would sniff me out quickly. He thought too much, while Ivaldr did not think enough.

Doran eyed me for a moment, his face blank. A tell-tale sign of his already developing suspicion. Ivaldr greeted him as he came to stand between us.

"I'm feeling much better," I directed towards Ivaldr. "It's as if the curse has been lifted!"

Doran **recoiled** in a way I had never seen before. His entire body seemed to move as he frantically looked me up and down. He did not say a word, but I assumed he was excited to hear. It was a baldfaced lie, as I currently felt the pulsing deep within my chest. Yet, I plastered a smile upon my face as I gazed between the men.

"I feel like a brand-new man." I added as a way to break the awkward tension that threatened to fill the space.

"That's... Great?" Ivaldr mumbled out, turning to look at

Doran. The men exchanged a nod, one that pulled at my intuition. *There was something amiss, and I wasn't sure what.*

"Shall we?" I asked, gesturing towards the doorway.

"A-actually," Ivaldr stuttered. "I must discuss something else with Doran. We'll talk later."

I knew I was right, and I knew there was something going on. I also knew there was nothing I could do, and it only stoked my desire to find Dallen. He might know. I nodded at the two men as they began to leave, Doran giving me a regal wave. *It all felt a little too much. The dream with Loreth. The woman. Ivaldr. Doran.* I shook my head, not sure where exactly to start. I didn't have an opportunity to dissect my thoughts, it would have to wait until tonight when I was alone. I let out a heavy sigh as I let my shoulders drop, not needing to stand so upright now. There was an ache in my left shoulder that I knew stemmed from my sleeping on the stone floor.

DALLEN WAS NOT in the training hall. He was not in the main hall. Nor was he in his cavern. I wanted to scream his name while I wandered the mountain. There were not many other places he would be, I thought. I had no idea where Asher and Kraka lived, or I would go there. I flexed my hands as the ache of closing my hands in tight fists began to set in. At one point during my fruitless wandering, the curse had begun to ache again. The cold began to settle into my bones, and I was fighting off shivers. **I wanted to throttle Dallen when I found him because I had wasted those few hours of feeling natural on looking for him.** I couldn't help but stomp as I marched my way back to my cavern; my day had been utterly wasted.

It was nearing evening meal now, and I knew I did not have it in me to be surrounded by others. Wasting more hours didn't mean much when the day had already been spent doing nothing. My legs were tired, my shoulder ached, and I was mentally exhausted. Anger still coursed through me, and I knew sleep would not be easy.

24

PITY AND SNOW

I WAS CORRECT IN THINKING I WOULD TOSS AND TURN ALL NIGHT. By the time morning came, I'd felt more exhausted than I had when I had first settled under the covers. Dawn was nearing, and the dread that came with it churned my gut enough that I felt it bubble up my throat. I wasn't sure how the morning would go with Esmeren. *I wasn't confident in my ability to pretend as if I wanted to be around her,* **but I knew it had to be done.** Most of the night had been spent thinking of the woman —the one who had disappeared and left me the bind rune. I'd stared at the parchment long enough that I had begun to see it when I closed my eyes.

I had no idea who she was, what she wanted, or what the bind rune meant. **Algiz** was meant for protection, but **I did not feel protected.** *Gebo* was a gift, but *I had gotten no gifts, only a curse.* *Dagaz* was a new beginning. *That was the one that I could relate to. Seeing as I was cursed now, that was sure a poor new beginning.*

Then there were the thoughts of what Doran and Ivaldr were up to, and I had come to the conclusion that it was about Esmeren. Doran had always supported our betrothal, and there would be no surprises if he assumed we would still be. I couldn't exactly figure out why he had hid when he could have arrived with Ivaldr. *It all felt odd, and my intuition was screaming that they were up to something together.* I had hoped to eat with the old men again to gather more information, but I would have to hope that I caught them tomorrow morning. *As long as Ivaldr didn't have any other plans for me.* I groaned as I threw my covers back, exposing myself to the cold air. The cold had seeped back into my body, but it did not feel as harsh as it once had. I knew that only time would tell if it followed some type of schedule, but I'd hoped that it would remain this faint.

I was quick to light a fire, and stayed huddled by it for a moment. My gut continued to roll as it threatened to send bile up my throat. I stared into the flames for a moment before raising my palms. I wove two strands of flames around my arms, close enough to feel the heat but not enough to burn. *If only the heat could penetrate the cursed cold that lingered.* I wished to go back in time and never go on the raid so that I would not have this sickness inside of me. I suddenly felt guilty for longing for the peaceful life I had gotten used to.

My people were suffering, and here I was feeling as if I were the only one.

I clenched my fists and sent the flames soaring back into the fire with a hiss. I would do this.

I would get myself together. **Fight the curse, kill Loreth, take down my father, and claim the crown.** *The people of Sidirna needed me, and I needed to save them.*

Shame and doubt swirled through me as I pushed myself to stand. *I feared my abilities. Feared that I wouldn't be able to accomplish the significant plans I had made. Worried I couldn't gain Ivaldr's trust. Terrified that the curse would take me before I could.* **Consumed by the thought of dying as the Lonely Heir of**

Sidirna who had accomplished nothing. *I was foolish, dull, and dishonorable.* *I could only hope to find redemption.* I was quick to wash myself and dress. Not knowing when I would need to set out and be seen with Esmeren was irritating. *What exactly did morning meal mean? The first round early in the morning?*

I groaned as I ran my hand over my head. The hairs were growing back, but not quick enough for my liking. It would take years before I had the growth I once had. I heard the shuffle of steps down the hallway and turned towards my curtain in anticipation. I needed the morning to go by quickly so I could find Dallen. I hoped he didn't see me out with Esmeren.

"Alfrikr?" Esmeren's squeaky voice rang out from the other side.

I sucked in a deep breath as I squared my shoulders. **I could do this**. I had done plenty of more difficult things. It was one meal and one walk. I let out the breath as I tilted my head to the sky. **I would play her games, but she would lose mine.**

"Be right there!" I shouted in response, snatching my pouch from the bed as I passed. *I didn't want to risk leaving the bind-rune around.* I debated on throwing it into the fire as I lifted my palm and settled the flames until it was mere coals.

Esmeren's face peeked into the cavern as she pulled it back, a wide grin on her rat-like face. I faked one in return as I walked towards her. "I'm so glad you agreed." She rushed out, stepping aside to let me through.

"Mmhmm." **I was not. I wished I had not.** *I'd never wanted to see her again, and here I was about to spend an entire winter with her.* **She was a liar, manipulator, and a stain from my past.**

"Do you mind if we skip the morning meal? I don't think

I'm ready to face the people yet..." Esmeren half whispered as we began our stroll down the hall. **The Gods were with me!**

"That's fine." The words tumbled out of my mouth, my excitement clear. I took another deep breath, holding it in for three seconds before continuing. "I'm not hungry anyway."

"So..." Esmeren flicked her braid over her shoulder. "What have you been up to?" I wasn't quite sure how to answer her, as *I'd still felt the sting of shame and disgust over what little I've accomplished in my life. Another breath in for three*, **out for three. Lie, I needed to lie.**

"Sparring, fucking, and working." I answered. I'd hoped that she would feel awkward enough to not respond, but I was not so lucky.

"That girl with the red hair?" Her tone was tense, and I hoped it was not jealousy.

"Siv? We don't spar together, but I'd bet she'd kick my arse if we did."

Esmeren huffed out a breath, and I couldn't help but chuckle. It was oddly satisfying to see her act this way. It was as if she had forgotten that she was the one who had stayed all those years ago. While I would rather not be around her at all, **I did enjoy seeing her irritated at the thought of me with another.**

"That's all?" Her voice was strained in a way that seemed impossible to figure out. *I couldn't tell if she was sad, mad, or confused.*

"Read plenty of books too, I guess." I shrugged my shoulders awkwardly. This entire thing felt awkward to the point where I longed to turn around and go back to my cavern alone. I wasn't sure how to speak with her, but I knew that she needed to believe I was on her side. *There was always the off-chance that Loreth and her had planned it to be this way.* Though I thought it to be more accurate than her claims to double-cross the man.

"That's nice." She finally responded, pausing in the middle of a common cavern. "Which way leads out?"

I pointed towards the sign above the middle doorway. "That one takes you to the main hall, and from the main hall you can."

She hummed in response as she set off towards where I'd pointed. I trailed behind her a bit, unsure of what else to say to her. **It was far too soon to dig for information.** I'd need to make sure that Esmeren was still pliable, and I had a feeling she'd grown a lot in the past nine years. Gone was the naive little girl I'd left behind.

"So..." I finally said as we neared the main hall. "What have you been up to?" I regurgitated what she had asked, *assuming that it was the polite thing to do.*

"My family kicked me out. I was forced to join the Valkyrie Guard. Your father had me betrothed to an evil, bitter, and dishonorable man. Then the man, Loreth, dragged me here." She bit out harshly. I was taken aback slightly at her bitterness. *Did she blame me for her fate?* I tried not to focus on the idea that she had been betrothed to Loreth, and **I was unsure why it stung deeply to hear the words from her mouth.**

Had she sucked his cock the same as I had? Did he invade her mind too? *Breathe in for three, out for three.*

"Oh... I'm sorry?"

"Are you?" Esmeren's voice was a squeak of a snark, but it hit all the same. **I wasn't sorry, but what else was there to say?** *Is that not what someone is meant to say when another tells them of something awful?*

"Umm..." I shrugged my shoulders, even though she couldn't see. "I don't know, probably?"

Esmeren laughed at that, which caught me off guard. It was a deep belly full laugh, as if I had said the funniest thing she'd ever heard. We continued to walk in silence, with her leading the way, until we hit the end of the hallway. It opened up into the main hall, which was already bustling with people. I could only hope Dallen was not among them. Esmeren froze a single step in, and I almost slammed into the back of her. Her body began to shake slightly as her head ducked down and shoulders slumped. *Odd. I would have assumed that a spy within our ranks would be more focused on interacting with as many people as possible.* I stepped around her and cleared my throat.

"Just across the hall, middle doorway." I lowered my voice as I spoke. Much like I would talk to a frightened animal. She was very rat-like, so it made sense. **It was not a pity I felt, it couldn't have been.** I took a deep breath in before blowing it out in small chunks. **By the Gods, I hoped Dallen was not around to witness this.** *I slung my arm around Esmeren's shoulders, quickly pulling her into my side.*

"Breathe." I mumbled to her as I felt her body shudder and shake. We made it across the hall in record time, with her small strides taking two for every one of my single steps. I recoiled away from her as soon as we hit the hallway, taking a step away from her for good measure.

"Thank you." She whispered as she moved to lean against the wall. Esmeren heaved breaths in and out with her eyes closed tightly.

It was a moment that would stick with me forever, but I didn't know it then.

I felt a surge of pity as I stared at her attempt to gather

herself. Tears welled at the corner of her eyes in a way that I doubted could be faked. Her hands shook as she fiddled with the end of her braid, and her knees wobbled just as badly.

"Are… are you okay?" I hesitantly asked. It was obvious that she was not, but I was unsure of what else to say. *Either she was a master at her game or I had overestimated her abilities.*

"Yeah…yeah, I'm fine." She rushed out between heaving breaths. My pulse picked up slightly as I weighed my thoughts. *Had I thought the worst of her? Just like those within the rebellion did of me because of who I was? Was she truly just a woman who had suffered after I had left?* I wasn't sure if I wanted to know the truth, and I wished it to be that she was faking.

We stood there for a few moments longer, until the distinct sound of footsteps echoed down the hallway. Esmeren jolted at the sound and tucked her chin to her chest to stare at her feet. The men passed us slowly as they conversed with each other, and they didn't spare us a single glance. *They looked to be Tyr's Enforcers, but I wasn't entirely familiar with their ranks.*

"Let's go." Esmeren muttered as she took off down the hallway at a brisk pace. I arched my brow before following her. She was quick to snap out of that. *So, it very well could have been a ploy.* **I was hesitant to believe in her in any form.**

The surrounding air got colder and colder to the point that I pulled my cloak tighter around my body. I hadn't had the chance to repair it, and the new furs still sat in the chest at the end of my bed. *I would need to find the time to do it soon.* I'd known this Cycle Winter would be rough, but I was not prepared for how quickly it had come upon us. I could hear Esmeren's teeth chattering from where she walked in front of me. *I almost offered to turn around,* but I knew that would be worse than the cold based on her reaction moments ago. I briefly wondered about her reaction before another gust of cold wind screamed down the hall. I shivered at the onslaught, and the pulse in my chest seemed to respond in delight to the cold. I felt the ribbons of ice weave their way around my ribs.

"By the Gods!" I heard a familiar nasally voice yell. Esmeren froze where she stood, and tucked her head down again. *Odd. Her reaction made me uneasy, and I wasn't quite sure why.*

"Good day, Jerrick!" I called out as I maneuvered around her shaking body. *I wasn't sure if she was shivering from the cold or from her reaction to people.* I assumed it was the first reason because my body shook for the same reason.

"Alfrikr!" Jerrick called out as he hobbled closer to us. There was a thin layer of snow atop his bald head and shoulders. He had a cane in his hand, one I must not have noticed before.

"That blind ol' coot was right! It's snowing!" Jerrick screeched out. I flinched at his voice. *I almost felt bad for him for having to live with a voice so unappealing.*

I chuckled as the man continued on, obviously not keen on having much more of a conversation. *Part of me had hoped he would stop and chat, if only to relieve me from the awkward tension of being with Esmeren.* Though, Jerrick wasn't much of a better option.

"Go sit by a fire!" I hollered at him, unsure of what else to say. He was far too old to be out in this weather.

"Aye! I'm going to die soon, I don't have time!" Jerrick responded, his voice taking on a shaky panic.

I let out a deep laugh, shaking my head. Jerrick had truly thought he was going to die, as I'd been informed the morning before. I had thought that it was an embellishment, or just simple gossip. I turned to look towards Esmeren, who now stared up at me with wide eyes. Her eyebrows quivered slightly before a full-body shiver wracked her.

"He… He's going to die?" She stuttered out.

I laughed at her question. *Had I not known, I would have assumed the same.* The man did, in fact, look old enough to be knocking on the door to Valhalla. I shook my head before responding, "The old fool has thought that for years he's going to die soon."

Esmeren shook her head with a confused look, and for a moment, I saw the *girl I once knew as she let out a small laugh. The girl that I had loved and cherished. The one who had known every thought within my head. It was a foolish thought, but one I could not stop from forming.* I smiled at her for a moment before nodding my head towards the hall. I turned and set off towards the impending snow. I knew it would be a cold Cycle winter, but the chill had surprised me. There was always excitement around the first snow. The first moment to truly show how we had transitioned from the leaves falling to the ground. **The long and cold months that would only bring relief when spring came.**

We usually held a feast, but the thought of a feast churned my gut. Pthun had been right about the snow, and I could only hope he would be wrong about what would happen if we had a feast. *How much worse could things get?* I knew we were at risk of starving, but I'd hoped that Ivaldr wouldn't be foolish enough to splurge right at the start of a Cycle Winter. The bitter wind slapped me in the face the second I took a step outside the mountain. I resisted the urge to turn around then, but I wanted to experience it, if only for a moment. There was a chill wrapped into the wind that could rival the curse within my chest. Esmeren came to a stop beside me, a small gasp falling from her lips.

I looked around, almost nervously, to see the steady flakes falling from the sky. There was a small dusting of pristinely white snow layered all around us. The pathway was covered enough that it was difficult to make out if not for the rocks that had lined it. *This would most likely be the last time I stepped out here until the start of spring.* It was an *odd* feeling, one that I couldn't really describe.

"The Cycle has begun." I called out to Esmeren as the wind whipped her braid from her hand. She shivered as she turned to look at me with wide and fear filled eyes. *Had she not known how bad this winter would be?* If she had not, it was obvious based on the drastic first snow. It was only a moment before we both turned and ran back into the mountain. We had only spent moments outside, but I felt that bone deep chill settling into my hands and feet. I cringed at the thought of it mixed with the icy cold pain of the curse. **This winter would be hard, but I knew I needed to survive it.**

Esmeren and I had not spoken much as I escorted her back to Ivaldr's caverns. He was nowhere to be seen, and I was glad for that. I had done my duty, and kept my word. It was not as dreadful as I had feared it would be, though I was unsettled at the pity I felt for Esmeren. She had obviously changed during the years, but I had not expected her to react the way she had around people. Esmeren had seemed fine at the last feast. She'd stood tall at Ivaldr's side and spoken to many, but I assumed it was probably a reaction based on how she knew the people felt for her. The walk back to my cavern felt unbearably long, as I struggled to walk with my feet still feeling frozen solid.

IT WAS NEARLY evening meal by the time Dallen burst through my curtain and into my cavern. He looked better than the last time I had seen him, but the grin on his face made me hesitant. *He was up to something, and I could only hope that it was not nefarious.*

"Riki! How are you?" He half-yelled as he strutted towards me. "You look better!"

"Better, yes." I responded as I set my book aside, scooting over to give him room on the bed. "And you, brother?"

"Better than I've ever been!" Dallen giddily said as he collapsed on my bed. "Enough about that, get ready! We have a feast to attend! With…are you ready?" I raised a single brow as I stared at him, trying not to focus on the fear that lanced through my heart. *A feast. There was going to be a first snow feast and Pthun had said—*

"FINNIAN'S STEW!" Dallen screamed out, his hand shooting out to grab my shoulder before he shook me roughly. I grunted as I moved away from him and gave him a half-hearted glare. I'd skipped both meals of the day, and Finnian's stew sounded amazing. *I knew there was no arguing with him,* so I heaved myself from the bed.

"Before we go," I started with a sigh. "If you see me around with Esmeren, just know that—"

"Esmeren?!" He shouted, pushing himself off my bed.

"Yes, I need you to know that—"

The curtain to my cavern flung open as Doran and Merelda entered. I held in the groan that threatened to slip out. *Of course, it was my luck that fate would work out this way.* I needed Dallen to know that I had not forgiven her, but I needed Doran to think that I had.

"Boys," Merelda greeted with a grin as she looked between

Dallen and I. "Are you ready? The feast starts soon, and I want to get a good place in line."

Doran said nothing as he nodded along. A small smile was plastered on his face as he tucked his hands into the pockets of his pristine trousers. I looked down at the clothes I wore and shrugged. *They would have to do.*

25

STAINS AND ANGER

We'd arrived early enough that the line to Finnian's was not incredibly long, which I was thankful for. The steady pulse of cold pain radiated through my body, but by this point **I had begun to normalize myself to the easier pains.** There were pains that ripped through my body and made it impossible to function. I had somehow found it easier to compare the levels so I could get through life. My body was slow to respond, but my muscles did not scream in pain.

"What say you, Riki?" Dallen called out, his voice entirely too loud for the faint hum of conversations surrounding us.

"Hmm?"

"Will the stew have everything?" Doran replied in place of his brother. Doran's face remained blank. *A tell-tale sign that he would be examining my response in the way that Doran often did.*

"Would it be stew if it did not?" I quipped back. While Doran's face showed nothing, his eyes told it all. ***They seemed to fill with emotion, though I wasn't quite sure which exactly.*** He nodded his head once before turning his head from me, leaning down to whisper something to Merelda. *It was odd.*

"That's what I said!" Dallen hollered as he slung his arm around my shoulder. He leaned in close to me, his lips brushing my ear. "Ivaldr asked Doran to keep an eye on you… Doesn't like ye hanging with other people that's upset about the winter preparation."

I gave him a single nod as he pulled away from me with a

wink. I needed to pull him aside and make sure he knew what was going on with Esmeren.

If I could go back in time, I would tell him right then and there.

Dallen was sure to misunderstand my intentions. I could only hope that he didn't assume that I had rekindled some sort of relationship with the vile woman.

"You're not… worried?" Doran drawled out his attention back to me. "With using supplies this early in the winter?" He was usually smoother than that. *It was odd to see him speak in a way that was not fully articulated and laced with undertones that weren't understood until hours later.*

"It's not my responsibility, nor my problem." I said with a shrug. **I'd found younger Alfrikr within me easily, almost too quickly. Not only that, but I had forgotten the thrill behind manipulation.**

"But…" Doran raised an eyebrow as he sucked in a breath. The wheels were surely turning in his mind now, and it was hard not to laugh. *He was just as easy as he was when we were children.* "You've been eating with the men, who also petitioned Ivaldr to prepare more for winter. You yourself have gone to him many times?"

"Aye, I did."

"So?" Doran snapped out before he quickly composed his features. *He was not one to act in anger, and it was an obvious sign that he held suspicions towards me.*

"Well, in case you forgot," I drawled out, a hint of dramatics woven into my tone. "I was cursed with blood

Sacredness. The only man who still knows much about it is Froggy, and I can't control who he mingles with."

Doran gave me a long look before he visibly exhaled. *We were at an impasse, and I was starting to feel suspicious. Why was he observing me so thoroughly?* It was known that I held different views than most within the rebellion, and the top reason why I had never moved up within the ranks. Yet, this moment brought me clarity and understanding; **I would need to be more cautious in my endeavors this winter.**

"That's where you've been during your morning meal!" Dallen exclaimed as he nudged my shoulder playfully. "I thought you were avoiding me!"

I huffed out a forced laugh as I shook my head. "It's harder to wake so early in the morning lately. I just happened to find the men, and figured it was a good time to pester Froggy about what he knows." I shrugged my shoulders, stealing a small glance at Doran's reaction. "If I want to pry this curse from my bones, then I need knowledge."

"How has it been? You haven't come to us lately." Merelda interjected into the conversation. Her voice was steady as she spoke, but *I noticed the way she glanced at Doran as if she needed permission to speak.*

"I thought you were better." Doran practically sneered, his eyebrows furrowing.

It was one of those things I had never noticed before, but the moment I thought about it, there were many times those kinds of things had happened.

There was a reason Siv detested Doran and while I had

listened to her drone on about it, I'd never put much weight into it. *He was my best friend, after all.*

"Aye, I've been managing. Just the same as before." It made me *anxious* **to speak of the curse,** *for I knew how easy it would be to put my foot into my mouth.*

"Such as?" Doran drawled out. Merelda closed her mouth as her permission to speak had obviously been revoked.

"I'm cold, my chest hurts, and every so often I pass out from the pain." I did not look at him as I responded, but kept my gaze towards Merelda. *I wanted to say something, to call him out for his transgressions, but I knew that I had bigger plans to change than how he treated her.*

"It's happened again?" Dallen asked with his voice hushed, barely audible.

"Aye, the night before last."

Merelda gasped, her hand flying up to her mouth. It felt a touch too dramatic, but she was a healer, after all. Doran's face scrunched in my peripherals, and **only for a second did his true colors display before the mask was placed again.**

"Was... Are... Well, you're still alive, so I won't ask." Dallen rushed out. A shiver wracked through his body just as I turned my gaze to him. Another thing I would need to talk to him about, **especially after that run in with that woman-Goddess-person.** *I understood the power he had felt, and now I needed to hear about what he had witnessed that night.*

"Aye, unfortunately for you lot, I've got plenty of years left in me."

"Did Froggy tell you that?" Doran responded quickly. I had barely finished speaking before his voice began.

"Hard to say what he has and hasn't told me." I shrugged again as a shiver ran through my body. "He doesn't speak plainly, and usually, it's pure nonsense."

The conversation died quickly as we found ourselves at the front of the line. The steaming hot bowl in my hands did little to warm my hands, but that was just the way it worked for me now. The stew was full of vegetables, meat, and a dark broth. Yet, the usual hunger I felt did not gurgle through my belly because it had been replaced by an all-consuming dread. *I tried not to think of Pthun's proclamation as I sat with my bowl in my lap, taking meager bites.* The conversation droned on around me, but all I could focus on was the knowledge that things were going to get a lot worse. *Ivaldr had doomed us all by arranging this feast, but a part of me had hopes that he would be intelligent enough to ration our food.*

I wanted to enjoy the meal, but deep-down it felt as if it would be my last.

"Don't look so happy to see me next time." Siv's voice floated through my thoughts as she plopped onto the bench beside me.

I tried to smile, but I was sure that it looked as pathetic as it felt. She scooted closer to me and leaned her body into my side. It was comfortable, natural, and *yet it did nothing to soothe the dread. She would die, I would die, Dallen would die, and everyone within this Gods-forsaken mountain would.* **There was no way for me to tell the others because they would think me as insane as those old men.**

"Are you okay?" Siv peered up at me. I didn't feel the same warmth that usually coursed through my body when I saw the woman. She was beautiful, and I could acknowledge that easily. *Yet, there was something different about it all that I could only attribute to my inner-turmoil.* Siv didn't consume me in the way I needed her to, but I could only hope that changed as the night went on.

"Aye," I pushed my bowl towards her with a nod. "Just not in the feasting mood, I think." She wasn't hesitant as she took the bowl with a smile, immediately spooning some into her mouth. *Perhaps I was bribing her to remain in her good graces so that she would invite me back to her cavern.* I needed the distraction just as much as I wanted to redeem myself for the last time I had been in her bed.

"Makes sense, I saw ye hanging around that awful wench. Must've sucked the happiness right out of ya!" Siv bit out through a mouthful of food. *I couldn't help but to chuckle at her antics, knowing that her jealousy was as superficial as her feelings for me.* I wasn't a fool when it came to understanding her feelings, but *I was foolish in many other ways.* I felt the dreadful nihilism in my gut lift minimally at her antics.

"You're quite perceptive tonight."

"Bleh, none of your pishy-poshy talk right now, please." She had nearly finished the bowl already, which did not surprise me. I felt more satisfaction in seeing her content and full than I did from eating the stew myself. **I may have been complicit in this feast—making me just as guilty as Ivaldr— but my guilt was significantly relieved by knowing that I wasn't participating in wasting needed resources.**

"Ye think good." I nudged her gently just as she took a bite, causing the spoonful to dribble down onto her smock.

She let out a sharp gasp before quickly refilling her spoon and flinging it directly at me. ***A quick, hot anger flashed through me, and the urge to react was difficult to resist. I wanted to grab her by her hair and slam her face into the table until she—****what the Hel kind of thoughts were these? They didn't feel like my own, but more as if they were placed within* *my mind.* It was a way I had never once felt towards her, but had felt many times about others.

"Aye, I deserved that." I finally settled on muttering as I tried to wipe away the remnants with my hand. It would stain, but I was sure it would stain Siv's clothes as well. "I better go wash this off." I added, knowing that would mean I wasn't going to her cavern tonight. *Though, I wasn't quite sure that I wanted to.*

"More of that pishy-poshy, Riki? We'll go together when I'm done." Siv grinned at me, obviously not as concerned as I was about the stains. "You'll wash, I'll watch." She added with a sly chuckle.

"Ye can stay… It'll be cold out by the river, the snows set in now." *The dread began to course through my veins again, threatening to consume my thoughts entirely.*

"Why are we going to fuck by the river? It's winter." Siv laughed out as her words intermingled with the melodic sound. *She was a beauty, one that I was lucky to be around. Though, that thought didn't amaze me as it once had.*

"No…our clothes?" I raised my brow as I stared at her. *I wasn't sure what she meant then when she said she'd watch me wash the clothing, but then mentioned fucking?*

"Are you that dull, or are you jesting?" Siv's tone had gone serious, and I felt my cheeks heat. *Ah, it was a veiled speech that I had never picked up on quick enough in the right moments.* Realistically, I should've known what she had been insinuating, and I could only hope that my brain felt slower to respond because of exhaustion and not the curse.

"Pathetic." Loreth's voice echoed out, causing me to jolt hard enough that I nearly fell from the bench.

"Oh!" I exclaimed as I scrambled back to sitting regularly. *Horrible timing, as always.* I wondered if he chose the times to enter my mind, and how he always seemed to know when the worst times to invade my mind. **I couldn't wait until the end of winter, when I could finally take the man down.**

Siv and I chatted as we walked to her cavern, more so her speaking than me. The pulsing pain in my chest had slowly released me from its grip as we walked, for which I was incredibly thankful. Part of me felt guilty for knowing that Loreth was watching through my eyes as I planned to fuck Siv, but I tried not to focus on it. It felt especially wrong as Loreth continued to hum that same tune in my head. *It was the one my grandmother had once hummed to me, but I didn't know the words.*

"Okay!" Siv finally exclaimed, snapping me out of my cycle of thoughts. "I can tell you're not listening to me this time, and you're never done that before. What's wrong?"

I had no idea how to respond, or rather how to lie. It wasn't as if I could tell her that *Loreth No Name was watching from my eyes.* **Oh yes, Siv, a lot is wrong. The tortuous, unredeemable, dishonorable, sick fuck was humming a tune in my head, and it makes it kind of difficult to listen to you babble about how much you hate winter.** *You're right, winter is horrible, and we're all doomed to die.* Let's just fuck to distract ourselves for a moment, except we have someone watching us, and I hope you're okay with that.

"I'm just tired, that's all." I ended up saying, giving her a tightlipped smile. "And admittedly nervous about the upcoming winter. It just doesn't feel like something we should be celebrating."

"But... We always celebrate the first snow? It's tradition." Her steps slowed as she gazed up at me.

"If she hates winter so much, why does she care about the first snow feast?" Loreth countered Siv, though she couldn't hear him. I agreed with him. *Which felt disgusting to admit, but he had a logical point?*

"Aye, but it's the Cycle of Winter. Maybe we should... I don't know." I was close to admitting to her how I felt about it all, but I wasn't sure how much I could trust her. *Doran was already sniffing around my thoughts about Ivaldr's lack of preparation.*

"You sure like to pick 'em dull, Lonely Heir."

"We should what? Sit around and be sad that it's a little more cold than usual?" She scoffed as she shook her head. While I understood what she meant, I knew that she didn't understand the intricacies of leading people during winter, let alone a Cycle Winter.

Many would die because Ivaldr was too foolish to admit that we needed to be cautious. I could only hope that those I cared about lived.

"She'll be one of the first to die."

"Aye, you're right." I agreed with her, but also unfortunately with Loreth. *Those who did not take it seriously were typically the first to die. I was sad to admit that, but I knew it to be true.*

Siv pulled back the curtain to her cavern and held a single hand up to stop me from following. "I'll only be a moment."

"Good Gods." Loreth grunted out, his voice not much more than a growl.

Siv's cavern looked as it usually did, and I wondered why she even bothered at this point to pretend as if it weren't always like that. Clothes were piled and strewn about, a few bowls littered near the fire, and it honestly looked as though someone had torn through her cavern looking for something.

"You don't have to…"

"Close your eyes!" Siv interrupted.

I groaned, but complied as the echoes of Loreth's laughter consumed me. *It shouldn't have been an attractive sound, but somewhere deep inside of me I wished to hear it more.* I had never heard him sound as carefree as he did at that moment. *I shivered in disgust.* **He was my enemy, he cursed me, and I would kill him. Loreth was not a good man, and my thoughts needed to end at taking advantage of his body.** That was all there needed to be.

"You're not really going to fuck her, are you?" Loreth growled out darkly. My stomach dropped in fear at the tone of his voice. I knew what he was capable of, but I had not truly witnessed him at his worst. There was nothing I could say as my heart began to beat wildly in my chest. *It was none of his business what I did and did not do.*

"Come in!" Siv's melodic voice rang out, and I hesitantly opened my eyes. The cavern was not much better. I honestly couldn't tell what she had tidied, but I took a step inside anyway. **Loreth could not stop me.** He was unable to find me during the winter, but I found myself fearing his reaction the next time I saw him. *How much could he hurt me within a dream? I didn't think he could kill me, but I wasn't sure.*

"So…" I said softly, stepping over a pile of clothes. "Can I clean your smock now, my lady?" I cringed after it came out, and I realized how awful it sounded. *The embarrassment only got worse as Loreth's laugh began again.*

"Oh, shut the Hel up." Siv laughed out as she began to pull the dress off her body. My gaze shot to the creamy, smooth skin of her shoulders. Beautiful, she was a beautiful woman. *Better than I deserved, but I did not feel I deserved her.* Siv stopped before she exposed her breasts, with her gaze locked on my face.

"I didn't get to touch you last time." She said simply, her head tilting as she looked at me. Loreth laughed again, and I felt my face begin to heat. I nodded my head in response, as I was unsure whether I could speak or not. She had rules that I would respect, even if Loreth looked at her the same as I did. *There was no stirring in my cock, no jolt of need, and it frightened me.* My body had never reacted this way, but it had always reacted in the opposite way.

"If she touches you, I swear I will cut off her fingers and shove them down her throat until she chokes and dies." His voice was low and menacing as he spoke within my mind.

My lungs seized, and my pulse thundered through my ears as I stood still, staring at Siv with my mouth half-open. *I was almost fool enough to believe it to be an idle threat.* I didn't understand why he would say that, or rather why he would feel such all-consuming anger. *How I knew what he felt, I also did not know.* Siv advanced towards me, her hips swinging in a sultry sway. One that would have had me on my knees begging her for more mere weeks ago.

Yet, my cock still slept peacefully, and my heart still thumped loudly. Now was not the time to be consumed by the thoughts swirling through my mind, but I couldn't seem to break out of the trance I was in. **On one hand, I wanted to anger Loreth because I hated him.** *On the other, I feared that he would make his threat a reality and that I would be the reason she died.* I didn't have much more time to think as Siv kneeled before me. Loreth growled like an angry dog as I stared down at the woman. Her copper hair was braided back neatly in a way that would once send a longing through me to use it as a handle as I pounded into her. Though it had never happened because of her strict rules, I had often found myself wishing for it. *However, right now, all I felt was the desire to turn my back to her and run away.*

I didn't say a word as her warm hands slid up my thighs in a provocatively slow manner. My eyes remained on the top of her head as she cupped my soft member, and my face began to heat. Embarrassment and confusion battled to take over my mind; *why was I not getting hard?* I could sense the anger and animalistic urge to kill her that flowed out of Loreth. **The feeling was strong enough that I almost wondered if it were my own.**

Her brows furrowed, confused, as she massaged my cock once lightly, but I felt no urge to buck into her hand. **I needed to leave.** *I needed to stop her before Loreth got any angrier.* There was once a time that a simple look from the woman had me tenting my trousers. It had to be the curse that was affecting my body, and I wouldn't allow it to be because I longed for a different, more masculine, hand gripping my cock. She gave me a hard squeeze with one hand as her other still trailed up and down my thigh. I grunted from the pressure, but still, my cock remained flaccid.

"I warned you, Alfrikr. She will pay for touching what is mine." Loreth's dark voice rang out, causing a shiver to barrel down my spine. My cock twitched at his words, and a sense of disgust was quick to follow. I was quick to take a step back. Quick enough that Siv lurched forward and yelped as she fell to her hands on the stone floor.

"It's too late. She's been marked for death." His cold voice seemed to whisper. My body moved faster than I knew I could move as I turned on my heel and ran from Siv. She began to yell after me, but I was too afraid to stop and make an excuse.

My vision began to blur as anger and bloodlust still thundered out of Loreth. *It was too much, it felt overwhelming, and I wasn't sure how he existed with such strong emotions.* My feet pounded on the stone steadily as I ran towards my cavern. **I was in trouble.** ***Siv was in trouble.*** *There was nothing I could do.* **I had doomed her.** *Loreth was going to kill her.* I turned into the common cavern that would lead me to my dwelling, my chest heaving in breaths from the exertion.

My steps slowed as the corners of my vision began to fade, and everything went black.

26

RUNNING AND HIDING

I RELAXED INTO THE FAMILIAR FEELING OF FLOATING AS I DRIFTED through the nothingness. There was no fear as the ribbons of foggy black twirled around my body. **I was safe. *I was protected.* I was calm.** *I wanted to stay in the darkness forever. I wanted it to **consume** me whole and keep me in its safe arms for all **eternity.*** **I had no need for Valhalla while the darkness held me.** *Safe. Safe. Safe.*

The feeling did not last long, as I blinked and pried my eyes open. **The darkness.** *I wanted to go back to the darkness, where it was safe.* I heaved in a breath and then another before looking at my surroundings. I was confident that I was in another dream as I looked at the trees around me because it was not winter. The air was warm like the nights of summer, and the foliage reflected that thought. The brush was thick around me, and I turned in a full circle as I took in my surroundings. I looked down at my clothes to see that I wore the same clothes as the last dream. It was an *odd* feeling as I looked at the clothes that I once wore, *so long ago.*

They felt too soft, new, and clean. I heaved in a breath as the panic began to **close in around me.** *I had tempted fate, or more so, that I had tempted Loreth through my inaction.* While I didn't understand why he had reacted in such a way, I took his threat seriously. *There was no way for me to warn Siv.* **If I were to warn her, then I would have to admit to the way that Loreth fell into my mind and how we shared dreams occasionally.** That I had gotten on my knees, much like she had for me, and how I had loved the feeling. Dread and panic consumed me as I struggled to pull air into my lungs. My hands shook as I brought them up to press into the sockets of my eyes.

I didn't know what to do. **I didn't know what was happening.** *I hated the curse, and I hated the feeling inside of me that felt a connection to Loreth.* He was terrifying. He was a bad man. Loreth did terrible things, and here I was thinking about the time I had sucked his cock. **There was something wrong with me, and I was scared to find out what.** *The curse,* **it had to be the curse messing with my mind.** I felt the familiar tug to my gut urging me to walk through the forest, but this time I was aware enough to know better. **That tug would bring me to Loreth, and I was afraid to see him.** *I didn't know how he would react. I didn't know if he would do to me what he had sworn to do to Siv.* By the Gods, I had doomed her.

She would die by his hand, and I knew it.

With a shaky breath that did not feel like enough, I turned on my heel and began to run in the opposite direction that my intuition told me to go. *If I could wait this out, I wouldn't have to see him. I could run and hide until I woke up in my body again.* There were no distinct trails as I started to run, and I could feel the branches tearing at the clothes on my body. *I knew I needed to go faster, but it was too thick this deep in the forest.* I leaped over a fallen log, my ankle twisting slightly as I landed. *I couldn't understand why this was happening to me, and I didn't want to think about it.* My thoughts wouldn't budge from the way Loreth's voice had sounded inside my head. **How I had felt the anger as if it were my own. How for a moment it was as if we had merged into one singular person?**

His feelings were mine. *Why had he felt that way? What* *claim did he have to me?* So, I had sucked his cock once in a dream, but that did not mean that I was his. I knew him to be a vicious man, and I could only hope that he didn't find me. I turned to the left as my gut began to pull me to the right. The brush seemed to get thicker, and it slowed me down considerably. Dread coursed through me as I heaved breaths in and out while I ran. *Loreth was not a man who acted upon his honor, nor was he a man who seemed to have any honor at all.* **He did what he wanted simply because he wanted to.**

He had cursed me, for God's sake! *Loreth had used blood Sacredness to curse my soul, and yet he viewed me to be his?* I didn't understand it, and I wasn't sure I wanted to. I stumbled over a root, yelping as I tumbled to the hard ground. My body ached already, and the fall did nothing to help. I laid there for a moment, feeling as if I had earned it. *I wanted to be back in my body.* I was slow to pull myself up to stand, wiping my dirtied and bloodied hands on my trousers.

Still, I ran through the thick brush as fast as I could. Sweat began to drip into my eyes, and my body began to heat up.

"ALFRIKR!" Loreth's voice called from somewhere behind me. "Come out, come out wherever you are!"

My heart simultaneously stuttered to a stop as it seemed to pick up its pace entirely. Fear shot down my spine as I willed my feet to move faster. *I couldn't let him find me, for I feared he would end me.* A pain lanced my side as I weaved around a tree, and I struggled to hold in a groan. *Faster, I needed to go faster.* A branch hit me square in the chest as I ran, causing my eyes to immediately fill with tears. I blinked past the blurriness, only to stumble over another root. I caught myself before falling, but my ankle screamed in agony. A fiery pain began to fill my chest as I heaved in breaths. One that was unlike typical pain as its fiery tendrils weaved their way between my ribs. My steps slowed as the trees began to get thicker. Nausea filled my gut, threatening to send the fiery liquid up my throat. I made it a few more steps before I heard the rustling behind me. *I wanted my body to move faster, but the pain made me sluggish.*

"I can smell your fear, I know you're close!" Loreth's voice rang out. **He sounded winded, which was good for me.** *Yet, I knew that it would still be difficult to outrun him in this forest.* I slowed for a moment, hoping to find a tree that would be easy to climb.

Fate was on my side for once as I spotted one close by. I sucked in a deep breath as I propelled myself towards it. My hands burned from the sweat filling the cuts where I had fallen, which did nothing to help me as I grabbed the closest branch. I gritted my teeth through the pain as I shimmied myself up the tree far enough that I hoped he would not see me. I stopped on a branch that looked thick enough to hold me and heaved my body onto it. I pressed my back against the trunk as I tried to control my breathing. The tree was thick enough that I couldn't see the ground very well, and I hoped that meant that Loreth would not see me either. I held on to the branch tightly as I tried to control my breathing to be quiet enough that he would not hear me. A loud rustle sounded below me and I felt my body begin to shake.

"Where, oh where, have you gone, little bear!" His voice was unsteady as he called out, angry and breathless.

I kept myself tucked into the tree as I waited. My heart thundered in my ears loud enough that I worried he would be able to hear it. *I couldn't let him find me, but I assumed he knew that I had scrambled up a tree if he was calling me little bear.* The pain continued to flow through my chest as it sent waves of heat through my body. My vision blurred as a harsh and burning heat began to pound into the center of my chest. I sat as still as I could, trying to listen for any movement below. It was silent, but I knew better than to climb down now. *If I thought Loreth was angry before, I was wrong.* **I had only angered him further by running.** A loud crack made me jump, almost losing my balance on the branch. I squeezed my eyes closed tightly as I pushed myself further into the tree.

A whoosh of air hit my face, and I opened my eyes to find Loreth standing atop a stone pillar. *Sacredness, why hadn't I used my Sacredness?* My heart thundered louder as I stared at his scrunched face. **If Loreth could kill me with a look, then I would be in Valhalla.** He said nothing as he curled his finger towards me, commanding me to come to him.

"H-hello?" I stuttered out weakly as I pushed my back into the rough bark of the tree.

"Come." Loreth commanded in a seething tone.

I stayed where I was and if I could go back, I would have flung myself from the tree and taken death.

That day was the moment that everything changed, and there was nothing more the Norns could do to save me.

"Do not anger me further, little bear." Loreth bit out through clenched teeth. I weighed my options as I stared at him. My entire body shook as the fiery pain continued to assault my chest. With a shaky breath, I began to scurry down the branch and towards the man. My hands burned in a bloody pain as I pulled myself onto the pillar.

Fear consumed me as I kneeled there, unwilling to meet Loreth's gaze. I stared down at his boots, noting how worn down and ragged they looked. Though that did nothing to save me as he used his Sacredness to lower us to the ground. My body shivered and shook from a mixture of fear and pain. *This would be the moment that I died, and I was sure of it.* Loreth was quick as his hand encased the back of my neck, squeezing roughly as he shoved me to the ground. I grunted in pain, but the heat that had coursed through me seemed to sputter out. I did not struggle beneath him because I knew it was futile. *It was a shameful way to go, and I could only hope that he made it quick.* His knees dropped to the ground on either side of my hips, where he held me tightly.

"Tsk, tsk." Loreth tutted as he leaned down to my ear. "You should not have run. Now I have to punish you." His breath was hot as he whispered darkly. I shivered beneath him as fear lanced my heart. *He would not make my death quick, and I feared how long he would draw it out. I could only hope that my body would not die if he killed me in this dream.*

"Nothing to say?" He grunted out as he shuffled above me. I tried to shake my head, but it was nearly impossible while pressed against the hard ground. *Words would not save me, and I would not waste them begging for my life.*

"You're almost tolerable when you're silent." He tutted out as his grip left my neck. "Roll over." He commanded as he let his weight up enough to allow me to move.

My body was slow as fear consumed me, but I listened all the same. With my eyes squeezed shut, I shimmied until I rolled onto my back. There was a rock beneath me now that dug into the middle of my shoulder blades, and **so I focused on that pain.**

"Open your eyes, little bear." Loreth growled out. I was unwilling to test his anger. I blinked my eyes open slowly as I adjusted to the light, staring at the man as he straddled me. *My cock twitched shamefully as I took in the sight of Loreth above me.*

There was a break in the trees above us and the sun shone through behind Loreth, making it appear as though he had a **God-like glow.** He was not a beautiful man, quite average looking, but the way he held himself seemed to boost his appeal. I found his lack of honor appalling, and his love of vicious torture even worse. *Yet, I found myself taking in the features of his face as if he were the most handsome man in this realm.* They were opposing feelings that I didn't have the opportunity to direct, and I feared that I would get stuck in a loop of thoughts, as I often did. I cleared my throat, coughing through the dryness.

"Hello, Loreth." I said, trying to feign a confidence I did not feel.

Loreth responded with a smirk that shot *fear* directly into my heart. His features twisted in such a way that you could almost see the vicious anger that I felt while I was in Siv's cavern. "You let another touch what was mine, and then you ran from me, little bear." He growled out in a tone that matched the look on his face.

I tugged my bottom lip between my teeth, worrying the skin, as I sucked in a breath. I wasn't sure how to respond because I was afraid to anger him further, but I also couldn't help how my cock seemed to respond to his words. It was an odd feeling to be so consumed with fear by a man I hated, but to equally feel the excitement that came with that. "Erm... I'm sorry?"

His eyes narrowed as he stared down at me, "Are you?"

"Yes?"

He tutted in response as he leaned forward, bringing his face closer to mine. Loreth's eyebrow raised a fraction as he wiggled his hips slightly, causing my own to buck into him. My face was filled with a red-hot heat almost immediately.

"What's this?" He growled out as he rested more weight down. My cock burned where it bulged against the confines of my trousers. Where I expected to feel shame, *I only felt excitement.* "Hmm." Loreth's head tilted slightly as he peered down at me with his soulless eyes.

"You like this, don't you, little bear?" His hand was fast to move to my neck, gripping it tightly as he leaned closer until his nose was brushing my own. "Admit it."

"Never." I rasped out as his grip restricted my breathing, only slightly. *I felt nothing but the need for Loreth. I wanted him to consume every piece of me until I reached that euphoric high.*

"Yet, your cock says differently. It certainly didn't react this way when that pretty little bitch had her hands all over it." He growled out, his breath hot on my lips. My tongue darted out to wet them as I breathed in a lungful of his cinnamon and cedar scent.

His scent seemed to fill a hole within me, but left me aching for more all the same. **Loreth was all my brain could focus on, and it was a better feeling than the fear and dread that had consumed me only moments before.** I had the urge to press my lips into his, an all-consuming need that sunk deep into my bones. I struggled against his grip on my neck until I could hastily and clumsily shove our lips together. Loreth grunted out a confused sound, but his confusion only lasted a moment before he pressed his lips roughly against my own. His lips were quick to part, and it was only moments before his tongue was aggressively demanding an entrance. I responded earnestly, my tongue rushing out to battle his own.

My hips bucked as I moaned into his mouth, pressing my aching cock into him. His tongue took dominance as they danced together, our teeth gnashing together roughly. Loreth's hand stayed locked around my throat as he ground his hips into me. I shivered beneath him as he growled out a moan into my mouth. The sound went straight to my cock, and I ached for more from him. I snaked one of my hands up and curled my fingers roughly into his hair. He moaned again as I forcefully yanked his head closer to me by my death grip in his soft locks. Loreth pulled away suddenly as he heaved breaths above me. My hand stayed locked in his hair as we stared at each other, the air charged with a need I had never felt before.

"Interesting." He drawled out breathlessly as I let my hand fall.

My cock ached and pulsed for more, but I did nothing but lay beneath him. *Shame threatened to ruin my mood as I gasped for breath, staring up at the man who had cursed me.* **I hated him just as much as I wanted him.** It was a battle that I didn't know which would win, especially as my hips bucked into him without a thought. Loreth stared for a moment longer as if he were peering directly into my soul. I stared back, not trusting myself to speak because I knew I would beg him. His hands moved to the ties of his trousers with a heavy sigh. A sudden wave of excitement rushed through me, and I couldn't help but moan at the sight. **I needed him more than I needed anything right now. I wanted to breathe in his scent as he choked me with his cock.**

He moved from me as he shucked his trousers off, and I moaned again as his thick cock came into view. "Off." He said as he pointed towards me, and my hands couldn't move fast enough. My fingers shook as I struggled to untie the knot before deciding to just shove them down. I lifted my hips as I pushed them down and kicked them the rest of the way off. I couldn't help the moan that slipped out as the air hit my cock, finally free from the tight constraints.

I wasn't sure what he had planned, but at that moment I didn't have a care in the world besides finally spilling my seed. My cock was painfully hard and pre-seed pooled at the tip. Loreth was slow as he straddled me again, his gaze never straying from my nakedness. He settled above me similarly to how he had been before, except his cock now rested directly above my own. I licked my lips in anticipation, fisting my hands to resist the urge to stroke myself to the sight.

With one hand, he gripped both of our cocks and squeezed. I whimpered as I thrust into him, and he growled in response. His cock was warm against my own, and *I was momentarily amazed at how large his hands were.* I felt the pressure building already, and I knew I would not last long like this. Loreth did not start slow, but instead pumped our cocks in sync with an almost painful grip. His head was tilted down as he watched, his brows furrowed deeply.

My balls began to tighten as the pressure at the base of my spine almost hit the point of no return. I turned my attention just as I felt the wetness of his pre-seed mixing with my own wetly, he fisted our cocks. *I didn't want this to end, but I knew there was little I could do to fight it.* Loreth was relentless as he tightened his grip further, a moan falling from my lips immediately. I squeezed my eyes shut as I felt myself racing towards the point of no return. Loreth's pace seemed to increase as another moan fell out as my hips bucked up against him. I moved my freehand to his thigh, digging my nails in as I tried to ground myself. Loreth let out a long growl as I dug my nails in deeper. **I was close, so very close, and I wanted this moment to last.**

I wanted to continue to breathe in his musky scent as the euphoric feeling of his cock against my own consumed my body.

I thrusted into Loreth's hand, unable to control myself, as I moved my other hand to grip his thigh as hard as I could. His pace quickened again, a long moan falling out of his mouth as I began to tip over the edge. Pleasure filled my body as I felt myself reaching the point of no return. Loreth squeezed roughly as I began to spill over his hand. I whimpered, almost in pain, and he began to pump his hand faster and rougher. It was only moments before Loreth moaned deep in his chest as he shot thick ropes of seed onto my chest. My hands fell from his thighs as I laid there, eyes closed, heaving in breaths. The euphoric high still flowed through me, and for a moment, *I wished to stay here forever.* Finishing with Loreth felt different from any other time I had spilled my seed. I couldn't exactly describe what the difference was, but it was distinct enough that I noticed it through the haze of my mind.

He moved from me with a grunt as he fell to the ground beside me, his breath uneven as he tried to catch it. We laid there in silence for a while, and I didn't dare to open my eyes. It was peaceful, for once, with the man and I didn't want to change that. However, Loreth had different plans as he cleared his throat from beside me.

"You're mine, Alfrikr." He grunted out. "Mine to curse, mine to chase, mine to torture, and mine to touch."

My high suddenly dropped as I processed what he said. I stayed silent beside him as I felt the familiar sense of dread flooding my being.

For once, I was thankful as everything went black.

27

SWIRLS AND FOG

I RECOGNIZED THE SMELL BEFORE I HAD OPENED MY EYES, groaning as I came to terms with once again finding myself within the healers caverns. Hilda's pine scented hand must have been the warmth I felt on my cheek. She mumbled something I couldn't quite understand. I was alive, and that was all that mattered. My eyes felt too heavy to open, so I laid there. I was cold, but not so cold that I felt pain. The ache in my chest has gone, but the familiar pulse remained. My head swam fuzzily with the memories of the dream, shame crashing down on me like a cresting wave.

I hated Loreth in his entirety. The way he shamelessly spilled blood in the name of my father. How he tortured innocent people for entertainment. *How much I wanted his cock.* The cruelty of the man was intimidating, but it did nothing to quell the pure hatred that I felt for him.

I hated him just as much as I wanted him.

I was not a weak man. I was larger than most, and I often won every sparring match. Yet, the brute strength of Loreth was so far above my own that *I felt like a weak fool. I didn't understand. How could I hate someone so much, but my body reacted so differently?* I'd felt the shiver of pleasure when he'd threatened me. I felt the ache to my core when he'd straddled me. **I would kill him**; he was an unredeemable soul that would suffer for all that he had done.

"This will do it," I heard Hilda croak out before the flash of pain against my cheek sent my eyes flying open and my upper half sitting straight up.

"What the Hel!?"

"Ah, boy," She smugly smiled at me. "You're awake!" I glared in response, the stinging on my cheek still pulsing.

"Alfrikr!" Froggy nodded my way, shuffling his decrepit body towards me. It was then I noticed that I laid naked upon the stone table. Laid bare for the world to see, yet I did not feel an ounce of shame. *I could only hope that they had not had to clean the seed that I knew stained my trousers.* I was never one to revel in my nudity, unless it was during a good fuck or to make someone leave my cavern. This felt different, in a way that I couldn't quite explain.

"Have you figured the curse out?" I hesitantly asked. I almost didn't want to know. Knowing and not knowing were equally intimidating. They were obviously aware that I had passed out again. Yet, I felt an ache of misery as I thought of no longer seeing Loreth. **I hated him,** *but why did I want him so badly?*

"Yes?" Froggy said, just as Hilda replied, "No."

"How long have you had this mark?" She pointed towards my chest, my eyes flying downwards quickly.

Right in the center of my chest sat a symbol, not quite matching the runes on my arms. The wound itself did not look fresh, more like it had been burned into my chest weeks ago and left to fester. **It looked like the algiz, gebo, and dagaz runes overlapped;** a straight line going down in the same order. Gebo meant gift, algiz meant protection, dagaz meant transformation. *The paper.* It was the same as the paper that woman had left me. I pushed a finger into the mark, flinching as the pain flared. I hadn't had the time to look into it more. Fear settled into my gut as I stared at the offending mark. *What did it mean?*

"Ah," Hilda hummed. "Not long then."

"Who has the match?" Froggy nodded three times, tapping the mark on my chest in nine quick successions. I flinched with each prod to the wound. Though I knew he had reasons for being as superstitious as he was. It was obvious that this was blood Sacredness.

"I..." It couldn't be. *There was no way that Loreth would have it.* Though, he hadn't taken his shirt off in the latest dream, and I had seen a mark upon his chest while he had looked at himself in the mirror.

I did not want to believe that this curse was equal. *Why would he curse us equally?* Yet, it made the connection between us more like the twins than I imagined. *Was that the reason he had felt so strongly about me being his? Did he curse me so that he could take ownership of me?* I could only hope that my mind would remain my own.

"I'm not...sure."

"Ah, I guess your generation does not know what it means." Froggy hummed out.

"What do you mean?"

"It's been a long time since I've seen one," Hilda agreed. Their lack of telling stoked the fire within my chest. I was still a scrambled mess; drowning in self-hatred and disgust. **I wanted to grab the pair of ancient fools and shake them.**

"Seen what?" I bit out harshly, gazing back down at the festered rune. The surrounding skin was red, with bubbles that almost looked like a healing burn. The marks themselves looked deep, the healing scan tinged with yellow.

"Since I was a child," Froggy agreed. That senile old man would meet his end soon, and I would happily be the one to lead him there. Though I still needed him this winter, so it would have to wait until spring. The both of them stood there staring at the mark upon my chest. I felt like I was an item upon a merchant's table; being silently judged without asking a price. *I wanted to shy away, but I knew there was no point.*

"By the Gods," I grunted out, looking between the two. "If one of you don't tell me what the Hel you are talking about..." Hilda was fast as she reached out to flick my nose.

"Hush, boy" She tilted her head back and forth, alternating closing one eye at a time to stare at it. "Do you remember it being like this?"

"I thought it was more like our runes," Froggy replied. "I must not have seen a fresh one."

"What the Hel are you—"

"I must have been a child the last time I saw one," Hilda brought her finger up to her lip, caressing the dry and cracked skin. "It is the right bind rune."

I had not heard much about bind runes, but I knew it was the same one on that parchment. I knew they were mostly used in complex blood Sacredness. Something that had been outlawed after the creation of the crown and barriers. The Rikr who had outlawed them assumed that no one would be able to break the barrier if they had no knowledge of bind runes.

"Aye," Froggy bobbed his head thrice. "There was a time that the Norns and Gods had looked upon us with joy, young heir." He had called me that before, but the term sounded foreign to me these days. *I would be the heir until my father produced a stronger son, and I doubted he would sire one in his old age.* **I could only hope that he could not.**

"Soul-ties were a rare but joyous bind rune," Hilda added, nodding her head towards my chest. "They were meant to signify that two people's souls were meant to be intertwined, for they were a perfect match in every way."

My heart froze within my chest before hammering the pulse into my ears. *There was no way.* **Loreth could not be my perfect match.** It made his possessiveness make sense, but why would he be my match? I had nothing in common with the man besides a mutual hatred…and sexual interest. **We wanted to kill each other!** He was a vile and cruel man! I was his sworn enemy; the one he'd vowed to kill more than once today! While he ran around brutally murdering Sidirnians; I was fighting for their equality and freedom. Though…perhaps I was not doing much fighting. *I was a hypocritical man who followed an idiot leader, much like Loreth.*

Yet, I did not see how that made us a match.

"Aye," Froggy added. "My grandfather and grandmother had one. They would rarely speak aloud because they could communicate within their minds." I tried to flatten my expression at his words. *Their minds. How had I been so dull?* The two men I regarded as brothers shared a soul; I'd grown up around the intricacies of souls and the mind.

"Soul-ties were once revered," Hilda added with a hum. "Two halves of one whole."

I sat there in silence. I couldn't wrap my head around knowing I had a soul-tie to Loreth. *I felt as if they were lying, but there was a part of me that could believe it.* **I was a despicable person, much like Loreth.** Yet, I felt the surge of disgust bubbling up again. I wanted to find the man and separate his head from his body. *How did that mean we were two halves of a whole? Was it because we had both wanted to kill the other? Were we bonded through being enemies?*

"I d-don't understand?" I finally sputtered out, cringing at the display of weakness. **I wanted to bash my head against the wall.** *I wanted to carve the mark from my skin.*

"The man, the one who you said cursed you? Where is he?"

"Hel's if I know!" *But I did know.* I knew he probably laid in his bed, pressed against the corner of a wall within the stronghold. I knew his noisy pet raven rested in a cage across the room. I knew he'd wake up with his trousers covered in seed. I knew he'd fall into my mind again, as I would his. I'd see him in a dream soon, and the urge to fuck would come over us like we were rabbits. *I knew I would want more from him.*

"Have you seen him since?" Froggy asked. I shook my head. There was nothing in this world that would make me admit the truth. *I would rather slit my throat than admit that it had felt so real only moments ago.*

That Loreth had held me down, choked me, and made me see stars as I finished by his hand. That I had sworn to myself, I would no longer be a weak man who followed a fool. How I had longed to wear the crown, and save our people.

We were enemies. We would never be soul-tied in anything but hatred.

"I wonder," Hilda hummed as she pursed her lips. "Perhaps the effects we thought were a curse are because of the distance."

"Then I will gladly die before I seek the man out. I will let the cold rot my bones within my body, steal my soul, and forever be left drifting without a hall."

Froggy hissed at me, much like a cat would. I gave the man a startled look, cautiously eyeing him as he narrowed his eyes at me. "You would disgrace the Norns?"

My body tensed as I prepared for an attack. *I wouldn't put it past the man to strike at me.* I wonder what Pthun would make of all of this. He seemed just as knowledgeable as Froggy.

"I would spit in their face before I admitted that beast of a man was meant to be my other half." I narrowed my eyes back. "Surely, you've heard of Loreth? The head of the Varangian Guard?" Froggy sucked in a breath at that, his body beginning to shake.

"Aye, I've heard of him plenty. Cruel man with eyes the darkest of blacks." Froggy seemed to forget that he was angry with me for denying the Norns spun fate. His body shook slightly, as if remembering those cold, dark eyes. "He came to me village," Froggy whispered, as if just speaking of the man would make him arrive. "He butchered every man and boy. Took many women. I'd been here when it happened." He shuddered as Hilda gasped. "When I returned…" His breath shook as he clenched his eyes shut.

"What?" I asked hoarsely. I wanted to know as much about the man that I could, like some part of me was fascinated. Mostly, I was afraid.

"He piled each body into the main hall, and lit it on fire. There were women huddled in the nearby forest. He'd made them all stand there and watch as he butchered their kin." He opened his watery eyes before continuing. "The women said he'd told 'em that weak men had no place in Sidirna. Any girl who cried was taken with him to be a Thrall. Only a handful of women remained."

I'd heard many stories of Loreth. Each one being so cruel that it turned my stomach. Doran had told me once about finding a man on the outskirts. The skin had been carefully peeled from his body; a bloody mass of muscles and tissue. There was a single arrow piercing his heart, holding a paper.

All that was scrawled on it was his name, Loreth. When he'd shown us the bloodstained parchment, Dallen laughed. "It looks like a child wrote it!" He wasn't wrong; it was lopsided and slanted, with each letter being a slightly different size.

I couldn't find it within myself to laugh because I knew just how poorly educated Thrall-born were. While a part of me felt sad for Loreth, an even larger part of me was disgusted by his actions.

"Now you see?" I asked Froggy, bringing my palms up to rub press into my eye sockets. I slid my hands down my face with a sigh. "What can I do to break it?"

"There is no breaking it, boy." Hilda said sadly. "I'll ask around—" I cut her off with a harsh growl.

"You will speak of this to no one!" The last thing I needed was my loyalty questioned further. Many already avoided me because of my status as heir. "Swear it!" I demanded, holding out my left hand. Froggy grumbled as he patted his pockets before pulling out the same dull knife he had sliced my arm with. The arm that was still bandaged, though no longer hurt. He slit each of our palms, slowly and methodically. I didn't understand the words he uttered, but nothing would be worse than the curse I had been stuck with.

Loreth would forever be tied to me.

"There," he said. "It is done."

I'd stumbled my way back to my cavern, using the wall to keep myself upright. While the pain had lessened, I still felt the chill to my bones. I'd apparently arrived at Hilda's with no clothes but had made use of an old sheet to cover my bottom half. I looked ridiculous, but I had no energy to care what the others thought of me. **They could choke on the spit from their laughs.** It was nearing dawn as I'd curled into my bed. I hoped sleep would take me quickly; with no dreams to be had.

THERE WAS a thick fog surrounding me, nothing but white haze as far as I could see. I took a step forward, and then another. This was different from my dreams with Loreth. *It wasn't safe darkness.* It was cold, quiet, and yet it felt more powerful than I had ever felt. I could almost feel the same power that I felt when that strange woman left.

"What the Hel?" I muttered, turning in a full circle.

Where was I? My heart began to race, a steadily increasing thump in my ears. *Why was I here? Why was this happening to me?* I looked down at my body, hoping that I had one again. It was a dream. It had to be one.

I had no body.

I had no hands.

"**Alfrikr, son of Alfrikr the Wretched.**" The fog seemed to whisper to me as if it were multiple voices twisted into one.

Was I dead? Did I die in my sleep? While I would be glad to have been rid of Loreth, I was not ready to pass yet. I needed to work harder at saving Sidirna. I was dead. I died. Loreth won. He killed me. He had to have killed me.

"**You will get your chance,**" The voices rang out. "**Still your mind so we may speak.**"

Still my mind? I had no body. The fog was talking to me! I must have gone crazy. This was all just a dream. I was simply exhausted after that dream, too much had happened in the last —

"**SILENCE!**" It boomed. "**You will listen.**"

The surrounding fog swirled until it took shape. Three hooded figures stood behind me; the fog within their outlines still swirling. This was odd. Yet, I was suddenly not panicking as deeply as I should have been. *Safe. I was safe. Protected.* So much had happened in the last few days that I was unsure of anything that would shock me. Including the sight before me. *I was safe. I was protected.*

I would live. Three. Three. Three.

"**Your threads have been woven**," They spoke as one. "**There is much you have done, are doing, and will do.**"

The Norns? Was I standing before the three sisters who wove the threads of fate? I wanted to say that is how living works, but I knew they would not appreciate the sentiment. Though, I guess they could hear the thoughts within my head. One of them had to have been the woman I had seen. Though, I was unsure which one it would have been —

"**It is not you who has been darning our weave**," Their forms took a step towards me. I tensed as fear seemed to break through the wave of calm that had come over me.

"I don't know what that means?" My voice came out garbled, like it had been consumed by the fog.

"**You must resist.**" They stepped closer again, and I wanted to retreat. I would never back down from a fight, but against the Norns was different.

"**The white winter is coming, Alfrikr. You must survive the winter. The wolf will come for you, and we cannot stop it. Survive the winter to change your fate.**"

"The wolf?"

"**You must resist the wolf.**" The fog began to swirl faster as they stood before me. *I wanted to cringe away. I wanted to run. Why would a wolf come for me? How did surviving the winter change my fate? I did not understand because I had assumed I* *would die this winter. Ivaldr had doomed us all, just as Pthun had said.*

"What wolf?" I asked quietly. The wolf could be Ivaldr, but it could also be Loreth.

"**This is all we can do for you.**" They said before the fog closed around me.

All I felt was pain. Unending pain that was worse than any pain I have ever felt. It flowed around me, through me, and did not stop. The fog began to glow brighter and brighter until bursts of yellow seemed to shoot out of my body.

I heard nothing but the echoes of my screams. The pain was familiar; cold and brutal before switching to fiery and harsh. I would die. I was dying. Pain. Pain. Pain.

I shuddered and screamed as the pain slowly receded. Cold, I felt cold. Yet, I welcomed the familiar cold over the pain I had just endured. The way it had flipped between burning and icy-cold made it the worst pain I had ever endured.

I would not be surprised if I had died. Another shot of icy cold pain shot through my chest and seemed to spin around inside me until my entire body felt cold. I could not stop myself from screaming as I wrenched my eyes open. Everything hurt, even if I was unable to see my body. I felt the shocks of pain still rummaging through my brain as I searched for the Norns. They stood where they had once been; close enough to make out their forms, but not so close that I could see anything but swirling fog.

"What did you do to me?" I croaked out.

"**Three Norns wove the threads of fate, two warriors on opposing sides, one curse that will change them forever. Three. Three. Three.**" Their voices chanted over and over. They got louder and louder before coming to a sudden stop.

"Wha—" I tried to ask again before they interrupted me.

"**<u>We have rewoven your fate as much as possible. Survive the winter. Resist the wolf.</u>**"

"What does that mean?" If I could fall to my knees, I would. I would beg them with all that I had, just like I had seen grown men beg before the executioners block. The same men that I had judged harshly, condemned for their weakness.

"**<u>Survive the winter, resist the wolf...</u>**" They began to fade into the fog, their swirling forms seeming to break away.

"Tell me!" I yelled, my throat screaming in pain.

"**Know the tie is a necessary curse...**" A single familiar voice rang out before they faded away.

WHAT'S NEXT?

This is not the end of Alfrikr and Loreth's journey, but it is simply the beginning. Keep an eye out for announcements about book two!

You can find updates, sneak peaks, and more on my Patreon!
Https://www.patreon.com/ledpaintsoup

Coming 2027, ON THE FENCE, a standalone cowboy romance.

AUTHOR'S NOTE

This all started with an idea, one that I never thought I would actually complete. I kept this a secret for over a year because let's be honest... I didn't believe in myself enough. BUT!! Here I am! I did it. I wrote a whole book. I've officially accomplished the dreams I had as a kid, and now I'm a published author. And WOW! **What a journey this has been**. One that I'm thankful to have taken.

If there's anything to be said, it is that you should do the things that scare you. Do the things you've always wanted to do. Write the book that lingers in your mind.

Big shoutout to my husband for always being supportive of me, and reading this book chapter by chapter as I finished it. Thank you for listening to my millions of ideas, and always being ready to listen to me blab. I don't know that I would have been able to do this without you. Your love and support have gotten me through so much. I don't know what I would do without you and your support.

Big thanks to River for beta reading, and always being there to bounce ideas around. I don't know that I would have finished this book if not for your constant show of support and encouragement. I'm so thankful to have you in my corner.

Big thanks to Caboose for always encouraging me and making sure that I knew this was something I could accomplish. For listening to my unhinged ideas. For being there for me whenever I needed to rant about these dudes.

I don't know what else to write here, this is my first book y'all.

P.s Dad, if you're reading this, I'm still embarrassed you've read some of these chapters.

ABOUT THE AUTHOR

Maxwell J Smith is occasionally funny. He loves to read, write, and blab about his books. He is a proud dad of three small children. He also has three cats, one dog, and one husband.

In 2024, he took the plunge and began to draft his first novel, Bone Chills, and finally achieved his dreams of becoming an author. His second book will be released in 2027, and he has no plans of stopping there.

MAXWELL IS MOSTLY KNOWN FOR HIS CONTENT ON SOCIAL MEDIA (@LEDPAINTSOUP) WHERE HE TALKS ABOUT BEING WRITING, BEING A STAY-AT-HOME DAD, AND MORE.

He also is not very good about talking about himself in third-person, especially when it comes to about the author. He should have given himself more time to do this, and not procrastinate it until the very end. Hi, I love writing queer books.

www.ingramcontent.com/pod-product-compliance
Lightning Source LLC
Chambersburg PA
CBHW060515160726

47991CB00001B/38